T0366644

DUMBARTON OAKS
MEDIEVAL LIBRARY

Jan M. Ziolkowski, General Editor

ARCHITRENIUS

JOHANNES DE HAUVILLA

DOML 55

Architrenius

JOHANNES DE HAUVILLA

Translated by

WINTHROP WETHERBEE

DUMBARTON OAKS
MEDIEVAL LIBRARY

HARVARD UNIVERSITY PRESS
CAMBRIDGE, MASSACHUSETTS
LONDON, ENGLAND
2019

Latin text reprinted from Johannes de Hauvilla, *Architrenius,* edited and
translated by Winthrop Wetherbee. Copyright © 1994 Cambridge
University Press. Reprinted with the permission of Cambridge University
Press.

First printing

Library of Congress Cataloging-in-Publication Data
Names: Johannes, de Hauvilla, active 12th century, author. | Wetherbee,
Winthrop, 1938– translator. | Container of (expression) : Johannes, de
Hauvilla, active 12th century. Architrenius. | Container of (expression) :
Johannes, de Hauvilla, active 12th century. Architrenius. English
(Wetherbee) 2019.
Title: Architrenius / Johannes de Hauvilla ; translated by Winthrop
Wetherbee.
Other titles: Dumbarton Oaks medieval library ; 55.
Description: Cambridge, Massachusetts : Harvard University Press, 2019. |
    Series: Dumbarton Oaks medieval library ; 55 | Text in Latin with
English translation on facing pages ; introduction and notes in English. |
This is Winthrop Wetherbee's second translation of the Architrenius; an
earlier translation was published by Cambridge University Press, 1994, as
volume 3 in the series Cambridge medieval classics. | Includes
bibliographical references and index.
Identifiers: LCCN 2018040034 | ISBN 9780674988156 (alk. paper)
Subjects: LCSH: Verse satire, Latin (Medieval and modern)—Translations
into English.
Classification: LCC PA8360.J65 A913 2019 | DDC 871/.03—dc23 LC
record available at https://lccn.loc.gov/2018040034

Contents

CONTENTS

vi

Introduction

THE POEM AND ITS AUTHOR

The *Architrenius* of Johannes de Hauvilla appeared toward the end of 1184,[1] when the author was not yet old (1.85–87). He was a Norman, probably from the village of Hauville near Rouen. His encomium on Paris at the end of Book 2 and the vivid account of student life that follows suggest that he had studied there. By 1184 he was probably teaching in the important cathedral school at Rouen, where the grammarian Gervase of Melkley was his pupil,[2] and he is named as a witness in a Rouen cathedral document of 1199. Since Gervase in his *Ars poetica* refers to his teacher in the past tense, Johannes must have been deceased when the *Ars* was produced, between 1208 and 1216.

The *Architrenius* is school-poetry through and through, proudly assertive of its pedantry and the cumbersome stylistic virtuosity for which its author was renowned, but it is also a worldly poem, moving with disconcerting freedom between topical satire and visionary allegory, the lower depths of Parisian student life and the utopian peace of the ancient philosophers, the cottage and the court. With occasional brilliance, it brings the resources of high Latin poetry into the secular world of the twelfth century and marks a stage in the literary movement that would eventually produce the fully realized comic worlds of Jean de Meun, Boccaccio, and Chaucer.

Architrenius (the "arch-weeper") is a young man approaching maturity but shocked to realize that all his thoughts and impulses tend to vice. Convinced that Nature is to blame, he resolves to seek out the goddess and confront her with his hapless state. His quest leads through a world that represents panoramically the ills of schools, court, and church: the bower of Venus, the house of Gluttony, the student world of Paris, the palace of Ambition, the mount of Presumption, and the site of a battle between the armies of Largesse and Avarice. Eventually he arrives in paradisiacal Tylos, where ancient philosophers instruct him on vice, the vanity of worldly things, self-discipline, and love of God. Finally, Nature appears, responds to his complaints with a long lecture on the order of the universe, and offers him the beautiful maiden Moderation as a bride. The poem ends with the celebration of their marriage.

The *Architrenius* defies categorization. I am not alone in my inability to see it as a fully achieved poem, but its social criticism is focused and coherent and reflects significant developments in western European society. During the later eleventh and twelfth centuries, urban culture, commercial and professional, had become a counterweight to the traditional dominance of aristocratic wealth and privilege. The bureaucratization of administration in Church and State had opened new avenues for advancement and created new functions for educated men. Higher education was increasingly the province of cathedral schools located in urban centers, and through the growing organization and specialization of teaching, the institution of the university was evolving. The intellectual had emerged as a social type, a professional class increasingly defined by its role in a secular society and expressing a new social awareness in new literary forms.[3] "Clerks" of this type composed the first vernacular romances, celebratory though often covertly critical of the courtly-urban culture of France and England. Works like the *Moralium dogma philosophorum* (ca. 1150) attributed to William of Conches, and the *Policraticus* (1159) of John of Salisbury brought classical ethical and political thought to bear on social institutions. And in Latin poetry of many kinds these clerks directed a barrage of satire, not only at the venality and greed of the rich and powerful, but at the corrupt ambition of men whose training and horizons were largely their own.[4]

The *Architrenius* was written for and largely about such "new men," and its purpose is secular and satirical. Though the presence of the goddess Nature and her discourse on cosmic order recall the great allegories of Bernardus Silvestris and Alan of Lille,[5] the poem offers no lofty philosophical or religious message. Hell and damnation are a recurring theme, and ancient philosophers admonish Architrenius on the fear and love of God, but the marriage that concludes his odyssey is devoid of religious meaning. Even the poem's ostensible theme, Architrenius's moral education, is less important than its criticism of a world where wealth and preferment are all-consuming concerns. There is no hint of the civilizing influence, which, as Jaeger has shown, was one of the educated courtier's duties to exercise.[6] The arrogance of power, flaunting wealth and abusing patronage, and the ambition, greed, and hypocrisy of the aspiring courtier or cleric are what bring Johannes's poetry to life.

Within this framework, the poet seems at times to resist the satirist. Some fine passages describe the material fabric of life on the heights of power: the elaborate dress (2.90–164; 4.285–300); the sumptuous and endlessly varied diet (2.184–247); the lavish decoration of palaces (4.179–90; 214–83). And this description can be unabashedly admiring, notably in the Palace of Ambition, where a magnificent tapestry displays the creation of the world and a panorama of scenes from ancient poetry (4.215–71). The artist has assumed the role of an "all-powerful Nature" (4.275–76) who exists to mirror and fulfill the capacities of mankind (4.182–90).[7]

Such passages, standing apart from their context, reveal an ambition inherited from Bernardus, Alan, and the Latin poets of the earlier twelfth century, Hildebert, Marbod, and Baudri of Bourgueil, an ambition which is central also to the project of the vernacular poets who produced the first romances: a desire to integrate the role of the poet as celebrant of urban or courtly culture with the traditional ideal of the poet possessed of universal learning.[8] It is hard at such moments to remember that the magnificence Johannes describes is always suspect, that it represents ambition, greed, or power, illusory and treacherous to those who obtain it. But the invectives of Cato, Democritus, Pliny, and Pythagoras against excess and immorality are already implicit in Johannes's tableaux. The sumptuousness described, beautiful in itself, never expresses significant cultural values, as it does in the *Anticlaudianus* of Alan of Lille.[9]

Indeed, the role of aristocratic values in the *Architrenius* is conspicuously limited. A brief discussion of kinship as grounds for preferment (3.454–62) suggests a grudging acknowledgment of hereditary prerogative, and *noblesse oblige* appears fleetingly in Gawain's assertion of his tireless generosity (6.4–8). The need for unstinting patronage is a recurring theme in the survey of the hardships of student life (3.323–471), and Democritus will center on enlightened giving as the one noble use for riches (6.286–316). But Gawain and the traditional nobility he embodies exist on their own plane, distanced from a "real" world dominated by the abuses of wealth and the workings of bribery and favoritism.[10]

Money is both the means and the all-consuming object of advancement for the courtiers who infest the poem, and Alexander Murray could be glossing the *Architrenius* when he explains the effect on European society of the growth of a money economy. Money facilitates social mobility, "liquefying" relations among and within classes and estates; and power, like cash value, is abstracted from individual merit to institutional status.[11] New social conditions generate new mental habits, and two such habits are fundamental: "the habit of desiring more and more money, which medieval theologians usually called avarice," and "the habit of desiring that power and dignity which society concentrates in its institutions . . . this usually went under the name of ambition."[12] Queen Money and her ennobling power were an established theme for satire,[13] and they are expressed nowhere more powerfully than in the *Architrenius*. Money's power transcends human relations: the courtier serves "not at the bidding of men, but of wealth" (4.445–46), Queen Money "takes precedence over justice" (5.95–97), and her effect becomes virtually organic: prompted by Juvenal,

Johannes makes his gluttons literally consume the gold that sustains the social status of which their feasting is the visible sign (2.248–56).[14] "The thirst is inherent in the money itself; the fever of possession rages in the things possessed" (5.289).

Repeatedly, the *Architrenius* sets ambition in an infernal perspective. Greed perverts aspiration, driving its victims to self-damnation, "extinguishing the sacred light of reason" (2.308–9) in men who are already "citizens of Tartarus" (4.164). Architrenius himself provides the fullest expression of this overpowering worldliness, which has left him haunted by images of hell (7.229–76), and he sounds the trumpet of apocalypse to warn of the judgment awaiting those whose power and wealth have driven them to abuse these resources (5.164–76, 232–35; 6.180–95).[15]

Other twelfth-century writers strike the same note. Walter Map depicts a court haunted by strange, dark forces: the courtier ostensibly serves his lord, yet his true "sovereign mistress" is Avarice, and his environment is a kind of hell.[16] John of Salisbury examines the pernicious effects of avarice, gluttony, flattery, and adulation, which alienate courtier and patron from themselves.[17] A passage in the *Policraticus* might have been uttered by an ancient philosopher in Johannes's Tylos:

> Prosperity, cruel stepmother of virtue, commends her favored ones to do them harm . . . The brighter she appears in her beauty, the denser the mist with which she clouds their wondering eyes. As darkness overcomes them, truth fades away, and when the root of virtue has been severed, the crops of vice sprout forth.

The light of reason is extinguished, and the whole man is brought headlong to a miserable fate.[18]

Architrenius and *Policraticus* are often strikingly close in tone and theme, and Johannes may have drawn on the earlier work for moral doctrine, in addition to emulating its use of classical precepts and exempla.[19] But the similarity is misleading. John of Salisbury's political ideals are grounded in biblical and patristic injunction. The *Policraticus* is charged with reminders that worldly conduct will be scrutinized by "the Angel of the Great Judgment": only divine grace can protect us from the consequences of our errors.[20] The right reason of John's ideal statesman depends on the rediscovery through grace of the image of the Creator within ourselves.[21]

There is no such religious purpose in the *Architrenius;* Johannes's religious rhetoric is part of his repertory as a satirist. Sin, grace, and *contemptus carnis* are in effect ethical rather than religious issues.[22] And despite the poem's debt to Bernardus and Alan, its visionary moments, though they reveal the infernal roots of wealth and power, do not penetrate the cosmic veil. Even before Nature introduces her own *religio nativa* to remedy Architrenius's misfortunes (9.242–49), the religious dimension of the poem has been reduced to questions of conduct. Christ is the prototype of generosity (5.67–68)[23] and a "gentleness" defined in secular as well as religious terms (8.45–52), and the secular note grows stronger as the poem approaches its conclusion. The wedding of Architrenius and Moderation is an unambiguously earthly affair: attendants like Reasonable Expenditure bustle about, and Fortune smiles on a union hallowed by practical good sense.[24]

THEME AND STRUCTURE

The tidiness of the poem's conclusion is misleading, for it suggests that Architrenius's journey has been successful, that his education, however practical, is complete. But evaluating the hero's experience is difficult. As Jung observes, the poem's allegory is static: a series of tableaux simply confront Architrenius, and he shifts abruptly from one setting to another with no indication of progress. In the absence of clearly marked stages, we can hardly feel that a quest or initiation is in progress.[25]

These difficulties have led to very different readings of the poem. Peter Godman sees the absence of a clearly evolving plot as intentional: the *Architrenius* is a parody of the poems of Alan of Lille, and the *Anticlaudianus* in particular, by Alan's "most devastating critic"; for Alan's *homo novus,* a perfect synthesis of knowledge and virtue, Johannes has substituted "the perfect idiot," who learns nothing from his experience, and whose marriage to Moderation is meaningless.[26] Bernd Roling, on the other hand, sees Johannes as carefully simplifying Alan's cosmic model to address the human condition in terms of practical morality; the theme of moderation, distilled from John of Salisbury and other twelfth-century sources,[27] is present throughout as the implicit standard against which the series of tableaux must be read. In paradisiacal Tylos, the "healing drinks" Architrenius receives confirm and order his experience and prepare him for Nature's "conclusive answer" to his fears about his place in the scheme of things.[28] For Roling, Architrenius finally exemplifies the ability of man to achieve a "harmonizing of affect," and a mature bodily and spiritual life.[29]

Both of these readings are problematic. Godman's pro-
vocative argument, which is not supported by close exami-
nation of the text, requires taking Architrenius at his word.
He is hapless by his own account, but despite his torrential
weeping and lengthy anticipations of damnation, he is not
often foolish; there is no clear indication of growth in moral
awareness, but his attacks on the vices of court and cloister
in Books 4 and 5 are as astutely probing as those of the phi-
losophers of Tylos.[30]

To this extent we can give qualified acceptance to Rol-
ing's view of Architrenius's experience. But later, haunted by
the sense of sinfulness as he listens to the philosophers, and
overcome by a final flood of tears in the presence of Nature,
he seems diminished, reduced to his own self-assessment.
Though the speech of Archytas on wrath has an immediate
salutary effect (6.73–74), his few subsequent responses to
the philosophers' discourses are almost entirely expressions
of hopelessness (7.231–76; 8.1–18). He has apparently become
again the creature of his vices, a moral *tabula rasa* to be
treated like a child (9.234–42). The quasi-prophet who had
denounced pride and cupidity in ringing tones (5.164–235,
256–342) is hard to reconcile with the "frail bridegroom"
(tenui sponso) whose only gift to his bride is submissiveness
(9.409–10). The marriage is perhaps Architrenius's reward
for having learned from his experiences, but it can also be
seen as a last recourse on Nature's part, a final attempt to
improve his otherwise incorrigible state.

Nature's long discourse (8.324–9.148) is also hard to as-
sess. It begins and ends by declaring grandly that the uni-
verse exists to serve mankind: "the greater world obeys the
will of the lesser" (8.326–27). But Nature's discussion of the

ordered universe is hardly Roling's "conclusive answer" to Architrenius's doubts; it conveys no hint of the moral or spiritual implications of her cosmic theme,[31] and leaves him amazed, but unenlightened and finally frustrated (9.1–10, 148–52).

Roling accepts Jung's distinction between the *Architrenius* and the allegories of Bernardus and Alan: in place of their utopian vision of universal harmony as a model for human aspiration, he sees Johannes and Nature offering a *consolatio;* practical morality replaces idealism, and there is no heavenly journey.[32] But Nature is problematical in herself. The cosmic dimension of her *religio nativa* has clearly been rendered ineffectual, and one may ask why Johannes finds it necessary to include her long astronomical discourse. Schmidt sees the *Architrenius* as an extension of Alan's *De planctu Naturae,* where the crisis of human sinfulness is left unresolved. But the role of Johannes's Nature is less a development than a contradiction of Alan's use of the goddess. The *De planctu* ends by showing the limits of Nature's power to regulate human life, and the necessity for intervention by a higher power, thus anticipating the *Anticlaudianus.* The crisis is finally theological in its implications. In the *Architrenius,* Nature deals with Architrenius's dilemma alone, but her remedy is reduced to the discipline represented by Moderation and the injunction to marry and procreate.

In the end I abandon the search for a coherent reading of the *Architrenius* and see the poem instead as it presents itself to its hero: a collection of vivid tableaux framed by the eloquence of the poet, the philosophers, and Architrenius himself, concluding with his passive participation in the pageant of the wedding feast.

The Poetry of the *Architrenius* and Its Sources

When the *Architrenius* sets its satirical purpose aside, not just the artistic beauty, but the purely human significance of what it describes engages the poet. A sense of the tragic aspect of human life can surface unexpectedly. The tapestry in the palace of Ambition is worked with scenes from the fall of Troy (4.236–51). Contemplating the death of Hector, Helen's tears, Priam pleading before Achilles, Johannes reflects that "it is sweet to sorrow for the sorrows of men, to grieve for their grief" (4.252–53). He quickly shifts to the sorrows of love, represented by the inevitable Pyramus and Thisbe, but he has felt and duly acknowledged the *antiquos labores* he describes (4.235–36). At times this feeling for the classical humane is incongruous, as when Architrenius compares the fallen Lucifer sympathetically to Ovid's Narcissus (5.214–19), or Pittacus acknowledges his fall with a gentle Horatian valediction (8.36–37). But such references attest an appreciation of ancient poetry that appears throughout in Johannes's assimilation of his *auctores*. Ovid is predictably the source of more borrowed phrases and formulae than any other author, and the influence of the *Metamorphoses* pervades Johannes's world-historical vision. Johannes also has Virgil at his fingertips and was clearly fascinated by *Aeneid* 6: the group of malevolent figures clustered on the threshold of Virgil's Dis (*Aen.* 6.273–89) inspired similar catalogs in the *Architrenius*. And he clearly appreciates the exotic qualities of Claudian. But he is closest in spirit to Horace and Juvenal and shares the satirists' versatility. He can sketch a parasite in a few brief strokes (4.387–90), and his philosophers are not mere names linked to set speeches, but present themselves as angry and abrupt (Cato, 6.123–29), self-absorbed (Crates, 6.396–99), obsessive (Xenocrates, 7.146–60), or avuncular (Thales, 7.277–85). His essays in classical style too often involve expanding a pithy formulation to several times its original length,[33] but at his best he catches the tone with remarkable fidelity. Stylistically, Lucan and Juvenal are his preferred models. His survey of the workings of ambition in Roman history (4.116–31) has Lucan's biting energy, and he is capable of Juvenal's caricatures of wealth and greed, as when his gluttons debate learnedly on sauces and modes of cooking (2.184–247). Like Juvenal, too, he is unfailingly responsive to poverty. His inventory of the furnishings and cuisine of a student's lodgings (3.55–80) is vivid, precisely detailed, and unusually free of the mannerisms of school poetry: he can capture a poor man's drunken fantasy of status (2.300–304), and his account of the rustic banquet of Baucis and Philemon (2.406–65) has a sympathetic delicacy.

But the *Architrenius* is also a product of its place and time. For every line in which we hear Lucan or Juvenal, there are dozens that could have been produced only by a virtuoso practitioner of the art of poetry as the twelfth century understood it. Such virtuosity disrupts passages in which Johannes comes close to classical gravity: the admirably concise *ardua tollit / Cras ruiturus homo* (man builds tall, though he will be brought to ruin tomorrow, 4.201–2) is followed immediately by four separate variations on the paradox of *tollit/ruiturus;* and after Pliny has brought his grim account of a ruined life to the *optata quies* (long-awaited peace, 6.382) of death, he unfortunately adds that in death, "wound is cured by wound, pain by pain, suffering by suffering" (385–86).

But Johannes was famous above all as a stylist, a master of the rhetorical figures prescribed by the *artes poeticae*. No less a figure than Geoffrey of Vinsauf could declare that the *Architrenius* surpassed all works of modern times in its complex figurative language *(tropicae locutiones)*.[34] Gervase of Melkley complains of its *durissimae translationes* (difficult metaphors),[35] but claims that careful study of the *Architrenius* is an education in itself.[36] He cites "a man of discernment" who declared that the poem's style was *too* perfect—flawed *(vitiosum)* only in that its lines were wholly free of *vitia*.[37]

Such a judgment must embrace tours de force like the fifteen varieties of fruit that grow on the mount of Ambition (4.37–52), the twenty-seven emblematic birds and animals that introduce the theme of Presumption (5.5–21), and the string of forty-five comparisons that illustrate Pythagoras's assertion that the world is filled with vice (7.204–19), as well as the over-predictable catalogs deployed repeatedly to illustrate presumption, cruelty, or the pains of hell. But as a comment on Johannes as a versifier, it is not too far off. Given his ambition as a classicizing poet, and with due allowance for twelfth-century *ornatus,* the verse of the *Architrenius* is on the whole correct and fluent.[38]

My Index includes not only proper names, which are given in their classical form, but also personified abstractions. The *Architrenius* abounds in these, and while it would be pointless to compile a complete list, Johannes's freedom in this respect makes his poem a likely catalyst for the explosion of personification allegory in later vernacular poetry. I have concentrated on personifications that are major themes *(Gula, Ambitio, Praesumptio)* and passages that include clusters of personifications (e.g., the companions of *Segnities,* 1.26–40; the climbers on the Mountain of Ambition, 4.79–110), or in which a personification is addressed or assigned a significant role (e.g., *Virtus pronuba,* 1.157; *Gula,* 2.339–49; *regina Pecunia,* 5.95).

FORTUNAE

The *Architrenius* did not enjoy the standing of the poems of Bernardus, Alan, and Walter of Chatillon but seems nonetheless to have become a canonical text. Johannes appears among the school authors in the *Laborintus* of Eberhard the German (late thirteenth century),[39] and the dozen surviving thirteenth-century manuscripts, with their often extensive glosses, make plain that the *Architrenius* was well known and was appreciated for its learning as well as its style.

La bataille des set ars of Henri d'Andeli (ca. 1240) was written in response to the changing intellectual milieu of the early thirteenth century and the increasing specialization of the university curriculum, which seemed to allow little scope to the humanistic pursuits that had flourished (or were wistfully recalled as having flourished) in the twelfth-century schools. In the course of a battle in which an army of poets, sages, and texts is routed by the forces of logic, "mon seignor Architraine / Un des barons de Normandie" is slain by "Parealmaine" (Aristotle's *Peri Hermeneias,* or "On Interpretation").[40]

Clear traces of the *Architrenius* in the work of other vernacular poets are few, but as Roling suggests, its structure may have provided a model for later allegorists.[41] As such, it could help account for allegories like the *Besant de Dieu* of

Guillaume le Clerc, which includes both a Castle of Maidens that harbors Chastity, Honor, Largesse, and other virtues, and a City of Pride peopled by Shame, Villainy, Felony, and other vices; allegorical journeys like the *Roman de Carité* of the Reclus de Moiliens, whose narrator visits all parts of Europe, including the papal court, in search of Charity; or the *Tornoiemenz Antecrit* of Huon de Mery, in which an army of vices led by Pride is defeated by an army of Virtues, augmented by Arthur, Gawain, and other heroes of romance.

Jean de Meun, whose portion of the *Roman de la Rose* is closer in spirit to the *Architrenius* than to the poems of Alan, which provide a foil to his own more worldly concerns, gives no sign of having known Johannes's poem.[42] Roling sees a correspondence to Johannes's plot in the *Tesoretto* of Brunetto Latini, where Nature reveals to the journeying hero the order of the universe and examples of good and bad conduct.[43] But Brunetto's cosmology is purposive where that of the *Architrenius* is not, and Alan seems a more likely source.

The later career of the *Architrenius* was largely confined to the work of teachers and commentators. The *Fulgentius metaforalis* of the fourteenth-century Franciscan John Ridewall includes quotations from Architrenius's encounter with the monster Greed and other passages on the same theme,[44] and the poem is cited frequently in the prose commentary to the fourteenth-century *Echecs amoureux*.[45] Coluccio Salutati (1331–1406) remarks on Johannes's knowledge of British lore concerning giants,[46] and Rabelais may later have borrowed the name of the giant Gabbara, father of Goliath, from the *Architrenius*.[47] The English antiquary John Pits reports that Hugh Legat, a fifteenth-century monk of St. Albans, greatly impressed by the *Architrenius,* renounced all other books and devoted himself entirely to a commentary on the poem.[48]

In 1373 the aged Petrarch was provoked by the treatise of a French friar, Jean de Hesdin, which extolled French culture at the expense of that of Italy, quoting at length from the encomium on Paris in *Architrenius* 2. Petrarch's rejoinder includes a scathing attack on Johannes's poem as tedious and inept.[49] Later humanists were more charitable. Josse Badius Ascensius published an edition of the *Architrenius* in 1517, though he introduced readings of his own to make Johannes's grammar and prosody conform to what he considered humanist standards.[50] Lilio Giraldi (1479–1552), while complaining of the poem's barbarity, considered that one would regret not having read it.[51] Johannes is the only medieval poet before Petrarch cited in the works of Ravisius Textor (1480–1542), who cites him many times.[52] Juan Luis Vives (1493–1540) pronounced the *Architrenius* exceptional for its age, one bright spot in the dismal history of Latin poetry between Sidonius Apollinaris and Petrarch,[53] and Konrad Gesner (1516–1565) cited Vives's judgment approvingly. This rather grudging praise was followed by silence. A few lines of the *Architrenius* surface unexpectedly in Gibbon's *Decline and Fall*,[54] and the poem receives a dozen sympathetic pages in the *Histoire littéraire*,[55] but it seems otherwise to have disappeared until the later nineteenth century, when Wright's edition and the appreciative study of Kuno Francke brought it back to life.

Translating the *Architrenius* a second time, I have drawn on careful reviews of my earlier effort by George Rigg and Antonio Placanica, and the scrupulous notes of Milena Minkova. In basing my text on that of Paul Gerhard Schmidt, I have been standing on the shoulders of a giant, and though I have examined most of the manuscripts, I could not improve on his selection of glosses. Closer to home, Robert Babcock and Danuta Shanzer have gone over my work to my great profit. Such expert scrutiny has made it easier to finally let go of a poem I have been wrestling with for fifty years.

<h2 align="center">NOTES</h2>

1 *Architrenius* 1.151–66 announce the imminent elevation of Walter of Coutances, Bishop of Lincoln, to the Archbishopric of Rouen. Pope Lucius III gave his approval in September or October 1184. Walter was installed on February 24, 1185. The poem must have been finished during this period: Schmidt, 16–17.

2 On Johannes's teaching, in addition to many citations in the *Ars poetica* of Gervase, Faral, "Le manuscrit 511," 88–100. Gervase quotes lines that may be from a now lost poem by Johannes on Caunus and Biblis, and he may also have written poems on Callisto and on Pyramus, though the lines quoted by Gervase could have been coined for teaching purposes: Faral, "Le manuscrit 511," 90–91; Schmidt, 22–26.

3 On these developments, Le Goff, *Les intellectuels,* i–x, 1–69; Jaeger, *Envy of Angels,* chapters 5, 8, 11.

4 See Murray, *Reason and Society,* 71–77; Yunck, *Lineage of Lady Meed,* 47–187; Uhlig, *Hofkritik,* 85–91.

5 In citing Alan's influence, I assume that the *Anticlaudianus* predates the *Architrenius,* a question that was long considered open, and for Schmidt still required discussion: Schmidt, 83–85; Wetherbee, ed., *Architrenius,* xxv, xxx–xxxii.

6 C. Stephen Jaeger, *The Origins of Courtliness: Civilizing Trends and the Formation of Courtly Ideals, 939–1210* (Philadelphia: University of Pennsylvania Press, 1985), 127–75.

7 Nature herself makes this claim at 8.324–33; 9.143–48, 218–21. Jo-

hannes's tapestry is perhaps conceived in imitation of the long poem in which Baudri of Bourgueil describes the bedchamber of Adela, Countess of Blois.

8 See Huizinga, "Über di Verknüpfung," 154–59; Adler, "*Roman de Thèbes*"; Jaeger, *Envy of Angels,* 161–68; Bond, *Loving Subject,* 63–67, 79–87.

9 On this aspect of the *Anticlaudanus,* see Jaeger, *Envy of Angels,* 284–91.

10 On the social situation to which this distancing corresponds, Le Goff, "Warriors and Conquering Bourgeois"; Thomas, *Secular Clergy,* 139–53.

11 Murray, *Reason and Society,* 59–61, 81–109; also Dunbabin, *France in the Making,* 277–86.

12 Murray, *Reason and Society,* 60.

13 Ibid., 71–77.

14 Glossing this passage, Schmidt aptly cites Juvenal, *Sat.* 11.14–16.

15 Petra Korte, *Antike Unterwelt im christlichen Mittelalter* (Frankfurt: Peter Lang, 2012), 252–59.

16 *De nugis* 1.1–5. Much of the *De nugis,* evidently completed in 1191, can be dated as early as 1181–82; Brook and Mynors, Introduction, xxiv–xxxii.

17 On avarice, *Policraticus* 7.16–17; 8.3–4, 13, 15; on gluttony, 8.6–7; on flattery, 3.4–7, 14–15.

18 *Policraticus* 1.1.19. The translation is mine.

19 Liebeschütz, *Medieval Humanism,* 67–73; von Moos, "The Use of *Exempla,*" 247–57; Roling, "*Moderancia*-Konzept," 186–88, 205–6.

20 *Policraticus* 1.Prol.18.

21 *Policraticus* 1.1, 2.20, 3.1.

22 Payen, "L'utopie," 392–93. Payen explains the exclusion of Christian spirituality by the poem's genre: it is a romance, aiming to convey humanist values, a "moralisme universel," to a lay audience.

23 In 7.324–37 generosity is discussed in conspicuously Christian terms, but Christ is not named. John of Salisbury cites Christ as an *exemplum* of secular virtue *(liberalissimus et civilissimus aut facetissimus paterfamilias), Policraticus* 8.9; see von Moos, "The Use of *Exempla,*" 251–54.

24 On the literary-historical significance of this ethical emphasis, Meier, "Wendepunkte der Allegorie," 61–62

25 Jung, *Études,* 118; Godman, *Silent Masters,* 318.

26 Godman, *Silent Masters,* 318, 320.

27 Roling, "*Moderancia*-Konzept," 184–94.

28 Ibid., 195–211. For a similarly positive reading, Piaia, "La 'filosofica famiglia,'" 118–22.

29 Roling, "*Moderancia*-Konzept," 214–15.

30 Gervase of Melkley calls Architrenius a "travelling philosopher" *(philosophus peregrinus)*, *Ars poetica* 3.

31 Johannes was not unaware of the larger meaning of cosmology in the earlier poets. 3.325–33 summarize in terms worthy of Bernardus the vision granted by the Muses of scholarship.

32 Jung, *Etudes*, 120; Roling, "*Moderancia*-Konzept," 216.

33 Schmidt, 54–55, analyzes Johannes's eleven-line recreation of Juvenal, *Sat.* 8.139–40 and lists similar elaborations on formulae from Horace.

34 This judgment appears in an excerpt from the longer version of Geoffrey's *Documentum de modo et arte dictandi* printed in an appendix to John of Garland, *Parisiana Poetria*, ed. Traugott Lawler (New Haven, 1974), 329.

35 *Ars poetica* 8, 17, 84, 136–37.

36 *Ars poetica* 3.

37 *Ars poetica* 8.

38 Schmidt, 87–89, lists a number of irregularly accented words and discusses Johannes's relatively conservative use of elision, which is twice as frequent in the *Alexandreis* of Walter of Chatillon, though almost nonexistent in the poetry of Alan and Bernardus.

39 *Laborintus* 629–30: *Circuit et totum fricat Architrenius orbem; / Qualis sit vitii regio quaeque docet.* (Architrenius goes about, scourging the whole world; each region shows us its particular vice.)

40 *The Battle of the Seven Arts*, 282–84.

41 Roling provides a very full discussion of the *Fortleben* of the *Architrenius*, "*Moderancia*-Konzept," 216–58.

42 Faral, "Le Roman de la Rose," 449–52, assumes Jean's knowledge of the *Architrenius* but cites only the two poets' frequent use of classical dicta and exempla.

43 Roling, "*Moderancia*-Konzept," 234–38.

44 John Ridewall, *Fulgentius metaforalis,* edited by Hans Liebeschütz (Leipzing: Teubner, 1926), 105–6.

45 There are twelve explicit citations of the *Architrenius* in the commentary, including a full chapter on the monster of Greed: Evrart, *Echecs,* 460.

46 *De laboribus Herculis* 3.39.

47 *Pantagruel* 1. Several editors cite *Architrenius* 1.289, where the name is given as *Gabbarus*. But Rabelais seems likely to have borrowed the name, as Johannes did, from Pliny, *Nat. Hist.* 7.16.74.

48 John Pits, *Relationum historicarum de rebus Anglicis tomus primus* (Paris, 1619), 568; Francke, "Der *Architrenius*," 475–76, notes that Hugh's glosses are probably those in Rome, MS Vatican Reg. Lat. 1812 (Schmidt's X).

49 Schmidt, 307–8; Ernest H. Wilkins, *Petrarch's Later Years* (Medieval Academy of America: Cambridge, Mass., 1959), 233–41. Petrarch seems nonetheless to have borrowed from the *Architrenius:* Pacca, "*De Thile Insula*," 606–8; Velli, "Petrarca, Boccaccio," 253.

50 On the shortcomings of this edition, Schmidt, 110–11; Francke, "Der *Architrenius*," 477–78; and my Note on the Text.

51 Francke, "Der *Architrenius*," 476; Max Manitius, *Geschichte der lateinischen Literatur des Mittelalters,* vol. 3 (Munich, 1931), 805–6.

52 Conde Parrado, "La recepción del *Architrenius.*"

53 Vives, *De tradendis disciplinis* 3.9.

54 4.171–72, 175–76 are quoted (with *nefas* for *notas* in 176) in *Decline and Fall of the Roman Empire,* chapter 22, n. 7, to characterize palatial Roman baths in Paris, which as ruins in the medieval period became "the scene of licentious love."

55 *Histoire littéraire de la France,* vol. 14 (Paris, 1817), 569–79.

xxvi

PROLOGUE

Architrenius quidam, cum ad annos virilis roboris devenisset, recordationis stilo retroacti temporis actus colligit universos. Secum quicquid egerit scrutabundus inquirit, nec moribus unquam invenit esse locum. Conqueritur igitur in Naturam, nam, quae maiora poterat, et illud utique potuisset, quod adversus scelerum motus et impetus inconsultos homo impassibilis perduraret. Post querelarum ergo lacrimas profusissimas "Quaeram," inquit, "Naturam, ut odiis expurgatis indignationis huius extergatur fermentum et amoris azymi vinculo solidato optatum Architrenio subsidium conferatur."

2   Mundum igitur pede circumeans vagabundo Venerem, Ambitionem, Avaritiam, Gulam et mundi ceteras invenit meretrices, quae fune multiplici ad rerum temporalium amplexus illicitos attrectant hominem et inclinant. Naturae tandem inventae genibus obvolutus, viae causam evolvit, et porro quicquid postulat impetrato pro subsidii summa de Naturae consilio uxor Architrenio, Moderantia nomine, desponsatur. Quos Deus coniunxit homo non separet.

A certain Architrenius, when he had attained the years of manly vigor, compiled, with the pen of recollection, all his actions of earlier times. Carefully investigating all that he had done, he found that there had never been a place in his life for morality. Therefore he complains against Nature, for she, who had been capable of far greater things, could certainly have ensured also that mankind withstand, impregnable, the contrary motions and unexpected impulses of wickedness. Then after copious weeping and lamentation he declared, "I will seek out Nature, so that when hostility has been cleared away, the ferment of this resentment may be purged, and when a bond of uncontaminated love has been established, she may grant Architrenius the assistance he seeks."

Traversing the world with wandering steps he encounters 2 Venus, Ambition, Avarice, Gluttony, and the other worldly prostitutes who seize a man with their many-stranded rope and draw him to the unlawful embrace of temporal things. Discovering Nature at last, and embracing her knees, he explains the cause of his journey, and when all that he demands has been granted, then, as the completion of Nature's provision for him a bride, Moderation, is married to Architrenius by Nature's decision. Whom God has joined together, let no man put asunder.

3   Architrenius iste ab eventu sic dictus est; nam locis fere singulis peregrinationis suae mundo compatitur sub vitiorum fluctibus naufraganti, et lamentis animum et lacrimis oculum impluit et immergit. Liber autem iste *Architrenius* nuncupatur; unde hic est titulus: "Ad Walterum Rothomagensem Archiepiscopum *Architrenius* incipit." Ex supradictis patet tam intentio quam materia. Ex titulo collige ad quem scribitur hoc opus. De quo autem aut quibus in libris singulis texatur oratio, posita in principio capitula te docebunt. Lege igitur. De actore si quaeras, dixisse sufficiat: Iohannes est nomen eius.

This Architrenius is so named from his experiences. For ₃
at nearly every stage of his pilgrimage he feels compassion
for a world foundering in the seas of vice, so that he floods
his heart with laments and fills his eyes with tears. The book
is also named "Architrenius," and hence its title is this: "Here
begins the *Architrenius,* dedicated to Walter, Archbishop of
Rouen." From what has been said the intention of the book,
as well as its matter, is clear. You may gather from the title to
whom the book is written. What it is about, and in what
several books the discourse is composed, the chapter head-
ings placed at the beginning will teach you. Therefore read
on. If you are curious about the author, suffice it to say: his
name is Johannes.

Capitula

Chapters

LIBER TERTIUS

Book Three

Liber Quartus

Book Four

Book Five

Book Six

Book Seven

LIBER OCTAVUS

BOOK NINE

BOOK ONE

Capitulum 1

De potentia laboris et ingenii et de impotentia desidiae

Velificatur Athos; dubio mare ponte ligatur;
remus arat colles; pedibus substernitur unda;
puppe meatur humus; pelagi Thetis exuit usum.
Salmoneus fulmen iaculatur; Daedalus alas
5 induit: ingenii furor instat, et invia praeceps
rumpit, et artifici cedit Natura labori.
    Languida Segnities, Veneris nutricia, tractat
otia, dilatrix operum, dissuada laborum.
Venativa morae, vix inceptura quod ipso
10 principio rumpit, hodiernos crastinat actus
et, quod praeteritum, numquam facit, usque futurat.
Ausus attenuat, animos premit, illigat artus,
contemptusque luto defoedat aromate morum
pectus odorandum. Famae secura, pudendae
15 assuescit vitae, vitiique paludibus haerens
sorde volutatur. Oculoque improvida caeco
mentis ab excubiis expellit inhospita curas
sollicitosque metus, currentibus urget habenam
ingeniis, fixoque modo conamina sistit,
20 torporisque iacet studii vigilantia somno.
Difficiles aditus, et, quo luctamine prono
nitendum est, odit; non invitata labores

Chapter 1

The power of hard work and ingenuity, and the impotence of sloth

Sails move over Athos; the ocean is spanned by a shaky bridge; oars furrow the hillsides; the waves are subjected to walking feet; ships move on dry land; Thetis has forsaken the ways of the deep. Salmoneus hurls his thunderbolt; Daedalus dons his wings: a frenzy of ingenuity is upon us, bursting headlong into regions uncharted, and Nature yields to the efforts of art.

Languid Sloth, the nurse of Venus, draws out the idle hours, putting off tasks, discouraging hard work. Hunting for an excuse to delay, she breaks off at the very outset what she has scarcely begun, puts off the day's work until the morrow, and ever postpones the past duties which she never performs. She wears down courage, oppresses the spirit, fetters the limbs, and befouls with the filthiness of her contempt any breast fragrant with the scent of morality. Heedless of reputation, she adopts a shameful life; keeping to the swamps of vice, she wallows in the mire. Blind and reckless, she inhospitably banishes care and anxious concern from the outposts of the mind, gives free rein to galloping ingenuity, yet resists endeavor in a determined manner, until zealous alertness succumbs to sleepy torpor. She hates what is difficult to attain, and whatever must be striven for by will and effort; she is attracted neither by praise, the crown of

laude coronanti nec, quo dulcescere sudor
edidicit, lucro, gladios in bella trahenti
25 facturoque leves freta, tela, pericula, caedes.
    Taedia Segnitiem comitantur, et invida laetis
Tristities; Luxusque vacans Lascivia pompis;
et Venus, et renum cinctus Petulantia solvens;
cognatusque Necis Sopor; et praecursor inermis
30 Torpor Egestatis; et amara Opprobria, vultu
maesta verecundo; salibusque Irrisio mordens;
et Pudor, et partes Infamia nuda pudendas;
et vaga propositi Levitas, et nescia fixis
Mobilitas mansisse rotis, et devius Error;
35 votorumque vices crebro Inconstantia versans,
et fluitans Animus, et non statura Voluntas;
pigraque Mollities, et Inertia parca laboris;
et fractus studii Languor, morbusque senectae
Debilitas; sterilisque brevi sub pondere manans
40 Sudor, et abscisis titubans Ignavia nervis.

Capitulum 2

De remotione arrogantiae

At ne desidia Musae mihi sopiat ignes,
nascitur et puero vagit nova pagina versu.
Propositique labor victorem spondet et audax

achievement, nor even by wealth, which teaches one the sweet taste of sweat, luring the swordsman into battle, and making light the perils of the sea, arms, and slaughter.　25

Boredom is the companion of Sloth, and Melancholy, jealous of those who are happy; Wantonness, given over to shows of Excess; Venus, and the Lewdness that loosens the girdle about the loins; Sleep, close kin to Death; and Torpor, the herald of helpless Poverty; and bitter Disgrace, her face　30 made grim by shame; Mockery, who wounds with her sallies of wit; and Shame, and Infamy, exposing herself in shameful nakedness; Fickleness, infirm of purpose, and Restlessness, whose wheels can never remain still, and wandering Error; Inconstancy, whose desires are ever changing; uncertain　35 Purpose and unstable Will; sluggish Effeminacy and shift-less Idleness; Apathy, broken in spirit; Infirmity, the afflic-tion of age; fruitless Toil, drenched with sweat by a small burden; and trembling Faintheartedness, whose strength　40 has failed her.

Chapter 2

A disavowal of arrogance

But lest idleness quench the fires of my Muse, a new work is born, and utters its first squalling verses. The labor of such a task, and the bold, unwavering zeal for great challenges

grandibus inceptis studii constantia; verum
45   inter Apollineas lauros fas esto myricae
deiectis vernare comis. Non praecinit omnem
ad digitum Phoebea chelys; non novimus aures
Aonia mulcere lyra; non pectinis huius
in plebem vilescit apex. Haec gloria vatum,
50   hoc iubar, hic titulus solos contingit Homeros.
Sufficiet, populo si suffecisse togato
hic poterit nostrae tenuis succentus avenae.
In Croesi ne sudet opes privatus Amyclas!
Contentum proprio faciunt me tuta facultas
55   angustique lares. Modico me posse potentem
metior ad multum, nec gutture rumpar anhelo
Sirenum insidias aequasse et funus oloris,
dum mea ieiuno mihi sibilet ore cicada.
Non ago praecipites sopire leonibus iras
60   pectine vel rigidos mores mollire ferarum.
Hoc precor, hoc satis est, si nostra haec arida plebis
aure sono tenui ieiunia solvat harundo.
Incola mergus aquae madidis ne provocet alis
surgentes aquilas lambentibus aethera pennis!

belong to the heroic spirit; but amid Apollo's laurels, be it   45
right that the myrtle, too, flourish with its drooping boughs.
The lyre of Phoebus does not give forth song at every touch;
we cannot charm the ear with Aonian chords; such high
artistry is not squandered on common folk. It is the glory
of true poets, a brilliance and distinction that belong only   50
to such as Homer. It will be enough if the lower note of
our slender pipe find acceptance among ordinary people.
A homely Amyclas should not aspire to the wealth of a
Croesus! My modest means content me, and my humble
dwelling. Though modestly endowed, I hold myself capable   55
of accomplishing much, and I will not become broken-
winded from striving to rival the treacherous music of the
Sirens or the death song of the swan, for mine is the thin,
whispering voice of the cicada. I do not propose to soothe
the lion's unbridled wrath with my lyre, or refine the savage   60
behavior of beasts. My prayer will be answered if hearing
the sound of my pipe, however dry and meager, may ease the
hard lot of common folk. A merganser whose wings are
drenched should not challenge eagles who rise toward
heaven on gleaming wings!

Capitulum 3

Contra depravationem
veterum modernorum

65 O mihi suspecta veterum mordacior aetas,
acrius in iuvenes decorrosiva Senectus!
Ne preme, sed pressa meritorum nomina tolle,
quae male tondenti decerpit forcipe livor.
Dulcescat gravium maiestativa virorum
70 lingua, nec invidiae fuso crudescat aceto.
    Deucalioneum pelagus vel naufraga Pyrrhae
saecula non vidi, vel quas solaribus ardens
vector equis radio sitienti sorbuit, undas.
Non me praeteritis iacto latuisse diebus
75 Maeoniumque senem mihi convixisse, nec aevi
lautius intitulor senioris laude, modernis
maior, ab ignotis famae lucrosior annis.
Sustineas quod me dederint haec tempora nec, si
videris auctorem, pretio leviore libellum
80 argue nec, si quem meruit, deperdat honorem.
Non me limes Atin, non barbarus edidit Atlas;
non apud Arcturi glaciem solemque Syenes
advena spectandos ordiri glorior ortus,
philosophum faciente loco, soloque verendum
85 externi terrore loci. Nodosa meretur
nondum ruga coli; nondum veneranda senectae
albet olore coma; non sum cui serviat auri

Chapter 3

An answer to the perversity of the old men of our day

O suspicious and backbiting generation, Old Age so eager   65
to judge harshly the deeds of the young! Do not attack, but
rather raise up the names of worthy men who have been at-
tacked, names which envy has wickedly damaged with her
sharp shears. Speak the sweet and ennobling language of
just men, not harsh words steeped in the acid of jealousy.   70

I did not witness Deucalion's flood or the shipwrecking
age of Pyrrha, or those waters which the ardent charioteer
of the horses of the Sun drew off with parching radiance. I
do not boast that I have mysteriously survived from ancient
times, that the old Maeonian was my contemporary; I do   75
not lay claim to a more elegant name in honor of my great
age, grander than those of modern men, and richer in re-
nown by virtue of my unnumbered years. Accept the fact
that this age has produced me, and do not, if you have seen
the author, value the book more lightly, or deny it whatever   80
honor it may deserve. Neither far-off Atin nor rough Atlas
gave me birth; I am no stranger who glories in a wondrous
origin amid the Arctic ice or beneath the sun of Syene, as if
the place itself made me a philosopher, to be regarded with
awe only because of fear of an unknown land. As yet I show   85
no venerable maze of wrinkles; my hair does not yet gleam
with the downy white of reverend age; I am not one whom a

turba vel argenti, cui rerum copia mundo
plaudat adulanti, cui Serum purpura vatis
90 attitulet nomen, cuius facunda smaragdus
disputet in digitis vulgique assibilet aures
attonitas gemmis. Liber est, non libra, Iohannes
quod canit; et Cirrhae modicum de fonte propinat,
hisque magis Phoebus cyathis quam Bacchus inundat.
95   Ha quod Alexander tetigit: "Decisor Homeri,
Zoile, tu laudum cynicus, tu serra bonorum;
magna doles, maiora notas, in maxima saevis.
Siste gradus solitos; odio tibi vapulo." Libro
parce, nec auctoris in opus iactura redundet.

Capitulum 4

De ortu eius ad quem scribitur

100 Gloria Pergameae sepeliri gentis Achiva
non potuit flamma; stetit occursante ruina
indilapsus apex; pulsanti cedere Fato,
non cecidisse tulit. Danais Fortuna caminis
excoxit non saeva Phryges; maioraque bellis
105 erudiit perferre viros, et diruta maior
stanti Troia fuit. Non est incensa, sed igni

heap of gold or silver may advance, whose sheer wealth might commend him to a fawning world, for whom China's purple robes might gain a priestly dignity, on whose fingers 90 eloquent jewels would speak for him, whispering in the ears of a multitude dazed by their brilliance. Johannes's song is a book, not a balance; his modest libation is from the fount of Cirrha, and it is Phoebus, not Bacchus, who fills the bowl.

How well Alexander said it: "Zoilus, you carp at Homer, 95 you sneer at praise, you tear at good men; greatness pains you, what is greater you defame, and at the greatest you rage. Give up your ever-aggressive stance; I am tormented by my hatred of you." Spare the book; let not the rejection of the author be extended to his work.

Chapter 4

The origins of him to whom the book is addressed

The glory of the people of Pergama could not be extin- 100 guished by Achaean fire; its loftiness remained unfallen in the face of disaster, and in yielding to the force of Fate, it did not succumb. Fortune was not cruel in subjecting the Phrygians to the heat of the Danaean forge: she taught their men to endure greater things than war, and Troy destroyed was 105 greater than Troy unfallen. It was not consumed by fire;

uberius lucrata iubar. Radiosque Pelasgae
Dardanios auxere faces; nec palluit illo
Sol Asiae fumo. Fines augusta potestas
110 indignata breves, iam fastidiverat Idae
artari plebeia iugis, mundique recessus
occupat et validis maiora supermeat ausis.
Plenior imperii Romanis Pergama pensat
fascibus, et tanto si quid de culmine Fati
115 diminuit livor, virtus reparavit: et orbi
hic urbem rapuit, haec orbem reddidit urbi.
      Prodiga, nec tandem niveis exhausta metallis,
utilium mater, dulcique puerpera glaeba,
absolvit Phrygiis affusa Britannia Graecos.
120 Immo Phryges Phrygius sanguis solatur, anhelos
exhilarat luctus, quem derivavit Iuli
postera maiestas nostroque insplenduit aevo.
Nec nisi nobilium medios intexuit ortus
ille Dei sedes, thalamus virtutis, honesti
125 hortulus et morum, vitiis impervia, Tempe
altera, quam nec hiems nec fervor marcidat, Hybla.
Ille procellosos innaufragus enatat annos;
inferius flantem scelerum premit altior Austrum,
nec mundi quatitur hac tempestate. Malorum
130 nubibus et ventis sublimior, alter Olympus
surgit, et explicitos apices extendit in ortus;
crescit, et in titulos maiores erigit Idam;
fulget, et aureolo populatur sidere noctem;
gaudet et impluvium maeroris siccat et imbres;
135 vernat et hiberna Walterus diluit, in quo
florida Troianum redimit Cornubia damnum.

instead its radiance gained a richer glow; Pelasgian torches enhanced Dardanian brilliance; the Sun of Asia was not dimmed by their smoke. Its august power, disdaining narrow confines, scorned to be basely contained by the ridges of Ida, reached forth to the ends of the earth, and overcame greater obstacles through strength and daring. A greater, imperial Pergama was augmented by the Roman fasces, and if envious Fate had diminished their once-great power , courage made good the loss: one robbed the world of a city, the other repaid the city with the world.

Britain, freely giving, not yet drained of her supply of gleaming metals, mother of resources, abounding in rich land, absolved the Greeks by pouring her wealth on the Phrygians. Indeed a man of Phrygian blood solaced the Phrygians, and brought them joy after exhausting labor, one whom the latterday majesty of the race of Iulus produced to lend its luster to our own age. For only among a noble people did this man trace his origin, this shrine of God, bower of virtue, garden of probity and character, immune to vice, this second Tempe, which neither winter nor summer heat can affect, this Hybla. He moves through our stormy time immune to shipwreck; his higher power suppresses the storm of wickedness raging below; he is unshaken by the turbulence of this world. Higher than the winds and clouds of evil, a second Olympus rises, and extends its lofty peaks toward the orient; grows, and raises Ida to yet greater dignity; shines, and robs the night sky of its starry brilliance; rejoices, and dries up the pools and rains of sorrow. Walter is the spring that dispels winter; in him flourishing Cornwall makes good the loss of Troy.

Vix tanti cyathum pelagi delibo, licebit
solverer in quaevis commendativa viroque
impluerem laudes. Nam morum praevolat alis
140   curriculum laudis; solus capit omnia Famae
nomina. Nec veris adventum percipit Aetnae
gloria; nec crescit Phoebus face, mundus harena,
saecula momento, nimbo mare, linea puncto.

Capitulum 5

De oblatione opusculi

O cuius studio, quo remige navigat aestu
145   mundanoque mari tumidisque exempta procellis
Linconiae sedes, O quem non praeterit aequi
calculus, O cuius morum redolentia caelum
spondet, et esse nequit virtus altissima maior,
indivisa minor; cuius se nomen et astris
150   inserit, et Famae lituo circumsonat orbem;
O quem Rothomagi sedes viduata maritum
sperat et aspirat, solidisque amplexibus ardet
astrinxisse virum, fragrantis odoribus uti,
morum deliciis, virtutis aromate, sponsi
155   pectore, quod Phoebum redolet, quod Nestora pingit.
Vere novo thalami florere expectat et illos

Even if it were granted me to pour myself forth in all manner of commendation and shower this man with praise, I would scarcely be drawing off a cupful from a vast ocean. For with wings of rectitude he outstrips the chariot of praise; he alone lays claim to all the titles of Renown. Glori- 140 ous Aetna does not notice the coming of spring; Phoebus's light is not increased by a torch, the world by a grain of sand, time by an instant, the sea by a shower, a line by a point.

Chapter 5

The dedication of the work

O you by whose zeal and guidance the see of Lincoln voy- ages unharmed through the raging ocean of this world and 145 its furious storms, you whom no degree of justice can sur- pass, the sweetness of whose character is a promise of heaven, whose supreme virtue cannot be made greater, nor its integrity diminished; whose name inscribes itself among the stars, and is proclaimed the world over by the trumpet 150 of Fame; O you for whom the widowed see of Rouen hopes and yearns as husband, eager to clasp you in firm embrace as a lover, to enjoy the fragrant scent, the charming character, the virtuous aroma, of a bridegroom whose mind is redolent 155 of Phoebus, the image of Nestor. She waits, ready to come to flower in the springtime of the marriage bed, eager to

ascendisse thoros, ubi Virtus pronuba, Christo
auspice, sacrati et sacrae conubia firmet.
Optat ut Arctois infusum manna Britannis
160 cedat et irriguum Normannis influat, urbis
aridulae deserta rigans, sitientia sacros
Linconiae fontes et vix libata recentis
gaudia prima favi, longum sperata brevique
degustata mora. Revocat, quem misit, alumnum,
165 depositumque petit et, quo videt, Anglia reddi
poscit inoccidui commissum luminis usum.
Virgo virum, matura thoros, innupta maritum,
orba patrem, mutilata caput, iactata salutem,
caeca ducem, tenebrosa iubar, nocturna lucernam
170 exigit. Et queritur tardanti mane, suumque,
eclipsata, sitit rediturum Cynthia Phoebum.
    O mihi Maecenas operis, tractique laboris
expectata quies, rudis indubitata Minervae
spes, adhibe coeptis oculi mentisque favorem.

enter that nuptial chamber where Virtue as brideswoman, with the sanction of Christ, will unite the consecrated bridegroom and sacred bride. She prays that the manna showered on the northerly Britons may remove, and flow 160 forth upon the Normans, watering the barren earth of the dry city, earth that thirsts for the sacred waters of Lincoln, and the first pleasure of this new nectar, as yet barely tasted, long awaited and only briefly enjoyed. She calls home the nursling whom she had sent forth, seeks him whom she had 165 committed to others and, discovering him, demands that England restore the unquenchable light entrusted to it. The virgin desires a man, the woman a marriage bed, the maiden a husband, the orphan a father, the maimed body a head, the fallen succor, the blind a guide, the shadowed a light, the benighted a guiding light. Cynthia, in eclipse, complains 170 that dawn comes slowly, and thirsts for the return of her Phoebus.

O thou Maecenas of my work, long awaited rest from my long labor, unquestioned inspiration of my rough understanding, grant to the work now begun the favor of your scrutiny and judgment.

Capitulum 6

De invocatione ad Deum

175 O qui secretas homini metiris harenas,
et numero claudis dubium monstrantia Fatum
sidera; qui nosti mundine intermina surgat
area, nec Stygiae noctis latuere recessus;
et solus solisque modum lunaeque meatum
180 scis, Deus, et celas incauto iudice visu
astrorum excursus (fallitque et fallitur idem
aethereae venans oculus secreta Minervae);
O divum Deitas, nusquam deflexa superni
linea consilii, divinae pagina mentis,
185 qua nec desit apex nec iota superfluat, una
singula complectens, quae dispertita quotannis
evolvit series nulli mutanda sororum;
cui Clotho, Lachesis deservit et Atropos, illa
stamina dispensans fusis vitalibus, illa
190 fila trahens operi, donec concluserit illa;
O Cirrhae latices nostrae, Deus, implue menti,
eloquii rorem siccis infunde labellis;
distillaque favos, quos nec, dum Tagus harenis
palleat aut sitiat admotis Tantalus undis,
195 horreat insipidos aetas vel livor amaros.
Dirige, quod timida praesumpsit dextera, dextram
audacem pavidamque iuva, tu mentis habenam
fervoremque rege. Quicquid dictaverit ori

Chapter 6

An invocation to God

O God, who measure out the hidden course of human life, 175
and subject to your harmony the stars that reveal uncertain
Fate; you who know whether the expanse of the universe is
unbounded, from whom the recesses of Stygian night are
not hidden; you alone, God, know the course of the sun and
the moon's wandering, and keep the courses of the stars hid- 180
den from the uncertain judgment of sight (for the eye both
deceives and is deceived when it pursues the secrets of heav-
enly wisdom); O God of gods, unalterable pattern of su-
preme wisdom, scripture of the divine mind, where not a
letter is missing, yet not a dot is superfluous, alone encom- 185
passing the single events, disposed year by year, which a se-
rial law unfolds that none of the Sisters may alter; you whom
Clotho, Lachesis, and Atropos obey, one meting out thread
for the spindles of lives, one working the threads into a pat- 190
tern which the third will bring to completion; O God, pour
the waters of Cirrha on my mind, moisten my dry lips with
the dew of eloquence; distill sweet springs which, though
Tagus be made yellow by its sands, or Tantalus thirst for
waters near at hand, the age will not reject as tasteless, or 195
envy find sour. Guide the work which a hesitant hand has
dared to begin, sustain my bold strokes and strengthen
my faltering ones, be both the curb and the inspiration of
my thought. Suffuse with the balm of your favor what a too

spiritus aridior, oleum suffunde favoris.

200 Tu Patris es verbum, tu mens, tu dextera: verbum
expediat verbum, mens mentem, dextera dextram.

Capitulum 7

Contra invidos

Hoc etiam votum facili bonitate secunda,
hoc nostris superadde bonis: ne transeat istud
ad limam Livoris opus; ne sentiat illam

205 iudicii formam, qua cancellatur honestum,
suppletur vitium; quae verba decentia radit,
turpia subscribit; quae praestantissima scalpro
mordet et omne bonum legit indignante labello.
Dulcius expectat examen pagina; iustas

210 pro vitiis latura notas, habituraque nomen
pro meritis, laudisque vicem, si forte venusti
quid ferat, auditu dignum punctoque favoris.
Sit procul Invidiae suspecta novacula, solis
ingeniosa dolis; procul haec sit vipera, nullo

215 corruptura nisi rerum momenta veneno.

barren spirit may have dictated. For you are the word, the   200
mind, the right hand of the Father: may that word, mind and
hand sustain my own.

Chapter 7

A prayer against the envious

Favor this prayer, too, in your ready goodness, and add to my
blessings this last: let not this work undergo the harsh ver-
dict of Envy; let it not know the sort of criticism by which   205
probity is rejected and vice promoted; which crosses out
seemly words and underlines vile ones; which cuts and
gnaws at excellence, and reads all good writing with a conde-
scending sneer. My page looks for a milder assessment; it is
ready to undergo just censure for its faults, but also to gain   210
recognition, and even praise, for its merits, if indeed it pos-
sesses sufficient charm to be heard and favorably received.
But let the slanderous razor of Envy, keen only in treachery,
remain far off, and far off be that viper which seeks with its   215
poison to destroy only significant things.

Capitulum 8

De recordatione Architrenii circa opera retroacta, et ibi incipit narratio operis

Dumescente pilis facie, radioque iuventae
obscuris pallente genis, cum mala viriles
exacuit nemorosa rubos nec primula mento
vellera mollescunt, virides quot luserit annos,
220 respicit et, quicquid tenero persuaserit aetas
floridior, recolit memor Architrenius. Imas
pectoris evolvit latebras mersosque profunda
explorat sub mente lares, nec moribus usquam
invenit esse locum, nec se virtutibus unum
225 impendisse diem. "Mene istos" inquit "in usus
enixa est Natura parens? Me misit ut arma
in superos damnata feram, divumque reatus
irritent odium? Legesque et iura meique
praeteream decreta Iovis? Vitiine potestas
230 mortales aeterna premit? Facinusne redundat
diis invisa palus? Mater quid pignora tantae
destituit labi, nec, quem produxit, alumno
excubat, ut nullis maculam scelus inspuat actis?

Chapter 8

Architrenius reflects on his past conduct, and here the story proper begins

As his face becomes overgrown with coarse hair, and the gleam of youth fades on his darkened cheeks, when his bushy jaws have grown sharp with manly bristles, and the fleece of early youth is no longer soft on his chin, Architrenius recalls to his mind how many springtime years he has given to revelry, the things to which a too-flourishing youth 220 has enticed his weakness. He delves into the shadowy depths of his breast, seeks out the ruling spirits buried in his innermost mind, and discovers that there has never been a place there for morality, that he has never devoted a single day to virtue. "For such purposes as these did mother Na- 225 ture give me birth?" he asks. "Has she sent me forth to wage impious war against heaven, that my guilty acts may provoke the gods to hatred? Am I to ignore laws and statutes decreed by my Jove? Does sin have power to oppress mortal 230 beings eternally? Is our guilt a swamp in flood, detested by the gods? Why has my mother abandoned her charge to such peril, why does she not keep watch over the child she has borne, so that his actions may remain untainted by guilt?

Capitulum 9

De Naturae potentia

"Illud enim supraque potest. Nullaque magistras
235 non habet arte manus, nec summa potentia certo
fine coartatur. Astrorum flammeat orbes,
igne rotat caelos, discursibus aera rumpit,
mollit aquae sphaeram, telluris pondera durat.
Flore coronat humum, gemmas inviscerat undis,
240 Phoebificans auras, stellas intexit Olympo.
    "Natura est quodcumque vides; incudibus illa
fabricat omniparis, quidvis operaria nutu
construit, eventusque novi miracula spargit.
Ipsa potest rerum solitos avertere cursus,
245 enormesque serit monstrorum prodiga formas;
gignendique stilum variat, partuque timendo
lineat anomalos larvosa puerpera vultus.

Chapter 9

The power of Nature

"Nature can do all this and more. There is no art that her hand has not mastered, and her supreme power knows no 235 limit. She kindles the starry orbs, makes the heavens revolve by her fiery energy, stirs the air with varying movements, makes the watery region fluid and hardens the bulk of the earth. She decks the land with flowers, buries precious gems in the deep, imbues the air with Phoebus's light, and adorns 240 the Olympian firmament with stars.

"Whatever you behold is Nature; all-creating, she works at her forge, produces anything at will, and spreads abroad a miraculous array of novelties. She has power to alter the normal course of events, and prodigally sows huge and mon- 245 strous forms; she varies the style of her conceptions, and by a fearful labor her fantastic fertility gives shape to abnormal creatures.

Capitulum 10

De monstruosis

"Mascula Gracchorum tribuit gestamina matri,
malleolosque ferens duplici cum folle viriles,
250   coniectura fuit gemini Cornelia sexus.
    "Nubit Aristonte mulier modo, nubitur illi
permutatque toros ea vir modo; foedere foedus
rumpit et efficitur illa ille, marita maritus;
passaque tritorem rursus terit area, ducit
255   femina, sulcus arat, fodit ortus, malleat incus.
    "Curio natales armato dentibus ore
exiit in luctus; acuit pro dentibus ossis
continui massam Prusiae filius. Ossa
Lygdamus extersis habuit concreta medullis,
260   qui tulit ad Siculos victoris praemia laurum,
quam dedit Herculei ludi servator Olympus.
    "Aethiopum naso facies non surgit; et oris
planitie strata, non delibantur odores
naribus, aut cerebrum lacrimosa foramina purgant.
265   "Sunt quibus excludit linguae iactura susurros;
eloquiique vices digiti facundia tractat;
interpresque manus animi secreta retexens,
obsequium vocis signis affabilis aequat,
et tacite rixans imitatur garrula lites.

Chapter 10

Strange creatures

"Nature assigned the actions of a man to Cornelia, the mother of the Gracchi, and it was supposed that she was of both sexes, possessing the little hammers of a man in their double pouch. 250

"Arescon first marries as a woman; then she changes marriage beds and, now a man, another is married to her; one bond is broken by means of another: she is made he, the wife a husband; having endured the thresher, she works the threshing floor; the woman takes a wife, the furrow plows, 255 the garden spades, the anvil hammers.

"Curio came forth into the pangs of childbirth with a mouth armed with teeth; the son of Prusia displayed, in place of teeth, a mass of solid bone. Lygdamus, who brought to Sicily as a token of victory the laurel which the Olympian 260 patron of the Herculean games first bestowed, had solid bones devoid of marrow.

"An Ethiopian's face has no projecting nose; the surface of the face being flat, no odors are taken in by the nostrils, nor do tear ducts provide purgation for the brain.

"There are those whom lack of a tongue prevents from 265 whispering: a witty finger performs the function of eloquence; the interpreting hand, unfolding the secrets of the mind, fulfills with signs the office of the friendly voice, and silently garrulous anger mimes a quarrel.

270 "Sunt quibus ora brevi coeunt obnoxia rimae,
qua bibulis stomacho cibus inspiratur avenis.
Vixque trahit cannis extorta liquamina Maurus,
quem dapis irrigua mediatrix lactat harundo,
dum calami rores angusta mamillula plorat.

275 "In pede bis binos digitos duplat accola Nulo.
Est qui monoculo vultu contentus et uno
crure potens cursus; plantam resupinat ad ignes
solis et erecti spatio pedis efficit umbram.

"Gens Librae vicina, carens cervicibus, inter
280 supremos humeros oculorum concavat orbes.
Sunt qui bis binis pedibus, sunt qui ore canino
degenerant; homines specie, sed monstra figuris.
Est cui cana comam puerilis liliat aetas;
maturusque putrem vetulam deliliat annus.

285 "Staturam cubitis septem distendit Orestes.
Bis senis Phrygios potuit movisse ruentis
Gemagog arduitas, Corinei fracta lacertis.
In bis quinque pedes produxit Gabbarus artus.
Aucta ter undenis cubitis mensura Metellum
290 terruit, et Flacci tenuit mirantis ocellos
corporis humani plus quam Titania moles.

"Gens Scytha spectatu geminis oculata pupillis
laedit. Et irata Bithia, quocunque rotatur,
enecat intuitus; oculis inserpit inurens
295 ira, peremptivi radiis interfica visus.

"Non est passa levi Crassum mollescere risu;
Antoniam Drusi sordente madescere sputo;

"There are those whose infirm mouths narrow to a small 270
slit, through which food is drawn into the stomach through
a straw. The Moor, to whom a reed, suckling like a nurse,
conveys liquid food, can scarcely take in even liquids
strained through a tube, as the tiny teat of the straw weeps
droplets.

"Those who dwell on Mt. Nulo have two sets of four toes 275
on each foot. There is a race content with a single eye in
their faces, and capable of running on one leg; they raise the
sole of the foot toward the blazing sun, and shade them-
selves in the space beneath the elevated foot.

"A race governed by Libra have no necks, and their eye
sockets appear between their upraised shoulders. There are 280
people disfigured by two pairs of feet, or a dog's face, human
in kind, but with the forms of monsters. There is a people
whose hair grows lily-white in childhood; mature years turn
this whiteness to decrepit age.

"Orestes stretched to a height of seven cubits. The tow- 285
ering height of onrushing Gemagog's twelve cubits could
disconcert the Phrygians, but was beaten down by the
strong arms of Corineus. The body of Gabbarus extended to
ten feet. The more than titanic mass of a human body grown
to a length of thirty-three cubits terrified Metellus, and held 290
the wondering gaze of Flaccus.

"A Scythian tribe whose eyes are equipped with double
pupils kill by staring. And when the Bithian is angry, her
look is deadly wherever she turns; burning wrath creeps into
her eyes and transmits death through the beams of her le- 295
thal gaze.

"Nature did not allow Crassus to relax in a gentle smile,
nor could Antonia, daughter of Drusus, perform the coarse

fumida Pomponii solvi ructatibus ora;
fulmine Fortunae Socratis pallescere vultus,
300 aut miseris letos rigidum flexisse tenorem.
    "Felices et paene dei, quos educat aura,
quam pomi praemellit odor. Fragrantia genti
panis agit potusque vices, hic Bacchus in eius
est cyathis, haec corbe Ceres. Sic Gangis alumno
305 vivitur, et redimunt oris ieiunia nares.
Non effusa gulae, non ventris tabida luxu
natio; nec sordet utero, nec gutture peccat.
    "Duritia Psyllum sic loricavit, ut atris
integer eludat pugnantes morsibus angues;
310 solaque pro muri cutis est insaucia vallo,
parma veneniferi iaculis impervia dentis.
    "At me pestiferis aliis exponit inermen
anguibus; et tortis vitiorum deteror Hydris.
Non mihi pacifico nudum latus asperat ense,
315 non Chalybum plumis loricae retia nodat,
non surgente caput animosum casside cristat,
non clipei telis obtendit moenia. Nec, quos
det Natura, timent scelerum Stymphalides arcus,
nec furtim laesura nefas deterret harundo.

act of spitting, or the steaming face of Pomponius find relief by belching. Socrates's countenance did not grow pale at Fortune's blows, nor alter its unvarying expression when 300 faced with the misery of death.

"Happy and almost godlike are those whom a breeze sustains, which the scent of fruit makes surpassingly sweet. Fragrance serves this people in place of food and drink: it is the Bacchus in their goblets, the Ceres on their board. Such is the life of those who dwell on the Ganges, whose nostrils 305 relieve the hunger of their mouths. This people are not abandoned to excess, not consumed by indulgence of the belly; they neither defile the stomach nor sin through gluttony.

"Nature has so steeled the Psyllian with toughness that he escapes unharmed from serpents attacking him with their black jaws; his skin alone, unscathed, serves as a pro- 310 tecting wall, a shield impervious to the darts of their poisonous fangs.

"But Nature has left me unarmed amid pestiferous vipers of another kind; I am overpowered by the twisting Hydra of my vices. She has not armed my defenseless body with the menace of a pacifying sword, nor bound the mesh of my 315 corselet with the feathers of the Chalybes, placed on my proud head a helmet with upright crest, nor offered me the protection of a shield. The Stymphalian birds of sin do not fear such bows as Nature provides, and the arrow that wounds by stealth does not discourage wickedness.

Capitulum 11

De proposito Architrenii

320 "Quid faciam, novi: profugo Natura per orbem
est quaerenda mihi. Veniam, quacumque remotos
abscondat secreta lares; odiique latentes
eliciam causas et rupti forsan amoris
restituam nodos. Adero, pacemque dolorum
325 compassiva feret et subsidiosa roganti
indulgebit opem. Flecti patietur, anhelas
hauriet aure preces, et mentis verba medullis
blanditiva bibet, lacrimisque pluentibus udas
siccabit mansueta genas. Ad vota parentem
filius inducet."
330   Spes solativa timorem
eicit et coeptis favet et temptasse repulsa
nil metuit peius: "ibo properantius, ibo
ocius et, quae sit miseris fortuna, videbo."

CHAPTER II

Chapter 11

Architrenius proposes to act

"I know what I will do: I must seek out Nature by roaming   320
the world. Wherever she dwells, secret and withdrawn, I
will come there; I will bring to light the hidden causes of her
hostility, and perhaps repair the broken bond of love. I will
appear before her, and in compassion she will assuage my   325
pain, and her succor will grant the aid for which I plead. She
will allow herself to be swayed, lend an ear to my breathless
prayers, draw my affecting words into the depths of her
mind, and gently dry these cheeks now wet with flowing
tears. A son will induce a parent to grant his prayer."   330

Consoling hope drives out fear and encourages his plan;
he fears no worse result than to have tried and failed: "I will
set forth at once, travel swiftly, and see what Fortune may
await the wretched."

Capitulum 12

De itineratione eiusdem

Rumpitur ergo morae sterilis dilatio; coeptum
335 promovet, urget opus, mundi circummeat axes,
et pede sollicito terit Architrenius orbem.
Montibus insudat, metit aegro poplite valles,
languet in abruptis, in planis praevolat auras;
ardua morbificant, relevant devexa laborem;
340 sicca pedum curru, manuum legit humida remo,
sese naviculae, sese vice remigis utens.
Nec suspendit iter, scopulos si planta queratur,
crura rubus fodiat, faciem ramalia caedant,
dumus aret vultus, Boreae furor ora flagellet;
345 ardeat ad radios cutis, extinguatur ad imbres,
sub Phoebo sitiat, pluviis adaquetur amictus;
saeviat aut aestus aut frigoris ira, caputque
alba ligustret hiems, nigra quod vacciniet aestas,
et face sol Maurum faciat, nive bruma Britannum.

Chapter 12

His journey

The fruitless hesitation of delay is interrupted forthwith; Architrenius sets about his task, presses forward, journeys 335 around the world, and wears away the earth with his anxious pace. He toils up mountainsides, crosses valleys on shaking legs, moves wearily up hills, outstrips the wind on level ground; steep places wear him down, but descending eases his labor; he crosses dry land with his feet as chariot, and 340 water with his hands as oars, making himself serve in place of a vessel, himself in place of an oarsman. He does not break off his journey though his feet complain of the rocks, brambles gouge his legs, branches lash his face, thorns dig into his cheeks, the rage of Boreas stings his lips; though his skin burns with the sun's rays, or is drenched with rain, 345 though he is parched by Phoebus, and his clothes are turned to water by the rain; whether cruel heat or raging cold assail him, whether winter white cover his head, or the black of summer stain it, and the sun give him the face of a Moor or the hoar frost that of a Briton.

Capitulum 13

De domo Veneris

350 Iamque fatigato Veneris domus aurea, rerum
flosculus, occurrit, monti superedita: qualem
cantat odorifero Philomena poetica versu;
quae, quibus intorsit odii certamina livor,
Rufinum vitiis, Stilichonem moribus armat,
355 alternansque stilos istum premit, erigit illum,
neutrum describit, tacet ambos, fingit utrumque.
    Hic dea virginibus roseum cingentibus orbem
praesidet et rudibus legit incentiva puellis,
inque viros faculas accendit et implicat hamos.
360 Ex quibus una, loci specie pictura, coruscat
stelligero vultu plus quam Ledaea, Dione
altera quae Lunam maiori praevenit astro;
et quam subradiat Phoebi minus aemula Phoebe.

Chapter 13

The house of Venus

At last Venus's house of gold, the flower of creation, set high 350
on a mountain, presents itself to the weary one: such a place
as poetic Philomena sings of in scented verse; she who,
describing men whom envious hatred forced into conflict,
arms Rufinus with vices, and Stilicho with virtues, varying
her style to put down the one and exalt the other, yet de- 355
scribes neither one, keeps silent about both, creates a false
image of each.

Here the goddess presides over a rosy world, surrounded
by maidens; she teaches the inexperienced girls her entice-
ments, kindles their torches and readies their hooks for
men. One among these maidens is in beauty an image of the 360
place itself, her face fairer than Leda's in its starry glow, a
second Dione who surpasses the Moon in light; Phoebe, less
envious of Phoebus, defers to her radiance.

Capitulum 14

De descriptione puellae

Verticis erecta moderatum circinat orbem
365   sphaerula; nec temere sinuato deviat arcu,
non obliqua means, ubi nec tumor advena surgit,
nec vallis peregrina sedet. Lascivit in auro
indigena crinis, nec mendicatur alumnus
pyxidis, exter honos, nec nubit adultera fictae
370   lucis imago comae; non exulat arte capilli
umbra, nec aurifero ferrum sepelitur amictu.
Haec capitis pretiosa seges nec densior aequo
luxuriat; iuncto descensu prona, nec errat
limite turbato, nec divertendo vagatur
375   transfuga, nec cedit alio pulsante capillus.
A frontis medio tractu directa supernae
verticis ad centrum via lactea surgit aranti
pectine, cuius acu geminas discessit in alas,
et tandem trifidum coma cancellatur in orbem,
380   divisoque prius iterum coit agmine crinis.
    Liber apex frontis nitidum limante iuventa
tenditur in planum, trito radiosa politu
et bysso, quo prima cutem vestiverat aetas.
Candida, nec maculae naevo nubescit, oloris
385   aemula, nec recipit vaccinia mixta ligustris.

Chapter 14

A description of a girl

The small sphere of her head, held high, has the shape of a well-formed globe; there is no random deviation from its 365 continuous arc, no divergent contour, for no unwelcome swelling rises, no intrusive depression subsides. Her natural hair luxuriates in its gold, and there is no need for external adornments, the products of the cosmetic case, no adulterating appearance of false radiance unites itself to her hair; 370 no darkness in her hair is banished by art, nor is any iron gray veiled by a mantle of gold. Her head's precious crop is luxuriant but not overly dense; easily drawn together as it falls, it does not stray about, resisting confinement, or escape to wander in all directions, and no strand submits to 375 the tugging of another. From the center of her forehead a milky way rises straight upward to the crown of her head, defined by the furrowing comb, at whose prompting her hair divides into twin wings, and is finally arranged in a threefold coil, and the hair whose ranks had been divided 380 draws together again.

The clear height of her forehead widens to an expanse glowing with a youthful sheen, its radiance born of assiduous scrubbing and set off by the linen headdress with which her youthful years have arrayed her. The whiteness of her complexion, vying with the swan, is not clouded by any mark or blemish, and its white bloom has received no 385

61

Qua propior naso frons ultima vergit, aperto
parvula planities spatio nudatur; utrimque
luna supercilii tenui succingitur arcu.
Nec coeunt medio distincta volumina fine;
390   gratius alternos prohibent divortia tactus.
Communisque rubo via non silvescit, eamque
non operit mentis pilus accusator amarae,
nec clausi loquitur fellis nemorosa venenum.
    Tortilis auriculae nodosaque cellula gyrum
395   explicat et tornata brevem complectitur orbem.
Mundaque, Naturae digito purgata, latenti
nusquam sorde rudis, scabros inculta recessus
erubuisse nequit verborum semita; planum
libera sternit iter, fruticoso calle, lutosis
400   non odiosa viis. Susceptam nuntia menti
portatura notam, vocisque domuncula, cuivis
semper aperta sono, tersisque penatibus hospes,
murmura vel timidos non exclusura susurros.
    Excubiae lampas, faculis ignescit ocellus
405   sidereis; in quo sapphiri flammata diescit
gemmula, quam rutili mediam circumligat auri
torquis; ad extremos tractus ardente beryllo.
Prima Pudicitiae testis mansuescit ocelli
Simplicitas, mentisque foris iuratur Honestas;
410   promittitque fides oculi sincera Sabinam.
    Egreditur nasi brevitas producta, magistro
permittente modo; quo praecurrente tumentis
ardua colliculi non dedecet aggere: turpes
excursus aquila nescit vel sima recursus.

admixture of dark berry juice. Where the lowest portion of her forehead tapers toward the nose, a little level area is exposed in this open space; on either side the crescent moon of an eyebrow is defined by a delicate arc. Separated by this middle ground, the two curves do not commingle; a divorce gracefully prohibits one from touching the other. The common road is not thicketed over; no bristling hair obstructs it, bearing witness to bitter thoughts, nor does bushy growth proclaim poisonous gall concealed within. 390

The whorled and intricate cell of her small ear defines a winding path, and is shaped to form a small circle. Unblemished, cleaned by Nature's own finger, never giving offense by any lurking impurity, the path of speech can never let its inner parts grow red and rough through neglect; it willingly maintains a smooth road, nowhere made unpleasant by overgrown or muddy stretches. It is a messenger ready to convey to the mind the information it receives, a little dwelling place for voices, ever open to any sound whatever, a hospice with well-swept chambers which does not exclude even murmurs or timid whispers. 395 400

Her eye, the lantern in the watchtower, shines with starry fire; in it a little blazing gem of sapphire shines bright as day, surrounded by a band of ruddy gold; the outer rim is glowing beryl. The gentle simplicity of the maiden's glance is the first evidence of her purity, attesting outwardly the decency of her mind; the good faith expressed in her eyes is a guarantee of her Sabine virtue. 405 410

The modest length of her nose is drawn forth in a masterfully controlled way; because of this precaution its gently swelling prominence is not of an unseemly size: it is neither the eagle's rudely jutting beak nor the receding snout of the

415 Dirigitur iusto spatio librata, venuste
     tracta, nec alterutro declinans regula; nasum
     non procul extendit refugove reciprocat arcu.
          Naris odoratae redolet thymus. Intimus extra
     non celatur honos; gemino dulcescit aroma
420 thuribulo spirans. Laetum fragrantia pascit
     aera vicinaeque lares imbalsamat aurae,
     et vacuos implent absentia cinnama tractus.
     Non ibi lascivis riget importuna pilorum
     silvula; nec naris tenui crinitur arista
425 munda, nec interius rudibus dumosa capillis.
          Ebriat aspectus, animum cibat; omne tuentis
     delicium facies et praedo, Cupidinis hamo
     piscatura viros. Haec Nestoris esse timori
     iam gelidis annis, haec sollicitasse Catonem
430 retia vel laquei vel pulmentaria possent.
     Hic color exultat placituro sedulus ori;
     incola flamma rosae, quam circumfusa coronant
     lilia, candentes vultus accendit; et ignes
     temperat et parcit faculis; et amicius urit
435 blandior extremi fusa nive purpura limbi.
          Haec rosa sub senio nondum brumescit; et oris
     hic tener in teneris puerisque puellulus annis
     flosculus invitat oculos, et cogit amorem
     mentibus illabi stupidis, Venerique ministrat
440 arma suasque faces, lunatque Cupidinis arcum
     pectoris in vulnus. Glacie contracta senectae
     non ibi languet hiems; illuc inserpere ruga
     non praesumit anus, subito circumvaga passu
     et faciem longo pede signatura viatrix.

ape. Charmingly formed, it is set carefully in the proper   415
place, its straightness deviating neither to one side or the
other; it neither extends too far nor turns quickly back.

The scent of thyme is diffused from her perfumed nos-
trils. The special quality within is not outwardly concealed;
a sweet aroma breathes forth from these twin censers. A fra-   420
grance enriches the happy air, imbues the spirit of the pass-
ing breeze with its perfume, and fills the open sky with un-
seen spices. No unruly little forest of hairs bristles wantonly
there; the clear nostrils are not fringed with fine hairs, nor is   425
there an undergrowth of rough stalks within.

Her face makes drunk the sight and feeds the mind; it is a
complete and treacherous pleasure for the beholder, draw-
ing men in with the baited hook of Cupid. Such nets, such
snares, such delicacies might disturb the chilly old age of a
Nestor, or trouble a Cato. Lively color flourishes in her   430
charming face; a natural rosy heat, which the surrounding
lily whiteness sets off, creates a warm light in her glowing
cheeks; it tempers its fire, does no harm with its torches;
and the softer red blended with snowy white at the edges of   435
her face has a gentler glow.

This rose has not yet been blighted by the chill of age; it
is this tender and girlish bloom in boys of tender years as
well that attracts the eye, causes love to infiltrate spellbound
minds, provides Venus with her weapons and torches, and   440
bends the bow of Cupid to wound the breast. Here is no
sluggish winter of cramped and chilly age; no old woman's
wrinkles have yet dared to insinuate themselves, those wide-
ranging travelers who so suddenly will inscribe her counte-
nance with their long footprints.

445　Vernanti minio suffusa labellula, nullo
　　　vulgari pictore rubent, nec protrahit artis
　　　obsequium, quam sola dedit Natura, rubricam.
　　　Non morsu solito, parcenti dente, labelli
　　　extorquetur honos; et, quo suprema loquendi
450　ianua vestitur, non huius texuit ostrum
　　　artificis pecten. Orisque accensa gemello
　　　limine sardonychis nativae prunula candet.
　　　Divite praecingit vallo redolentia linguae
　　　atria dentis ebur, qui nec livescere morbo
455　erubet aut putris olida ferrugine sordis.
　　　Nec male radicum solidata sede minuto
　　　agmine rarescit; nec, dum comes improbus instat
　　　proximus, urgenti cedens extrarius errat,
　　　nec minor est speciem merito vicinia fine.
460　Nec linguam reserat foribus distantia ruptis,
　　　aut clausos aperit spatii caesura penates.
　　　　Colle tumens modico convexi argentea menti
　　　area descendit, quantum studiosa venusti
　　　nobilitas formae decreverit, omnia iusto
465　philosophata modo. Praetenditur ordine lecto
　　　meta; nec effusum praegnanti porrigit alvo
　　　curvatura sinum, teretisque licentia clivi
　　　non nimis ausa brevi sinuatur fine, decenti
　　　monticulo surgens, humili lascivula dorso.
470　　Ningit in albenti mansura pruinula collo;
　　　nec quatitur ventis, nec anhelo carpitur aestu
　　　verna; nec hiberno Boreae cessura tyranno,
　　　nec metuens Parthi dominum latrasse Leonem,
　　　cum fumante furit, timor anni, Sirius arcu.

Her lips, suffused with flourishing vermilion, owe their 445
redness to no common painter, for the rubric which Nature
herself has conferred shows no trace of the services of art.
The beauty of her lips is not painfully attained by the cus-
tomary biting, for her teeth have spared them; and no arti- 450
san's loom has woven the purple with which the outermost
portal of speech is decked. The warm glow of her mouth
is brightened by twin rows of natural sardonyx. The ivory
of her teeth surrounds the sweet-smelling chamber of the
tongue with its sumptuous rampart, which is never shamed
by the blackness of disease or the stinking foulness of rot 455
and decay. Her teeth form no straggling line, since their
roots are securely fixed; none yields to pressure and strays
out of line when an impudent companion stands too close,
nor shows less well in its rightful position among its neigh-
bors. Her tongue is not allowed to move far abroad when 460
the gates are opened, nor does a gaping aperture reveal the
inner chambers.

Modestly swelling, the silvery surface of her well-rounded
chin descends as far as the standard of graceful and noble
and form decrees; every detail expresses a philosopher's idea 465
of order. The tip of the chin conforms to this careful stan-
dard; its curve does not protrude like a stomach expanded
by a pregnant womb, and the freedom of its rounded swell,
discreetly bold, takes shape within modest limits, a graceful
little hill that entices by its gentle rising.

Perpetual snow gleams on her white neck; its vernal pu- 470
rity is never assailed by winds, nor sullied by panting heat; it
does not yield to the wintry tyranny of Boreas, nor fear the
roar of the lordly Parthian Lion at that fearful season when
Sirius rages in the blazing firmament.

475   Gutturis illimi speculo contendit ad unguem
       tersa superficies. Cupidos vix lubrica tactus
       sustinet, ut possit digito labente repulsam
       erubuisse manus. Non hic montana torosos
       multiplicat pinguedo gradus, testata gulosam
480   finitimis clivosa iugis; non proxima nudos
       gutturis orbiculos cutis exprimit, ossibus arto
       nubilis amplexu, paulo placitura recedit.
       Nec, carnis mediae quod epenthesis addit avarae,
       syncopat exertis macies ingloria nervis.
485   Omnis in hac una species consedit, ubique
       inseritur, nusquam declinativa, modumque
       iactitat in quovis spatio librasse venustum.

The surface of her throat, polished to perfection, rivals a 475
spotless mirror. Its softness hardly endures a wanton caress;
one's hand might blush to have its straying fingers repulsed.
No mountainous fleshiness overlays its firm contours, no
hilliness that attests to gluttony with its surrounding ridges; 480
the skin is not so closely drawn, so wedded to the bones of
her neck, as to expose the protrusion of the gullet, but main-
tains a pleasing distance. No degrading leanness with pro-
truding sinews removes what was added by insertion to the
middle of the greedy flesh. A uniform beauty, all-pervading 485
and unvarying, informs her, proclaiming that the standard
of grace has been observed in every part.

BOOK TWO

Capitulum 1

De residuo descriptionis puellae

Uritur, et caecum fovet Architrenius ignem,
spectandoque faces acuit, vultuque ruentes
inserit intuitus. Facies praesentior aestum
asperat, et tandem, visu sibi pestifer omni,
5   mollibus ad partes alias divertit ocellis.
   Parcior attollit diffusio pectus; amarum
in muliere sapit membrorum sarcina. Dulce
virginis est animo, non corpore, pondus; honorem
attenuat, pugiles quicquid densatur in artus.
10   Est brevibus maior, magnis minor; omne recidit
staturae vitium medio statura venustas.
Consuluit Natura modum, cum sedula tantum
desudaret opus, ne qua delinqueret; utque
artificis digitos exemplar duceret, ante
15   pinxerat electi spatii mensura puellam,
ne male Pygmaea sedeat, Titania surgat.
   Circumcisa, brevis, limata, mamillula laxum
non implet longaeva sinum, puerilibus annis
castigata sedet. Teneroque rotundula botro
20   pullulat, et nondum lacrimante puerpera lacte,
clauditur, et solidum succingit eburnea nodum.
   Bina mamillarum distinguit pomula planum
vallis arans sulcum descensu libera, donec

Chapter 1

The rest of the description of the girl

Architrenius burns, feeds the hidden fire, and makes the flame keener by gazing, fixing his eager sight on her face. Her too-vivid beauty intensifies the heat, and since he does himself harm with every glance, he finally diverts his sensitive eyes to other parts.

The swelling of her breast is modest; a large body is an unpleasant thing in a woman. The charm of a maiden's presence is a matter of spirit, not bulk; whatever makes for brawny limbs detracts from her dignity. She is taller than short, yet less than tall; her gracefully moderate stature avoids any fault of height. Nature deliberated carefully, eager as she was to produce such a work, so that nothing should be lacking; to ensure that the ideal pattern would guide her fashioning hand, she had first imagined the girl in terms of her proper size, that she might neither crouch like a Pygmy nor rise to Titanic heights.

Her breasts, small, restrained, and clearly defined, are not the full, slack bosom of an old woman, but remain slender, as befits her girlish years. The little sphere puts forth a tender bud, and since milk for a newborn child is not yet weeping forth, it remains closed, and the ivory breast encircles a tight little node.

A valley divides the twin fruits of her breasts, plowing a smooth furrow in its unhindered descent, until a nice sense

73

ventriculum tollat spatii cautela, brevemque
25 obvius enodis uteri tumor erigat arcum.
Qua teres astricti mediam domat orbita cinctus,
contrahitur flexo laterum distantia lumbo.
Plenior ad pectus, tenuatur ad ilia, donec
luxuriet renum gremio crescente volumen.
30   Invius, exclusae Veneri, secretior hortus
flore Pudicitiae tenero pubescit. Ibique
vernat, inattritus, nec adulto saucius aevo,
nondum praeda pudor vacua qui regnat in aula,
solus habens thalamos ubi non admittitur hospes.
35 Temperat innocuas iuvenilis flamma favillas;
nec Venus intrudit quo mores pruriat ignem,
nec divertit Amor ad inhospita tecta pudoris.
Nec nocet hic vel ea, mater face, filius arcu.
Improba non aperit vitii praesumptio clausas
40 clavigera Virtute fores; adamante ligatur
ianua, quam voti gravitas infracta sigillat.
Pro foribus lanugo sedet, primoque iuventae
vellere mollescit, nec multa in limine serpit,
sed summo tenuem praeludit margine muscum.
45   Subtiles patula digitos manus extrahit, unguem
caesilis urbano praemordens forcipis usu.
Lenta verecundos amplexus bracchia spondent,
nata puellares collo suspendere nexus.
Plena, tenella, teres surarum pagina leves
50 pumicis attritus refugit, non indiget huius
auxilio limae. Tactum non decipit isto
morsa diu scalpro, non hoc sentosa pilorum

74

of proportion gives rise to her stomach, and her smooth 25
womb raises its modest swell to meet it. Where the encir-
cling roundness of the confining girdle draws tight about
her middle, the width of her flanks narrows down to the
supple loins. Fuller at the breast, her body narrows toward
the stomach until the space of the loins swells sumptuously
with the full curve of her womb.

A more secret, undiscovered garden, where Venus is ex- 30
cluded, puts forth the tender bloom of Chastity. Here there
flourishes, unsullied, undisturbed by adulthood, a still invio-
late Purity that rules over an empty court, in sole possession
of that chamber to which no guest is admitted. The warm 35
glow of youth tempers its harmless fires; Venus does not in-
fect her with the flame that provokes wanton behavior, nor
does Love visit this unwelcoming home of purity. Neither
he nor she, the mother's torch or the son's bow, afflicts her.
No basely presuming vice opens locked portals of which 40
Virtue holds the key; the door is bound with iron bands, on
which the unfailing power of a vow has set its seal. A down
spreads about the portals, soft with the first fleeciness of
youth. It does not stray much over the threshold, but con-
fines its tender moss to the outer borders.

Her open hand extends delicate fingers, for it trims the 45
nails by the graceful exercise of sharp scissors. Her slender
arms promise modest embraces, ready to entwine them-
selves girlishly about one's neck. Full, yet delicately rounded,
the smooth skin of her calves shuns the light rasping of 50
pumice, and does not require the aid of such polishing. It
does not deceive the touch by virtue of long scraping with a
razor, and no bristly thicket of hairs dreads having the roots

turba timet rastrum, fruticum radice revulsa;
hanc meliore polit nativa novacula cultu.
55   Orbiculum tollit communis fibula crurum
surarumque, genu, nec, quem internodia lunant,
angulus incurvi corrugat poplitis arcum.
Non distorta rudi procedit tibia torno
recta, nec agricolam meminit male nata parentem.
60 Sublimata brevem cogit pedis area calcem,
articulosque ligans tersis decet unguibus ordo.
        Incisiva cutem scabies non asperat; illic
nullus inhorrescit scopulus; nec laedit acuto
exterretque manus caro limatissima rusco,
65 nec simulat sparsa cristatam cuspide rhamnum.
        Haec oculis partim notat Architrenius et, quos
non videt, a simili visorum conicit artus,
nudaque pro speculo velatae gratia servit.
Haec placet, hanc voto, quod vix respiret, anhelat,
70 cernendique favum cupidis delibat ocellis,
nec sitis infuso minor est hydropica melle.

of its bushes torn up by the rake; a natural grooming adorns her with surpassing elegance.

The joint connecting shin and calf is capped by the little sphere of the knee, and the angle which the joint forms in bending does not mar with wrinkles the arch of the rounded knee. The shin extends straight, undistorted by any awkward bending, and no innate flaw recalls peasant parentage. The finely arched sole of her foot requires a small shoe, and its orderly constraint sets off her toes with their well trimmed nails.

No scarring disease roughens her skin; no mole menaces there; her perfectly smooth complexion does not cause pain or irritate the touch with sharp bristles, nor imitate the buckthorn, armed with scattered spears.

Architrenius takes partial note of these things by sight, and infers the parts that he does not see from the evidence of things seen; the grace exposed serves as a mirror of what is veiled. She pleases him, and panting for her, he offers a scarcely whispered prayer, he feeds his eyes, eager to examine this honeycomb, and his thirst for the honey within is no less feverish.

Capitulum 2

De studio Cupidinis

At vagus intuitu flexo miratur Amoris
suggestus alios, iuvenum dum pectore fraudes
implicat Idalias. Non maiestate sedendi
75 quam deitate minor, teneris tener ille magister
discipulis pharetram nunc sumit, cuius aperto
carcere, vulnificum numerando colligit agmen.
Quid declive meet oculo monstrante, sagittas
dirigit et cote mucronibus asperat iras,
80 cuspidibusque minas acuit; quasdamque recisis
aligerat pennis, filique superpolit orbes,
unde maritatur volucri teres hastula plumae.
    Nunc stat, et obsequiis genuum cessantibus, arcum
lunat et accedit humeris, flexisque recedit
85 renibus, inque latus laevam praeporrigit ulnam.
Obliquoque pedes spatio diducit, et ecce!
Cornibus ad coitum nitentibus effugit arcus
ex oculis, ad quos retrograda serpit harundo
in digitis, nervo mox progressiva relicto.

Chapter 2

Cupid's occupation

But as he wanders with roving gaze he is struck with wonder by the further enticements of Love, as he weaves his Idalian deceptions through the inclinations of young men. No less grand in the majesty of his dwelling than in his divinity, the soft master of soft disciples now takes up his quiver, and having opened the case, gathers a carefully chosen, wound-inflicting company. Keeping an eye on whatever passes below, he aligns his arrows, sharpens their fierce points with a whetstone, and adds barbs to the shafts; some he wings with trim feathers, and binds them neatly with bands of thread, so that the round shaft is closely united to the winged plume.

Now, having ended his kneeling tasks, he stands, strings his bow and brings it to his shoulder, draws back, bending at the waist, and pulls his left elbow back against his side. Setting his feet at an angle, he draws, and lo! As the straining horns are on the point of meeting, the bow springs away from his eyes, and the arrow, which had been drawn back in his fingers, glides off, quickly gaining speed as the string is left behind.

Capitulum 3

De vestitu eiusdem

90 Aliger, et nullos alias dignatus amictus,
purpureo vestis ardebat sole. Stupetque
omnia, sed cultum magis Architrenius. In quo
succinctae medio soleae diffusior ante
et retro forma sedet. Soleae substringitur arcu
95 calceus obliquo, pedis instar factus, ut ipsos
exprimat articulos, cuius deductior ante
pinnula procedit, pauloque reflexior exit
et fugit in longum tractumque inclinat acumen.
Exterior lateris paries coit integer, intra
100 calceus admisso spatio discedit, et ambas
alterno laqueus morsu complectitur oras.
Artatur caligae descensus ad infima, donec
plenior occurrat pedis area. Portio summa
fluxior assurgit, caute crescentibus illa
105 indulget spatiis. Crurum magis ampla tumori
pars facit, et—posset offendi poplitis arto
curvatura sinu—longo sub poplitis arcu
stringitur excursu caligae pars cetera, presso
tensior amplexu, ne, si spatiosior amplos
110 porrigat anfractus, intus vaga fluctuet, extra
turpiter assurgat rugarum tibia dorso.
Gratior irrugat ritu lascivia bracas
Teutonico. Crispatque sinus amplexibus artis

Chapter 3

Cupid's costume

The winged god, disdaining garments of any other kind, is   90
resplendent in the sunlike brilliance of his purple robe.
Architrenius marvels at everything, but most at his adorn-
ment. The form of his sandal, bound in the middle, remains
wider at front and back. The boot, bound to the sandal   95
across the arch, is made in the shape of the foot, so that the
very toes are defined. A little plume extends slightly for-
ward, then curves abruptly and retreats extending its point
far to the back. The surface of the boot is unbroken on the
outer side, but the inner side is split, leaving an open space,   100
and a lacing, crossing back and forth, grips the two edges
and draws them together. The boot is close fitting as it de-
scends, until the broader surface of the foot meets it. The
upper portion grows looser as it rises, making careful allow-   105
ance for an increasing fullness. There is ample space for the
swell of the shank, and since the bending of the leg might
have been inhibited by a tight gathering, the rest of the boot
is bound just below the long hollow behind the knee, caught
in a tight embrace, for if its increasing fullness spread too   110
freely, the inner part would flap loosely, and outside the shin
would raise an unseemly ridge of wrinkles.

A more pleasing wantonness gathers his breeches to-
gether in the German manner. A belt crimps the billowing

balteus undantes, teneros dum mollia surgunt
115 suppara per renes, oculis factura repulsam
arcanosque virum praevelatura recessus.
    Prodigus in latum, nec castigatus avaro
forcipe, procedit tunicae discursus, et idem
peccat in interula vestis modus. Omnia Luxus,
120 ignavus provisor, agit; sola exit in artum
luxuries manicae, summa castratior ora.
Multiplici laqueo manicae mordetur hiatus;
artificis qua cessat acus, pars cautius illa est
sutrici neglecta manu, nam colligit oras
125 fibula distantes nodoque extrema maritat,
ut manus artanti manicae iunctissima nubat.
Ilia substringens spatiosum cinctus amictum
contrahit et ruga tunicam depingit anili,
rugarumque togam senio iuvenescere cogit.
130   Qua toga laxat iter capiti, qua nobile pondus
pectoris erigitur collo confine, coruscant
gemmarum radiis stellata monilia, noctis
sidereae mentita diem. Flammatur in auro
pectus, et ardenti dulcescunt fulmina collo.
135   Ne coma liberior erret, ventoque feratur
importuna genis, vultusque exire volentis
caelatura iubar, succedit circulus alto
incumbens capiti. Cedit statura comarum
mobilitas; cedit servire licentia, pressis
140 orbe coacta comis. Vultusque erumpit aperta
gratia, dum gemina suspenditur aure capillus.
    Mollibus exultat spoliis tunicata, suaque
lascivit manus ipsa toga, quae a pollice tractis

folds with its close embrace, while soft linen spreads over 115
his tender loins, to thwart the gaze and veil the place where
his manly parts are concealed.

His tunic flows in profusion, unchecked by the miserly
shears, and the same style runs riot in the blouse beneath.
Excess, idly provisive, sees to everything; the extravagant 120
fullness of the sleeve becomes narrow only when cut off at
the open end. The open side of the sleeve is made fast by
elaborate basting; where the work of the needle leaves off, it
is due to careful omission on the part of the seamstress, for a 125
brooch draws together the sundered edges, and unites them
in a knot at the wrist, so that the hand is intimately wedded
to the confining sleeve. A girdle, drawn about the loins,
draws the voluminous robe together, inscribing the tunic
with an old woman's wrinkles, and by these very marks of
age emphasizes the youthful cut of the robe.

Where the robe ceases its ascent toward the head, and 130
the noble mass of the chest rises toward the base of the
neck, necklaces gleam with the starlike radiance of gems,
feigning the brightness of a starry night. The breast is aflame
with gold, and its lightning flashes become charming on the
gleaming throat.

Lest his hair stray too freely, and be indecorously blown 135
about his cheeks by the breeze, hiding the brightness of a
face eager to show itself, a circlet comes to rest on his lofty
head. The movement of his hair agrees to be stilled; its free-
dom agrees to submit to constraint, as the hair is bound by 140
this circle. The fairness of his face shows forth openly, while
the hair falls over his two ears.

He rejoices, clad in his effete finery; even his hand sports
a garment of its own, the length of which extends from the

decurrens spatiis media plus parte lacerti
145　induit et summum cubitum delibat, utrimque
clausa iacens. Ipsaque manus scribente figuram,
certius in digitis nodi numerantur et ungues,
quos male tornatos incudi reddit amictus
pressior et formae vitio mendicat honorem.
150　　Crimina surgentis uteri, si quasque tumoris
desidior Natura notas incauta reliquit,
has nova providit industria demanicatis
occultare togis, quarum contracta supremos
artat forma sinus, humerisque angustior haerens,
155　crescit et inferius spatiosos exit in orbes.
Ultima lascivit luxu chlamys ebria; dextrum
dedignata latus, humero iurata sinistro.
　　Arguit exterior animum status; intimus extra
pingitur affectus; levitas occulta forensi
160　scribitur in cultu, cultu monstrante latentis
copia fit mentis. Habitus qui cetera velat
pectora develat, aperitque abscondita morum
garrulus interpres; et mentem veste loquenti,
praedicat exterior internas pagina leges.

fingers to cover more than half of his arm, and finally takes   145
in the elbow, closing about it on either side. As it defines the
shape of the hand the joints of the fingers may be more ac-
curately counted, and also the nails, which, if ill shaped, the
glove sends back to the forge, or by its tight fit seeks to dig-
nify their defective form.

Should Nature have grown lazy, and carelessly left traces   150
of the scandal of a bloated belly, modern enterprise has
made provision for concealing them by means of sleeveless
garments, whose narrow cut clings closely to the upper body,
and more closely still to the shoulders, but grows fuller as it   155
descends, and ends in spacious folds. A final outer robe rev-
els in drunken luxury; scorning to cover his right side, it is
fastened to his left shoulder.

His exterior condition declares his mind; the inner dispo-
sition is painted on the surface; a concealed shallowness is   160
declared by the public display, and suggests what the inner
resources amount to. A costume which conceals all else un-
veils the mind, and provides a garrulous reading of the hid-
den flaws of his character; the clothes bespeak the mind, a
page proclaiming outwardly the laws that rule within.

Capitulum 4

De Ingluvie

165　Haec stupet, et coepti memor Architrenius inde
　　　transit. Et ecce, locus visum ferit obvius in quo
　　　affectus varios hominum trahit una colendae
　　　sollicitudo Gulae, molli studiosa palato
　　　deliciis lactare cibos; varioque paratu
170　extinctas animasse fames; dispendia noctis
　　　producto breviasse mero, longasque dierum
　　　corripuisse moras; Baccho vigilante dolores
　　　et sensum sopire malis, mentisque labores
　　　fallere, ieiuno redituras pectore curas.
175　　　Hic ieiuna modi, transgressus ebria, ventris
　　　ingluvies humiles fastidit prodiga mensas,
　　　privatosque lares, vel quod prae fascibus ipsis
　　　Fabricius morderet, holus, trabeatus aratro
　　　Serranus posito riguis fovisset in hortis.
180　Nescit ut humanae redimat dispendia vitae
　　　quam modicum Natura petat: producere vitam
　　　sola Ceres Nereusque potest, illudque beatum
　　　vivere, quod foliis rudibusque innititur herbis.

Chapter 4

On Gluttony

Architrenius is astonished by this, and mindful of his under- 165
taking he moves on. And lo, a place presents itself to view
where a single preoccupation governs the desires of every
one: to cater to Gluttony, and attentively nurture the tender
palate with delicacies; to revive extinguished appetites with 170
varied menus; to make the long nights short and speed the
slow pace of day by protracted drinking; to lull pain and the
sense of misfortune to sleep with Bacchic vigils, evading
burdensome thoughts, the cares that will return with the
pang of hunger.

Here the prodigal greed of the belly, starved of modera- 175
tion, drunk with sheer excess, scorns the humble board, the
modest dwelling, the cabbage that Fabricius would eat with
the very fasces before him, or Serranus, though having aban-
doned the plow and put on the robes of consul, had raised in
a well-watered garden. Gluttony does not know how little 180
Nature needs to meet the expenses of human life: Ceres and
Nereus are sufficient by themselves to ensure longevity, and
it is a blessed way of life that is sustained by simple herbs
and vegetables.

Capitulum 5

De quaestionibus ventricolarum

Inter ventricolas versatur quaestio: pisce
185 quis colitur meliore lacus; quis fertilis aer
alitibus; quae terra feras effundat aedules;
quos assare cibos, quos elixare palati
luxuries discincta velit; quae fercula molli
iure natent, quae sicca gulae trudantur Averno;
190 quo iuris iactura meri redimatur in unda;
quot capiat fartura modos; quo foedere nodet
oppositos mixtura cibos; quo frixa paratu
exacuant gustus; quae corpora cura nepotum
dictet aromatico panis mandare sepulcro.
195 Quae novitas adiecta cibis epulonis acutum
commendet studium? Nam quaevis prima voluptas
delicias novitate capit; nam gratia rebus
prompta novis pretiumque venit; praecepsque bonorum
gloria temporibus recipit fragmenta favoris.
200 Quid prosit variare dapes, possitve cadentem
erexisse famem? Nam prona paratibus isdem
occurrit saties; recipit fomenta ciborum
alteritate fames. Diversaque fercula gustus
invitant, similesque creant fastidia mensae.
205 Quis pretio leviore cibus, quis plure refertos
emungat loculos? Nam condimenta palato
plus sapiunt, quae pluris emis; pretiumque paratus

Chapter 5

The gluttons' disputation

A debate is going on among the belly worshippers: what lake 185 is home to the finest fish; what climate is best for birds; what lands are rich in game animals; which foods the unbridled appetite prefers roasted, which boiled; what dishes, by their soft rule, should swim, which ones should be plunged still dry into the Avernus of the gullet; and how an infraction 190 of the rule can be made good with a flood of wine; how many forms stuffing may take; in what combination one may mix different kinds of food; what way of preparing a fricassee whets the appetite; in what cases family piety decrees that the corpse be consigned to an aromatic tomb of bread.

What new way of preparing a dish will flatter the keen 195 discernment of the feaster? For any pleasure is delightful at first because of its novelty; gratitude and reward are ever ready to greet what is new; the fleeting glory of good food after a time gains only scraps of favor. What will serve to 200 lend variety to a banquet, or have power to revive the flagging appetite? Surfeit is the likely response to menus that are ever the same; appetite draws its stimulus from different kinds of food. A variety of dishes appeals to the taste, while familiarity breeds a distaste for dining.

Which foods cost less, and which inveigle more from the 205 well-stuffed purse? For those dainties are sweetest to the taste which cost you more; the menu derives its value from

a pretio sumit. Refert, quo vivitur, asse
veneat an libra; mensae spectatur in aere
210 nobilitas, censuque sapor maiore iuvatur.
    Quae raro molles exornent fercula mensas?
Namque voluptates offendit copia. Raris
accedunt momenta bonis; convivia raro
sumpta iuvant; rarusque venit iucundior usus.
215 Distat utro piscis an dulci ventre palatum
plus iuvet an tergo tenero; quis crure, quis ala
ingluviem plus ales alat; quae prima ferarum
nobilitas mensis veniat pictura potentum.
Exceptis excepta viris, non Baucidis ollae,
220 non Codri sperata casae, convivia regum
delicat et numquam mensae popularis ad usus
degenerat; nullique togae partitur honorem,
quem proprium praetexta rapit; sublimis ad aulas
convolat et sese raro committit Amyclae.
225 Par labor et studium, quo fercula fine parata,
quo frustata modo, qua scissa libidine possint
ardorem fudisse Gulae. Nam forma paratis
delicias pretiumque parit, multumque tenetur
materies formae. Nam, si labor improbus assit,
230 materiam superabit opus, opibusque paratus
addet opes, acuetque gulis ardentibus ignes.

its price. It matters whether one's sustenance costs a penny or a pound; the excellence of the feast is assessed in cash, and its taste is enhanced by a greater expenditure. 210

What dishes rarely adorn the gourmet's table? For a ready supply detracts from enjoyment. Importance is assigned to rare delights; meals rarely consumed are pleasing; the rare enjoyment is the more agreeable.

Opinion varies as to whether the plump belly or the ten- 215 der back of a fish is most tasty; which bird's leg offers the glutton most, and which bird's wing; which beast by virtue of its nobility should come first to adorn the tables of the great. A privilege of the privileged, unhoped for in the kitchen of Baucis or Codrus's cottage, it graces the feastings 220 of kings, and never degrades itself by providing for common people's tables; the honor that robed dignity claims as its own is not imparted to the toga; it flees on high to palaces, and rarely bestows itself upon an Amyclas.

An equally grave concern is the design with which dishes 225 are prepared, how they are divided, and what pleasure the carving may provide to Gluttony's burning appetite. For it is the style of a banquet that creates the effect of pleasure and expense, and the ingredients are valued largely for their appearance. And if wicked toil is brought to bear, the finished 230 work will transcend its materials, add a rich effect to the richness of the food, and intensify the ardent appetite.

Capitulum 6

De sollicitudine circa salsas

Amplius in salsis labor amplior, ambitiosas
facturis avidasque fames, maioraque magno
laturis momenta cibo. Properatur ad Indos,
235 ardentemque polum, secretaque sidera strati
aetheris, ut toto cogantur aromata mundo,
et condimenti surgat lascivia mensis,
auctior et calido subsidat flamma palato.
Curritur ad Macedum fines Nilique recessus,
240 et nudam sub sole Pharon, qua sidera Memphis
non oculo languente videt, dum cuncta sereni
libertate legit; qua semper utrumlibet axem
vel neutrum demergit Aren; qua dirigit ortus
occasusque pares oculorum meta colurus.
245 Itur ad Eoas species messemque perusti
axis odoriferam. Ventris devellere toto
nititur orbe dapes et condimenta libido.

Chapter 6

The importance of sauces

Still more effort is lavished on sauces, which make appetite eager and all-embracing, and lend to grand dishes a still grander significance. They rush to India, to the burning pole, to stars far withdrawn in the vast heavens, that flavors may be drawn together from the entire universe, the wanton stimulus of spice enhance the feast, and a more intense flame descend on the burning palate. They hasten to the land of the Macedonians and the upper reaches of the Nile, and Pharos, open to the sun, where the man of Memphis gazes on the stars with unblinking eye, while he ponders all things in the freedom of a tranquil mind; where Aren continually sees one of the two poles, or neither one, sink below the horizon; where the colural band, marking the limit of our vision, balances the risings and settings of the Sun. Eastern spices are sought, and the sweet-scented harvest of the torrid south. From every corner of the world the lust of the belly labors to draw seasonings for its banquets.

Capitulum 7

Contra vescentes auro

O furor, inque nefas egressa licentia mensae,
prodigiumque Gulae! Labor est in prandia quamvis
250 flectere naturam; mollis fit cena metallum,
ingenitusque rigor epuli peregrinat in usus.
Principibusque cibum mentiri cogitur aurum.
Ergo aurumne gulae vivendi protrahit auram?
Et Crasso concludit idem? Crassosne iuvabit
255 et Crasso nocuit? Absit, pudeatque pudorem,
quod vitium surgat, quo virtus corruit, auro.

Capitulum 8

De vini optimi quaesitione

Sudor et attritae superest vigilantia curae,
excoctusque labor, studiumque quod occupet omne
ingenium: quaesisse merum. Nam gratia mensis
260 absque mero decisa venit; nec plena voluptas
est mensae quae fundit aquas, facinusque receptis

Chapter 7

Against those who feed on gold

O madness, o wickedly indulgent feasting, monstrous Gluttony! It strives to transform any natural thing into food; 250
even metal becomes soft and edible, and its inherent hardness is drawn into the service of the feast. Gold is compelled
by princes to masquerade as food. Will gold, then, draw out
the breath of life for the glutton? Did it achieve this end for
Crassus? And will it benefit other Crassi, though harmful to 255
Crassus himself? God forbid, and let shame be cast on the
gold that gives rise to such wickedness, by which virtue is so
corrupted.

Chapter 8

The search for the finest wines

Sweaty work and the wakefulness of gnawing anxiety remain, an exhausting task, a problem demanding the utmost
ingenuity: the quest for wine. For the charm of dining is cut 260
in half without wine; the feast at which water is served cannot be fully enjoyed, and it is a crime to consign the food

naufragium fecisse cibis. Solemnia mensae
Bacchus agit; maestos animi devellit amictus.

Capitulum 9

De commendatione Bacchi

"Bacche, corymbiferis Phrygiae spectabilis aris,
265 quem Iove maiorem Thebae venerantur alumnum
Parnassusque deum, cunctis deus inclite terris,
quam bonus es! Meliusque sapis; plus sole sereni,
plus splendoris habes auro Phoeboque nitoris.
Plus auro Phoeboque potes; tu cetera pleno
270 obnubis radio, sidus plus sidere, luxque
luce, diesque die. Plausus seris, otia tractas,
et thiasis thyrsisque iuvas. Tibi maeror et omnis
cedit hiems; vernusque venis. Lugubris amaram
pectoris abstergis lacrimam, sepelisque sepulcra
275 laetitiae, curas. Refoves felicius aegro
pectus hebes luctu; per te tranquillior omnis
intima luxuriat pax, expirante tumultu.
"Praetimidos audere facis, leporique leonem
inseris, et nervis animos, ut vina ministras.
280 Imbelles in bella vocas, animosque iacentes

one takes in to a watery grave. To Bacchus belong the rites of the feast; it is he who plucks the mantle of sorrow from the mind.

Chapter 9

In praise of Bacchus

"Bacchus, honored by the ivy-laden altars of Phrygia, whom 265 Thebes and Parnassus revere as a divine protector greater than Jove, god renowned in every land, how good you are! Yet your taste is better; you are fairer than the Sun, more splendid than gold, more radiant than Phoebus. You are more potent than gold or Phoebus; you overshadow all else with thy full radiance, more stellar than a star, more lumi- 270 nous than light, a day surpassing day. You are the source of rejoicing, the patron of leisure, the inspiration of the Bac- chic dance and the thyrsus. Grief and all the chill of winter give way before you; your coming is spring. You wipe away the bitter tears of the heavy hearted and bury cares, the 275 tombs of happiness. You restore happiness to the spirits of the the sick, dulled by suffering; through you there abounds the utter tranquility of inner peace, as tumult fades away.

"As you proffer wine, you endow the timid with daring, imbue the hare with the spirit of the lion, stiffen men's re- solve. You summon the unwarlike to war, rouse the dormant 280

in Martem mortemque rotas; Mavortis in usum
invalidos Mavortis agis; dextramque trementem
sub senio vinoque regis. Tuus ensis in enses,
in galeas galea, quemvis rapit, ignis in ignes.

285   "Fecundo fecunda mero facundia surgit,
et vino verbisque fluit; sic lingua Liaeum
Mercuriumque sapit, gemina sic aestuat unda,
eloquii torrens. Etiam prudentia vino
uberior fervet. Exsurgis, Bacche, caputque

290   et linguam pectusque moves: capitique Megaera,
pectoribus Nestor, linguis inserpit Ulixes.
        "Tristibus oppressos animos in laeta relaxas.
Maeroris tumidam curas hydropisin; aegro
Paeoniis animo medicina potentior herbis.

295   Languores languere facis, sensumque doloris
cogitur ipse dolor posuisse, malisque malorum
eripis effectum, relevas servire paratae
paupertatis onus. Totiens quod sensit, egestas
dediscit sentire iugum. Felicia fata

300   et rerum momenta creas; sortemque beatam
pauperis esse iubes, et qui servire steterunt
consedere duces; et Bacchi stante corona,
surgit ad hos paterae dominus septemplicis Aiax
Anglicus, et calyce similis contendit Ulixes."

305   Haec ibi funduntur Baccho praeconia, tales
multiplicat plausus plebes, devota refertis
incubuisse scyphis, erroris prodiga, mente
saucia languenti, rationis dedita sacrum
exstinxisse iubar rapido submersa Liaeo.

spirit to meet death in battle; you drive those too weak for
warfare into the service of Mars, you steady with wine the
hand that trembles with age. For those whom it inspires,
your wine is their sword, armor, valor, in the face of swords,
armor, valor.

"Abundant wit arises from abundant drinking, and be-   285
comes a stream of wine and words; thus the tongue tastes
both Bacchus and Mercury, and a double surge, a torrent
of eloquence wells up. Even wisdom grows more fertile
when inspired by wine. Your power, O Bacchus, gives rise
to thought, speech, and spirit: Megaera infests the brain,   290
Nestor claims the breast, and the tongue becomes a Ulysses.

"To spirits oppressed by sorrows you grant ease and hap-
piness. You cure the swollen dropsy of grief; your medicine
is more efficacious for the diseased spirit than Paeonian
herbs. You make faintness grow faint, cause pain itself to   295
lose the sense of pain, rob our evils of their evil effects, and
ease the burden of a poverty resigned to serfdom. Need,
whenever it feels your effect, forgets the weight of its yoke.
You make the Fate of the poor seem blessed and consequen-   300
tial; you decree that their lot be a happy one, and those who
have stood in attendance sit at the feast like lords; so long as
they wear the garland of Bacchus, the English Ajax himself,
lord of the sevenfold bowl, rises to toast them, and Ulysses
raises a competing goblet."

Such are the tributes poured forth to Bacchus, such the   305
applause that the throng raises again and again, devoting
themselves to reclining with brimming goblets, full of con-
fused thoughts, stricken with dullness of mind, dedicated to
extinguishing the sacred light of reason in the swift Lyaean
flood.

Capitulum 10

De potu superfluo

310 Ergo vagante scypho, discincto gutture "wesseil!"
ingeminant "wesseil!" Labor est plus perdere vini
quam sitis; exhaurire merum studiosius ardent
quam exhaurire sitim. Commendativa Liaei
est sitis, et candens calices iterare palatum
315 imperiosa iubet. Ad Bacchi munera dextras
blandius invitat, pluris sunt pocula, pluris
ariditate sitis; Bacchusque ad vota perustae
candentisque gulae recipit crementa favoris.
    Non modus est calicis, nisi sarcina sumpta redundet,
320 et primum repetatur iter. Data nausea reddit
altera vina scyphis; luteo corrupta veneno,
a venis in vasa venit, sua munera Baccho
indignata refert, reditumque urgente palude.
Bacche, retro properas, versaeque recurritis undae.
325 Sic male libratos castigat nausea sumptus;
et fugat excessus Naturae parca voluptas.
    Non satis est haurire satis se credere citra
naufragii discrimen aquis, pede summa profundi
carpere nec mergi. Rerum Gula praeterit usus
330 improba felices; ieiunia sustinet aegre,
nec librante modo novit deponere. Rebus

Chapter 10

On drinking too much

Then, waving the goblet about, shouting unrestrainedly, 310
they cry out "Wassail!" and again "Wassail!" Wine, not thirst,
is what they strive to do away with; they are far more eager
to exhaust the supply of wine than to ease the pressure of
thirst. Thirst is Bacchus's ambassador, and delivers his im- 315
perial decree that the tingling palate taste repeated drafts.
Thirst sweetly draws the hand to Bacchus's gifts, drafts that
have a greater value due to the dryness of a greater thirst;
Bacchus is the more honored when he answers the prayer of
a parched and burning gluttony.

There is no limit to the drinking, unless the bellyful taken
in overflows and retraces its original journey. The gift of 320
nausea restores the wine again to the cups; tainted with yel-
low bile it comes forth from the belly into the bowl, and an-
grily returns Bacchus's gifts, since the morass within de-
mands their rejection. How quickly you return, Bacchus,
rushing forth on the turning tide. Thus does nausea punish 325
ill-judged indulgence; for Nature's pleasures are temperate
and she rejects excess.

It is not enough to have drunk enough that one feels one-
self just short of the risk of shipwreck, to tread the surface
of the abyss yet not be submerged. Shameless gluttony is be-
yond the enjoyable use of food; it can scarcely endure priva- 330
tion, and cannot submit to the dictates of moderation. Its

utitur ad poenam dum ventrem copia iusto
plenior attollit, dum parcius esse beatus
vellet homo, damnatque suas habuisse faventes
335   in sua vota manus. Gula quas Natura creavit
delicias tormenta facit, sumptusque minores
pauperis absolvit. Heu numquam sobria, numquam
nacta modum, recipit ieiuna et plena flagellum.

Capitulum 11

De exclamatione in Gulam

Ha Gula, quae mundum penitus scrutatur et usus
340   torquet in illicitos Terrae praedulcia matris
pignora, quae gremio defovit blandius, ipsis
egregio factura deis miracula partu.
Ha Gula, quae mundum modico concludit in utre,
omnia detrudens stomachi ferventis in Aetnam,
345   vivendique lares Naturae vile sepulcrum,
tabificansque rogus, et edulis funeris urna.
Ha Gula: delicias cuius perferre quis aequa
mente potest? Cunctis opibus circumflua mundi,
tot non posse dolet uno concludere ventre.

enjoyments become punishments when excessive abundance swells the belly; when a man longs to have been blessed more sparingly, and curses his hands for having 335 granted his wishes. Gluttony turns to torment what Nature created to give delight, and spares only the meager consumption of the poor. Alas, never sober, never capable of restraint, it feels the pains of both want and surfeit.

Chapter 11

An outcry against Gluttony

Such is Gluttony, who endlessly ransacks the world and perverts to forbidden uses the beloved offspring of Earth, their 340 mother, whose bosom provides tender nurture, and who in her extraordinary fecundity produces things that astonish the very gods. Such is Gluttony, who holds the world shut up in a mere wineskin, and thrusts it all into the Aetna of the seething stomach, the sanctuary of life a foul burial place of 345 Nature, a pyre of decayed matter, an urn filled with the remains of the funeral feast. Such is Gluttony: who can endure her pleasures with an untroubled mind? Surrounded by all the world's goods, she grieves that a single belly cannot contain them all.

Capitulum 12

De statu gulosi in commestione

350 Fercula metitur ventrisque palatia, tantis
invenisse studet capientem rebus abyssum.
Gutturis ergo vias latebrosaque viscera tendit.
Est satius rumpi quam mensae parcere, ventrem
distraxisse cibos quam non consumere dulces.

355 Increpat angusta ventris praesepia; monstrum
ventre licet sit homo, stomachi piget esse recessus
tam modicos, et ea Naturae damnat avaras
parte manus. Reliquo Pygmaeus corpore mallet,
ventre fuisse Gigas; augeri cetera ducit

360 membra supervacuum. Mallet se cetera nano,
plenius augmentum ventris pigra sarcina penset.
Respicit ergo dapes, circumfususque paratus
iam votis oculisque vorat, circumspicit omnem
luxuriem mensae. Sed cum non possit ad omnes

365 suffecisse cibos, nescit Gula, nescit, an istis
irruat aut istis, sed et illis ardet et illis.

Chapter 12

How the glutton feels as he eats

The glutton measures the dishes, ands measures the palace 350
of his belly, eager to find a cavern that can contain so much.
Then he stretches open the channel of his throat and the
shadowy innards below. For it is better to burst than to stint
at the feast, to tear the belly apart rather than fail to con-
sume delicious food. He inveighs against the narrow con- 355
fines of his belly; though he be a man with the belly of a
monster, he feels shame that the recesses of his stomach are
so small, and curses the hand of Nature, so stingy in this re-
gard. He would prefer to have been a Pigmy in the rest of his
body, but a Giant in belly; and he considers the growth of his
other limbs unnecessary. He would gladly be a dwarf in other 360
respects, if the sluggish bulk of his belly might gain greater
expansion. Thus he looks over the banquet, already devour-
ing the array spread before him with wishful thought and
glance, and takes in every sumptuous detail of the feast. But
since he cannot possibly deal with the entire meal, gluttony 365
is at a loss, uncertain whether to pounce on this dish or that,
but lusting equally for both.

Capitulum 13

De statu eiusdem post satiem

Ut satis est ventri, nec iam vacat angulus, escis
invita parcente Gula, longumque momordit
versavitque diu, pleno cogente repulsam
370 gutture; iam veniam fessis poscentibus aegro
dentibus attritu, nec plus datur esse facultas,
iam cumulum capiente cibo; cum postulat aequam
ne vergat dapis unda Gulam; tunc cogitur esse
tandem larga manus; partitur, si qua supersunt,
375 convivis conviva satur. Transferre necesse est,
quod retinere nequit; cui non licet, ut sit avarus,
cogitur, ut largus. Trahitur dare dextera, dando
paenitet, et sequitur redeunti munera voto.

Chapter 13

His condition after he has had enough

When the belly has had enough, and no cranny remains empty, and gluttony, reluctantly ceasing to eat, has gnawed at length and turned over again and again what a full gullet compels it to reject; when at last the exhausted jaws beg for relief from their now feeble grinding, and he lacks the ability to consume more, since the food within has attained full measure; when he requires an equally gluttonous effort to keep the feast from pouring forth again; then at last the hand is compelled to be generous; the sated feaster shares whatever is left with his fellow feasters. What one is incapable of retaining must be given over; he who cannot be greedy must become generous. His hand is drawn into giving, but the gesture pains him, and he follows the gift with a prayer for its return.

370

375

Capitulum 14

De sobrietate alborum monachorum

Haec indignatus et abhorrens omnia secum:
380 "O sancta, O felix, albis galeata cucullis,
libera paupertas, nudo ieiunia pastu
tracta diu solvens nec corruptura palatum
mollitie mensae. Bacchus convivia nullo
murmure conturbat nec sacra cubilia mentis
385 inquinat adventu. Stomacho languente ministrat
solemnes epulas ventris gravis hospita Thetis
et paleis armata Ceres; si tertia mensae
copia succedat, truncantur holuscula, quorum
offendit macies oculos, pacemque meretur
390 deterretque famem, pallenti sobria cultu.

Capitulum 15

De sobrietate Fabricii et Baucidis

"Haec sunt Fabricius quae legit holuscula, quorum
asperitas, modico sale fracta et simplice limpha,
rustica non novit molli mansuescere cultu.

Chapter 14

The sober life of the white monks

Angered and revolted by it all, Architrenius says to himself: "How blessed, how happy the voluntary poverty helmeted 380 by the white cowl, which breaks its long-protracted fasts with simple food and will never contaminate the palate with the delicacies of the feast. Bacchus does not disrupt their communal meals with noise, nor pollute the sacred chambers of the mind by his intrusion. When the stomach grows 385 weak, Thetis, stern mistress of the belly, and coarsely clad Ceres provide sober meals; if a third course follows, small cabbages are cut up, whose spare austerity and pale robes, offensive to sight, obtain peace and keep hunger at bay. 390

Chapter 15

The sobriety of Fabricius and Baucis

"These are the small cabbages that Fabricius chose, whose country coarseness, tempered by a pinch of salt and fresh water, was not subjected to delicate preparation. Such were

Consulis hae dulces epulae lautique paratus,
395　quasque probat Natura, dapes.
　　　　　　　　　　　　　"O terque quaterque
Baucida felicem, sociumque Philemona lecti,
pauperis et mensae cuius pes tertius impar
aequa subinducta tenuit mensalia testa.
Ille beatorum cenae modus; illa beata
400　mensa viris optanda fuit, quam larga profudit
fecundo Natura sinu mundoque paravit,
ingenio contenta suo, non indiga victus
artifices quaesisse manus; sollertior artes
respuit humanas. Pretiosa Philemonis illa
405　fercula, quae Baucis studio tractavit anili.

Capitulum 16

De mensa Baucidis

"Panis triticea de messe siligine mixta,
quam volvente manu mola rustica fregit. Et illum
Baucis sub tepida coxit studiosa favilla,
detersitque sinu, digitoque abrasit adusti
410　corticis extremam quam pruna momorderat horam.
Pro vino miscentur aquae, quas, putris avenae
corruptaeque solo turbatas pulvere, primum
coxerat et lutea mox fermentaverat olla.

the rich meals and sumptuous banquets of a consul, feasts 395
such as Nature herself commends.

"O Baucis, three and four times blessed, and Philemon,
companion of her bed, and of that poor table whose uneven
third leg was kept steady by a tile slipped beneath the board.
Such are the feastings of the blessed; such a blessed feast is 400
what men should long for, a feast which generous Nature
has poured forth from her fertile womb and offered to all
the world, content with her native skill, needing to seek no
artful preparation for her food; her resourcefulness disdains
mere human art. Precious are those dishes which Baucis, 405
with an old woman's care, prepared for Philemon.

Chapter 16

Baucis's cuisine

"Her bread was made from the flour of ripe wheat, which a
rude millstone turned by hand had ground. Baucis baked it
carefully under a low flame, wiped the loaf on her apron, and
rubbed off with her finger a charred edge of crust which the 410
coals had nipped. In place of wine water was mixed, clouded
only by the dust of dry and decayed oats, which she had first
boiled and then fermented in an earthen jug. There was

Addit holus, quod item cum ruris edulibus herbis
415 legerat, et calidis rigidum defregerat undis
imbueratque bovis, riguo quam paverat horto,
lacte novo, pinguique suis condiverat osse.

   "Caseus accedit vetus; et quem fiscina nuper
miserat; et sinum qui nondum liquerat infans;
420 et tener et tepidi servans cunabula sini;
et qui flere gena nondum desueverat uda.
Additur agresti contractum lance butyrum:
quodque superducto solidi curvamine lactis
continuoque sinu clausit sollertia maior
425 seduliorque manus — rurisque urbanior usus.

   "Dulcia succedunt nivei libamina lactis;
idque quod, extorta solidae pinguedine massae,
exeso macies vultu viridavit; et illud,
tempore quod tracto solidatum, reddit aceto
430 rustica cognatum. Quid plura? Beatior omni
divite pauper anus lactis genus omne ministrat.

   "Addit apis quas fudit opes, ancilla potentis
sedula Naturae; dat mella, et coniuga cerae,
et viduo iam passa favi divortia lecto.

435   "Ovaque largitur tepidis admota favillis
et versata diu, partim submollia pruna
parcius urenti, partim solidata favilla
acrius ignita. Digito quae morsa superne
corticibus ruptis iterantis pollicis ira,
440 sordescente salis lapidosi fragmine Baucis
sparserat, et tandem festucae fixa rigentis

cabbage, too, which she had picked along with the edible herbs of the countryside, softened its toughness in warm 415 water, then steeped it in the fresh milk of the cow she had fed from her well-watered garden, and flavored it with the fatty bone of a sow.

"There was aged cheese; and cheese newly emerged from the basket; infant cheese which had not yet forsaken its bosom; soft cheese keeping to the cradle of the cool vat; and 420 cheese which had not yet learned not to make its cheeks wet with tears. There was also butter, piled on a rough dish: when a rounded lump of congealed milk had been produced, her skillful and attentive hand had quickly enclosed it in a 425 mold, the more than urbane practice of country folk.

"Sweet libations of snow-white milk come next; and milk to which the thinness of its pinched face gives a greenish pall, after the solid, fatty mass has been churned away; and milk which, when it has congealed over the course of time, the countrywoman turns into something close to vinegar. 430 Why should I say more? The poor old woman, more blessed than any rich man, serves milk of every kind.

"She adds those riches which the bee produces, that eager handmaid of powerful Nature; she offers both honey still united with its wax casing, and honey that has already been divorced from the widowed bedchamber of the comb.

"She offers eggs that have been placed close to a warm 435 fire and turned for a long time, some soft within, since the coals have scorched them lightly, and some hard, where the embers have been hotter. When the top had been broken by a finger, and the shell torn off by a ceaselessly aggressive thumb, Baucis had sprinkled it with rough fragments of 440 coarse salt, and at last proffers it to her spouse, whom she

cuspide praemorsa, lauti ieiuna paratus,
sponso non alio luxu placitura propinat.
Mille modos cultus recipit tractabilis ovi
445 mollities, sed eos, uno contenta, cucullis
parca voluptatis senio vergente reliquit.
     "Poma dat, et mellis et aceti proxima, poma
quorum verna genis primae lanugo iuventae
texitur, et poma quae filia ruga senectae
450 exarat, intorta senio nodante cicatrix.
Utraque corticibus tunicata: nec ille nec illa
caesilis ingenio ferri devellit amictum.
Ultima tornato pomi devellere giro,
non fortuna casae, non ruris curia novit.
455   "Dat pira, dat tenero corna inflammata rubore;
dat ficus, dat pruna, rosae quae purpura velat,
et, quae pallidior blando crocus induit auro;
et, quibus exterius ferruginis enatat umbra;
et quae Naturae studio mixtura colorum
460 gratior, et dulcis oculo discordia pingit.
     "Nux datur, et nemorum quae dumos incolit, et nux
Puniceo nuclei peplo generosior; et nux
nobilior gustu, quam gessit amygdalus; et nux
exteriore toga pallentibus ebria succis,
465 mansuramque diu digitis factura lituram.
     "Has inopis mensae dat opes, et cetera, pleno
cetera si qua dedit horti sacra Copia cornu,
liberiore manu Baucis dedit omnia, si quo
plenior arrisit Autumni gratia mensae
470 tempore. Nam multis opibus Natura parandis
tempora multa parat, et rerum temperat usus

would better please with no other delicacy, impaled on the sharpened point of a stiff straw in lieu of a serving dish. The soft and adaptable egg lends itself to a thousand kinds of preparation, but contented with one, she leaves the rest in their shells, grown frugal in her pleasure with the onset of age.

"She brings fruits whose taste is close to both honey and vinegar, fruits whose cheeks are covered with the fresh down of youth, and fruits which wrinkles, daughters of time, have furrowed, the twisting scars of gnarled old age. Each fruit is still clad in its rind, and neither he nor she plucks away this garment by the artful use of a sharp knife. To divest a fruit of its outer covering in a twisting spiral is not a cottager's lot; it is unknown to the rural court.

"She offers pears, cornel cherries flushed with a delicate red; she offers figs; she offers plums, some clad in rosy purple, some imbued with a yellow more delicate than white gold; some over whose surface float shadows of rusty red; and some painted by artful Nature with a charming blend of colors, a discord pleasing to the eye.

"The nut is served which is found in woodland thickets; the nut ennobled by the purple cloak of its kernel; the nut, nobler in taste, which the almond tree bears; the nut with an outer cloak of drunken red and pale juice, which will leave a long-lasting stain on the fingers.

"These, the riches of a poor table, she offers, and others, if Plenty has bestowed further blessings on the garden. Baucis generously offers all she has, whenever the kindness of Autumn has favored her table more abundantly. For in disposing her many rich gifts Nature disposes many seasons as well, and does not restrict the enjoyment of her resources to

445

450

455

460

465

470

tempore non uno; variat successio tractu
successus vario. Nec sic parit ista quod illa
nil veniat paritura dies: felicia reddit
475 tempora distincto superum clementia cultu.
   "O Deus, humanis circumspice; frena palato
pone, modumque cibo. Mundum lascivia maior
exeat, aut alio dispenset Copia cornu.
Parcius effusam tractet Moderantia mensam,
480 admissusque pati venter doceatur habenam."

Capitulum 17

Quod Architrenius Parisius venit

Haec fatus lacrimas non ultra continet; illo
devenisse dolet, alio festinat. Eunti
exoritur tandem locus: altera regia Phoebi,
Parisius, Cirrhaea viris, Chrysaea metallis,
485 Graeca libris, Inda studiis, Romana poetis,
Attica philosophis; mundi rosa, balsamus orbis,
Sidonis ornatu, sua mensis et sua potu.
Dives agris, fecunda mero, mansueta colonis,
messe ferax, inoperta rubis, nemorosa racemis.

a single season; the procession of time brings varied results in its varied course. No season yields so much that another will come yielding nothing; the kindness of the gods blesses each season with its own tasks. 475

"Oh God, look down on humankind: set a curb on appetite, a limit on consumption. May this great wantonness depart from the world, or let Abundance issue from another source. May Moderation govern a table more frugally laid, and may the belly grow submissive and be schooled in restraint." 480

Chapter 17

Architrenius arrives in Paris

Having spoken thus, he restrains his tears no longer; grieving that he should have encountered all this, he hastens away. At length a place rises before him: Paris, the second palace of Phoebus, Cirrhaean in its citizenry, Chrysaean in its wealth, a Greece in its libraries, an India in its schools, 485 a Rome for poets, an Attica for philosophers; the flower of the world, balm of creation, a Sidon in its splendor, uniquely itself in its feasts and drink. Its soil is rich, its vineyards productive, its land readily cultivated, its harvests abundant, bare of brambles but dense with clustering vines.

490   Plena feris, piscosa lacu, volucrosa fluentis.
      Munda domo, fortis domino, pia regibus, aura
      dulcis, amoena situ; bona quolibet, omne venustum,
      omne bonum, si sola bonis Fortuna faveret!

Game is plentiful, the lakes are full of fish, many birds haunt 490
the streams. Its houses are handsome, its barons bold, its
rulers godly, its air fresh, its situation delightful; it is good in
every respect, endowed with every grace, every good, if only
Fortune favored the deserving!

BOOK THREE

Capitulum 1

De miseria scholarium

At diis paulo minor plebes Phoebea secundos
vix metit eventus; quicquid serat undique tortis
vapulat adversis. Gemit Architrenius agmen
Palladis a miseris vix respirare, beatos
5   pectore philosophos Fato pulsante flagello
asperiore premi, nulla virtute favori
divitis annecti. Studio sudante malorum
continuare dies, senium prohibentibus annis
praecipitare malis, pubisque urgere senectae
10 damna rudimentis; dum vitae abrumpit egestas
gaudia, dum tenuem victum Fortuna ministrat
ad modicum torpente manu.
                        Ruit omnis in illos
omnibus adversis. Vacui furit aspera ventris
incola longa fames, formae populatur honorem
15 exhauritque genas. Macies pallore remittit
quam dederat Natura nivem, ferrugine texit
liventes oculos, facula splendoris adustam
exstinguit faciem. Marcent excussa genarum
lilia laborumque rosae, collique pruina
20 deicitur livore luti, maestissima vultu
mortis imago sedet. Neglecto pectinis usu
caesaries surgit; confusio crinis in altum
devia turbat iter; digito non tersa colenti

Chapter 1

The wretched life of scholars

But this Phoebean people, though all but gods, reap little
good fortune; whatever seed they sow is blown about by
hostile whirlwinds. Architrenius laments that the ranks of
Pallas are all but exhausted by their misfortunes, that phi-   5
losophers gifted in mind are beaten down by the cruel lash
of violent Fate, that their virtues gain them no favor from
the wealthy. They prolong their days of misfortune by their
exhausting studies, bring upon themselves the debilitating
ills of the elderly, and impose the ruin of age on their early   10
youth; for poverty deprives them of the joys of life, and For-
tune's listless hand provides only a scant and meager suste-
nance.

Evils rush upon them from every quarter. Cruel, raging
hunger, long at home in the empty belly, lays waste all grace
of body and makes the cheeks grow thin. Leanness substi-   15
tutes its pallor for the snowy white which Nature had be-
stowed, traces lines of rust on the inflamed eyes, deprives
the seared face of the spark of brightness. The blighted lilies
of the cheeks and the roses of the lips are withered, the
whiteness of the neck is defiled by spots of dirt, and the face   20
assumes the ghastly appearance of death. Since the task of
the comb has been abandoned, the hair bristles; random
confusion drives it upward; untouched by any grooming

pulverulenta riget. Secum luctamine crinis
25 dimicat alterno; non haec discordia paci
redditur intortum digito solvente capillum.

Capitulum 2

Quod egestas a corpore cultum amoveat petulantem

Non coluisse comam studio delectat arantis
pectinis, errantique viam monstrasse capillo.
Languenti stomacho nitidi non sentit egestas
30 cultus delicias; dissuada libidinis odit
pectinis arte coli, formae contenta venusto
quod Natura dedit. Maior depellere pugnat
sollicitudo famem, graviorem gentis Erinyn,
quae, Thetin ore bibens, animo bibit ebria Phoebum.

finger it grows stiff with dirt. The locks struggle in battle among themselves; and the discord is not reduced to peace by the fingers that might unsnarl the tangled hair.

Chapter 2

How poverty does away with stylish grooming

Poverty takes no pleasure in tilling the hair by applying the furrowing comb, and defining a path for the straying locks. Poverty, when its stomach is faint with hunger, does not know the delights of elegant grooming; disinclined to indulgence, it loathes the hairdresser's art, content with that bodily grace which Nature has bestowed. The graver concern is the struggle to fend off hunger, the besetting Fury of all those whose lips taste Thetis, while their minds grow drunk with Phoebus.

25

30

Capitulum 3

De tenuitate vestitus

35 Quem scopulum mentis (scopulo quid durius?) illa
horrida non flectat logicorum turba? Rigorem
quis non excutiat et toto pectore dulces
derivet lacrimas, quotiens occurrit honesta
philosophi fortuna minor? Defringitur aevo
40 qua latitat vestis. Aetatis fimbria longae
est, non artificis; ipsa est quae abrumpit amictum,
portandique labor quodque omnibus unus adesse
cogitur obsequiis. Varios damnatus ad usus,
respirasse dies nullo sudore meretur.
45 Quem dederint noctes venti suspirat ad ictus,
litigat ad Boreae flatus; assibilat Euris
mollibus et Zephyri clementes ridet ad auras
laetior, et madidis eadem lacrimatur ab Austris.
Paenula tot lassata malis propiusque senectae
50 forcipe tonsa pilos. Aut si qua est gloria cultus,
exit ad aspectum: veris praetexitur umbra
intima vestis hiems. Laedit minus abdita claustro
divite paupertas; oculos deludit amictus,
dum tenui Croesum praescribit imagine Codrus.

Chapter 3

Their threadbare clothes

What rocklike spirit (and what is harder than rock?) is not moved by the plight of this shaggy horde of logicians? Who would not put off severity and give forth tender tears with all his heart, whenever he encounters the philosopher's honorable but ignominious condition? The cloak in which he covers himself is ravaged by time. Its fringe is the work of great age, not tailoring; it is this that has torn the garment, and the labor of enduring all the duties this one garment is compelled to perform. Condemned as it is to such a variety of uses, it never wins a day of rest by any amount of effort. It sighs at the buffetings of the wind which the night brings on, and protests at the blasts of Boreas; whispers to soft Eurus, smiles happily at the touch of Zephyrus's gentle breeze, and is reduced to tears by rainy Auster. A cloak assailed by so many ills is too soon torn apart by the shears of old age. Or if any trace of style remains, it is all on the surface: the wintry chill within is veiled by the springlike surface of the garment. But poverty is less painful when concealed in a rich covering; the garment deceives the eye, when Codrus presents the surface appearance of Croesus.

Capitulum 4

De indigentia rerum familiarium, et cibi maxime

55　Parva domus, res ipsa minor. Contraxit utrumque
　　immensus tractusque diu sub Pallade fervor
　　et logices iucundus amor. Tenuisque laboris
　　emeriti merces, et quod de more sophistas,
　　miror qua invidia Fati, comitatur egestas.
60　Pauperies est tota domus; desuevit ad illos
　　ubertas venisse lares, nec visitat aegrum
　　Copia Parnassum, sublimior advolat aulas,
　　his ignota casis, ubi pauca annosa supellex,
　　languida sordet anus, admoto murmurat igni
65　urceolus; quo pisa natat, quo caepe vagatur,
　　quo faba, quo porrus capiti tormenta minantur,
　　quo rigidum pallescit olus; quo fercula festo
　　atriplices libanda die, quo vilior horti
　　ieiunam expectat quaevis farrago Minervam.
70　Hic unde assiduo conflictu litigat unda,
　　hic coxisse dapes est condivisse. Libido
　　mensae nulla venit, nisi quod sale sparsa rigorem
　　esca parum flectit. Solo fit amicior usu
　　cenula, luctanti minus obluctata palato.
75　　Maior in angustis si accedat copia, mensae
　　gloria solemnis aries truncatur, et ollae
　　maiorique minor undae mandatur, ut unctae

Chapter 4

The lack of household goods, and food most of all

The house is small, the furnishings still more so. Great and 55
long-protracted effort in the service of Pallas and the sweet
love of logic have diminished both. For the reward of such
worthy work is meager, and Poverty, I know not by what
malice of Fate, is the customary companion of the man of
learning. The house is utterly impoverished: plenty is un- 60
used to enter these chambers; Abundance does not visit a
stricken Parnassus, but flies on lofty wing to the court, un-
known to such houses as this, where the aged furnishings
are few, a feeble old woman sits in squalor, and a little pot,
set close to the fire, murmurs; within, a pea swims, an onion 65
wanders, bean and leek threaten torment to the head, a stiff
cabbage leaf grows pale; there will be a dish of orache on
feast days, and a humble sort of vegetable stew awaits the
starving student. Here, when the very water seethes with 70
hostility, to cook food is only to soften it. No pleasure visits
the table, unless the scanty fare is made a little less tough
by a pinch of salt. Only through habit does the paltry meal
become more agreeable, less intolerable to the embattled
palate.

If an increase in resources should occur in these narrow 75
circumstances, a small sheep is slaughtered to grace the fes-
tive board, and entrusted to a larger pot of water, so that the

asperitas mansuescat aquae, mox carnibus esis
suppleat hausta cibum panemque absorbeat atrum,
80 ardua dum pleno superet structura catino.

Capitulum 5

De vilitate servientium

Nudus in annoso tunicae squalore, ministrat
Geta dapes, dum vile meri libamen in urbe
Birria venatur, pretio vestitus eodem,
muricis eiusdem. Luteus, macer, horridus, ore
85 languidus exsangui, plumarum squameus hirtam
agmine caesariem, festucae extantis in altum
cuspide cristatus. Crinis silva intima denso
pulvere pressa iacet, sed et his peiora latere
suspicor, attritum digito scrutante capillum,
90 nescioquid facilem dum saepe adducit ad unguem.

water's brackishness may be softened by its fat and then
sopped up with black bread as an extra course after the meat
has been eaten, when only a gaunt skeleton survives from   80
the full platter.

Chapter 5

The low condition of the servants

Geta, all but naked in the ancient squalor of his shirt, serves
the banquet, while Birria hunts up a measure of cheap wine
in town, clad in robes of equal value, and of the same splen-
did color. He is dirty, lean, unkempt, his face dull and pallid,   85
his scabrous head bristling with an array of plumage, a crest
of straw standing stiffly upright. The dense forest of hair is
covered over with thick dirt, but I suspect, from the finger
that scratches at the sparse scalp, that worse things lurk
within, since he readily draws forth I know not what with a   90
deft fingernail.

Capitulum 6

De cubilibus

Sobria post mensae tenuis convivia, frenum
suscipiente gula satiem quod praevenit ante
dimidiasse famem, scabra farragine strati
contrahitur macies, quo vix depressior infra
95   area descendit, ut ferrea paene iacentem
proxima frangat humus. Illic pugil improbus heres
sudat Aristotelis, oculum mordente lucerna.
Dum pallens studio et marcens oleo, ardet utroque;
languidus, insomnis et ocello et pectore, noctes
100 extrahit alterutro vigiles. Oculusque lucernae
pervigil et lippit et lippum torquet ocellum.

Capitulum 7

De nocturno studio

Imprimit ergo libris oculi mentisque lucernam,
et libro et cubito dextraeque innixus et auri,
quid nova, quid veterum peperit cautela, revolvit.

Chapter 6

The scholar's bed

After the sober cheer of the meager meal, when the appetite receives a curb that forestalls satiety before hunger has been cut by half, the meager pallet is burdened by the weight of this meal of coarse stew, a pallet than which the floor itself is scarcely lower, so that the closeness of the almost ironlike ground bruises the recumbent body. Here the embattled bastard heir of Aristotle toils, with a lamp that makes his eyes sting. Pale from study, and sleepy from the oil lamp, he is eager for both; he grows faint, eyes and mind in need of sleep, but he demands nocturnal vigils of each of them. The watchful eye of the lamp becomes blurred, and strains his own blurred vision.

Chapter 7

His nights of study

Thus he applies the light of eye and mind to his books, and attaching his elbow to the page and his hand to his ear, ponders what modern and ancient inquiry has produced.

105 Omnia, Castaliis pede quae sudaverat antris
Pegasus, exhaurit oculis et mente fluenta;
nunc oculo, nunc mente bibens, nunc haurit utroque,
illo plus illaque minus. Nunc lecta camino
decoquit ingenii, memorique in pectore nodo
110 pressius astringit; nunc delibata reducto
praeterit affectu, non invitantia pectus,
deliciosa minus, altaeque in scrinia mentis
digna venire parum. Nunc, quae minus ardua parcunt
reptanti ingenio, facilis transcurrit aperta
115 planitie clivi; nunc, quod nodosius obstat
ingeniumque tenet, ne tollat in altius alas,
instanti rodit studio. Conamine toto
pectoris exertus, pronisque ignescit ocellis,
immergitque caput gremio, longumque volutat
120 praecipites reserasse vias, cursumque negantes
oppositas fregisse fores. Oculumque reducit
saepius ad librum, digitique et mentis acumen,
inque diem limat tenebras. Decrescit ocelli
angulus in rugam; reliquam ferit obvia silvam
125 silva supercilii; vario frons ignea sulco
monticulosa coit; studio crispatus in altum
contrahitur nasus; animae luctamen anhelum
pressa labella iuvant. Sese procedere toto
dimicat, obicibus ruptis suspiria tractim
130 proicit et gemitus efflat, vultumque cruentat
ignibus, ambustis oculis, totusque furore
effluit. Ingenii tandem studiique ruenti
fulmine cogit iter et liber in ardua figit
intuitum, totumque iubet sibi cedere caelum.

He gulps with eyes and mind all that the hoof of Pegasus   105
caused to flow forth from the Castalian cave, drinking now
with the eye, now the mind, now both together, yet more
with the former than the latter. Now he boils down what he
has read in the furnace of thought, and secures it tightly
bound in the vault of memory; now he leaves behind mat-   110
ters skimmed less attentively, matters that did not elicit
thought or give pleasure, and were of too little worth to en-
ter the storehouse of the inner mind. At one moment he
glides smoothly along on the open and level ground of sub-
jects that present less difficulty to the mind as it creeps
ahead; at another, he gnaws in intense concentration at a   115
knotty passage that resists him, and keeps the understand-
ing from spreading its wings for flight. Exerting the utmost
power of his mind, he inflames his drooping eyes, then low-
ers his head to his chest, and ponders at length how to clear   120
the steep path, and break open the obstructing doors that
deny him access. Repeatedly he brings back to the book his
eyes, his pointing finger, and keenness of mind, and strives
until dawn to clear away the shadows. The corner of his eye
becomes wrinkled; one bushy eyebrow strikes against the   125
other; the hilly swell of his burning brow is contracted into a
series of furrows; his nose, wrinkled by concentration, is
drawn upward; and pursed lips assist the effort of the pant-
ing mind. He strives to advance with his whole being, gives   130
forth long-drawn sighs, pants and groans as the barriers are
broken, brings the hot blood into his face, and with blazing
eyes puts forth his utmost furious effort. At last with a sud-
den flash of insight and application he forces a path, is free
to raise his gaze to the heights, and bids all heaven yield to

135 Immensumque probat, quo mundus clauditur, orbem,
si, quod nulla ligat metae orbita, dicitur orbis.

Capitulum 8

De singularium Artium Liberalium capitulis paucis

Aethera directe cernit, contraque reniti
quamlibet oblique stellam, solisque rotari
orbe parallelo. Quae sidera fixa vocavit
140 segnior occursus aperit; quae forma, quis ordo,
quae natura latens, quae vis distorqueat axes
sideris errantis; fixis quae musica cursus
vincla parallelent—eadem quae perficit aetas,
annosusque dies et in ordine firmat eodem,
145 qui situs est idem.
　　　　　　　Nunc mente et pulvere circos
lineat et sphaeras et, quod quadrangulus orbem
quadruplet, evolvit, laterum qui ductibus exit
et quibus hoc cingit mediumque hoc dividit orbem.
Quodque orbem sphaerae maiorem quadruplet eius
150 curva superficies stupidae sollertia menti
nobilior monstrat. Nunc elimasse laborat

him. He explores the vast sphere by which the universe is   135
enclosed, if that which no circling path encompasses may
properly be called a sphere.

Chapter 8

A few themes of each of the Liberal Arts

He observes that the etherial sphere moves in a direct path,
and that each planet strives obliquely in an opposing path,
its circling controlled by the parallel orbit of the Sun. He
discerns those stars which their slower advance has given
the name of "fixed"; what form, what order, what underlying   140
natural principle or force distorts the orbit of a wandering
planet; what bonds of harmony ensure the parallel courses
of fixed stars—laws which an eternal power, ever the same, a
day embracing all the years, has ordained, and maintains in
an order ever the same, while being itself unmoved.   145

Now he draws circles and spheres, in his mind and in
sand, and proves that a rectangle formed with sides whose
lengths correspond to the circumference and the diameter
of a circle has four times the area of the circle. And a splen-   150
did feat of concentration reveals to his dazed mind that the
surface area of a sphere is four times that of the plane of its
circumference. Now he strives to refine more precisely the

pressius Euclidis numeros, cogitque quod esse
linea non possit numeri divisa secundum
extrema et medium, quodque est asymmetra costae
155 in duo quadratum partita diametrus aut est
par impar numerus.
           Nunc ad miracula limam
rhetoricae flectit reserans, qua molliit Orpheus
rhetore dura cheli, quanto facundia linguae
robore Threicii defregit roboris agmen;
160 qui fit, ut hanc vitae populus fastidiat auram,
seque sibi mortis pugilem spontaneus armet,
et rupto gladium fatalem sorbeat alvo,
dum nocuas in luce moras mundique retractat
Hegesias luctus, contemnendumque perorat
165 hoc Lachesis munus et apertum pestibus orbem,
poenarum pelagus, scelerum mare, cladis abyssum,
foetoris puteum, vitiorum sorde palustrem.
    Nunc, quo vera latent scrutatus scrinia, caecis
a latebris vellit, quid verum semper idemque
170 semper erit falsum: nec corpus corpore plures
tenditur in partes; nec harena maius harenam
partibus excedit.
            Nunc pessum figit acumen
grammaticae cunis et vocum circuit apta
foedera, mensus ubi geminum constructio rectum
175 transitione ligat, sicut contraria recto
obliquum ratio sine transitione maritat.
    At si quid studium celat caligo, retusam
elidens aciem, clivoque relangueat ardens
cursus in ascenso, desperantemque relabi
180 arduitas cogat, id sola mente, vel illa

138

formulas of Euclid, and proves that a line cannot be divided according to the ratio of extreme and mean; and that the diagonal which divides a rectangle into two equal parts must be incommensurable with the side of the rectangle, or else be at once an even and an uneven number.

Now he scrutinizes the wonders of rhetoric, and discovers how Orpheus's eloquent lyre made hard things grow soft, by what power the Thracian's charming words caused the oaks to break ranks; how it comes to pass that a people grow contemptuous of this life, willingly take up arms to wage deadly war against themselves, and thrust the fatal sword into their own torn bodies, when Hegesias speaks repeatedly to them of the perils of lingering in this life and the hardships of the world, concluding that the gift of Lachesis must be repudiated, that the world is a place of sickness, an ocean of pain, a sea of wickedness, a maelstrom of slaughter, a pit of decay, a foul swamp of vice.

Now, probing to where the annals of truth lie hidden, he plucks forth from the dark shadows both what will always be true and what always false: that no one body is amplified by more dimensions than any other body; not even one grain of sand can exceed another in this respect.

Now he directs his probing mind to the cradle of grammar, and traces the proper connections of words, studying constructions in which two nominatives are bound together in a transitive relation, just as a contrary rule joins a word in an oblique case to a nominative without such a transitive link.

But if a cloud should obscure any inquiry, defeating the dulled keenness of his mind, and his eager rush up the steep path is slowed, and difficulty makes him fall back in despair,

et calamo currente, notat, clausumque reservat
crastina quod maior possit reserasse Minerva.
Et menti et calamo rerum velamina mandat,
quae develanti possint venisse magistro
185 mentis in aspectum, cum Phoebi auriga fugabit
lutea purpureo stellas Aurora flagello.

Capitulum 9

De sopore scholaris studio fatigati

Talibus insudans olei librique lucerna,
tabidus illanguet, toti nupsisse Minervae
sedulus ardet amor. Dum strato Phoebus ab axe
190 Antipodum surgat, et paucis distet ab ortu
iam gradibus, tenui tum primum spargit ocellos
nube quies somni. Calamumque et cetera laxis
instrumenta rapit digitis, declive libello
suscipiente caput. Sed in illa pace soporis
195 pacis eget studii labor insopitus. Et ipso
cura vigil somno, libros operamque ministrat
excitae somnus animae. Nec prima sopori
anxietas cedit, sed quae vigilaverat ante
sollicitudo redit, et maior summa laboris
200 curarum studiis insomnibus obicit Hydram.

he merely makes a mental note, or perhaps quickly jots it down, and keeps closed what tomorrow's greater wisdom may be able to unfold. To such thoughts and jottings, too, he entrusts veiled matters, which may become accessible to his mind through the master's unveiling, when golden Aurora, 185 Phoebus's charioteer, has put the stars to flight with her purple lash.

Chapter 9

The sleep of a scholar exhausted by study

Toiling at such tasks by lamplight and the light of learning, he grows faint with exhaustion, yet burns with eager love to make Minerva wholly his own. Only when Phoebus has arisen from the low-lying Antipodes, and drawn within a 190 few paces of the horizon, does the calm of sleep first spread its gentle mist over his eyes. It takes the pen and other tools from his slack fingers, while the book receives his drooping head. But even in the peace of slumber the unceasing labor 195 of study finds no peace. Care remains wakeful amid sleep, and sleep is still proposing books and projects to the restless mind. His former anxiety does not yield to sleep; instead the preoccupations that earlier had kept him awake return, and the vast amount of work to be done presents a Hydra of 200 troubles to his nightmarish cogitations.

Capitulum 10

De vexatione eiusdem in dormitione
per somnia

Nulla quies somnus! Nec enim cessura quieti
cura soporatur. Nec nulla potentia somni,
cum quod in astrictis rerum perplexio nodis
torserat evolvit, quod non speraverat ante
205   segnior intuitus vigilantis. Multa magistro
nox aperit somno; cum strati corporis extra
sarcina dormitet, vigilant in pectore sensus.
Disputat oppresso strepitu, clausoque tumultu
argumenta iacit, tacitoque instantius ore
210   et digito laevam ferienti clamat, utroque
garrulus immoto. Nec numquam lingua loquenti
temptatam seriem titubanti murmure turbat,
nec nexu explicito somno ligat ebria voces;
et somni meminit cunas infantia linguae.
215   Nec minus et digiti suspecta audacia laevae
surgere conatur, sed deside pressa soporis
mole, retardatur, et solum palpitat, icto
aere vel libro (nam libro inversus inheret,
exanimisque iacet sub mortis imagine, somno).
220   Sic varia pectus ambage insomnia vexant,
sollicitumque trahit curarum turba, soporis
indepasta fame. Iamiamque Aurora diei
nuntiat adventum, cum Phoebo praevius ortum

Chapter 10

The student is troubled by dreams as he sleeps

It is sleep, but not rest! For care will not let itself be lulled to rest. Yet sleep is not wholly without effect, since it opens up what his earlier perplexity had twisted into tight knots, what the flagging insight of the waking mind had not hoped to solve. Night reveals many things through the tutelage of sleep; while the bulk of the sprawling body is outwardly 205 slumbering, understanding is awake within. He disputes soundlessly, throws out arguments in silent excitement, exclaims vehemently with silent lips, striking his index finger 210 against his palm, though both remain unmoved as he runs on. At times his tongue, with a faltering murmur, disrupts the intended order of his speech, and drunkenly joins words with no clear connection to his sleeping thoughts; the mute babbling of slumber recalls the cradle of speech. So too the 215 censorious boldness of the index finger struggles to reach the left hand, but is held back, burdened by the dull weight of sleep, and only flutters, tapping at the air or the book (for he is still bent over his book, lying as if lifeless in a sleep that is the image of death). Thus dreams trouble his mind with 220 random thoughts, a throng of cares continue to worry him, and his craving for sleep is unsatisfied. And already Aurora announces the advent of day, while Phoebus's precursor

Lucifer explorat, primumque excerpere rorem
225 mane novo sudante parat, ne semita Phoebi
polluat uda togam clamidisque elidat honorem.

Capitulum 11

De excitatione eiusdem
a somno

Ecce sopor, Phoebo vigili cessurus, ocellis
philosophi cedit, somno nutantibus astris
iam vigilante die, stellis citus insilit hospes,
230 hospite mutato. Miser ecce excitur ocellus,
Luciferi clamante tuba. Damnoque lucerna
ardet adhuc, extincta die caelique sepulta
lumine. Non oleo summam aspergente papyrum,
obsequiove manus vasi revocantis olivum,
235 post alios pastus, se depascente papyro.

Lucifer explores the horizon and prepares to sweep away
the dew of the fresh early dawn, lest a wet path stain Phoe-   225
bus's tunic and mar the glory of his robe.

Chapter II

How the scholar is aroused
from sleep

Lo, sleep, giving way to wakeful Phoebus, withdraws from
the philosopher's eyes, while the stars nod off to sleep as the
day awakens, and the swift traveler, leaving his place of rest,
leaps forth among the stars. Lo, an unhappy eye is jarred   230
open by Lucifer's clamorous horn. To his ruin the lamp still
burns, though eclipsed by daylight and lost in the light of
heaven. There being no olive oil to keep the top of the wick
moist, since no attendant hand has replenished the oil in the
bowl, the wick, having consumed this other meal, now feeds   235
on itself.

Capitulum 12

De preparatione eiusdem
ad studium profecturi

Excutit ergo caput vultuque assurgit, et ora
turbidus et crines. Digitorum verrit apertam
pectine caesariem, somnoque madentia siccat
summa labella sinu, noctisque laboribus ore
240 respirante gemit. Oculosque in faece natantes
expedit, a nodis cilii texentibus umbram
extricatque manu, partesque effusus in omnes
undique discurrit oculus, dum tempore digna
nomina deprendat. Et ubi dinovit ad ortum
245 surgere Solis equos, queritur dispendia somni
plus iusto traxisse moras, nimiumque citato
axe diem raptam. Praecessurusque, magistrum
praecessisse timet, et iam pro parte diurna
intonuisse tuba, fontisque secunda propinet
250 pocula Cirrhaei. Domitos torporibus artus
increpat; et maestos irae indignatio risus
excutit, et tumidos flammato pectore quaestus
evomit, in lacrimas tandem vergente querela.

Chapter 12

The scholar prepares
to set out for school

Then he shakes his head and looks around, his face and hair alike confused. He sweeps back his uncovered hair with the comb of his fingers, dries his lips, moist from sleep, on his tunic, and groans with a mouth still panting from his night- 240 time labors. He clears his eyes, swimming in dross, frees them with his hand from the tangled lashes that shadow them, and his gaze moves quickly forth in all directions, while he gropes for words worthy of the hour. And when he realizes that the Sun's horses are rushing toward the hori- 245 zon, he laments that time spent in sleep has caused him to delay unduly, that the day has been carried too far on its swift wheels. Eager to arrive first, he fears that the master has preceded him, that the horn has already sounded for the daily lesson, and he is now proffering a second round of 250 Cirrhaean libations. He curses his body for succumbing to fatigue; indignation evokes a sneer of bitter anger, and he spews forth the complaints welling up in his burning bosom, laments that come at last to the point of tears.

Capitulum 13

De amatore qui amicae pactus est accessum de nocte

Sic Veneris miles furtivum pactus amatae
255   postibus accessum, cum Luna retorserit ignes
fratris ad occasum, Veneris minus apta rapinis
lascivisque dolis. Dum nocti infuderit umbram
anxius expectat; tandem titubantia somnus
lumina furatur dubiisque inserpit ocellis.
260   Quos ubi torporem Venus indignata vigilque
somno extorsit Amor; et iam tenet ultima caeli
coniuga Luna solo, sternitque cubilia fessam
susceptura Thetis; umbramque extendit in ortus
pressa soror Phoebi; rabie crudescit amator,
265   deside deludi somno ratus. Irrita languet,
quam facit hora ratam, modicis spes saucia causis.
Increpat excubiis oculi se credere; iurat
damno praeteritae quod vota fefellerit horae,
quodque semel lusa numquam potiatur amata.
270   Seque suique pudet, Veneris se intrudere castris
degenerem damnat.
                  Stimulos tamen invenit; et spem
consolatur Amor, et amans ad limen amatae
ocius igne volat. Rapiturque Cupidinis alis,

Chapter 13

The lover who has arranged to visit his beloved by night

It is thus that the soldier of Venus arranges to come in secret to his mistress's door, at nightfall when the Moon casts back her brother's reflected flames, a time ill-suited to the thefts and wanton stratagems of Venus. He waits anxiously while she steeps the night in darkness; but at length sleep steals away his faltering vision and seeps into his wavering eyes. When Venus, indignant at such slothfulness, and wakeful Love snatch him from slumber; when the Moon has already reached the edge of the sky and united with the earth, and Thetis has prepared a bed to receive the weary one; when the sister of Phoebus as she descends casts long shadows toward the eastern horizon; the lover grows fiercely angry, knowing himself idly mocked by slumber. That hope which the naming of the hour had made real has withered to nothing, blighted by this mere accident. He curses himself for having trusted his eyes to keep watch; he declares that his prayers have been rendered vain by the loss of the hour now past, that he may never enjoy a beloved once deceived. He is ashamed, and condemns himself as one unworthy of admission to the camp of Venus.

Yet even now he finds inducements; Love revives hope, and now the lover flies swifter than fire to the beloved's door. He is borne along by the wings of Cupid, and gazing

suspiciensque simul terras metitur et astra,
275 has pedis, haec oculi cursu. Quod sole prematur
signum, quod medium teneat sublimius orbem,
mens oculusque vident. Quantum est de nocte relictum,
aethere scrutatur et cuncta loquentibus astris.

Capitulum 14

De transitu scholaris ad scholam

Non secus et miles Phoebi ad loca pacta Minervae,
280 discendique Lares, properat, luctamine toto
et pedis et mentis, Aurorae ad limen eundo
saepius aspectans, oculisque amplectitur ortus,
et pedibus terras. Quantumque Aurora superni
aetheris ignito chlamydis succenderit ostro,
285 et quantum a Phoebo declinet linea Librae,
hoc oculis, hoc mente legit. Devellit ab illis
quae mora, dum Tethyos medius superenatet arcum
sol, ubi philosophis est ianua prima diei.

about he takes the measure of earth and heaven, the one 275
with his hastening feet, the other with sweeping gaze. Eye
and mind observe which constellation is dominated by the
Sun, which one has attained the zenith. From the sky and
the all-revealing stars he discovers how much of the night
remains.

Chapter 14

The scholar's journey to school

In the same way the soldier of Phoebus hastens to the pre-
cincts of Minerva, the sanctuary of learning, exerting feet 280
and mind to the utmost, continually glancing at Aurora's
threshold as he proceeds, spanning the horizon with his
eyes, and the earth with his feet. He gauges how much of the
upper sky Aurora has set aflame with her glowing purple
mantle, and how far the line of Libra is withdrawn from 285
Phoebus, the first with his eyes, the second with his mind;
thereby he determines how long it will be before the Sun
swims forth from amid the swell of Tethys, the opening of
the philosopher's day.

Capitulum 15

De statu eiusdem in magistri praesentia

Ut ventum est Pallas ubi mitior agmina Cirrhae
290 armat, et est studii mens sudatura palaestram,
suscitat ingenii flammas, conamina mentis
contrahit, exacuit animam, totusque coacti
pectoris incumbit oculis, riguaque magistrum
aure et mente bibit, et verba cadentia prono
295 promptus utroque levat. Oculique et mentis in illo
fixa vigilque manet acies, aurisque maritat
pronuba dilectam cupida cum mente Minervam.
Hanc sitit, hanc ardet studii Venus altera; maior,
alter anhelat amor. Totumque impendit acumen
300 expenditque diem, dum Phoebi roscidus orbis
crescit in occasu, sublataque redditur astris
flamma suusque dies, cum limina sole fugato
et noctis reserat et lucis Vespera claudit.

Chapter 15

His behavior in the presence of the master

Having arrived where a gentler Pallas arms the Cirrhaean host, and the mind prepares to exert itself in the gymnasium of study, he stirs up the fire of understanding, musters his powers of thought, sharpens his wits, gives himself wholly to the perceptions of his attentive mind, and drinks in the master's words with open ear and mind, alert to gather with both the cascade of words. Eyes and mind remain keenly focused on the teacher, and the ear as brideswoman marries the eager mind with its beloved Minerva. For her a second, scholarly Venus makes him thirst and yearn; for her another, a greater love makes him pant. He devotes to her all his energy and spends the day, until the orb of Phoebus grows large in its evening descent, and the withdrawal of his fire restores their day to the stars, while Vesper, as the Sun departs, opens the portals of darkness and closes those of daylight.

Capitulum 16

De compassione rerum saevissimarum
erga scholares

Hoc studii pondus, haec est congesta malorum
305   philosophis moles. Cui compassura quiescat
monstrorum rabies: scopulus Scironis amico
degeneret fletu; veniat clementia praeceps
in Diomedis equos; Busiridis ara cruorem
compluat humanum lacrimis; curvata recursum
310   haud Sinis arbor agat; dirumpat vincula carcer
ferrea Sullanus; vinctis minus uda Neronis
parceret ebrietas; Phalaris pietate iuvencus
mugiat; et pacis sit Cinna et Spartacus hospes.
Auderent Stygii canis obmutescere fauces;
315   mutaret Cocytus aquas aliisque maderet
fletibus; et Phlegethon clementi aresceret igne.
   Quae feritas illis non esset inaspera? Talem
redderet absenti Labyrinthus Thesea filo;
sterneret intortos orbes mansueta Charybdis,
320   nec laesura rates; placidum cessante latratu
Scylla susurraret; et libertate profundi,
mitior innocuis premeret vada Syrtis harenis.

Chapter 16

Some sympathy for scholars and their harsh lot

Such is the burden of study, such the mass of evils heaped 305
upon the philosopher. Would that the monsters' rage might
fall silent in compassion for him: that Sciron's rock might
dissolve in friendly weeping; kindness suddenly overcome
the horses of Diomede; the human blood on the altar of
Busiris be washed away by tears; that Sinis's bowed tree 310
might recoil no longer; Sulla's dungeon burst its iron fetters;
Nero become less sodden in drink and spare his victims; the
bull of Phalaris bellow in pity; and Cinna and Spartacus be
at peace. Would that the jaws of the Stygian dog might dare
to fall silent; Cocytus transform its waters and brim with 315
tears of another kind; and the plain of Phlegethon burn with
a gentle fire.

What savagery would not end its harshness for their
sake? The Labyrinth would release such a Theseus without
a thread; Charybdis, grown mild, would calm her swirling
waters, and no longer destroy ships; Scylla would cease bark- 320
ing and whisper peacefully; and a milder Syrtis, as free of
access as the open sea, would reduce her shoals to harmless
sand.

Capitulum 17

Quod scientia favorem
potentum diminuat

Cedere duritiem scopulis, et in obvia flecti
Naturam his spero, quibus est immota potentum
325 pectoris asperior rupes. Non subsidet illis
quod veri extergunt tenebras, rerumque retrusas
altius effodiunt causas; nec praeterit illos
uncia totius orbis, vel si quid ab orbe
cedit in immensos tractus. Nec sufficit arto
330 pectore diffusi clausisse volumina mundi,
quin procul a superis acies admissa, nec ullo
limite fracta volet, surgatque relinquere mundi
ausa supercilium. Nulla haec suffragia Musis,
subsidiique ferunt fomenta; scientia nullo
335 robore flectit opes. Sed et haec novisse favorem
divitis elidit; et risu morsa sciendi
gloria laesa iacet. Laudisque scientia damnum
ludibriosa dolet, et in aula maius habetur
ignorasse magis. Risu laedente notatur
340 grandiloquis Famae titulis incognita virtus.
    Praemia quae Davus recipit meruisset Homerus.
Ipsa sibi virtus odium parit: aulica rodit
serra virum mores, et laudis eclipticat astrum

Chapter 17

To possess knowledge is to be less favored by the great

I wish that hardness might depart from rock, and Nature be induced to favor these scholars, toward whom the hearts of the great are unyielding rock of a harder kind. It gains them 325 nothing that they cleanse truth of darkness, and unearth the deeply hidden causes of things; that not an atom of the entire world eludes them, nor whatever exists withdrawn from the world in the immensity beyond. It is not enough to have 330 enclosed within the confines of the breast a voluminous knowledge of the vast universe, or indeed that their keen vision is admitted afar by the heavenly powers, soars unsubdued by any limit, and rises undaunted to leave behind the scornfulness of the world. These feats gain no applause for the Muses, and no substantial aid; knowledge has no power 335 to sway the wealthy. To possess such knowledge is rather to make the rich man's goodwill vanish; the glory of learning is harassed by mockery and cast down. Science, an object of scorn, bemoans its lack of praise, while at court the greater ignorance is considered greater. A virtue that is not made 340 known by high-sounding claims to Renown is scathingly mocked and censured.

Thus Davus receives the rewards that Homer deserved. Virtue even brings hatred upon herself: the sawteeth of the court gnaw at men's characters, envy eclipses the star of

livor, et in tenebris ingloria pallet honestas
345 et Virtus titulos, sua mater pignora, perdit.

Capitulum 18

Quod artes a divitibus approbantur saltem in conscientia

Forsitan ad laudes linguae contraria sentit
pectus, et occulto rerum sub iudice Cirrhae
exaltatur honos; foris os condemnat, et intus
divitis absolvit melior mens testis, et ore
350 proditor accusat, animo commendat honestum.
    Non adeo tenebras serit ignorantia, mitrae
et solii morbus, ut tantae transeat illos
prosperitatis odor; lateatque incognitus aulae
sol melior mundi? Fallatque altissima tantos
355 lux oculos, maiorque dies? Sidusque lucernam
praeradiat; vincuntque faces fulgore favillas.
    Absit ut haec lateat sceptratos gloria; fusum
non cohibet lux tanta iubar quin splendeat aulae
limine. Sed quae sunt studiis aliena potentum
360 sunt et eis famosa parum. Diversa professos

praise, worthiness languishes in shadowy ignominy, and 345
mother Virtue is deprived of those tributes which are her
proper offspring.

Chapter 18

That the rich preserve a respect for learning at least in their hearts

Perhaps such minds harbor thoughts that contradict the
praises of the tongue, and the honor of Cirrha is esteemed
in their secret judgment; perhaps the voice outwardly con-
demns, and the mind within, the rich man's better testi-
mony, absolves, and he betrays by accusatory words those 350
whom in his heart he considers praiseworthy.

Surely ignorance, the plague of miter and throne, has not
spread such darkness that the philosopher is denied even
the scent of prosperity; can the world's truer Sun remain
hidden, unknown to the court? Can that most brilliant light, 355
that greater day, escape such noble eyes? A star shines
brighter than a lamp; the light of a torch surpasses a mere
spark.

Far be it that such glory should remain hidden from scep-
tered power; so great a light does not so curb its radiance
that it may not shine within the court. But whatever differs
from the pursuits of the great is little esteemed by them. 360

rarus amor nectit; contemnitur obvia curae
cura, favorque minor studiis discordibus exit.

Capitulum 19

Quare qui Artes noverint
sint divitibus odiosi

Forsan inaccessis lux haec splendoribus aulae
mollibus occurrit oculis, et lumina lumen
365 elidunt maiora minus, visusque reflectit
impetus excursum; tantumque ingloria solem
aulica celatur acies, carumque putatur
vile, sed ignotum. Laudis iactura beatis
imminet occultis; bona commendantur operta
370 parcius, et meritam premit ignorantia famam.
　　Forsan et ex illis aliquis laudare veretur
quod nescire pudet, vel quo reptasse facultas
libera nulla datur, dum torpidus illigat artus
desidiae languor, et segnis in otia vires
375 pectoris aegrescunt. Studiique in mollibus ardor
stinguitur, et plenis inserpit inertia rebus.
Desidiam cornu mutato Copia fundit,
ingenii tensum laxat opulentia nervum.

Scant love is bestowed on those who declare other interests; concerns at odds with their concerns are scorned, and little favor is extended to divergent pursuits.

Chapter 19

Why those versed in the Arts are hateful to the rich

Perhaps the light of learning strikes the feeble vision of the court with an unapproachable splendor, its greater light effaces the lesser, and its impact causes the gaze to recoil. 365 Perhaps the inglorious vision of the court is blind to such radiance, and what is precious is deemed worthless, though unknown. Loss of praise is the fate of sacred objects that remain hidden; concealed goods are sparingly commended, 370 and ignorance suppresses deserved Renown.

But perhaps there are also some at court who fear to praise what they are ashamed not to understand, matters in which they have been denied the capacity even to grope their way, since the dull lethargy of sloth fetters their limbs, and the powers of their sluggish minds lapse into idleness. 375 Zeal for learning is extinguished in these effete creatures, and their abundance is infected by inertia. The horn of Plenty, transformed, pours forth mere dissipation, and opulence slackens the taut sinews of intellect.

Forsan et est mentis tumidae suspectus in aula
380   Palladis hic miles, ne sit felicibus aequo
altius elatus, faciatque incauta bonorum
moribus offensam deiuncta superbia Musis.

Capitulum 20

De remotione elationis
a philosophis

Forsan id innocuam Cirrhen accusat, at illam
insita philosophis absolvit, et excipit omnem
385   Mansuetudo notam. Pax est cognata Minervae,
et iucunda Quies; et frenum passa Voluntas,
et lacrimis rorans Pietas; et prona fideles
amplecti sincera Fides; et conscia recti
Dulcedo, facilisque bonis Clementia flecti.
390   Non datur exactum Famae decus; omne venustum
creditur elatum, sine limo gloria nulli
affluit. Immeritis aliena superbia culpae est,
summaque Luciferi Boreis afflata putatur
nobilitas, virtusque venit suspecta tumoris.
395   Hac macula tanti non delibatur honoris
integritas, ubi verus honos, ubi cognita Phoebo
maiestas et fervor inest; ubi pocula Musis
consecrata bibit verus conviva Minervae;

Perhaps too the court suspects the knight of Pallas of a   380
presuming mind, as though he might aspire to more than
equality with the happy few, and a reckless and unbridled
pride in the Muses might offend the morals of good people.

Chapter 20

Philosophers are far removed
from vainglory

It may be that such an accusation is brought against unof-
fending Cirrha, but the inherent Mildness of the philoso-
pher absolves her, and exempts her from all censure. Peace   385
and happy Repose are Minerva's kinswomen; Will submis-
sive to restraint, and Pity, brimming with tears; untainted
Good Faith, ever ready to embrace the faithful; the Sweet-
ness of conscious rectitude, and Mercy, readily moved by
goodness. Yet the required honor of Renown is not granted;   390
every grace is deemed vanity, and glory comes to none with-
out some taint. Pride is alien to these blameless men, yet
their high nobility is presumed to be puffed up with the
winds of Lucifer, and their virtue is taken for haughtiness.
But the integrity of great honor is not diminished by this   395
taint when it is true honor, when the dignity and zeal that
Phoebus acknowledges are present; when the worthy guest
at Minerva's feast drinks from goblets consecrated by the

veraque Cirrhaeum perhibent insignia numen,
400   commendatque datam mens Phoebi conscia laurum.

Capitulum 21

Contra superficiales philosophos

At sunt philosophi, qui nudum nomen et umbram
numinis arripiunt, qui vix libasse Minervam
exhausisse putant. Tenuisque scientia pectus
erigit, et properata pudent insignia Musas;
405   raptaque temporibus nubit, sed adultera, laurus.
Hii sunt, qui statuae veniunt statuaeque recedunt;
et Bacchi sapiunt, non Phoebi pocula, Nysae
agmina non Cirrhae. Baccho Phoeboque ministrant,
hoc pleni, hoc vacui.
                Puer intrat Delia miles
410   castra, recessurus, dicta sumptaque salute
et dicto sumptoque vale; temereque magistri
praecipitatur honos. Rudibus praesumptio Musis
insilit, et primos audacia decipit annos.
Iamque in bella venit imbellis, inermis in arma.

Muses; then true tokens bear witness to the Cirrhaean god, and the mind that acknowledges Phoebus's power justifies 400 the awarding of the laurel.

Chapter 21

Against superficial philosophers

But there are philosophers who snatch at the bare name and shadow of this power, who suppose that to have barely tasted of the cup of Minerva is to have drained it. A little learning swells their chests, and their hastily acquired titles bring shame on the Muses; stolen laurels lend a false grace to 405 their brows. Such students arrive as statues and as statues they depart; they drink from Bacchus's cup, not Apollo's, for they are of the company of Nysa rather than Cirrha. They serve both Bacchus and Phoebus, but are full of the one, devoid of the other.

The boy-soldier enters the Delian camp only to depart 410 again, having given and received a greeting and given and received a farewell; and the title of master is carelessly thrust upon him. He sallies forth presumptuous in his crude learning, deceived by the boldness of his early years. Unfit for warfare, defenseless though armed, he immediately goes to war.

415   Haud ea sunt Famae Zephyris mandanda. Nec aulae
hunc ego commendo, nam se maioribus aequat,
contemnitque pares, indignaturque minores.
Nulli iucundus, gravis omnibus, omnia praeceps
imperiosus agit, et pacis nulla tumoris
420 fulmen habena premit. Modico quod novit in astra
conscendisse ratus, alienum scire labello
progrediente notat, et coniventis ocelli
invidia mordet, et quod tetigisse veretur
laudibus attenuat pressis, oculoque susurrat
425 subridente notam. Livoris cuncta veneno
conspuit, ipse suis avidus laudator in actis.
Et librata diu sed turgida verba loquendi
maiestate trahit, et gutture tracta tonanti
excutit, et linguam digito gestuque loquaci
430 adiuvat, et vultus animo maiora fatetur.

Capitulum 22

De venia divitum
ab auctore postulata

At super his aulae veniam peto; supprimat irae
impetus excursum, frenoque modestia pacem
imperet adducto. Cirrhaeas scimus ad aulam

Such things ought not to be consigned to the breezes of 415
rumor. I cannot even commend this youth to the court, for
he equates himself with his superiors, scorns his equals, and
disdains his inferiors. Pleasant to none, gruff to all, he
adopts always an abrupt and haughty manner, and no re-
straining gentleness curbs the thunder of his bombast. Con- 420
vinced by the little he knows that he has ascended to the
stars, he criticizes the learning of others with outthrust lip,
gnaws at it with enviously squinting eye, and belittles with
faint praise things which he would have feared to attempt,
muttering censure while his eyes continue to smile. He 425
sprays all others' work with the venom of his envy, though
eager in praise of his own achievements. And with majestic
eloquence he draws forth words long pondered but still tur-
gid, emitting them slowly from his sonorous throat, and aid-
ing the tongue with eloquent gestures of the finger, while his 430
expression speaks far more grandly than his mind.

Chapter 22

The author begs the indulgence
of the wealthy

But in speaking of such matters I beg the indulgence of the
court: may it resist the impulse to act in anger, and may
moderation, plying the reins, impose peace. We know that

divertisse deas, totumque infundere Phoebum
435 pluribus; et geminum contingit regia solem.
Criminis unius hos colligit, excipit illos
linea, paucorumque nota non tangimus omnes.
Hos cum declinet vitium, declinat ad illos;
hos vel eos tetigisse licet, veniamque peroret
440 excepisse bonos; redimatque exceptio culpam.

Capitulum 23

Quae sint causae dandorum redituum

Et tamen admiror, quam dandi caeca potentum
sit reditus sparsura manus; nam prodiga fundit
immeritis, et avara tenet, cui larga tenetur.
Ad data prona datis, pollutaque munere munus
445 restituit, munusque putat quod munere vendit.
    Expectata bonis rapiunt bona prona cupido
in pretium pretio; nullique incognitus aulae
ambitus; et laterum falerato multus in ore
Tullius; et celso cumulus speratus honori;
450 et furtim mitrata Venus; scelerisque minister
conscius; imperiique metus; vitaeque nocenti
histrio suspectus; et adultae gloria laudis;

the Cirrhaean goddesses have visited the court, and the full
power of Phoebus has inspired many; the palace acknowl-   435
edges a double Sun. The roster of this particular crime in-
cludes some and excludes others, and in censuring a few we
do not implicate all. The vice avoids some, while it adheres
to others; though it should happen that it implicate this or
that person, yet it may claim in its behalf that it has ex-   440
empted the good; let that exemption free it of guilt.

Chapter 23

The reasons for giving rewards

And yet I wonder at how blindly the hand of the powerful
strews the rewards it offers; for it pours forth prodigally on
the undeserving, and avariciously withholds from those to
whom generosity is owed. Readily giving in return for a gift,
it is corrupted by gifts, offers gifts in return, and considers   445
that a gift which it sells for a gift.

Thus good men are robbed of their expected reward, by
greed, ever ready to exchange gift for gift; by ambition, with
which no court is unacquainted; by the Cicero who abounds
in the ornate speech of faction; by the treasure given in hope
of a lofty title; by the Venus who wears the miter in secret;   450
by the minister who condones wrongdoing; by fear of power;
by the actor suspect for his vicious habits; by the glorifying

dando non meritis; nimiumque alterna potentum
gratia; cognatusque movens praecordia sanguis;
455 consimilesque ligans animorum fibula mores;
implicitaeque dolis venundata copia linguae.
    Nec noto, quod sanctum Naturae lege: propinquis
astringatur amor; truncique a robore ramus
robora derivet. Surgatque in sanguine sanguis
460 idem in eodem; ortusque sui Natura memento.
In genus est proclivis amor; maiorque minores
tollat honos, generisque genus sub sole diescat.
At quantum liceat libeat; tollantque propinqui
dona propinqua modo, reditusque in parte relinquant
465 philosophis; unum capiant, qui cuncta merentur!
    Detur; et hoc aulae fateatur Pallada munus;
significentque data solium novisse Minervam,
et studii quaedam consortia dona loquantur.
Impigra sit dandi meritis manus. Infima laus est
470 cuncta dari, cum nulla bonis. Quas sorbet in hora
histrio dantis opes, logicus delibet in anno.

of false praise; by gifts to the undeserving; by the too-uncertain favor of the great; by kinship of blood, which stirs the affections; by the bond that unites the souls of men of   455
like character; and by wealth, bribed through the wiles of a designing tongue.

I do not censure what is sanctioned by Nature's law: let love be a bond between kinsmen; let the branch derive its strength from the strength of the trunk. The same blood must flow in the veins of men of the same stock; let Nature   460
be mindful of her origins. Love is responsive to the bond of family; let dignity of ancestry uplift the young, and the family be illumined by the Sun of their lineage. But let this be granted only insofar as it is right; let kinsmen carry off only the fruits of kinship, and let them leave some small reward for philosophers; let them receive something, who de-   465
serve all!

Let this much be granted: let this reward be the court's tribute to Pallas; let gifts attest that majesty acknowledges Minerva, and the giving declare some friendship toward study. Let the hand be unwearied in its gifts to the deserving. Giving all deserves scant praise when nothing is given to   470
the virtuous. The largesse that an actor gulps down in an hour a logician would sip at for a year.

BOOK FOUR

Capitulum 1

Compassio Architrenii super scholarium egestate

Lilia Castalii Veris marcentia Fati
sub Borea brumante gemit, Nysamque negantem
subsidium Cirrhae. Verum praesentia laedunt
fortius adversa, contra distantia sensum
5   diminuunt poenae; nec compassiva dolendi
tot stimulos lamenta ferunt, et segnius urit
fax admota minus. Igitur maeroris in unda
naufragus, inde meat alibi siccandus ocellus.

Capitulum 2

De monte Ambitionis

Mons surgente iugo Pellaeam despicit urbem,
10 astra supercilio libans, lunaque minorem
miratur longe positam decrescere terram.
Sideribus vicinus apex, ut saepe meantem
ocius offendat, cum cursu est infima, lunam
augis in opposito, cum visu maxima pessum

Chapter 1

Architrenius's compassion for the students' poverty

Architrenius mourns to see the lilies of the Castalian spring withering beneath the wintry blasts of Fate, and Nysa denying support to Cirrha. But present misfortunes wound us more severely, and as they become more distant the sense of pain is diminished; compassion and lament do not bring such pangs of grief, and the torch burns less keenly when less close. So foundering in a sea of grief, Architrenius departs to dry his eyes elsewhere.

Chapter 2

The Mount of Ambition

From its lofty height a mountain looks scornfully down on the Pellaean city, its brow touching the stars, and wonders that the earth, lying far below, grows smaller than the Moon. So near the stars does it rise that its peak often obstructs the swift-moving Moon when, at the low point of her orbit,

15 vergit in orbe brevi, mediumque aspectibus offert
    quadratura iubar. Partem directior omnem
    vix aliqua vergit, facilemque admittere nescit
    arduus ascensum. Sola hic latus omne pererrans
    Ambitio reptat praedilexitque colendum
20 pro laribus montem, Zephyris ubi succuba tellus
    Veris alumnat opes passimque intexit amara
    dulcibus. Et fruticum nodis armantur olivae;
    et laurus cristata rubis; suspectaque dumis
    quercus; et horrenti crudescit coniuga rusco
25 aesculus; et rigidis spinae vallatur aristis
    astra comis abies superum concivis inumbrans.
    Hic, quaecumque virum fit gloria crinibus arbor,
    gratia montis habet et, si qua audacius alto
    vertice diis certat. Ibi nulla licentia pressae
30 arboris, ut surgat; montique assurgere nano
    crine myrica timet. Steriles ibi verberat auras
    infecunda salix, riguisque libentior alnus
    ascendisse vadis, aeternaque testis amorum
    populus Oenones, platanusque et, si qua neganti
35 Natura haud recipit partus ingloria fructum.

opposite to the apogee, she appears largest, and her quar- 15
tered surface presents only half of her radiance to the sight.
One face of the mountain hardly rises more sharply than all
the others, and its steepness affords no easy ascent. Only
Ambition creeps about here, roving over every slope, for
she has chosen this mountain as her abode, where the Earth, 20
offering herself to Zephyr, nurtures the fruits of spring, and
intersperses bitter and sweet at random. Olive trees are
girded with clusters of shrubbery; the laurel is crowned with
brambles; the oak menaces with thorns; winter oak be-
comes the rough consort of bristling broom; and the fir, fel- 25
low citizen of the gods, shading the stars with its boughs, is
fortified with stiff clusters of thorn. The mountain extends
its favor to any tree that may serve to adorn the brows of
men, and any that is so bold as to challenge the gods with its
lofty crest. But it is not permitted a shorter tree to grow 30
here; the myrtle with its tiny leaves is afraid to grow on these
slopes. Here the barren willow whips the sterile breeze; the
alder, which prefers to grow on well-watered banks; the
poplar, eternal witness to the love of Oenone; the plane, and
any inglorious tree to which Nature has denied the power to 35
bear fruit.

Capitulum 3

De quibusdam montis illius
arboribus et floribus

Hic pinus graciles succingitur alta capillos;
palmaque centennis tardante puerpera fructu;
et pretiosa rogos fumo condire cupressus;
et meliore libro cinnamolgi cinnamus hospes;
40   et lacrima felix nostrae sacra balsamus arae;
et ficus geminis depingens floribus annum;
et bina nucleum quae claudit amygdalus arca;
et sitiens Bacchi primaevum pessicus imbrem;
et tunicata croco germanaque coctanus auri;
45   et rugosa genam producto dactylus aevo;
et pirus huicque sacrum tituli dat Regulus omen;
et pirus hancque volae plenus denominat orbis;
et pirus, huicque dedit matrina angustia nomen;
et pirus, Augusto quae patrinante vocatur;
50   et pirus, haec nota est et filiolata Roberto;
et pirus, est huius alius baptista Iohannes;
et pirus a quovis pretio signata, vel oris
cena vel aspectus. Coit uno quaelibet arbor
ambitiosa sinu, quo pictae prodiga formae
55   rumpitur in vernos montis lascivia risus.
Gratus ibi livor violae, dulcique rosarum
flamma cruore natans; terrae devinctior auras

Chapter 3

Some trees and flowers
that grow on the mountain

Here the tall pine wreathes itself in graceful boughs; and the
palm, pregnant a hundred years with its slow-growing fruit;
and cypress, prized for steeping the pyre in its scent; and
cinnamon, with its even finer bark, home to the cinnamol-
gos; and balsam, blessed for the tears which hallow our al-   40
tars; and the fig, which adorns the year with twin flowerings;
and the almond, which encloses its kernel in a double coffer;
and the peach, thirsting for the early rain of Bacchus; and
quince, jacketed in a yellow that is close to gold; and the   45
date, its face wrinkled as if by great age; and the pear on
which Regulus conferred the sacred token of his own title;
and the pear named for the rounded the hollow of the hand;
and the pear to which the narrow passage of motherhood
gives its name; and the pear for whose naming Augustus
stood as godfather; and the pear that was acknowledged and   50
christened by Robert; and that pear whose baptizer was a
second John; and pears distinguished by any and all attri-
butes, whether of taste or of appearance. Ambitious trees of
all kinds come together in this single space, so that a wanton
profusion of bright shapes bursts forth into the merry   55
springtime of the mountain. The violet's pleasing purple is
here, and the flaming red of the rose, swimming in sweet
gore; the crocus, kept close to the ground, sweetens the

mulcet odore crocus; et notus amantibus hospes
exaequasse nivi praesumit lilia pallor.
60 Floribus egregiis solum pubescit, ut absit
gloria pauperibus hortis: vilesque ligustra
ornatura rubos et, quae certasse ligustris,
nigra licet, cogit Zephyrus vaccinia pingens.

Capitulum 4

De rivulo in eius apice demananti

In planum descendit apex, variusque superne
65 rivulus exultat. Conflictantisque susurrat
ludus aquae, ripasque ioco pulsante lacessit.
Solis unda vacat pretiis: haud ulla profundo
vilis harena sedet lapidumque ignobile vulgus.
Ditia luxuriant ridentibus ima metallis,
70 exundatque iubar lapidum generosa propago,
ut gelidus mixtis delectet in ignibus humor.
Illic illimes bysso candentius undas
liliat argentum, partimque argenteus auro
amnis inauratur. Gemmarum turba nitore
75 auget aquae radios: hic iaspidis, hic amethysti
gloria lascivit; hyacinthi caerula plaudunt;

breeze with its scent; and the lily's pallor, a guest well known
to lovers, presumes to rival the whiteness of snow. The 60
mountain flourishes only with special flowers, so that there
is no place for the glories of humble gardens: privet, which
beautifies the rough thorn hedge, and those berries which,
black though they are, Zephyrus compels to compete with
privet.

Chapter 4

The stream that descends from the summit of the mountain

The peak descends into a plain, and a winding river leaps 65
down from above. The play of its turbulent waters creates a
murmur as it dashes with sportive force against its banks.
The water admits only precious things: no lowly sand lies at
the bottom, no ignoble crowd of pebbles. The rich depths
abound in happily shining metals, and the noble family of 70
jewels diffuse their brightness, so that the chill water de-
lights in their mingled fires. Silver, whiter than fine linen,
gleams through the clear waters, and the silvery stream is
gilded here and there by gold. A host of gems enhance the 75
water's radiance with their glow: the glory of jasper and am-
ethyst is flaunted here; sapphires display their deep blue;

et pretium praebet nutricibus unio conchis;
et fruitur viridis aeterno vere smaragdus.

Capitulum 5

De incolis eiusdem montis

Hic vaga discurrit, animi gravis incola, numquam
80 Cura soporis amans, Curaeque annexa parenti
Anxietas; tacitique Metus et vota Voluntas
dissimulans et Spes dubio vicina Timori;
donaque nobilior populis sparsura Cupido;
et sceptri secretus Amor, nimioque vacillans
85 Credulitas voto; soliique occulta casarum
laudativa Sitis; et honorum sedula Plausus;
muneribus pavisse Fames; audaxque favores
alternos emisse Favor; Famaeque sititor
Impetus expensae; donataque Gratia gratis,
90 sed reditura datis; vultusque Modestia raro
gratior arrisu; Gravitasque affabilis oris
non animi plausura ioco; mansuetaque linguae
Canities; verbique virum testata Venustas.
    Hic promissa volant, discursant dona, fidesque
95 pollicitis proclivis adest; dandique facultas
libera spargit opes; plenoque Pecunia cornu

the pearl gives value to its nurturing shell; and the emerald rejoices in the green of an eternal spring.

Chapter 5

Those who frequent the mountain

Care, who infests the troubled mind, and has no love for 80
sleep, wanders restlessly here, and Anxiety, clinging close to
Care, her parent; unspoken Misgiving, and a Will that keeps
its wishes hidden, and Hope that is close to timid Fear; the
Greed that ennobles itself by strewing largesse among the
people; a hidden Love of royal power, and the hopes of too- 85
uncertain Credulity; the Thirst for a throne that conceals
itself in praise of the simple life; Adulation, eager for hon-
ors; Hunger to be fed with rewards; Favor that boldly seeks
to buy the favor of others; Recklessness, still thirsty for the
Reputation it has squandered; Goodwill, bestowed at no ex-
pense, but sure to be repaid with gifts; a Modesty of de- 90
meanor set off by rare smiles; Gravity, pleasant of voice,
though not of thought, in commending a jest; a gentle Ven-
erability of speech; and a Charm in speaking that claims to
express the man.

Here promises flit about, gifts speed back and forth, and
trust gives ready credence to assurances; an artful liberality 95
scatters its riches; Money's cornucopia pours forth friend-

fundit amicitias; emiturque in mutua nexus
foedera, venalique datis succumbitur aulae.
Hic fictus Virtutis odor; fabricataque vultus
100 Religio; clausoque tumens Elatio vento;
et Recti mendax species; et simia morum
Hypocrisis neglecta genas; aucepsque favoris
Eloquium; vernusque rudis Facundia causae
flosculus; et turpem redimens Sollertia vitam.
105 Hic in amicitias hostem complectitur hostis,
blanditur Feritas, Odium favet, Ira salutat,
Saevities palpat, Libertas servit, oboedit
Imperium, premitur Maiestas, Gloria languet,
cedit Apex. Omnique via reptatur ad aulam,
110 omnique Ambitio saltu venatur honores.
      Hic puer imperii cupidus ludebat: alumnus
Martis, Alexander. Sceptrique infudit amorem
Ambitio nutrix, totumque armavit in orbem
praecipites animos, tenerisque induruit annis
115 bella pati, votumque duos extendit in ortus.

ship; commitment to mutual contracts is purchased, and depends on gifts to a mercenary court. Here are the odor of feigned Virtue; a contrived Religiosity of manner; Self-esteem puffed up by a bellyful of wind; the false semblance of Rectitude; and Hypocrisy, aping goodness with unpainted cheeks; Eloquence, laying its snares for favor; Glibness, the spring flower that adorns an awkward appeal; and the Craftiness that redeems the shameful life. Here enemy embraces enemy in friendship, Savagery grows mild, Hatred is kind, Wrath is courteous, Cruelty caresses, Freedom is submissive, Command obeys, Majesty is humbled, Glory fades, Authority yields. Ambition creeps toward the court by every path, and stalks preferment with every step.

Here there played a boy, greedy for dominion: Alexander, the ward of Mars. Ambition, his nurse, instilled the desire to rule, armed his impulsive spirit against all the world, steeled his tender youth to the hardships of war, and stretched his aspirations to the two horizons.

Capitulum 6

Quod ex Ambitione
bella ortum habuerint

Primos Ambitio remos et prima furori
vela dedit ventosque rudes, Martique volanti
cum sole et luna primas innexuit alas.
In Magni iugulos animavit Caesaris enses,
120   corrupitque fidem soceri, pavitque Philippos
sanguine civili. Pugnavitque hostibus hostis;
et Romana leves iuverunt proelia Parthos,
instantesque fuga supplerunt pila sarissas.
Hac duce sunt Latii totum diffusa per orbem
125   vulnera. Poenorum subsedit gloria Romae,
fulminea pulsante manu bibuloque cruoris
Hannibal ense furor. Mundumque doloribus emit
Caesareumque iugum Romae defessa iuventus
Ambitionis acu. Gaudensque laboribus omnes
130   indolis extorsit titulos, fuditque furore
Martis et Herculeo nitentem sanguine Pyrrhum.

Chapter 6

That wars originate from Ambition

Ambition first gave oars, sails, and the rough winds to our madness, and provided wings to a Mars who flies with the Sun and Moon. She drove Caesar's sword against the throat of Pompey, caused a father-in-law to break faith, and steeped 120 Philippi in civil bloodshed. Warring against Rome's enemies she was herself an enemy; Roman campaigns were a boon to the swift Parthians, and javelins hurled in flight served them in place of menacing pikes. With Ambition as leader, Latian slaughter was spread throughout the world. The glory of 125 Carthage, the fury of Hannibal, with his thunderously pounding arm and bloodthirsty sword, submitted to Rome. Driven to exhaustion by the goad of Ambition, the youth of Rome reduced the world to the yoke of the Caesars by their sufferings. Rejoicing in their hardships, they grasped 130 all lordship as if by natural right, and overthrew even Pyrrhus, glorying in his Martial fierceness and his Herculean lineage.

Capitulum 7

In quo genere hominum
Ambitio conversetur

Hinc hominum tortrix, Alecto maior, Erinys
summa, potestates urget violentius. Ardor
arduus, Ambitio, solitaeque accendere corda
135   nobiliora faces, indignatusque caminus
degeneres animos timidosque invadere votis.
Integrum imperium, summamque capessere mundi,
et diis esse pares superumque instare favori,
Fortunaeque sequi tollentis in aethera dextram.
140   Contentos habitis, submissaque pectora spernit,
et votum quod serpit humi; nam prodiga voti,
sperat in immensum, nullique indulget habenae
Ambitio secura modi. Spes ardua sola est
quae timuisse facit, et anhelans summa voluntas,
145   et desiderii sitientis sceptra libido.

Chapter 7

The sort of men in whom Ambition resides

Then this tormentor of men, this greater Allecto, this arch-Fury asserts her power still more violently. For Ambition is a lofty passion, a torch that ever inflames noble hearts, a fiery heat that scorns to inspire the mean-spirited, or those timid in their hopes. She seeks absolute dominion, supreme worldly power, to be equal to the gods and enjoy their acclaim, to follow the guidance of Fortune that raises her to the heavens. She scorns those content with their lot, submissive spirits, and the prayer that creeps along the ground; for Ambition squanders prayers, her hopes are vast, and she recklessly admits no restraint. Only her high hopes make her anxious, her will that pants to gain the heights, and the goad of her thirsting desire to rule.

Capitulum 8

De aula in montis eius
vertice constituta

Huc nova visurus fastigia surgere, fessis
luctatur pedibus. Et iam superatur Olympus
tertius, alter Atlas, et adest quae sidera dorso
culminis aula quatit. Contendit in ardua caelo
150   invidiam factura domus; sublimis in altum
ad modicum statura volat. Transcendit et auras
et pacem quam summa tenent, seque inserit astris,
sollicitatque deos iteretne proelia Phlegrae.
Haud aliter caelestis homo, suspecta minanti
155   arduitate, Iovem repetita in fulmina cogit;
armatusque manus hominum securus et arces
despicit, et terrae digna scelus expiat ira.

    Tollitur alta solo regum domus aula, deumque
sedibus audaci se vertice mandat. At umbras
160   fundamenta premunt; regnisque silentibus instat,
ultima Tartareos aequans structura recessus.
Radices operis, ne verticis ardua preceps
sarcina subsidat, Stygias demittit ad undas.

    Tartareus iam civis homo: Stygis incola, mortis
165   non expectato laqueo, venit, illa supremo
vis rapitur Fato. Mavult praecedere liber,

Chapter 8

The court established at the top of the mountain

Architrenius, his feet grown weary, labors to reach the summit and behold new heights. At last this third Olympus, this second Atlas is conquered, and a hall stands before him which strikes the stars with its roof. Rising steeply, the building seeks to create envy in heaven; sublimely tall, it 150 seems almost to soar on high. It transcends both the atmosphere and the peace which the higher realms maintain, installs itself among the stars, and makes the gods take care lest the battle of Phlegra be renewed. In the same way a sky-born race, the menace of whose great height bred mistrust, 155 once drove Jove to hurl repeated thunderbolts; but Jove, armed and fearless, scorns the arms and citadels of men, and his just wrath gains satisfaction for the crimes of the world.

This royal dwelling, this hall rises high above the earth, and claims with its audacious height a place amid the homes of the gods. But its foundations encroach on the under- 160 world; it is set above the realms of silence, and its lowest supports are as deep as the depths of Tartarus. Lest the towering bulk of the roof come crashing down, it sends down its roots to the very waters of Styx.

For man is even now a citizen of Tartarus; he comes to Styx as a native, seized by the unsuspected snare of death, 165 robbed of his strength by all-powerful Fate. He thinks to

Fatorum quam iussa sequi; iam tramite caeco,
ad Styga rumpit iter. Vivus venisse laborat
quo defunctus eat. Descendit ad infima, mundi
170 centro fixa domus, medioque innititur axi.
    Explicat aula sinus, montemque amplectitur alis
multiplici latebra scelerum tersura ruborem.
Ipsa loco factura nefas: erroribus umbram
caeca parat, noctisque vices, oculique verendas
175 decipit excubias, pereuntis saepe pudoris
celatura notas, Venerisque accommoda furtis.
Nam tenebras qui peccat amat, latebrisque pudorem
excusat, noctemque facit velamina culpae.
    Marmor, et attriti quicquid splendore politus
180 aspectum pavisse potest, aut nobile reddit
et Famae commendat opus, pretiosa domorum
materies laudisque venit. Fecunda bonorum,
luxuriem largitur humus, mundique nefandis
obsequitur votis. Rerum Tellure ministra,
185 aedificat securus homo, nam terra paratum
iurat in auxilium. Quidvis Natura potentis
expedit ad nutum: lapides et ligna ligandis
aedibus, et quicquid pretiosior exigit usus.
Exhibet et gemmas, quarum fulgore diescit,
190 sole suo contenta, domus. Sed gloria paucas
haec visura moras; cursum felicibus aufert
temporis occursus, laetis venit obvia fati
ianua, summa dies, metuenda potentibus hora.

survive, a free man, rather than submit to the commands of the Fates; but already wandering blindly, he is forcing a path to the Stygian shore. It is his life's labor to reach the place where he will go when dead. This house, rooted in the earth's very core, fast bound to the center of things, extends to the lower depths. 170

The palace reveals inner chambers, and its corridors spread over the mountain, with countless hiding places to efface the shame of wrongdoing. The place gives rise to crime by its setting: its darkness, like night itself, provides a veil for error, and deceives the wary sentinels of sight, concealing many a tale of the loss of purity, suited as it is to the stratagems of Venus. For the sinner loves shadow, excuses his shame by concealing it, and makes night a cloak for his guilt. 175

There is marble, and whatever may feast the eye by the splendor of its well-polished surface, whatever creates a noble appearance and bids for Renown, costly material for building and for gaining praise. The earth, so productive of good things, bestows luxury, serving the base desires of the world. Man builds confidently, when Earth provides the means, for she pledges her ready assistance. At the great man's nod Nature brings forth whatever is desired: stone and beams for framing houses, and whatever else a costlier undertaking may require. She proffers gems, in whose splendor the palace basks, content with its own sun. But this glory will know only a brief sojourn: the onset of time checks the course of happy mortals, and amid their bliss there appears before them the fatal gateway, the final day, the hour so fearful to the great. 180 185 190

Capitulum 9

Exclamatio Architrenii in eos qui opes aedificando consumunt

Hoc fatui caelum mundi videt inque dolentes
195 excutitur risus: "Heu, quae dementia, tantis
erexisse domos studiis, tantosque labores
perdere, tot census! Quod crastina diruat aetas
instruit instanter labor irritus; ocius ista
otia tollantur; ad inania mundus anhelat.
200 Deflectatur iter, totusque in seria sudet!
Nam risu aut digito quid dignius? Ardua tollit,
cras ruiturus, homo. Furor est sublimibus uti
sedibus ad lapsum properanti; improvida montes
accumulat casura manus. Nam sufficit unam
205 contraxisse casam morituro, cum irrita surgant
quae Fati pulsante manu fastigia nutant.
    "Haec tamen et, quicquid auget ludibria vitae,
sunt desperantis animae solatia; Fati
postera deterrent dubiae praesagia mentis.
210 Crastina celamur, hodiernis utimur. Iram
iudicis expectat incauti audacia mundi,
conscia delicti. Suadet praesentia; clausos
expositura metus series occulta futuri."

Chapter 9

Architrenius inveighs against those who squander their wealth on mansions

Architrenius beholds this, the heaven of a foolish world, and breaks into grim laughter: "Alas, what madness, to take such pains to build houses, to squander so much labor, so much wealth! It is a fruitless endeavor to build with such care what another generation will destroy; such idle pleasures are swiftly swept away; the world pants after vanities. Would that it might change its course, and work only at serious things! For what is more deserving of laughter and derision? Man builds tall, though he will be brought to ruin tomorrow. It is madness for one rushing toward disaster to claim a lofty dwelling; with no foresight the hand of a doomed man heaps up mountains. To build a single hut is enough for one condemned to die, since those high roofs are raised in vain which totter at the powerful blows of Fate.

"And yet these things, and whatever else may increase the foolishness of life, are the comforts of the despairing spirit; they allay the presages of the troubled mind about the Fate to come. We blind ourselves to the morrow, and enjoy the present moment. But the bold and reckless world, aware of its wickedness, awaits the wrath of the judge. The present seduces us; the unknown course of events to come will bring our hidden fears to light."

Capitulum 10

De pictura aulaeorum

Hic auro Parias onerant aulaea columnas.

215 Nobile surgit opus, levius quod torsit Arachnes
pollice Lida manus, et vestibus impluit aurum;
pectinis ingenio nulli cessura, licebit
Pallas anum simulet. Hermi satiatur harena
gloria picturae: florum lascivia ductu

220 pectinis accedit, et veris gratia maior
vestibus arridet. Series depingitur anni,
temporis excursu vario distincta, sed illic
aurea vernat hiems, et item Saturnius annus
ver habet aeternum. Picturae clausula quaevis

225 saecula clausa tenet; annosaque tempora vestis
colligit una dies, cuius brevis explicat ordo
omnia. Nascentis ibi mundi vagit origo;
et iam cana redit teneris infantia rebus,
praeteritumque Chaos iterum puer induit orbis.

230 Nec minus horrescit mundum clausura, suasque
Asperat hora minas, et adusto murice candens,
Purpura iudicii supremum ventilat ignem.

Temporis expressus medii praetermeat ordo,
ut vero videas succedere saecula tractu,

235 nec spatio confusa brevi. Pictura labores
antiquos meminit: Danaos ibi Pergama fleres
diruta flere dolos; lacrimis dum purpura sudat,

Chapter 10

Designs in tapestry

Tapestries heavy with gold adorn the Parian columns. A no- 215
ble work spreads forth, which the Lydian hand of Arachne
has delicately woven, showering the cloth with gold; she will
give place to none in the weaver's skill, though Pallas should
play the old woman. The glory of the design is amply set off
by the sands of Hermus: a riot of flowers appears at the 220
needle's bidding, and a more than vernal charm smiles from
the cloth. The cycle of the year is depicted, marked by the
changing course of the seasons, but here a gilded winter
shines springlike, and again a Saturnian age enjoys perpetual
spring. The enclosed space of the design holds captive all 225
the ages; the tapestry's single day draws together the years
of time past, and its compact scheme unfolds it all. Here it
begins, with the squalling of the newborn universe; now the
ancient infant state of budding creatures returns, and the
young world assumes once again its former state of Chaos.
The hour that will end the world, too, fraught with terror, 230
offers its harsh threats, and purple dye, flashing forth from
its dusky shell, quickens the fire of the ultimate judgment.

The procession of intervening time is presented in due
order, so that you may observe the ages joined in their true
sequence, not disordered by the limited space. The imagery 235
recalls ancient sufferings: here you might weep for fallen
Troy, weeping because of Grecian guile; kingly purple is

dum latus Hectoreum maior fodit Hector, Achilles,
succumbitque Paris Graeca Venerisque sagitta,
240 et Venus Atridae gladios iramque ministrat.
Hic fletus teneros Priami vomit uda senectae
ariditas, redditque dolor quod perdidit aetas,
Hectoreos casus morte ausa. Hic sensus Ulixis,
hic Pyrrhi gladius pugnat, conatibus ille
245 pectoris, ille manus. Hic flet Ledaea; nec oris
gloria diluitur lacrimis; sed fletibus ipsis
vultus ridet honor. Hic Graeca, hic Dardana pubes,
illa stat, illa cadit; tractantur bella, sed inde
ensibus, inde fuga. Et dum, respirantibus armis,
250 consulit in dubios Atrides Nestora casus,
ille vir, ille senex Phrygio iuvenescit in auro.
    Dulce virum luctus lugere, dolere dolores
et lacrimis lacrimas, planctu rescribere planctum.
Dulcius est oculo dulci decurrere casus
255 Fortunaeque vices Veneris quas alea versat,
et pasci lacrimis quibus invitantur amantum
gaudia: dum tenero dulcescunt oscula fletu;
et lacrimis inserpit amor, miserisque fovetur
maior in adversis.
                    Intextos pecten amorum
260 exprimit eventus. Ibi serum Pyramus ense
vindicat egressum, Thisbe lugubria Fati
pondera morte levat; tua non formidat ad umbras,
Pyrame, fata sequi, sequiturque dolore dolorem
et gemitu gemitum, producit funere funus.
265 Hic patris amplexus usurpat Myrrha, noverca

drenched with tears as that greater Hector, Achilles, pierces
the side of Hector, Paris is overcome by the darts of Greece
and Venus, and Venus herself lends arms and fierceness to   240
the son of Atreus. Here the withered age of Priam becomes
moist and spews forth feeble tears, and grief brings back
what was lost to the world, when death dared to claim Hec-
tor. Here the astuteness of Ulysses and the sword of Pyrrhus
make war, the one by feats of mind, the other by strength of   245
arm. Here Leda's daughter sobs; the glory of her face is not
dimmed by her weeping; indeed the grace of her expression
rejoices in her very tears. Here the youth of Greece stand
firm while those of Troy fall back; war is waged, on the one
side with weapons, on the other by flight. And when, during
a lull in the combat, the son of Atreus consults with Nestor   250
about the uncertain situation, the mature and the elderly
man grow young again, set off in Phrygian gold.

It is sweet to sorrow for the sorrows of men, to grieve for
their grief and answer tears with tears, lamentation with
lamentation. Sweeter still to survey with tender gaze the fa-
tal errors and shifts of Fortune to which the hazards of Ve-   255
nus give rise, to feed on the sorrows to which the joys of love
invite us: for kisses are made sweet by tender weeping; love
insinuates itself in tears, and is cherished all the more by un-
happy lovers in their adversity.

The weaver's art sets forth embroidered tales of love.   260
Here Pyramus pays with the sword for his late setting forth,
and Thisbe by her death eases the sorrowful burden of Fate;
fearlessly she pursues your fate, O Pyramus, into the realm
of the shades, matching grief with grief, mourning with
mourning, adding her funeral to yours. Here Myrrha usurps   265
the love of her father, herself a stepmother more pleasing to

gratior ipsa sibi; Byblisque sororia fratri
gaudia mentitur. Iolen ibi mollis amictu
induit Alcides, rigidoque et pensa stupenti
pollice turbat opus. Ausus latus ardua doctum
270 edocuisse colos, fuso meminisse cadenti
cogitur Alciden, positamque resumere clavam.
 Haec et si qua iuvant oculos pictura iubenti
pectine producit; homines et bruta creanti
pollice tela parit. Operis laudisque magister,
275 omnia doctus arat; Naturae cuncta potentis
induit ille manus: vigilant ibi sidera caelo,
aequora piscis arat, vario discurritur aer
alite, terra feris. Nostrique superbior oris
maiestate, parit homini quod serviat, omni
280 obsequiosa bono, quovisque iuvantibus usu
sedula deliciis. Ibi laeta et tristia spargit
ambigua Fortuna manu; Fati exitus omnis
texitur, et tenui dependent omina filo.

herself; and Byblis dissembles to her brother her sisterly pleasure. Here an effeminate Alcides wraps Iole in his cloak, and botches his work with stiff fingers baffled by the task of spinning. Bravely striving to teach his hard-schooled limbs to ply the distaff, he is compelled by the fall of the spindle to recall that he is Alcides, and to take up again the club he had laid aside.

These scenes and whatever else may please the eye the design displays at the weaver's bidding; under his creating hand the tapestry gives birth to men and beasts. Praiseworthy master of his craft, he knows every kind of husbandry, and assumes the role of all-powerful Nature: here stars keep watch in the sky, fish furrow the sea, the air is traversed by birds of many kinds, the land by beasts. Made proud by the majesty of our countenance, he brings forth whatever may be of service to man, attentive to his every need, and eager that delights may enrich his every pursuit. Here too Fortune's equivocating hand scatters joy and sadness; all the workings of Fate are woven here, and great consequences hang by a slender thread.

Capitulum 11

De luxu vestium

Luxuriem cultus nullo modus ordine, nullo
285 limite metitur; Luxus non claudit honestas
praetereuntis iter. Pretium quaesisse laborant
vestibus uda Thetis et fecundissima Tellus,
mater opum: calido tenuis mandatur ab axe
carbasus, et Pharii linum de litore Nili
290 tollitur, ut nudam gemat Isida nudus Osiris;
vellera dant Seres. Studiique Britannia maior
ingeniique potens, quocunque vocaverit usus
ausa dedisse manus, raptique paratior ala
fulminis, ut pretio queat exaequasse laboris
295 altera Naturam Natura, Minerva Minervam.
Fervescit Tyrius sudor fudisse cruorem
muricis, aequoream penitus scrutatus abyssum,
ut falli facilis roseo flammata veneno
vellera miretur oculus, mundumque beari
300 sic putet, interius animam torquente reatu.

CHAPTER II

Chapter 11

Sumptuous dress

Moderation exercises no control, sets no limit to the lavish-   285
ness of apparel; no decency bars the way to luxurious excess.
Watery Tethys and the teeming Earth, mother of riches,
strive to gain the prize for raiment: fine flax is sent from the
hot south, and linen is brought from the banks of the Egyp-
tian Nile, so that a naked Osiris bemoans his naked Isis;   290
China provides fleecy cocoons. Thus does Britain, great in
learning and richly inventive, presume to extend her grasp
wherever opportunity may beckon, swifter than the flight of
the hurled thunderbolt, that a second Nature may equal Na-
ture in the fruits of her industry, a new Minerva rival the   295
old. The Tyrian, ransacking the depths of the sea, sweats to
pour out the bloody dye of the murex, that the eye, so easily
deceived, may wonder at woolen robes inflamed by this
bright poison, and suppose the world a blessed place, even   300
as the mind is racked inwardly by guilt.

Capitulum 12

De pictura vasorum

Divitis ingenio picturae gaudet, et auri
gloria vasorum rutilo pallore coruscat,
nec pretii nec laudis egens. Miratur in illis
artificis Natura manum, seseque minorem
305   agnovisse pudet; nam gratia surgit in auro
plenior, et quaevis facies ornatior exit.
    Blandius invitat ad pocula, vasis in imo,
stans hominis signum, Baccho superante futurum
naufragio felix, nisi quod Gula saepe paratis
310   subvenit auxiliis, hominemque urgentibus undis
humanum servasse putat. Volat ebrius ales,
inferius tardante mero; serpente bibenti,
innocuus conviva bibit; bibit angelus, uda
sanctificans dextra; blandum fremit ira leonis,
315   poturae tranquilla gulae; mansuescit in unguis
pace minax ursus; Nerei mutasse profundum
piscis amat, Bacchique lacus et litora servat.
    Gratia picturae, picturaque gratior, aurum
gemmarumque dies, Bacchum latura favoris
320   nectare vasa replent. Vasis pictura decorem
Exhibet ornatus, decus aurum, gemma nitorem.

Chapter 12

Painted vessels

A glorious array of drinking vessels rejoices in the skill of their rich decoration, and gleams with the ruddy pallor of gold, in want of neither costliness nor praise. Nature wonders at the skill of the maker of these objects, and is ashamed to realize herself inferior; for a fuller grace emerges in gold, 305 and whatever shape it assumes appears more elegant.

The image of a man, standing in the bottom of the goblet, cheerfully bids one drink, happy at the shipwreck that Bacchus's powerful effect would portend, were it not that gluttony is so often at hand with ready aid, thinking to save a 310 fellow human from the whelming tide. A bird hovers drunkenly, as wine retards its flight; a banqueter drinks unharmed while a serpent shares his drink; an angel drinks, blessing the board with his dripping hand; a raging lion roars softly, remaining calm while a glutton prepares to drink; a fierce 315 bear draws in his claws in peace; a fish gladly forsakes the Nerean depths, and frequents the lakes and shores of Bacchus.

The beauty of the images, and gold and brilliant gems, more beautiful still, fill vessels meant for Bacchus with the 320 nectar of their charm. The images on the vessel set off the beauty of the handiwork, the beauty sets off the gold, and the gems emphasize its splendor.

Capitulum 13

De accidentibus aulae et eius incolis

Illic Ingluvies, illic Venus effluit; illic
texitur occulto studio Dolus; aemula veri
Fabula praevelat Fidei Periuria peplo.
325 Pacis habent vultus Odii secreta; venenum
Fraudis Amicitiam tenui mentitur amictu.
Occulit immanes animos Clementia vultus.
Pectoris Asperitas, risu praetexta sereno,
interius fervens, laqueos innodat et hamos
330 curvat in insidias, rabiemque in pectore fixam
armat in omne nefas. Non est quod abhorreat aulae
incola delictum: facie describit amicum,
hostem mente premit; linguam dulcedine lactat,
mentis amara tegens; animo blanditur operto,
335 laedit in occulto; praesenti parcit amico,
vulnerat absentem. Quicquid praesentia pacis
spondeat, a gladio non est absentia tuta.
  Nulla fides aulae, nulla est reverentia, nullus
committendo modus. Vitiis indulget, honestum
340 Ambitione premit. Aequum declinat in omni
materia lucri, studio quocumque laborat
ut loculus crescat, linguae suffragia vendit
ad pretii libram. Rapiunt maiora patronum
munera, nec numquam partitur puncta favoris

Chapter 13

What happens at court and who resides there

Here Gluttony and Venus run free; here Deceit is wrought by hidden skill; Falsehood imitating truth shrouds its Perjury in the mantle of Good Faith. Lurking Hatred wears a face of Peace; and the poison of Fraud disguises itself in a thin cloak of Friendship. An appearance of Kindness hides monstrous thoughts. Cruelty of spirit, veiled by a serene smile, but seething inwardly, sets its snares and barbs its hooks for treachery, and arms the madness rooted in its heart for any wicked action. There is no crime too awful for the courtier: he presents the face of a friend, burying enmity in his heart; imbues his tongue with sweetness, concealing the bitterness of his mind; his outward expression offers a caress, but he wounds in secret; he spares a present friend but he attacks an absent one. Whatever pledges of peace one gains in his presence, in absence one is not safe from his dagger.

There is no good faith at court, no reverence, no limit to what is perpetrated. It indulges vice, and keeps down worthiness in favor of ambition. The courtier abandons justice at every opportunity for gain, works at whatever pursuit will make the purse grow fat, and trades his vocal support for a cash reward. It is the greater gift that obtains patronage, and sometimes the mark of favor is bestowed

325

330

335

340

345 partibus adversis; unum promittit utrimque
obsequium, neutrumque iuvat; qui utrique tenetur
proditor amborum. Nam vel bellator utrimque
arma negat, vel utrique favens utrique minatur.
    Prodigus eloquii, vultu non mente serenat
350 aulicus affatum. Zephyro vernantior, oris
lilia verborum cuivis largitur, et omnes
nectar amicitiae redolenti pace salutat.
Quid doleas, quid non, quid dulce, quid utile, quid non,
sollicitus quaerit. Et tantum verba daturus,
355 singula promittit, crescentibus omnia spargit
pollicitis, sed nulla manu. Spem mandat inanem
pectoribus, dextraeque nihil; spes credula fallit
pectora, verba manum. Sese ligat aulicus omni
omnia facturum, largoque enititur ore
360 quilibet ut speret. Sic imminet ardua multis
sarcina, dum verbis temere fiducia surgit,
dum spes caeca iacet, subiti secura flagelli.
Heu facinus! Multos in summa pericula misit,
naufragioque fuit linguae tranquillior aura.
365 Mobilis, et nullos solide complexus amicos,
mente vagus dubia, nullis nisi foedius uti
foederibus novit; odiis alternat amores,
mutat amicitias, has exuit, induit illas,
quosque minus constanter amat constantius odit.
370 Vagit amicitiae teneris infantia cunis,
gratior ad veteres numquam perducitur annos,
nec senii matura sapit; fastidia ferret,
si senio marceret anus. Dum spirat odorum

on opposing factions; a single service is promised to both,   345
but helps neither; he who is committed on either side be-
trays both. For this warrior will either refuse to take up arms
in either cause, or pose a threat to each side by supporting
the other.

Lavish of fine words, the courtier makes his speech fair
by his expression, not his thoughts. More springlike than   350
Zephyrus, he bestows verbal flowers on all alike, and the
nectar of his friendship greets one and all with the sweet
scent of peace. Solicitous, he asks why you are sad, or why
not, what may please or serve you and what will not. Though
words are all he will give, he promises anything, spreading it   355
abroad in expansive promises, but with an empty hand. He
bestows vain hope on the spirit, but puts nothing in your
hand; hopeful credulity betrays the spirit, empty words the
hand. The courtier pledges himself to perform all things for
all men, and strives by his generous speech to keep everyone   360
hopeful. Thus a heavy blow awaits many people, when confi-
dence rises foolishly at his words, when hope remains blind,
unmindful of the lash about to strike. Alas, such wickedness!
It has cast many into extreme peril, and the too-favorable
breeze of speech has led to shipwreck. Fickle, embracing no   365
one in firm friendship, inconstant in his anxiety, the courtier
has no use for promises unless to betray them; he shifts be-
tween love and hatred, changes friendships, shaking off one
to put on another, and he is constant in hatred of those he
has inconstantly loved. His friendship is a feeble infant that   370
squalls in her cradle, never so favored as to survive to later
years, or know the ripeness of age; should she become an old
woman, withered with age, she would incur his contempt.
Even as it inhales the scent of its first fruits, his love expires.

primitias, expirat amor. Sic aula diurnos
375 eligit, et tractos ultra fastidit amicos.

Capitulum 14

De adulatoribus aulae

Principis ad nutum servi inconstantia nutat.
Quodlibet ad votum didicit versare favorem
clausus adulator. Ad quodvis "nolo" paratum
"nolo" relaturus et, si "volo" dixerit ille,
380 reddet et ille "volo"; semel hinc "non" dicitur, inde
ingeminatur "non"; semel hinc "ita" dicitur, inde
ingeminatur "ita." Quicquid laudaverit, illo
nil melius, quicquid animo non sederit, illo
nil visum est peius. Si quid iubet acrius, ipsum
385 iuratur licuisse nefas, si mitius, ipso
tollitur ad superos melior Iove; quicquid agatur,
"Id bene, dii melius!"
          Hic est qui, pulvere nullo,
excutiat nullum, cauteque absolvere quaerat
crimen ubi non est, suspectam sordis amictus
390 munditiam reddens, ut quo placet inde mereri
debeat offensam. Servi manus illa ministrat,
non reprimit culpam, domino male sedula servit,
obsequio laedens. Hic est, qui adversa volenti

So too the court prefers friendships of a day, and scorns those that endure longer. 375

Chapter 14

Flatterers at court

Servile inconstancy nods at the nod of the great man. The secret flatterer has learned to adapt his assent to whatever wish is expressed. To each "I will not" he returns a ready "I will not"; if the lord has said "I will" he replies "I will." The 380 moment "nay" or "yea" is uttered on the one side, "nay" or "yea" is repeated on the other. There is nothing finer than whatever the lord has praised; nothing worse has ever been seen than what has not caught his fancy. Should he issue an overly harsh command, the wickedness is declared to be 385 lawful; if he is lenient, one greater than Jove himself is exalted to the heavens. Whatever is done, "Well done! May the gods grant it!"

This is he who, where there is no dust, sweeps away that dust, who takes pains to absolve guilt where none exists, bringing a clean robe under suspicion of being soiled, so that 390 when he is pleasant he is most deserving of censure. His servile hand assists guilt, rather than reproving it, and his very attentiveness serves his lord badly, wounding by obsequiousness. For such a man calls favorable what is against his

prospera diffinit; dominoque in fata ruenti,
395 iurat in eventus dextros, laudatque sinistri
augurium Fati, quicquid Fortuna minetur
mentis pace ferens, placeat modo. Pauca dolorem
altius infigunt. Hic est, qui gaudia mente
supprimit, ore gemit, et rursum gaudia vultus,
400 pectus habet gemitus. Vultus accomodat omni
fortunae domini, nusquam vestigia mutans.
Solvitur in risus in quos se solverit idem,
ore pluit lacrimas animo quas pluverit idem.
    Cum dominus tali facinus committit amico,
405 ille doli vulpes, dominique domesticus hostis,
omne domus vitium mordenti ridet ocello,
et pede vel cubito socios et crimina tangens.
Quod lingua reticet loquitur pede; cuncta loquentis
garrulitate pedis domini commissa revelat,
410 et fidei fracto reserat secreta sigillo.

CHAPTER 14

lord's interest; even as his lord rushes on a fatal course, he promises a successful outcome, and applauds the omens 395 of adverse Fate, bearing with tranquil mind whatever Fortune may threaten, provided he remain in favor. Few things pain him deeply. Such a man suppresses the joy in his mind and weeps outwardly, or, again, preserves a joyful countenance while grief possesses his heart. He adapts his face to 400 every shift of his lord's fortunes, never straying from his footsteps. He is seized by the very laughter to which the master gives himself, and sheds outwardly the tears which the other sheds from the heart.

Should the master entrust to such a friend the punishing of wrongdoing, this guileful fox, this familiar enemy of his 405 lord, laughs with mocking eye at all the misconduct of the household, nudging his cronies and their crimes with foot or elbow. What his tongue withholds his foot declares: by the chattering of his eloquent foot he reveals his lord's commission, and lays bare his secret orders by breaking the seal of 410 trust.

Capitulum 15

De potentum
impotentia et caecitate

Has aliasque notas notat Architrenius, ergo,
"Heu! Quem divitiae, quem mundi vana loquuntur
gaudia felicem, vitiique ancilla beatum
gloria mentitur! Gladiis linguisque suorum
415 caeditur ipse; manus non evasisse ministras
fortior ipse potest, non extorsisse latentem
perfidiam novit, animo non prendit apertum
crimen adulantis, oculo quod praestat et auri.
Non oculo non aure videt, popularibus auris
420 auribus assurgit, laeta praeconia vulgi
dulcia mente bibit. Circumfusisque favorem
plausibus indulget nec laudibus artat habenam;
sed sibi iam melior et maior laude videtur.
Ipse nefas totusque nihil, se credit ad omnes
425 esse satis laudes, pretiumque in laudibus esse
concipit. At nescit: pretium non laude meremur,
sed pretio laudem; nescit quod turpibus ipsa
laus damnosa venit, cum sit derisio pravis
laus, pictura bonis. Ipsa est quae exultat honestis,
430 insultat vitiis, illis arridet et illa
cautius irridet. Nescit, dum lingua redundat
laudibus, omne malum mentis secreta loquuntur.

Chapter 15

The impotence and blindness of great men

Architrenius takes note of these bad signs, then cries, "Alas for him whose wealth, whose vain worldly pleasures proclaim him happy, whom glory, the handmaid of vice, falsely calls blessed! He is wounded by the swords and tongues of 415 his own household; for all his power he cannot escape the clutches of his servants, realize the need to force lurking treachery to show itself, or grasp with his mind the barefaced guilt of the flatterer, though it is plain to his eyes and ears. He neither sees nor hears, but pricks up his ears to the 420 breeze of his people's talk, happily drinks in the sweet celebrations of the many. He bestows his favor on those who surround him with applause, and imposes no restraint on their praise; indeed he imagines himself a better and greater person because of it. Utterly base and empty, he considers himself sufficient to all praises, and supposes such praises to 425 be the measure of his worth. But he is wrong: worth is not attained through praise, but praise through worth; he does not know that even praise is destructive when it is visited on unworthy objects; for the praise of depravity is mockery, though it is an adornment to good men. Praise delights in worthy men and makes merry with them, but scorns vice 430 and inwardly mocks it. He does not realize that while the tongue abounds in praises, the hidden meaning is utterly malicious.

"Non aperit clausura dolos facundia servi
quo prosit domino, sed quo delectet. Ad aures
435 verborum cum melle venit, nec pectore librat
utile suspenso; domini securior usum
praeterit. Eloquii vallo, ne capta recedat,
gratia munitur. Verbo vallante favorem
claudere fervescit, et dum sua tuta ferantur
440 lintea, praecipiti domini non subvenit alno.
    "Vulgus ad obsequium numquam dominantis honestas
invitat, sed dantis opes. Servire minores
maiori non suadet amor; sed cogit egestas,
imperiique timor, et in aspera prona cupido.

Capitulum 16

Quod opibus non hominibus deservitur

445 "Non hominum votis, sed opum servitur; ab illis
imperium mendicat homo, famulantis ad illas
servus anhelat amor; et cui devinctior haeret
vellet ut exiguo dominum mutaverit aere,
iuranti licet ore neget, testatus et ipsam,

216

"The charming speech which conceals the servant's deception is never used in an open way to serve his lord, but only to gratify him. He visits the lord's ears with honeyed words, and no thought of being useful weighs on his mind; he ignores the lord's interest without concern. The lord's goodwill is kept secure by a rampart of eloquence, lest having once been captured it should escape again. He works furiously to imprison favor with a wall of words, and while his own sails bear him safely along, he does not seek to aid the careening vessel of his lord.

"It is never the worthiness of the man of power that draws the common people to his service, but his bestowal of wealth. Love does not compel the lowly to serve the great; it is need that compels them, and the fear of authority, and greed ever ready to endure harsh treatment.

Chapter 16

Obeisance is accorded not to men, but to wealth

"Service is given not at the bidding of men, but of wealth; from wealth men's authority is gained, and it is for wealth that the servile love of the attendant yearns; he would willingly change for a meager sum of money the master to whom he clings so closely, though he denies this with a mouthful of

450 horrendam superum, fidei Styga, quaelibet ausus
testanti factura fidem. Periuria venti
non reditura ferunt; aura rapiente recursu
non laesura volant. Non est, cui lingua minorem
postponat dominum, quicquid mens obvia linguae
455 liberior dictet, quicquid suppressa susurret
libertas animi, nullius passa tyranni
imperiosa iugum nulloque absterrita monstro.

Capitulum 17

Quod adversitas adulatorum detegit falsitatem

"Si linguae ad phaleras, si detur ad omnia verbi
condimenta fides, domino nil maius in ipsis
460 excellit superis; nec habet pretiosius illo
area fortunae; malletque et luce carere,
et se, quam domino, fortunae ad vota fruenti
uberiore bono. Sed si modo dando solutam
contrahat illa manum, raptamque in tristia verso
465 urgeat orbe rotam, dominum quem multa ministri
turba loquebatur, servus modo, pocula fati

oaths, calling to witness Styx itself, which the very gods fear   450
to swear by, and fearlessly names whatever might lend credi-
bility to his testimony. The winds bear perjuries away, never
to return; they float off on the swift breeze and will not
damage him by returning. There is none to whom his tongue
would acknowledge his master inferior, however much his
franker thoughts might oppose his words, however the sup-   455
pressed freedom of his spirit might mutter, that haughty
spirit which endures not the tyrant's yoke and remains un-
afraid in the face of terror.

Chapter 17

Adversity unmasks the falseness of flatterers

"If one give credence to the embellishments of the flatter-
er's tongue, and all the spices of his speech, there is none
more excellent than his lord among the gods themselves;   460
the domain of Fortune holds nothing more precious than
he; and one would rather lose the light of day, or one's very
self, than this lord, so long as Fortune decrees that this lord
enjoy her goods in abundance. But should Fortune close
that hand now generously open, seize her wheel and drive it
around its circle into sorrow, then he whom a great throng   465
of servants called master, now become a slave, drinks alone

solus amara bibit; sibi soli applaudit amico
qui premitur Fato. Sepelit quos laeta creavit
maesta dies Fati; servi celaverat ante,
470 nunc aperit fraudes. Domus extunc cogitur omnem
exseruisse dolum; dominum non decipit ultra.
    "Mundi nulla fides! Et quae latuere secundis
cernit in adversis. Hominem quid prospera celet,
asperior Fortuna docet; felicia Fati
475 excaecant animos. Distinguere nescit amicos,
qui fruitur laetis; Fortunae quicquid ab alto
sidere despectet, unum celatur amari."
    Ut satis est visum, viso indolet; intimus exit
exclamatque foris gemitus. Solitumque recurrit
480 maeror ad impluvium, positumque resuscitat imbrem
vivus item luctus; et pectore rivus aquoso
enatat et notis oculorum spargitur undis
alveus et gemina lacrimarum rumpitur urna.

the bitter cup of Fate; he whom Fate has cast down has no friend to acclaim him but himself. The sad, fatal day sees the burial of those friendships to which happier times gave rise; the servant's dishonesty, concealed before, now appears openly. Henceforth the house is compelled to lay bare all its deceptions; the lord is deceived no longer. 470

"There is no good faith in the world, and a man perceives in adversity what had been hidden in happier times. Adverse Fortune teaches a man what prosperity conceals; Fate's blessings make us blind. He who enjoys a happy life cannot distinguish his true friends; whatever he may see as he gazes down from Fortune's starry realm, bitterness alone is concealed from him." 475

Having seen enough, Architrenius grieves over what he has seen; his inner sorrow emerges and proclaims itself openly. Again his grief has recourse to the accustomed cistern, and fresh weeping renews the sunken water level; a stream flows down his dripping bosom, and the basin is splashed with the eyes' familiar streams as the double vessel of tears is unsealed. 480

BOOK FIVE

Capitulum 1

De colle Praesumptionis

Transit ab aspectis, nondum rorantia siccus
lumina, nec tersus oculos maerore palustres.
Nec mora; finitimo tractu Praesumptio collem
stringit, et insolido nitens pede sarcina pessum
5   nutat; ubi testudo volat, fastidit in alto
mergus aquae sedes, aquila cessante ministrat
arma Iovi milvus; spolio contendit olori
corvus, id est ferrugo nivi; strepit anxius anser
Actaeam vicisse lyram; caecusque pererrat
10 bubo diem, nisumque fugat torpentibus alis;
dum mendicata sequitur cornicula penna.
Hic lepus insurgit animo pallente leoni;
simius, humanae naturae simia, vultus
despuit illimes; bubali bos cornua cornu
15 praevenisse putat; admissam tigrida barri
segnities inflexa fugat; lupa, nupta Molossis,
iactitat insignes thalamos, Lycaonis ausa
coniugii rupisse fidem; contraque leaenam
pardus, asellus equam, praesumpto foedere lecti,
20 ducit, et hircus ovem; solioque pudendus, adulter
semimari partu Pasiphen taurus honustat.

Chapter 1

The Hill of Presumption

Architrenius turns away from the spectacle, still not having dried his brimming eyes or cleared their standing pools of sorrow. There is no delay; Presumption is assailing a nearby hill, struggling with uncertain tread and staggering backward under her burden. Here the tortoise flies; the diving gull disdains its home on the deep ocean; the kite bears the arms of Jove while the eagle gives place; the raven competes with the swan in plumage, rusty brown with snowy white; the anxious squawk of the goose strives to excel the Attic lyre; the blind owl wanders abroad in daylight, and with its sluggish wings drives away the hawk, while the crow, in borrowed plumage, gives chase. Here the fainthearted hare rises up against the lion; the ape, aping human nature, rejects an unbemired countenance; the cow imagines her horns to surpass those of the buffalo; the unbending sluggishness of the elephant puts to flight the eager tigress; the she-wolf, mated with the Molossian hound, boasts of her illustrious marriage bed, boldly breaking her wedding vow to Lycaon; conversely, the panther claims the lioness, the ass the mare, the goat the ewe, in presumptuous union, while the adulterous bull, disgracing the throne, burdens Pasiphae with her half-human progeny.

Capitulum 2

De quibusdam Praesumptionis exemplis

Hic Niobe multa Latonam prole lacessit
ardua, sed numerum tam Sol quam Cynthia pensat.
Surgit in aurigam, dum Phoebi sanguine Phaethon
25 nititur, et nitido temere confidit in ortu;
errantemque diem, mundo nimis obvius, urit.
Miraturque citum Boreas ardere Booten,
indomitosque regi spargens auriga iugales,
praecipiti Fato meriti mercede laborem
30 claudit et in patria tandem se novit habena.
Amplexus Cereris dulces avellit opaci
insipidus Plutonis amor; regique Molosso
Idaeum dat praeda thorum; Nessusque biformi
Alciden deludit equo; caelique litura,
35 Lemnius, innuptae conubia Palladis ardet.
   Hic furit in superos Tellus armasse Gigantes,
et nivibus montes galeatos Ossan, Olympum,
Pelion et scopulis populosa cacumina pacem
tollit in aetheream, securaque fulminis instat.
40 Hic sibi rhetoricos Theodentis gloria flores
deputat, auctorem titulo mentitus inani;
assumptumque notae mens conscia damnat honorem;
nec meritam laudem maiestas nominis aequat.
Ardua Pierides ineunt certamina Musis,
45 sed rapitur rapto laurus cum nomine. Laurus

Chapter 2

Some examples of Presumption

Here haughty Niobe taunts Diana with her numerous prog-
eny, but the Sun god and Cynthia together even the score.
Phaethon, since he exalts himself as the child of Phoebus,
ascends his chariot, foolishly trusting in his glorious origin; 25
passing too close to the earth, he brings upon it the fire of
the straying Sun. Boreas is amazed to see a swift, burning
Bootes, and the charioteer, allowing the uncontrollable team
to scatter, concludes his work in a fitting manner with a fatal 30
plunge, and recognizes at the last that he has taken on his
father's task. The unappealing love of shadowy Pluto steals
away the beloved child of Ceres; and theft bestows a Tro-
jan bride on the Molossian king; Nessus, in his semiequine
form, deceives Hercules; and the Lemnian, a blot on the 35
heavens, yearns for marriage with unwedded Pallas.

Here Earth madly arms the Giants against the gods, and
thrusts up the snow-capped peaks and rock-strewn slopes of
Ossa, Olympus and Pelion against the peace of the heavens,
forgetful of the thunderbolt in her defiance. Here the vain- 40
glory of Theodectes claims for itself the flowers of rhetoric,
feigning authorship on the strength of an empty name; but
the mind that recognizes this infamy condemns the claim-
ing of honor; the grandeur of title is no equivalent for praise
well earned. The Pierides engage in difficult competition
with the Muses, but the laurel is snatched away, together 45

ornat et in memori victoria nomine vivit;
aeternumque negat laurum marcescere nomen.
Persius in Flacci pelago decurrit, et audet
mendicasse stilum satirae. Serraque cruentus
50 rodit, et ignorat polientem pectora limam.

Capitulum 3

De Praesumptione personarum
ecclesiasticarum et magistrorum

Hic puer, insolidus et mente et corpore, laesae
indolis, et teneris animo nervoque solutus,
quem renum senior lascivia mollit et aevi
ardescens novitas; emptas in devia praeceps
55 ecclesias auriga rapit, superumque regenda
suscipit innumera lactandus ovilia pastor.
Omnibus ecclesiis haud contraxisse veretur,
centigamusque novo superis de iure ministrat
presbyter, in sponsi spolio praeclusus adulter.
60 Moribus insipidus, nostri Iovis inquinat aram,
accessuque notat. Veneris Bacchique sacerdos,
numen utrumque sitit, lumbosque et guttura solvens
sedulus his servit.

with the stolen name. For the adorning laurel and the victory itself live on in the name that recalls them; since the name is eternal, the laurel will never wither. Persius plunges into the great sea of Horace, and dares to counterfeit the style of the satirist. Bloodthirsty, he hacks away with his saw, 50 and knows nothing of the file that gives polish to thought.

Chapter 3

The Presumption of churchmen and teachers

Here is a boy, unstable in mind and body, his natural endowments ruined, spirit and sinew slack and feeble, one whom the wanton desires of an old man's loins and a young man's burning love of novelty have dissipated; in his lurching chariot he descends abruptly on churches he has purchased 55 and, still unweaned, undertakes to be the shepherd guiding countless flocks of God. This centogamous priest, an adulterer wrapped in the despoiled robe of a bridegroom, would not hesitate to plight his troth in every church, for he serves as God's priest by a new dispensation. A moral weakling, he 60 defiles the altar of our Jove, and defames it by his approach. He is the priest of Venus and Bacchus, and thirsts for the inspiration of both, eagerly giving over his loins and gullet to their service.

Liceat scelus esse locutum
quod fit inoccultum; vitium facit ipsa loquendi
65 materiae sordes, irae furor imperat ori;
circumcisa minus movet indignatio verba.
Pauperibus dandos reditus inviscerat et, qui
cuncta dedit, nulla contingit portio Christum.
Emungitque bonis ara ventris numinis aram,
70 cuius delicias uteri deperdit in utre,
dum quod in ore sapit stomachi corrumpit Averno.
    Hic vulgus cathedras, rapta deitate magistri,
insilit, et vacua de maiestate tumorem
concipit. Impubis et mento et mente, virenti
75 crudus adhuc succo, iuvenem solidosque viriles
praeveniens culmos, nec maturata senectae
praecipiti lauro non exspectasse veretur.
Hos ego praetereo tactos sine nomine; nosque
praeterit ignotus, insania nota, magister.
80 O rabies! sedisse rabbi, dulcique Minervae
intonuisse tuba nondum patientibus annis!
Hic in philosophos ausa est saevire flagello,
mortis alumna, fames, animoque potentia Phoebi
pignora pauperies curarum verberat Hydra.

Be it lawful to speak of crimes that are practiced openly; the foulness of the subject matter makes it sinful to speak of 65 these things, yet the force of wrath governs my lips; indignation evokes undisciplined speech. He gorges himself on offerings intended for the poor, and no portion is assigned to Christ, who bestowed it all. The pigsty of the belly defrauds the altar of God, and the fruits of this womb are abandoned 70 to the bladder, for what is sweet to the taste is destroyed in the Avernus of the stomach.

This low creature clambers into the teacher's chair, usurping the divine title of master, and becomes pregnant of bombast by this empty dignity. Though both chin and mind are beardless, though he is still unripe and green, it causes 75 this youth no fear that he has arrived before his stalk was strong and mature, that with his laurel hastily bestowed he has not awaited the ripeness of age. But having touched on such as these I will leave them unnamed; the master will pass us by unknown, though his folly is well known.

Madness! to have sat as teacher, and sounded the clear 80 clarion of Minerva before one's years allowed it. Here hunger, the foster child of death, has dared to wield her lash against philosophers, and poverty assails the strong-spirited disciples of Phoebus with a Hydra of woes.

Capitulum 4

Quod Praesumptio est Senectutis ad regem Angliae divertisse

85 Hic ubi delegit summam Praesumptio sedem,
inserpit festina comis crispatque Senecta
Henrici faciem, quem flava Britannia Regem
iactat, eoque Duce titulis Normannia ridet
et belli et pacis. Totumque supermeat orbem
90 indole quam belli numquam fregere tumultus,
dedidicitque virum gladio matura iuventus.
His vernare genis aeternum debuit aevi
flosculus, et nulla senii marcescere bruma.
   Hic vitii fecunda parens, soliumque domanti
95 imperiosa iugo, regina Pecunia iuri
praeminet, ausa suis astringere legibus orbem,
quas ratio nescit. Sed ei devincta cupido
dictat et indicit avidi facundia quaestus,
et loculos ardens discinctae audacia linguae.
100 Census censura fiunt, iniuria iura,
pura minus pura, sacra littera sacra litura.

Chapter 4

How Age has presumed to visit the King of England

Here where Presumption has established her principal 85
dwelling, premature Age has crept into the hair and wrin-
kled the face of Henry, whom golden Britain proudly calls
King, while Normandy rejoices to name him her Leader in
war and peace. He surpasses all the world by a strength of 90
character which the violence of war has never broken, and
his mature youth has unlearned the role of the man of war.
The youthful bloom should have flourished on his cheek
eternally, and the frost of age should never have sullied it.

Here Queen Money, the teeming mother of vice, im-
periously imposing her control on the throne, takes pre- 95
cedence over justice, having boldly subjected the world to
laws of her own, unknown to reason. But Greed, her insepa-
rable companion, instructs her, while the glibness of the ea-
gerly acquisitive speaks for her, and the unbridled audacity
of the burning desire for wealth. Property performs the of- 100
fice of judgment, injustice does the work of justice, purity
grows less pure, and the sacred word gives way to sacrile-
gious forgery.

Capitulum 5

De Superbia

Vicinos germana lares attollit, et astris
invidet, inferior cognata Superbia, terris
impatiens habuisse parem caeloque priorem.
105 Surgit in articulos, summos descendit in ungues,
crure stat inverso, renes obliquat in arcum,
ventre parum cedit, suspendit ad ilia laevam,
educit cubitum, flexam procul arduat ulnam,
tenditur in pectus, declives vergit in armos,
110 grandiloquum guttur et garrula colla supinat;
et, nisi pro voto respondent omnia, vultu
candet, et ignitis oculis prognosticat iram,
et digito nasum ferienti magna minatur.
Sed laesura parum; solo nocitura tumultu.
115   Ortu sidereo sublimis, proxima caelo,
haec dea nobilium mandat se mentibus, illas
adventu dignata suo. Torquentis Olympum
sedibus orta Iovis, patrio desuescit ab ortu
degenerare, casas vix intratura minores.
120 Sic sublime volat, sceptrisque domestica, reges
incolit. His pugnat iaculis, hoc militat ense.
Et tamen interdum claustris invecta, potentum
atria commutat casulis. Illicque profanam
continuat sedem, sanctis illapsa cucullis.

Chapter 5

Pride

Her sister Pride has raised her dwelling nearby, and envies the stars, seeing herself lower than they, unable to endure an equal on earth or a superior in heaven. She rises on her toes, and walks on tiptoe; stands with her leg turned in, arches her loins, draws her belly in a little, rests her left hand on her stomach, thrusts out her elbow, holds her bent arm away from her body, pushes her breast forward, draws her shoulders down, pulls back her high-sounding throat and garrulous neck; and then, if all does not conform to her wishes, her face grows hot, her flashing eyes give notice of her anger, and with a finger tapping on her nose she threatens terrible things. But little harm will come of it; her menace is only noise.

Exalted by her sidereal lineage, her proximity to heaven, this goddess commends herself to the minds of the nobility, and honors them by her visitation. Born in the palace of Jove, who holds sway over Olympus, she is not used to lower herself from her high birthplace, and rarely enters humble cottages. At home with royal power, she soars aloft, and dwells with kings. Scepters are the javelins and swords with which she wages war. But sometimes she is brought into the cloister, and exchanges the great man's hall for little cells. Here she maintains her profane way of life, though reduced to the holy cowl.

235

Capitulum 6

De monacho elato

125 Ecce supercilium monachi lunatur in altum,
sublimis rapitur vultus declivis, ocellus
surgit in obliquum. Ventremque Superbia festo
plus epulo tendit: duplex sic regnat Erinys
interius, venterque Noto turgescit utroque.

130 Quid cum turbatur animi pax intima, verbis
intonat, ardescit oculis vultuque minatur?
Quid quotiens pastor erranti publica monstrat
vel privata gregi iuris vestigia? Nonne
dictat in oppositum tumidae Praesumptio mentis,

135 et leges alias deceptae immurmurat auri?
Quid, quotiens morbos ovium nocuosque tumores
subsecuisse parat, reliquum patienter ovile
pastoris sequitur virgam, pacemque flagellis
exhibet ut monitis, sed claustri haec belua de qua

140 fabula narratur mansuescere verbere nullo
sustinet aut verbo, domitores odit et instat
asperior virgis, oculisque vomentibus iram
fulminat, et monitus fumanti despuit ore.

Hic quarum vita est humili deiecta cuculla
145 spernit oves, et eas audet praesumere de se
delicias: in quem pretium totius ovilis
confluat; et solus virtute, supernatet omnes.
Si quando careat baculus pastore, suoque

Chapter 6

The proud monk

See how the eyebrows of the monk are arched upward, how   125
his bowed head is lifted high, and his eye looks askance. It
is Pride, even more than the festive board, that swells his
stomach: a double Fury rules within him, and his belly is
swollen by two winds. What is it that resounds in his words,   130
flashes from his eyes and makes his face threatening, when
the inner peace of his mind is disrupted? What happens
whenever the pastor instructs his erring flock on the pat-
terns of public and private conduct? Does not the presump-
tion of a prideful mind speak out against him, and deceive   135
the ear by insinuating rules of another kind? When the ab-
bot seeks to cure his sheep of diseases and harmful growths,
why do the rest of the flock patiently accept the chastise-
ment of the shepherd, and remain quiet under his blows and
admonitions, while this cloistered monster whom my tale   140
concerns cannot bear to submit quietly to words or blows,
but hates his superiors and resists more fiercely for having
been beaten, fulminates while his eyes pour forth anger, and
rejects admonition with fuming lips.

This monk spurns those sheep whose life is shrouded in
the cowl of humility, and dares to anticipate delightful   145
things for himself: that the whole flock might be awarded to
him; that he, unique in virtue, might rise above them all.
Should the pastoral staff ever be in need of a shepherd,

rege vacet sceptrum moniale, haec belua sedem
150 iam sibi sortitur viduam. Dextramque maritat
absenti baculo, vacua iam regnat in aula,
iam subiecta iubet. Omni se concipit unam
imperio dignam, vacuam spem figit in alto,
praesumitque sibi baculum, quem perdere virtus
155 et vitium rapuisse solet. Iam fulgurat astri
alterius radiis, iam tollit in ardua mentem,
iam Iovis alterius ruituro pectore fulmen
tractat, et alterius animo praelibat honores,
induiturque prius animus quam dextera sceptrum.
160 Sic fit apud claustrum; ventosque Superbia praeceps
velis praerapidos nigris infundit et albis,
mundanique maris rapto per inania cursu
naviculam scopulis perituram mandat acutis.

Ut, cui nota domus famuletur, novit: "O" inquit
165 "O vitii radix primaeva! novissima Christum
accedit visura Deum, sed prima recedit;
nativumque sibi propriumque, hunc deligit usum,
ut non unanimes faciat quos inquinat una.

"Magna quidem molles animos ligat unio; magna
170 conciliat cupidas pacis clementia mentes.
Pax quoque firma leves animos amplectitur, immo
pax alios vitae sumptos communiter usus
nectit; et unus amor studiis inservit eisdem.
Verum par tumidis venit indignatio praeceps
175 mentibus, alterno factura tonitrua vento,
discordesque secat morum concordia mentes.

should the monastic scepter lack its proper king, this mon- 150
ster already assigns the widowed office to himself. He weds
his hand to the absent staff of office; already he rules over
his phantom court, already gives orders to subjects. He
imagines himself uniquely worthy of high authority, fixes
his empty hopes on lofty objects, and presumes to claim for
himself that staff which virtue is too apt to lose, and vicious- 155
ness ever ready to usurp. Already he glows with the radiance
of another star, already his mind ascends on high, already in
precarious thought he wields the thunderbolt of a second
Jove, enjoys in his mind another's dignity, and his mind is
granted the scepter before his hand. Such things come to 160
pass in the cloister; Pride fills sails both black and white
with her too eager winds, and drives in headlong flight
through the world's vast sea little vessels that sharp rocks
are bound to destroy.

As he realizes to whose service this familiar house is de-
voted, Architrenius cries: "Oh most ancient root of sin! This 165
fault is the last of all to behold God in Christ, but the first to
withdraw from him; and it determines, as a thing natural
and proper to itself, that there can be no unanimity among
those whom this one sin defiles.

"There is to be sure a great bond among degenerate
spirits; a great mutual forbearance brings greedy minds into 170
agreement. A stable peace draws unstable spirits together,
as indeed peace embraces other ways of life practiced com-
munally; a single love informs their common pursuits. But
an anger equally strong descends headlong on these arro-
gant minds, creating storm and thunder of another kind, 175
and their common style of life brings these unruly spirits to
ruin.

Capitulum 7

De casu Luciferi

"Hoc animi fulmen solio detrusit ab alto
Luciferum, Iovia dum se miratur in aula.
Partitusque polos superum, sibi destinat axem
180 devexumque Iovi, sua cui decreta vel astris
mandet suppositis. Igitur rapturus ad Arcton
imperium, fatuo conceptis pectore regnis,
affigi Boream iubet, indignatus ad Austrum
sub pedibus regnare Iovis. Sed gloria caecis
185 fidit in auguriis, et amara Superbia dulces
vix habet eventus. Melior prudentia fastus
irritat, et rigidus lentescere cogitur arcus.
    "Ecce novos flatus, et prima tonitrua pacis
aethereae, strepitusque rudes et semina belli,
190 primitias odii, fraudis cunabula, mortis
primaevam faciem, vitae nova funera, mentis
Iupiter arcano circumspicit; et periturae
compatitur proli. Caelo iunctissima, culpam
excusat Pietas, manifestaque crimina velo
195 palliat erroris. Vindictam fixa supernae
sanctio iustitiae dictat, iustamque reatum
evocat in poenam. Nec enim Iove maior ad axes
imperet astrigeros: velit ipsa Superbia tantum
non voluisse gradum; caveat suspecta ruinae

Chapter 7

The fall of Lucifer

"This same spiritual thunderbolt drove Lucifer from his lofty throne, even as he wondered at finding himself in the court of Jove. Dividing the heavenly realm, he assigns himself a region withdrawn from Jove, where he may impose his 180 decrees at least on subordinate stars. Preparing to seize dominion over the North, having imagined such a kingdom in his foolish spirit, he thus commanded that the Northern realm be seized, for he disdained to rule the South beneath the feet of Jove. But vainglory trusts in blind auguries, and 185 bitter pride rarely enjoys sweet success. A superior wisdom reduces his pride to nothing, and his tensed bow is forced to grow slack.

"Jupiter in the depths of his wisdom contemplates new storms, thunder for the first time disturbing the peace of heaven, rough clamor and provocations to war, the first 190 fruits of hatred, the birth of deception, the primal face of death, a new ending of life; and he feels compassion for his offspring who must perish. Pity, intimately joined to heavenly power, excuses the guilty act, and seeks to clothe manifest crime in the mantle of error. But the unalterable 195 ordinance of divine justice decrees vengeance, and summons the guilty one to a just punishment. For none greater than Jove may govern the star-bearing heavens: let Pride itself wish never to have wished for so lofty a place; let the

200 summa deum sedes. Igitur sententia poenae
cum nequeat flecti, Pietas secedit; et iram
Iupiter induitur et anhelos concutit axes;
fulmineisque manum iaculis armatus et ira,
praecipitat tonitrus, poenamque in fulmine mandat,
205 et superum patriis civem deturbat ab astris.
　　"O miserum civem, cuius sub fulminis ictu
detumuit flatus! O gloria dulcis amaras
eliciens lacrimas! O lux augusta, profundis
pallescens tenebris, solii pictura superni,
210 deliciae caeli! Pretio solidata perennis
materiae, proles, omni circumflua formae
imperio, Phlegethontis aquis assatur, Averni
fundamenta tenens, Cocyti sorbet abyssum
luctificam. Felix, nisi se tot fonte bonorum
215 Lucifer agnosset! Alter Narcissus, et oris
dotibus et fati lacrimis. Solatia concors
praebeat eventus, communis sarcina damni
pondus utrumque levet. Miser ille, sed ille quod ultra
quam liceat temere speciem quam vidit amavit.

high realm of the gods beware the threat of ruin. Since,   200
then, the punishment decreed cannot be averted, Pity with-
draws; Jupiter becomes wrathful and shakes the breathless
heavens; armed with bolts of lightning and with wrath, he
hurls down thunder, assigns punishment to lightning, and   205
casts out a citizen of heaven from his starry home.

"O wretched citizen, whose windy pride shriveled at the
blast of the lightning bolt! O sweet glory that now elicits
bitter tears! O majestic radiance, vision of a lofty throne and   210
heavenly delights, now growing pale in deep darkness! A
child of God sustained by the gift of eternal substance, en-
veloped in the utmost dignity of form, is now broiled in the
waters of Phlegethon, lurks in the depths of Avernus, drinks
the sorrowful waters of Cocytus. Happy Lucifer, had he not
beheld himself in a well of such bounty! He was another   215
Narcissus, in the rich beauty of his face and in his tearful
fate. Let their consonant ending be a source of solace, and
the shared onus of self-destruction ease the burden for
both. He is miserable, because he rashly loved beyond mea-
sure the beauty he beheld.

Capitulum 8

Invectio in Superbiam

220 "O caeli scabies, terrae contagia, mortis
initiale malum, ventosa Superbia, cuius
flatu fletifero pax est excussa superne,
et superis extincta dies! O prima reatus
clausula, prima deum confusio, prima dolendi
225 ianua, vas vacuum, pondus leve, robur inane,
de facili turgens animi vesica, potentum
addita saevitiae pestis, corrumpere vatum
pectora prompta lues, facilisque inserpere plectris
dulcibus, et teneris praeceps dare cornua Musis!
230   "O abies, quae nunc peregrino ad sidera ramo
serpis, et abiectum fugis indignante comarum
maiestate solum! Praeceps hanc imminet hora
suppressura fugam; non haec pede gloria firmo
nititur; invalidis truncus radicibus haeret,
235 exiguum Boreae subito casurus ad ictum."

Chapter 8

An outcry against Pride

"O blight on the heavens, earthly plague, first of deadly   220
evils, stormy Pride, whose grief-bearing blast drove peace
from heaven, and extinguished the light of day for heavenly
creatures! O first guilty ending, first disruption of the life of
the gods, first gateway to sorrow, empty vessel, weightless   225
burden, hollow force, quickly swelling blister on the mind,
disease that increases the cruelty of the great, plague ever
apt to corrupt the hearts of poets, creeping over us with
soft music, then suddenly providing the gentle Muses with
trumpets!

"O tree, that now creeps upward toward the stars with   230
roaming limbs, rejecting the lowly earth in the disdainful
majesty of its foliage! The hour is at hand that will suddenly
curb this flight; this striving after glory is not firmly
grounded; the tree clings to feeble roots, ready to fall at the   235
lightest blow from Boreas."

Capitulum 9

De monstro Cupiditatis

Dixit, et extrema lacrimis immersit, et imbre
detumuit ventus quem linguae intorserat ira.
Iamque pererrat, per plana, per aspera, mundo
parte tenus magna, monstrum reperitur, eunti
240 insolitus terror; nam caelum vertice pulsat,
et patulis terrae digitis superoccupat orbem.
Et Phoebe medium fraternos amovet ignes,
et Christi radios melioraque lumina tollit.
Mater Avaritiae, somni ieiuna cupido,
245 aeternam damnata sitim producere nullis
exsatiata bonis. Lucri studiosa, rapinis
artifices factura manus, visura recessus
Antipodum, noctisque dies umbrasque sinistras,
ardentis secreta sinus. Mollesque Sabaeos,
250 et rigidos sine sole Getas, primaevaque Phoebi
limina cum scopulis, quibus exulat ultima Thule,
ut varias rerum species emungat, avari
orbis opes animi longo sudore secuta,
ut tandem modico loculis deserviat aere.

Chapter 9

The monster Cupidity

Thus Architrenius spoke, drenching his last words in tears, and with this shower the storm wind aroused by his angry words subsided. And now, when he has traversed a great part of the world, on smooth roads and on rough ones, a monster appears, a terror unfamiliar to the traveler; for its head 240 strikes against the sky, and it extends its long claws over the earthly sphere. Phoebe half conceals her brother's fires, and takes away the radiance, the truer light of Christ. This is the mother of Avarice, the starved Greed of a dream, con- 245 demned to produce an endless thirst, satisfied by no good thing. Zealous for gain, she creates hands skilled in theft, and she will see the depths of the Antipodes, the daytime of night and sinister shadows, the secret places of the heart's desire. She visits the effete Sabaeans, the sunless land of the 250 rough Getae, and the rocky threshold where Phoebus first appears, lands from which farthest Thule is exiled, that she may defraud them of their various resources, exhausting her greedy spirit in a long search for the world's riches, to provide her coffers at last with a little money.

Capitulum 10

Quid de Cupiditate Architrenius sentiat

255 Horruit, et noto quid erat, suspexit et inquit:
"Haec Stygiae, superis infelicissima, noctis
filia fas abolet, cancellat iura, resignat
foedera, pacta movet, leges abradit, honestum
damnat, amicitias rumpit, divellit amorem
260 succinditque fidem. Plena est discordia; quaestus
ardor ubi pugnat, studio concurritur omni
ad loculos; nam sola potest reverentia nummi
quodlibet ad libitum mundano quolibet uti.
Haec vaga commutat solidis, quadrata rotundis,
265 solvit amicitias veteres iterumque renodat
quas prius abrupit. Alternos gratia nodos
vix recipit, nisi quos alterna pecunia nectit.
    "Dulcia sunt cupido lucrosa pericula; dulci
Aeolus armatur horrore, Ceraunia fluctu;
270 blanda Charybdis aqua, Phorcis cane, Syrtis harena.
Emollit scopulos lucri dulcedo; diurnas
absolvunt hiemes lucri momenta; labores
expiat innumeros lucrum breve; sarcina lucro
fit levis, et rutilo sudor siccatur in auro.

Chapter 10

Architrenius's views on Cupidity

Architrenius is horrified, and realizing what she is, eyes   255
her askance and exclaims: "This daughter of Stygian night,
utterly unwelcome to the gods, abolishes good, nullifies
justice, rescinds promises, alters agreements, cancels laws,
repudiates honor, destroys friendships, severs the bond of
love, and subverts trust. She is full of discord; when the de-   260
sire for profit causes strife, all rush to man the moneybags;
for only when money is revered can one enjoy any and all
worldly goods according to one's every desire. She changes
fluids to solids, makes square things round, destroys old   265
friendships and reunites again those whom she had once
sundered. Little favor can attend a mutual bond, unless an
exchange of money has reinforced it.

"To the greedy man the perils of the quest for Gain are
sweet; there is a sweet terror in the power of Aeolus, in the
Ceraunian waves; the waters of Charybdis, Phorcus's daugh-   270
ter with her dogs, and the shoals of Syrtis are pleasant. The
sweet love of gain softens rocks; the motive power of gain
reduces winter to a single day; a little gain makes good un-
numbered labors; a burden is made light by gain, and the
ruddy glow of gold dries the sweating brow.

Capitulum 11

Quod cupidus nullis habitis
sit contentus

275 "At licet Hesperiae fluvios Bessique meatus;
vincula Macrobii; Chryses vada; lina Neronis;
Hesperidum ramos; Martis penetralia; Danes
impluvium; Bacchi tumulum; Phariique tyranni
naufragium; tenerosque Iovis spoliaverit annos,
280 et Phoebi tulerit, sapientum praemia, mensam,
et geminos axes una congesserit arca;
cura tamen numquam residet suspensa soporis
pace; nec alternam requiem delibat avarus.
Inter opes mendicus opum; non temperat unda
285 qua natat ipse sitim. Semper post parta laborat
in partus alios, nulloque retunditur aere
mentis acus cupidae. Loculo vix sufficit uni
quicquid Fabricius sprevit Crassusque probavit.
Haeret in aere sitis; habitis furit ardor habendi.
290 Pullulat in quaestu quaestus amor. Omnia nullum
pondus habent, nisi sint unum simul omnia pondus.

Chapter II

Nothing he possesses will content the greedy man

"But though he should have plundered the Hesperian 275
stream and the winding Hebrus; the Macrobian's chains; the
shoals of Chryse; the nets of Nero; the tree of Hesperus's
daughters; the sanctuary of Mars; the shower of Danae; the
tomb of Bacchus; the shipwreck of the Egyptian tyrant;
though he should despoil the age that saw the infancy of
Jove, carry off the table that was Phoebus's reward from the 280
wise men, and place the twin poles on his heap of treasure;
even then his anxiety can never be quieted by the peace of
sleep; the greedy man never enjoys an interval of rest. Amid
his wealth he begs for more; the flood in which he swims 285
cannot ease his thirst. After every increase he labors to pro-
duce still more, and no amount of money can dull the keen
edge of his greedy mind. All that Fabricius scorned and
Crassus tasted are scarcely enough for his one purse. The
thirst is inherent in the money itself; the fever of possession
rages in the things possessed. The process of acquisition 290
only spreads the love of acquiring. Nothing has value, unless
all things can be possessed at once.

Capitulum 12

Quod sola morte Cupiditas terminatur

"Infelix cupidis omnis fortuna; sitimque
nulla levant quae cuncta sitit. Sed meta malorum,
mors, sola innumeras curas expellit, et una
295   falce metit varii quicquid peperere labores.
Et bene de cupido tandem mors sola meretur,
cum longo vigiles somno suffundit ocellos.
Vix tamen a quaestu studium subducitur: ipsum
mortis ad imperium sensus vigilantia census
300   aeternum meminit. Loculis, in morte cadentes,
assurgunt oculi. Tenero super omnia voto
dilectus suprema rapit suspiria nummus.
Iamque Stygis medium perlabitur umbra, memorque
nunc etiam quaestus, in carnis claustra reverti
305   nititur, ut nummo rursum potiatur amato,
et loculum loculo superaddat, Pelion Ossae,
colliculum monti, fluvio vada, flumina ponto.
At nullos reditus regis dispensat opaci
sanctio. Sic dominam saltem suspirat ad arcam,
310   extremumque vale Stygiis mandatur ab undis:
'O loculi dulces, iocunda pecunia, nummi
deliciae, Sirenes opum, Philomena crumenae,
cuius ad auratae vocis modulamina cedit
Orpheus, fastiditur olor, delirat Apollo.'

Chapter 12

Cupidity comes to an end only with death

"All Fortune is misfortune to the greedy; nothing can relieve a thirst which thirsts for everything. Only death, the terminus of evil, banishes his countless worries, and with a single sweep of its scythe reaps all that his various efforts had produced. And surely in the end only death deserves the greedy man's thanks, when it suffuses his watchful eyes with lasting slumber. Yet scarcely is his eagerness for gain subdued: even as he submits to the eternal dominion of death his still-wakeful thoughts dwell on his property. His eyes, dimming as he dies, open to gaze on his moneybags. It is his beloved money above all else that claims his final breaths in a faint prayer. And even as his shade is borne through the Styx, even now, recalling its profits, it struggles to return to its fleshly prison, that it may once again enjoy the money it loves, and add yet another bag to the heap, a Pelion to Ossa, a knoll to the mountain, a brook to the river, a river to the ocean. But the decree of the shadowy king admits of no returnings. Thus he can only sigh for his coffer, his mistress, and a last farewell issues from the Stygian depths: 'O sweet moneybags, O charming money, delightful coin, O Sirens of wealth, Philomena of the purse, at the sweet sound of your golden voice Orpheus yields, the swan is scorned, Apollo raves.'

315   "O geminos solis ortus amplexa, cupido,
alterutrumque diem, cuius radicibus omnis
perplexatur humus, caelumque cacumina terrent.
Vae terrae! Superis cum sis suspecta, nec eius
divitiis contenta; vocas Titanas in astra,
320 sollicitasque Iovem superosque in monstra resolvis,
dum petitur caelum per Pelion, Ossan, Olympum.
    "Heu sortis miserae quibus est angusta bonorum
portio Sol oculis quicquid metitur habere!
Indepulsa manent cupidae ieiunia mentis;
325 quam non exsatiant uno minus omnia; pontum
exhausisse nisi bibulas emungat harenas.
Heu, pugnaturos plus quam civiliter enses,
alternaeque necis gladios accincta, Cupido;
mille modos leti rerumque pericula tractat,
330 ut mundi lacrimas loculi transfundat in usus.

Capitulum 13

Exclamatio in praelatos

"O utinam sanctos haec citra viscera patres
ecclesiae pupugisset acus; ne vilior auro
ara foret, sed libra libro, sed numine nummus.
Non Davo caderet morum censura, Catonis

"O Greed, encompassing the two sunrises and both day-   315
times, every soil is infested by your roots, and your treetops
menace heaven. Alas for the earth! For you are not content
with her wealth, but threaten the very gods; you bid the
Titans assail the stars, you harass Jove and open the heavens   320
to monsters, as the sky is attempted from Pelion, Ossa,
Olympus.

"Alas for those ill-fated ones to whom the possession of
whatever the eye of the Sun encompasses seems a meager
share of the world's goods! The hunger of the greedy mind
remains unsubdued; all things are not enough for it if one   325
thing be missing; it is not enough to have drunk an ocean
unless it may also loot the thirsty sands. Alas for Greed,
girded with weapons for a conflict worse than civil war, the
swords of mutual slaughter; it conducts its perilous affairs in
a thousand deadly ways, to conduce the world's tears to the   330
service of its treasury.

Chapter 13

An outcry against prelates

"O would that a needle had punctured the bellies of the holy
fathers of the Church before this; the altar would not now
be less precious than gold, but wealth would defer to wis-
dom, greed to godhead. Moral judgment would not condone

335 limatum totiens temere morsura rigorem.
Non partiretur, consulto Simone, Petri
curia vel baculos Christi vel cornua. Virtus
surgeret excessus circumcisura, beatos
illustres factura viros; librasset honores
340 ad meriti libram. Nec ea sub iudice possent
iura peroranti loculo succumbere; numquam
Birria sufficeret, ubi defecisset Homerus."

Capitulum 14

De bello inter Largos
et Avaros

Fine dato verbis, subitos bibit aure tumultus.
Et ruptas gladiis Martisque tonitribus auras
345 haurit, et horrisonis qua litigat ictibus aer,
flectit iter stupidum. Dubiisque allabitur ausis,
Mars ubi saevus agit, gladius necis eliquat imbres,
sidera texuntur iaculis, superosque sagitta
territat, et densa noctescit harundine caelum.
350 Gemmis vernat apex galeae; lorica nitoris
ridet in argento; mucro splendore minatur;
reptat in umbone leo flammeus; igneus aurum
ventilat in hastis volitans draco; mortis odore
cuspis inescatur. Ignes equus arduus efflat;

a Davus, while daring to carp endlessly at the tempered   335
discipline of a Cato. The court of Peter would not dole out
Christ's staffs and miters on the advice of Simon. Virtue
would rise up to cut away excess and ensure that men of holy
life were renowned: honors would be weighed on the scale   340
of merit. Under such a judge laws would not be defeated by
money, pleading its case: never would a Birria succeed where
a Homer had failed."

Chapter 14

The war between the Generous
and the Avaricious

As he finished speaking, his ear took in a sudden tumult. He
heard the air shattered by the clash of swords and martial
thunderings, and made his astonished way to where the air   345
clashed with the terrible sound of blows. Moving forward
with faltering courage, he arrived where cruel Mars was at
work, swords dripped with the rain of slaughter, the stars
were crossed by javelins, arrows menaced the gods, and the
sky grew dark with the dense flight of missiles. The crown of   350
the god's helmet is adorned with gems; his breastplate re-
joices in gleaming silver; his sword arouses fear by its sheer
brilliance; a flame-red lion crouches on his shield; on his
spear a fiery dragon beats the golden air as it flies; his spear-
head is steeped in the odor of death. His bold steed breathes

355 sanguine crudescunt phalerae; spumescit, habena
indignata regi. Freni natat ardor in ira,
ungula summa volat. Raptos iuba verberat armos.
Pectoris excussus aries terit obvius hostem.
   Caelum Marte tonat; gladii face fulminat aer.
360 Sanguine luget humus, eadem mare purpura vestit.
Morte natantur aquae, terram bibit unda cruoris.
Aera mugit equo, lituo sinus aetheris hinnit.
Ictibus exclamat gladius, conflictibus umbo.
Turbine saxa fremunt, taedae igni, tela volatu.
365 Subticet adventum plumbi impetus, ala sagittae,
et nec funda neces nec vulnera praecinit arcus.
Insilit arma Furor, acies Discordia nodat,
Terror agit currus, Feritas auriga iugales,
efferat Ira viros maiorque Audacia Martis
370 filia, vexillumque ferens Dementia belli.
Mucroni gladius occurrit, harundo sagittae,
cornipedi sonipes, lateri sinus, ungula cornu,
umboni clipeus, lituo tuba, missile telo,
loricae thorax, galeae iuba, fraxinus hastae.
375 Mars in morte natat, feriens furor inserit enses,
dumque fodit, foede caedis cadit unda redundans.

fire; his trappings are caked with blood, and he froths at the 355
mouth, disdaining to be ruled by the reins. Anger at re-
straint gives rise to burning rage, and he speeds along on the
tips of his hooves. His mane is hung with captured arms. His
chest strikes against the enemy like a battering ram.

The sky resounds with war; the air is bright with the flash
of swords. The earth weeps tears of blood, and the same 360
dark red coats the sea. The waters teem with death, and a
tide of blood soaks the earth. The air echoes with the
whinny of horses, and the depths of the sky are full of the
clarion of their neighing. The sword resounds as it strikes,
and the shield as it receives the blow. Rocks roar in their
whirling flight, the torches roar as they burn, and spears as
they fly. The impact of lead shot and winged arrow comes 365
silently, and neither sling nor bow foretells wounds and
deaths. Madness rushes to arms, Discord confuses the bat-
tle lines, Terror urges the chariot forward, Savagery is the
charioteer who guides the team, Wrath and Boldness, elder
daughter of Mars, make the warriors fierce, and Folly bears 370
the standard of war. Sword clashes with sword, arrow with
arrow, hard-hoofed steed with loud-hoofed steed, flank with
flank, hoof with hoof, shield with shield, trumpet with
trumpet, missile with missile, breastplate with breastplate,
helmet with crested helmet, spear with spear. Mars wallows 375
in death, madness lends force to swords, and at their deep
cut, a copious stream of gory death pours forth.

Capitulum 15

Sermo Walgani ad Architrenium
de Corineo

Quod metuit, vidisse iuvat, novitasque videndi
affectus et vota facit. Miratur et ecce,
improvisus adest miranti miles, anhelo
380   pulverulentus equo. Dantur redeuntque salutes
pace relativa: quis sit, quo tendat, uterque
discit, uterque docet. Tamen Architrenius instat
et genus et gentem quaerit studiosius; ille:
"Tros genus et gentem tribuit Lodonesia. Nutrix
385   praebuit irriguam morum Cornubia mammam,
post odium Fati Phrygiis inventa smaragdus.
Hanc domitor mundi, Tirynthius alter, Achillis
Atridaeque timor, Corineus, serra Gigantum
clavaque monstritera, sociae delegit alumnam
390   omnigenam Troiae; pluvioque faviflua lacte
filius exilio fessae dedit ubera matri.
A quo dicta prius Corineia, dicitur aucto
tempore corrupti Cornubia nominis heres.
    "Ille Giganteos attritis ossibus artus
395   implicuit leto, Tyrrheni litoris hospes.
Indomita virtute Gigas, non corpore, mole
ad medium pressa, nec membris densior aequo,
sarcina terrifico tumuit Titania monte.

Chapter 15

Gawain's speech to Architrenius concerning Corineus

Though the sight is fearful, it pleases Architrenius to behold it, and the novel spectacle elicits sympathy and prayers. He looks on in wonder, and lo, as he gazes, a knight unexpectedly appears, covered with dust and on an exhausted steed. 380 Greetings are exchanged in mutual goodwill: each learns and explains who he is and where he is going. Yet Architrenius eagerly and earnestly asks the other's nation and lineage; he replies: "My people are Trojan, and Lothian gave me birth. Cornwall, that gem discovered by the Phrygians after the hateful blow of Fate, was the nurse whose flowing breast 385 sustained my upbringing. It was this place that Corineus, the world-conqueror, the second Tirynthian, the terror of Achilles and the Atrides, the cutter-down of giants and batterer of monsters, chose as the all-producing nursery of a 390 new Trojan society; a son granted breasts flowing with milk and honey to a mother worn out by exile. The place, first named for his sake Corineia, over the course of time assumed the corrupted name of Cornubia.

"Sojourning on the shores of Italy, Corineus destroyed the limbs of giants with a deadly, bone-crushing embrace. 395 Himself a giant, not in body but in his indomitable heroism, confined to medium stature, and with limbs not disproportionately thick, he seemed to swell to a Titanic size, massive

Ad Ligeris ripas Aquitanos fudit, et amnes
400 Francorum pavit lacrimis; et caede vadoque
sanguinis ense ruens satiavit rura, togaque
Punicea vestivit agros, populique loquacis
grandiloquos fregit animosa cuspide fastus.
Integra, nec dubio bellorum naufraga fluctu,
405 nec vice suspecta, titubanti saucia Fato
indilata, dedit subitam Victoria laurum.

Capitulum 16

De adventu Bruti et Corinei in Angliam et de Gigantibus

"Inde dato cursu, Bruto comitatus Achate,
Gallorum spolio cumulatis navibus, aequor
exarat; et superis auraque faventibus utens,
410 litora felices intrat Totonesia portus,
promissumque soli gremium monstrante Diana,
incolumi census loculum ferit Albion alno.
    "Haec eadem, Bruto regnante, Britannia nomen
traxit in hoc tempus. Solis Titanibus illo
415 sed paucis famulosa domus, quibus uda ferarum
terga dabant vestes, cruor haustus, pocula trunci,
antra lares, dumeta thoros, cenacula rupes,

and terrifying. On the banks of the Loire he routed the Aquitanians, and fed the rivers of the Franks with tears; 400 wreaking havoc with his sword and steeping the countryside in carnage and streams of blood, he decked the fields in a purple robe, humbling the haughty eloquence of a loquacious people with undaunted arms. Total victory, unhindered by the perilous tides of war, untroubled by any rever 405 sal and marred by no vacillation of Fate, rapidly earned him laurels."

Chapter 16

The arrival of Brutus and Corineus in England and concerning Giants

"Pursuing his destined course, accompanied by Brutus, his Achates, Corineus plowed the waves, his ships laden with Gallic booty; enjoying the favor of gods and winds, and 410 guided by Diana to this destined lap of earth, he enters safe harbor on the Cornish coast at Totnes, and, with his vessels unharmed, comes ashore in that rich treasury Albion.

"This same land has borne the name of Britain, from its ruler Brutus, to the present time. But then it provided a 415 home only for a few Titans, whose garments came from the damp bodies of wild beasts; their drink was blood, their goblets wooden, their homes caves, their beds brush, their

praeda cibos, raptus Venerem, spectacula caedes,
imperium vires, animos furor, impetus arma,

420 mortem pugna, sepulcra rubus. Monstrisque gemebat
monticolis tellus, sed eorum plurima tractus
pars erat occidui terror, maiorque premebat
te furor, extremum Zephyri, Cornubia, limen.
    "Hos avidum belli Corinei robur Averno

425 praecipites misit. Cubitis ter quatuor altum,
Gemagog Herculea suspendit in aera lucta,
Antaeumque suum scopulo detrusit in aequor.
Potavitque dato Thetis ebria sanguine fluctus;
divisimque tulit mare corpus, Cerberus umbram.

Capitulum 17

De conceptione Arturi et ortu
eius ad quem scribitur

430 "Nobilis a Phrygiae tanto Cornubia gentem
sanguine derivat. Successio cuius Iulum
in generis partem recipit, complexa Pelasgam
Anchisaeque domum. Ramos hinc Pandrasus, inde
Silvius extendit, socioque a sidere sidus

435 plenius effundit triplicatae lampadis ignes.

tables rocks, their food game, their love rape, their enter-
tainment slaughter, their rule brute strength, their courage
madness, violence their warfare, their death battle, their   420
tombs thickets. The land complained of these mountain-
dwelling monsters, but they were for the most part the
terror of the western region, and their mad ravages most
afflicted you, Cornwall, uttermost threshold of Zephyrus.

"The might of Corineus, ever ready for battle, drove
these creatures headlong into Avernus. In a Herculean   425
struggle he lifted Gemagog, thrice four cubits tall, on high,
and cast his Antaean enemy from a rock into the sea.
Drunken Thetis drank the stream of blood he gave forth;
The sea received his sundered limbs, Cerberus his shade."

Chapter 17

The conception of Arthur, and the origins of him to whom the book is addressed

"To such Phrygian blood noble Cornwall traces its ancestry.   430
Succeeding generations inherited Iulus as a contributor to
their lineage, joining the house of Anchises and that of
Greece. Pandrasus extended the royal line in one direction,
Silvius in another, and the star derived from this union of
stars poured forth the fuller radiance of a triple light.   435

"Hoc trifido sole Corinei postera mundum
praeradiat pubes, quartique puerpera Phoebi
pullulat Arturum, facie dum falsus adulter
Tintaiol irrumpit. Nec amoris Pendragon aestum
440   vincit, et omnificas Merlini consulit artes.
Mentiturque ducis habitus et rege latenti,
induit absentis praesentia Gorlois ora.

"Ecce Furor lucis! Maiori sidere quintus
enituit Phoebus, ad cuius lumina quivis
445   sol alius Saturnus erit. Splendore planetas
vesperat; obscuro brumescit Falcifer igne
caecus ea sub nocte senex. Iovis erubet astrum,
Marte verecundo; peplo Venus occulit ora,
Mercurius mitra. Phoebe ferrugine vultus
450   Aethiopes odit faciemque intersa lutosam
plena latet nodo; germanaque turbida fratrem
et modicum lucis vocat et causatur avarum.

Capitulum 18

De Ramofrigio

"Hunc Ramofrigius mundo intulit, anchora iuris
impatiens nutasse ratem. Se Tydea bello
455   exhibuit, se pace Numam, scelerumque procellas

"The later progeny of Corineus spread the radiance of this triple Sun over the world, and the birth of a fourth Phoebus produced Arthur, when the adulterer under a false appearance broke into Tintagel. For Pendragon could not overcome the strength of his love, and appealed to the all-capable arts of Merlin. Feigning the behavior of the duke and, hiding his kingly identity, he assumed the outward appearance of the absent Gorlois.   440

"Behold a frenzy of light! A fifth Phoebus gleams with yet greater brightness; any other sun is a Saturn in comparison.   445
His splendor eclipses the planets; the aged Scythe-bearer dwindles to a faint glow, hardly visible in this darkness. Jove's star blushes, while Mars grows shy; Venus conceals her face with her robe, Mercury his with his helmet. Phoebe loathes   450
her face, Ethiopian in its duskiness, and though full, hides in eclipse, her tarnished face uncleansed: the distraught sister appeals to her brother for a little light and complains that he is stingy.

Chapter 18

Ramofrigius

"Ramofrigius, an anchor who would not allow the vessel of justice to be shaken, brought this sun into the world. He proved himself a Tydeus in warfare, a Numa in time of peace;   455

propulit infracto securus navita clavo,
quem praecessiva Ratio dedit, excuba tanto
cum socia Virtute viro. Se moribus ipsis
praebuit exemplum nec honesti flexit habenam
460 alter, sed melior, hic Nestor, Nestore primo
annis inferior, par pectore, celsior actis.
  "De genitore fidem genitus facit: optimus ille
extitit, existit superoptimus ille, bonorum
maximus absque gradu. Non est quo surgat honestum
465 supra summa situm, nec novit linea morum
infinita gradum. Reliquus sic orbis ab uno
exsuperatur, uti, quem contingentia curvat,
angulus a recto. Numquam descendit ad Austrum
Arcticus, et pleno radiat fulgore dieque
470 integra Sol iste superlativus, et illo
pro gemma voluit mundi teres anulus uti.
Hoc aurifrigio Tellus redimitur, eoque
stella Rothomagi lascivit palla sabelo,
gemmescitque novo Christi sacra nupta monili.
475   "Hic sinus hos, hominum rosulas et lilia, vernat.
Regula: nil gignit olidum Cornubia. Partus
expolit illimes, et ab ubere pignora tersis
morigerat vitiis, et plus quam cetera scabram
limat Avaritiam, quae nostrae saepius Arcto
480 institit, et gelidum violenta lacessiit orbem.
  "At nos pro patria semper pugnavimus, armis
elidendo minas. Latiumque repellere monstrum
cura laborque fuit, et adhuc, ne tanta nepotes
belua subvertat, pugili sudamus in ense.

a steadfast sailor who thrust forward through storms of wickedness with that helm unbroken which foresighted Reason provided, keeping watch, with her companion Virtue, over such a man. He proved exemplary in character, and never swerved from the course of probity, a second, but better, Nestor, inferior to the first Nestor in years, but equal to him in wisdom and superior in deeds. 460

"The offspring gives clear evidence of his progenitor: if the one excelled, the other is superexcellent, great beyond any measure of goodness. Having attained the highest level worthiness can rise no higher, and his unlimited strength of character cannot be measured. The rest of the world is surpassed by this one man, just as a contingent angle of curvature is less than a right angle. This Polestar never descends to the south, this supreme Sun shines with the full brilliance of a perfect day, and the round ring of the world is glad to make him its jewel. Earth derives a new value from this orphrey, the starry vestments of Rouen luxuriate in this sable, and the sacred bride of Christ is resplendent in this new necklace. 465 470

"Such are the men the springtime of this small place produces, the roses and lilies of humankind. Take it as a law: Cornwall can produce nothing rank. Her offspring are flawlessly formed, and at her breast she imbues her progeny with character, obliterating vicious habits and above all cleansing them of the itch of Avarice, which has too often infested our northern clime, and assailed the cold region with its blast. 475 480

"But we have always been at war for our country, resisting threats by force of arms. To drive back the Latian monster has been our anxious labor, and even now we must strive with the sword of war lest this terrible beast undo our

485 Reppulimusque suas acies hucusque, necesque
   fudimus innumeras, sed adhuc cum multa supersint
   milia, non prono rapitur victoria cursu.

Capitulum 19

De ducibus castrorum Avaritiae

"Marte potens miles, nimbo populosior, illis
semper agit castris, et ea de parte magistri
490 bellorumque duces sunt, quos aeterna notabit
   et notat illa lues: Parthorum victima, Crassus,
   Septimulusque, suo qui Graccho praetulit aurum;
   et loculis donans ne tutus Cassius esset;
   quique necis propriae Ptolomeus rettulit hosti
495 praemia, ne census ageret divortia pontus,
   naufragioque daret dilecta pecunia poenas.

descendants. We have repelled her attacks until now, and   485
have produced boundless slaughter, but when so many thou-
sands still survive, the path to victory is not easy.

Chapter 19

The leaders of the forces of Avarice

"A powerful army, a throng more dense than a storm cloud,
is always on duty in their camp, and the strategists and   490
generals of their campaign are those who bear and will bear
forever the mark of this disease: Crassus, the victim of the
Parthians; Septimulus, who valued gold more than his friend
Gracchus; Cassius, who enriched his treasury rather than
ensure his own safety; and Ptolemy, who presented the rich
reward of his own death to his enemies, rather than let the   495
sea divorce him from his property and allow his beloved
money to suffer shipwreck.

BOOK SIX

Capitulum 1

De Arturo, Ramofrigio, Walgano in Avaritiam dimicantibus

"Ex alio belli cuneo sumus: alter Achilles,
Arturus, Teretis Mensae genitiva venustas;
et Ramofrigius, dandi non unda sed aequor;
et Walganus ego, qui nil reminiscor avara
5   illoculasse manu. Non haec mea fulgurat auro
sed gladio dextra; recipit quod spargat, et enses
non loculos stringit. Nec opes incarcero miles
degener, et cupide cumulato rusticus aere.
At me bella vocant, et te tua forsitan urget
10 sollicitudo. Vale."
                    Non expectatus eunti
reddidit ille vale, meditativusque recedit,
corde querelanti, quod scrutativus et Austrum
viderit et Thetide miranti merserit Arcton,
effusoque vagus oculo perlegerit orbem,
15 nullaque propositi datur exoptata facultas.

Chapter 1

Arthur, Ramofrigius, and Gawain wage
war against Avarice

"We are an army of another kind: Arthur, a second Achilles, founder and glory of the Round Table; Ramofrigius, not a stream but an ocean of largesse; and I, Gawain, who do not recall consigning anything to my purse with stinting hand. 5 This right hand of mine shines, not with gold, but with a sword; what it receives it spreads forth, and it grasps weapons, not purses. I am no base knight who hoards his wealth, no peasant with greedily acquired money. But battle calls me, and perhaps cares of your own draw you away. Farewell." 10

Architrenius returned a farewell which the departing one did not wait for, and then withdrew, pondering, and complaining inwardly, for in his search he had seen even the southern world, caused the Bears to sink beneath the waters of an astonished Thetis, and cast his sweeping gaze over the wide world in his wandering, yet the opportunity for what 15 he hoped to accomplish was not granted.

Capitulum 2

De transitu Architrenii in Tylon

Intimus ergo tumet, vultusque superfluit ira;
purpureisque furor animi coquit ora caminis.
Nec mora, dum fervet nec tempore temperat ignem,
floridulum mundi thalamum Verisque penates,
20 advenit usque Tylon, ubi numquam labitur absque
praeterito praesens, plus quam perfecta venustas.
Perpetuatur honos rosulis, intacta senectae
lilia pubescunt senium; nec bruma nec aestas
advehit, et Veris aeternativa iuventam
25 floribus ipsa loci deitas nativa perennat.
Hic, ubi planities patulum lunatur in orbem,
philosophos serie iunctos circumspicit; in qua
Archytas varios excessus explicat Irae
et docet, hac mentem Furia vexante, labores.

Chapter 2

Architrenius's entry into Tylos

Thus he seethes within, and wrath suffuses his countenance; the rage in his heart steeps his face in its purple flames. But soon, while he still rages and time has not tempered the fire, he comes to the world's flourishing bower, the abode of Spring, Tylos, where a present that knows no past, a more 20 than perfect beauty, never fades. Here the glory of the rose is perpetual, lilies bloom untouched by age and decay; for neither frost nor the heat of summer intrudes, and an eternizing power, a deity native to the place, grants the flowers 25 a perennial youthful spring. Here, where an open plain formed a broad circle, he sees around him an ordered gathering of philosophers; in their midst Archytas is explaining the various disruptive effects of Wrath, and showing the hardships with which this Fury assails the mind.

Capitulum 3

Oratio Archytae de Ira

30 "Ira malum deforme viris: quo pectus acescit,
sensus hebet, languet studium, sollertia lippit,
caecatur ratio, pietas tepet, alget honestas,
macrescit virtus, vitium pinguescit, inundat
livor, adest facinus, lex nutat, norma vacillat,
35 pax titubat, surgit odium, clementia vergit,
cedit amor, crescit hostis, rarescit amicus,
insidiae serpunt, ruit impetus, evolat ardor,
bella fremunt. Bellona tuba, Mars intonat ense;
vita fugit, vitaeque sopor mors ultimus instat.
40   "Ira, malum quo non aliud velocius, alas
urget in errorem, pennasque in devia versat.
In faciem surgit et pectore nascitur Ira;
interiusque cremat et vultibus exsilit ardor;
praecipitesque furor animos rotat, ora perurit.
45 Hic rogus exterius celari nescius urit,
accensoque labor animi vulgatur in ore.
Nec tacet arcanum mentis facundia vultus.
    "Imperat haec dextris rabies, natosque parentum
immergit iugulis, contraque in pignora patres
50 efferat; et fratris frater bibit ense cruorem.
Cognatas acies alterno sanguinis haustu
polluit, et gladio Naturae foedera rumpit.

Chapter 3

Archytas's oration on Wrath

"Wrath is an ugly evil in men: through it the heart is embittered, understanding grows dull, alertness lapses, apprehension becomes sleepy, reason is blinded, devotion grows weak, probity fails, virtue starves, vice grows fat, envy floods the mind, crime appears, law nods, rule falters, peace trembles, hatred arises, mercy wanes, love is defeated, hostility thrives, friendship fades away, treachery creeps about, violence rampages, passion soars, war rages. Bellona's trumpet and the sword of Mars resound; life flees, and death, life's final slumber, impends.

"Wrath, than which no other evil is swifter, flies eagerly into error, and its flight is drawn into false paths. It is born in the heart and wells up into the face. It burns inwardly and its heat bursts forth through the face; its madness stirs up the impulsive spirit, and causes the face to burn. The blaze of this pyre cannot be concealed from outward view, and the labor of the spirit is manifested in the burning face. The eloquence of the face does not conceal the hidden state of mind.

"This madness controls our actions, makes sons pierce the throats of parents, and conversely drives fathers to savagery against their children; a brother's weapon drinks a brother's blood. Wrath defiles the blades of kinsmen with reciprocal bloodshed, and severs the bonds of Nature with a

Caedibus accedunt caedes, et caeca nefandis
implicat in facinus pugiles audacia sensus.
55   "Irae fida manus cladesque ancilla ministrans
surgit, et exilium Pacis molitur, iterque
rumpit in omne nefas: Rabies, germana Furoris;
pronus in arma Furor; stricto vagus Impetus ense;
indocilis flecti Feritas; et cognita sceptris
60   Seditio; caecusque Tumor; regnique Tyrannis
et soror et coniunx; et belli semina, Lites
Litigiique tubae; crudoque Insania vultu;
Rixarumque faces et Iurgia plena cruoris;
caedeque Saevities Irae clausura tumultus.
65   "Ira iuventutis solitus calor, ardor amantum
Acrior in poenas stragique paratior ense,
maturasque neces laqueo, face, cuspide cogens,
cum Veneris voto contraria ludit amantes
alea, nec motus animi Fortuna secundat,
70   nec ferit ad libitum voti quo tenditur arcus.
"Ira parens Odii, quod proles tertia Livor
subsequitur, pestis utriusque diutior heres."
Audit, et incinerat gelidis fornacibus ignes,
et sepelit vivam prius Architrenius Iram.
75   Pascitur auditis, propius sedet, erigit aurem,
cor patulum solvit; etenim sermone carenti
Gloria praecessit. Sequitur Plato verba secundans.

sword. Slaughter is added to slaughter, and a boldness blind to its own wickedness draws warlike minds into guilty actions.

"A faithful retinue stands ready to serve Wrath with violent acts, strives to banish Peace, and forces a path to wickedness of all kinds: Madness, the sister of Rage; Rage herself, ever ready to take up arms; Violence, rushing about with drawn sword; incorrigible Savagery; Sedition, well known to kings; blind Vanity; Despotism, the sister and wife of royal power; Dispute and loud Litigation, the seeds of open war; Frenzy with bloody face; the torches of Brawling and bloodthirsty Quarrel; and Cruelty, who concludes wrathful quarrels in slaughter.

"Wrath is commonly the heat of youth, the ardor of a lover too ready to brave pain and too ready for a swordfight, imposing untimely deaths by hanging, fire, or steel, when at Venus's whim a contrary throw of the dice mocks a lover, and Fortune does not favor his inclination, nor the arrow strike to gratify the hope with which it was aimed.

"Wrath is the parent of Hatred, from which a third offspring, Envy, is descended, a disease that long outlives either of the others."

Architrenius listens, and his fires are reduced to ashes as his furnace cools, and he extinguishes his once-active Wrath. He feeds on what he hears, draws closer, pricks up his ears and opens his heart wide; for even though speech is absent, he anticipates a glorious discourse. Plato follows, adding to the previous speech.

Capitulum 4

Oratio Platonis de Livore

"Ecce furor Livoris, acus maiorque Megaera
Invidiae, Famae cumulum raptura beatis.
80 Non pudet in mundos maculas iurasse, notatis
adiecisse notas. Erebum fastidit Erynis
maternamque Stygen, nostras peregrinat in aedes;
hospita dente gravis, didicit revocasse favores,
exacuisse dolos, clausos aperire reatus.
85 Ipsa scelus fictura nefas, tortura flagello
pervigili mentes, successibus aegra, sinistros
ad casus lugubre canens, lacrimosa secundis,
gavisiva malis. Ideo maerore serenum
et risu lacrimans fatum comitatur amaro.
90 "Livori assistunt Rabies animosa; Tumultus;
Pax armata Dolis; suspectum Foedus; Amoris
umbra; latens Odium; gladio Mars igneus; 'Arma,
arma, viri,' Bellona tonans; et pronuba belli
Seditio; primumque ferens Discordia pilum.
95 "Livor in insidias et in ebria tela veneno
irruit; et varia cumulantur pocula morte
exundantque neces. Nec inexpugnabile praestant
divitiae vallum, sed vino purpura cedit
mortibus hamato; damnique incauta, potestas

Chapter 4

Plato's oration on Envy

"Behold the raging of Envy, the goad and greater Megaera of Jealousy, who seeks to snatch away the reward of Reputation from the fortunate. She is not ashamed to charge the blame- less with faults, casting her aspersions over their known qualities. This Fury disdains Erebos and her native Styx, and journeys abroad to our halls; a sharp-toothed guest, she has learned to retract gifts, incite treachery, and lay open guilty secrets. In her wickedness she invents wicked acts, torment- ing our minds with her tireless lash, made wretched by our successes, mournfully celebrating our failures, weeping at good fortune, rejoicing at misfortune. Thus she is compla- cent in the face of sorrow, and responds to tearful Fate with a bitter smile.

"Envy's attendants are agitated Madness; Violence; Peace armed with Guile; untrustworthy Covenant; the false shadow of Love; lurking Hatred; fiery Mars with his sword; Bellona thundering 'To arms! to arms!'; Sedition, sponsor of war; and Discord bearing the spear of the senior centurion.

"Envy is quick to prepare ambushes, and weapons drunk with poison; her goblets are full of different forms of death, and overflow with slaughter. Even wealth does not provide an unassailable rampart: the purple robe succumbs to wine barbed with death; heedless of danger, the man of power

100 illud easque bibit. Aliudque infunditur ostro
quam Tyrium virus; hoc enitet, enecat illud;
erigit hoc fastus, illosque ulciscitur illud.
   "Detulit a superis radicem Livor, et ortu
summus summa petit, superisque simillima pulsat.
105 Certamenque deis plus quam civile minatur,
divitis et caelo. Redolentis lilia Famae
Livoris decerpit hiemps, insultat honori,
extenuat laudes. Adimit virtutis odorem
nariculis Famae, superos fragrantia morum
110 balsama delimat, virus inspirat et atro
polluit afflatu. Dens improbus omnia carpit
nec sibi depercit: in cetera Livor et ipsum
saevit in auctorem; roditque et roditur idem.
   "Livor opem pressis et opes sublimibus aufert,
115 provectumque bonis. Meritis infesta Celaeno,
aeternum fornax odium coctura novercae.
Et puto philosophis laterum Livore potentum
tollitur accessus, metuendaque gratia sceptri;
nam Livor titulum, quem non habet, odit haberi."

drinks the one and the other. It is the taint of something ₁₀₀
other than Tyrian dye that infuses his purple splendor; the
one ennobles, the other is deadly; the one gives rise to
arrogance, the other avenges it.

"Envy traces her origin to heaven, and being of lofty birth
she seeks out lofty realms, and attacks those places that
most resemble the heavens. She threatens the gods, and the ₁₀₅
heaven of wealth, with an attack worse than civil warfare.
The winter of Envy cuts down the lilies of sweet-smelling
Renown, reviles honor, and subdues praise. She withdraws
the sweet scent of virtue from the nostrils of Renown,
scrapes away the fragrant balsam of good character from ₁₁₀
superior people, and infuses poison and pollution with her
black breath. Her wicked tooth snaps at everything and
does not spare herself: Envy is cruel to others, and cruel to
the one who gives her rise; as he gnaws at others, he himself
is gnawed by her.

"Envy begrudges aid to the oppressed, wealth to the
great, and preferment to the good. She is a Celaeno in ₁₁₅
her cruelty toward merit, a furnace that glows with a step-
mother's undying hatred. And I think it is through Envy
that philosophers are denied access to the company of the
great, and the awesome favor of sceptered power; for Envy
is moved to hatred when any distinction is granted that she
does not possess."

Capitulum 5

Invectio Catonis contra divitias

120 Ut modus est verbis, subeunt partita favorem
murmura, nec serpunt vacui Livore susurri.
Nec mora, dum linguis immissa licentia fandi
materias versat, iuvat exclamasse Catonem:
"O inopes virtutis Opes! O gloria paucos
125 productura viros, caeloque invisa potestas!
Nec loculis factura deos! Felicia molles
seducunt animos; nec sunt commercia regnis
cum Iove, nec mitra superis accedis; inopsque
plus animae quam dives habet. Levioribus alis
130 pauper in astra volat, dulcique pecunia mole,
quos aluit, laesura premit. Nec Croesus in auro
Fata fugit, perdensque deos non perditur umbris.
    "O Erebi descensus, Opes, et maior Averni
introitus mortisque fores, quas Cerberus alter,
135 Ambitus, exstruxit, medioque erexit in orbe.
Qua surgit cum divitibus factura Megaera
colloquium, notaque diu cum prole susurrat,
et iacit amplexus et plaudit et oscula miscet,
incautoque doli ridenti arridet alumno.
140 Interdum Stygias attentius edocet artes,
sollicitumque minus intorto verberat hydro,
effusumque iacit Stygium per viscera virus,
quo nequeat non velle nefas; scelerumque soporem
nesciat et numquam facinus succumbat honesto.

Chapter 5

Cato's invective against wealth

As the speech ends, murmured expressions of approval arise, and no hollow, envious whispers insinuate themselves. Without delay, even as the intervening opportunity for talk is giving rise to various topics, Cato is moved to cry out: "O Riches poor in virtue! O glory that advances so few, power hateful to heaven! You will not create gods with your money! Your pleasures entice weak spirits; your kingdom have no commerce with Jove, nor do your mitered ones enter heaven; the poor have more spiritual treasure than the wealthy. On his lighter wings the pauper soars to the stars, while the cherished mass of money proves an injurious burden to those whom it has enriched. Croesus amid his gold cannot elude the Fates: though he lose his gods, he is not lost by the underworld.

"Wealth is the pathway to Erebus, chief entrance to Avernus, gateway of death, which a second Cerberus, Corruption, has built, and placed in the midst of our world. Here Megaera emerges to commune with the wealthy, whispers with her long-familiar progeny, bestows embraces and praise mixed with kisses, and smiles on the smiling pupil unmindful of her guile. While she carefully instructs him in her Stygian arts, she strikes him unawares with a writhing serpent, and its bite spreads through his bowels a Stygian poison, so that he is unable not to will evil; he may know no rest from wrongdoing, and his wickedness may never yield to probity.

Capitulum 6

De transitu Megaerae et Mortis
ab inferis in potentes

145 "Hac solitum decurrit iter, totumque Megaera
advehit infernum. Quicquid Plutonius axis
educat immundum, vitiorum turba, sinistra
progenies noctis, matrem complexa feruntur
emerguntque sinu bibulasque paludibus aulas
150 aspergunt Stygiis. Propiusque vocantur, et omni
assunt consilio. Verum cum sorde fluenti
polluti satis est, et fusae latius orbem
afficiunt maculae (nec Ditem evadere Dites
dant delicta fidem), Mors ecce, extrema dierum
155 vespera, pallenti subito procedit amictu,
accensamque tenet sicco Phlegethonte cupressum,
quae decisa rogis pigmentet odoribus auras,
divitibus supremus honos. Praenuntia Fati,
noctua praecedit properanti morte, propinquos
160 occasus infausta canens, buboque, sinistri
augurii vates. Aevumque in dulcibus annis
Atropos abrumpens, Fati comitatur euntis
indivisa vias. Lacrimae Planctusque sequuntur,
et Gemitus, fletuque madens Decisio Vultus,
165 funeribusque comes Ululatus, et horrida crinis
Arduitas, scissoque comae Iactura capillo,
diruptique sinus et maestae vestis Honestas,
et manuum presso coeuntes pectine nodi.

Chapter 6

The passage of Megaera and Death from the underworld into the mighty

"Controlled by this Fury, he pursues his accustomed course, 145
and Megaera summons all the powers of hell. Whatever foul
thing the Plutonian deep produces, the teeming vices, the
evil progeny of night, are borne along in their mother's em-
brace, and come forth from her bosom to sprinkle the dank 150
waters of Styx over a court eager to absorb them. They are
hailed familiarly and take part in all deliberations. But when
there is enough pollution from their foul effluent, and the
widespread taint afflicts the whole world (for his wicked
deeds ensure that no Dives will evade Dis), behold, Death,
the evening of all our days, suddenly comes forth in her 155
pallid robe, bearing a cypress torch kindled in waterless
Phlegethon, hewn for the pyre to adorn the breeze with its
scent, a final tribute to wealth. The night owl, herald of Fate,
flies before as Death draws on, singing ominously of immi- 160
nent downfalls, with the screech owl, priest of unlucky au-
gury. Atropos, breaking off life in its sweet prime, follows
closely the fated path of the departing one. Weeping, Com-
plaint, and Mourning follow, and Clawing-at-the-Face,
drenched with tears, Howling, the companion of funerals, 165
disheveled Hardship and Deprivation, tearing her hair, the
Honorable Gesture of the battered breast and robes of
mourning, their knots held fast by the comb of tightly
clasped hands.

"Inserit ergo manum trabeis gremioque reducto
170 exuit, et dextrae sceptrum, diadema revellit
crinibus, et Stygiae spoliatum mandat harenae.
Funebrique tuba victrix circumsonat aulam,
et superis vindex clangoribus aethera pulsat,
optatumque deis reserat clamore triumphum;
175 et de divitibus nota est victoria caelo.

Capitulum 7

Exclamatio in divitias

"O subito lapsurus apex! O pendula rerum
ardua, praecipitem gravius factura ruinam!
O mundi lugubris honos et debile robur,
divitiae, Fati dubio quassabile flatu!
180 Haud procul a mentis oculo ventura recedat
illa dies, quam clausa Dei prudentia differt
occultamque videt, quae, tandem cognita, regum
mordeat excessus, poenamque excedere crimen
vindicet; et laqueis doleant crudescere regna.
185 "Nec solio parcet superum clementior urna,
nec poenam redimes, quod mundum polluit, auro,
cum, trabea tandem cessura moribus, ignis
quem Phlegethon sudat gemmarum diluet ignes,

"Death then grasps the robe of state and pulls it away from the body within, plucks the scepter from the right 170 hand, the crown from the head, and relegates the despoiled body to the Stygian strand. Victorious, she causes funereal trumpets to resound through the court; and as heaven's avenger she makes the skies throb with loud music, announcing clamorously a triumph pleasing to the gods; a victory 175 over wealth is acknowledged in heaven.

Chapter 7

An outcry against wealth

"O pinnacle destined for a sudden fall! Your steep and precarious height will make the headlong fall harder! Riches, the world's sad honor, a fragile bulwark, easily shaken by the random winds of Fate! Let that coming day not be hidden 180 from the mind's eye, that day which the hidden Wisdom of God holds in store and secretly foresees, and which, made known at last, may attack the excesses of kings, and avenge penalties that exceed the crime; and royal power, in chains, will lament its cruelty.

"No merciful decree of heaven will spare the throne, nor 185 may you pay the penalty with gold, which pollutes the world, when the robe of state will at last succumb to virtue, when the fire which Phlegethon exudes will dim the blaze of your

vernabitque deum solio trabeata casarum
190 sobrietas. Tandemque dato fulgebit in ostro
gaudebitque, velit Dominus!, vitale Iohannes
aeternare iubar, roseis ardere coronae
sideribus, quam non odium, non fortior aetas,
immo nec invidiae rabies suspecta venenis
195 excutiat; vitemque metet quam plantet honestas."

Capitulum 8

Oratio Diogenis de contemptu mundi

Hic subicit, nec amara timens nec dulcia sperans,
Diogenes, fixus animo, sed mobilis aede:
"Si quicquid gemino Phoebus complectitur arcu
imperio stringas, tumulo non maior humandus
200 occidis; et tandem, cui non suffecerat orbis,
magnus Alexander parvae non sufficit urnae.
Si Paridis formae rosei praecellere oris
gloria, nec vultus maculae nubesceret umbra,
occiduus sol ille perit, floremque iuventae
205 vel fati caesura terit vel lima senectae.
    "Si praelustre genus, si regius ortus adusque
innumeros decurrat avos, non sanguinis illa
lux addit meritis; patrem dediscit in ense

jewels, and the sobriety of the cottager will shine in royal splendor on a divine throne. Then at last, God willing, Johannes himself will glory in the gift of a purple mantle and rejoice at the eternally living radiance that flashes from the glowing stars of a crown which no hatred, no more violent age, which not even the hateful malice of envy may remove; then will worthiness harvest what it sows."

190

195

Chapter 8

Diogenes's oration on scorning worldly things

Next spoke Diogenes, who neither feared hardship nor yearned for pleasure, steadfast in mind, but of no fixed abode: "Though you should subject to your dominion whatever Phoebus's double arc encompasses, you will not be too great to be buried in a tomb when you die; in the end great Alexander, for whom a world was not enough, was himself not enough to fill a small urn. Though the glory of a rosy face surpass the beauty of Paris, and no trace of a blemish mar the countenance, this sun too is doomed to set, and either a sudden blow of fate or the file of old age will efface its youthful bloom.

200

205

"Though your family is distinguished, though your royal heritage extends back to countless ancestors, this distinction of blood does not enhance your merit: the son of

Neptanabi proles, matremque absolvit in armis.
210 Si Famae radies titulis insignis et alto
nomine gemmescas, animae non tergis olentes
sub Fama redolente notas, nam mentis inumbrat
laudis oliva rubum, nec spinam pectore vellis.
Si quicquid Socratis exundat Fama capaci
215 hauseris ingenio, nihil est hausisse: tuumque
insipidum scire est, nisi quod condivit honestas;
nec morum redimit cumulata scientia damnum.
Si longo senii fastidia traxeris aevo
Nestor, et ad quarti numerus processerit annos
220 limitis, exiguam sub morte crepuscula lucem
claudunt; et sedes superest suprema sepulcrum.
Si toto physicae lucteris robore lucis
continuasse moras, stamen tamen Atropos aevi
rumpit, et in mortem non est praescriptio. Vitae
225 producitque dies sed non medicina perennat.
    "Si quicquid Tyrius accendit murice pecten
aut Sidonis acus, naturae simia, Serum
velleribus fecunda parit, si quicquid ubique
vestis abest, habeas, uni toga sufficit una.
230 Si quicquid gremio nutrit Rhea, lactat in undis
Nereus aut Bacchus pressa vomit ebrius uva,
affluat, et pretio cultuque arrideat ori
copia, quo turges, uterum non amplius imples.
Si variae sedes, si sit populosa domorum
235 turba tibi, si mille lares, si milia, sola

Nectanabus disavowed his patrimony with his sword and absolved his mother by force of arms. Though you gleam with the emblems of Renown and the splendor of a lofty title, you do not wipe away the foul-smelling vices that lurk beneath the sweet odor of fame, for the olive tree of praise overshadows the thicket of the mind, but you cannot pluck the thorns from your breast. Though you should drink in with capacious understanding all that redounds to the fame of Socrates, it is nothing to have done this: knowledge is of no value, unless it be steeped in worthiness; no amount of knowledge can redeem a ruined character. Though you be a Nestor, protracting by longevity the tedium of old age, though the number of your years extend to the fourth generation, evening will close up your feeble light in death; the final resting place is the tomb. Though you strive to prolong the light of life by all the power of medicine, Atropos still breaks the stem of life, and there is no prescription against death. Medicine can prolong the days of your life, but not make them last forever.

"Though you should possess all that the Tyrian shell has illumined with its purple dye, whatever design the Sidonian needle, aping nature, has brought to birth on the cloths of China, or whatever sort of garment is anywhere to be found, a single robe is still enough for anyone. Though you should be amply possessed of all to which the womb of Rhea gives life, all that Nereus nurtures with his tides, or drunken Bacchus spews forth from the wine press; though an abundance of costly delicacies should grace your mouth so that you become swollen, your belly will be none the fuller. Though you possess several dwellings, or a cluster of houses filled with retainers, though you have a thousand abodes, or thousands,

te capit una domus; et frustra, nanus, in astra
turribus accedis, casula contentus Amyclae."

Capitulum 9

Oratio Socratis de commendatione Diogenis, Cratetis et Democriti

Vix ea, cum Socratis surgens facundia verbo
continuat verbum; reliquos affatur et ora
240 sermonemque simul socias convertit ad aures:
"Haec rigui virtus Cynici, quam nulla soluti
polluit ebrietas luxus. O sobria pransi
laetaque ieiuni saties! O rara verendae
maiestas casulae! Soliumque volubilis aulae
245 doliolum, cuius patula fore ianua numquam
limine nodatur; non obiectura frequenti
hostia convivae, nec mandatura repulsae
dedecus occursu. Fervorem, frigus, utrumque
evasura malum nec conquestura molestas
250 aeris esse vices. Properanti terga periclo
obicit, et versae faciem non verberat Austris
Aeolus, imber aquis, nive bruma, vaporibus aestas.

a single house alone can still contain you; it is vain, dwarf
that you are, to raise your towers to the stars, when Amy-
clas's hut can accommodate you."

Chapter 9

Socrates's speech commending
Diogenes, Crates, and Democritus

Scarcely has he ended when the lofty eloquence of Socrates
adds speech to speech; his expression engages the others as   240
he directs his words to their friendly ears: "Such is the virtue
of the water-drinking Cynic, which no drunken fit of unbri-
dled excess has defiled. O sober, happy sufficiency of a fru-
gal meal! O spare dignity of a dwelling small yet venerable! A
little cask is the throne of his rolling court, whose wide en-   245
trance is never obstructed by a barrier; it imposes no obliga-
tion of sacrifice on a throng of would-be dinner guests, and
issues no insulting message of rejection by closing. It avoids
the evils of both heat and cold, and does not complain that   250
changes of weather are troublesome. It turns its back at the
approach of danger, and Aeolus's autumnal stormwinds, the
spring rains, the snows of winter and the summer's heat do
not strike its averted face.

"Magni sprevit opes, curarum pondus, et aurum
insidiis plenum. Suspectaque munera leti
255 horruit, intactus gladios ridere latronum
maluit et iuguli vacuus servasse cruorem.
Erubuit transisse modum, quod flumina ligno
hauserat, et calicis digitos collegit in orbem,
libandoque manus docuit servire fluento,
260 omnifico facta Naturae pocula torno.
Indolis activa placuit, passiva laborum
paupertas, vitii declinativa, malorum
ablativa, virum genitiva, dativa bonorum.
    "Flevit opum risus lacrima, mordente Platonis
265 Sidonio fastu corrupta cubilia mente
et pede calcavit. Naturae fercula numquam
fastidivit: olus pallenti maluit unda,
quam linguae phaleris Siculum mollire tyrannum,
alter Aristippus; vestiri cannabe liber
270 quam trabea servus; et se quam regibus uti
integer. Haud sapido praetextae laesus odore,
uberius felix animae quam vestis in auro.
    "Cum peteret, voto studii, Thebanus Athenas
philosophus Crates, notumque potentibus agmen
275 collegisset, opes socias, dissuada Minervae
pondera, mersit eas, ne mersaretur ab illis,
passus, ut expensis impensa pecunia pessum
pessima pressetur, meritamque ut naufraga poenam
naufragii lativa ferat.

"Diogenes spurned the riches of Alexander, his burdensome worries, and his gold fraught with treachery. He recoiled from gifts which carry the threat of death, preferring 255 to laugh unscathed at the robber's sword, and to preserve his throat's blood in freedom. He was mortified at having transgressed his own rule and drunk water from a wooden cup; he formed a circular bowl of his fingers, and taught his hands, a goblet fashioned on the all-creating lathe of Na- 260 ture, to assist him in drinking from the stream. Poverty pleased him, as active in disposition, passive in enduring hardship, and declinative of vice—ablative of evil, genitive of manliness, dative of virtue.

"He wept at the laughter of the wealthy, and in thought 265 and act he trampled on the bed of Plato, corrupted by a Sidonian pride that stung him. He never rejected Nature's food: he chose to soften cabbage with clear water, rather than mollify a Sicilian tyrant with ornate language, like Aristippus; to be a free man dressed in coarse cloth rather than a 270 slave in a robe of state; to be true to himself, rather than to kings. Never infected by the rich aura of a purple garment, he was more abundantly blessed in the riches of mind than of dress.

"When the Theban philosopher Crates, wishing to study, was sailing to Athens, and had assembled a company of the sort well known to great men, a body of riches, a burden in- 275 compatible with Minerva, he cast it overboard, rather than be drowned by it, allowing his money, an evil thing devoted to spending, to sink under its own weight, that a thing productive of shipwreck might suffer the shipwreck it deserved.

"Cum tenderet illo
280 isdem Democritus studiis accensus, avari
sacra suosque deos, loculos, abiecit. Avitos
distribuit census, librisque extructa Minervam
sorbuit, inserto consurgens mantica Phoebo.
Plena sophismaticis set opum ieiuna, Camenis
285 intumuit, gravida concusso Pallade dorso."

Capitulum 10

Oratio Democriti quod divitiae non sunt habendae nisi ut expendantur

Haec ubi, Democritus: "Nulli placuisse merentur
quae Styga pro fructu pariunt. Haec omnia tractu
duratura brevi, nimias mentita carenti
delicias, illumque minus factura beatum
290 cui magis accedent. Reprimantur vota sitisque
extinguatur opum; nec clauso pectore census
ardor agat rimas.
          "Opibus tamen omnis in omnes
omnia posse potest; per eas suspectus ab hoste
extorquetur amor, nodoque adversa ligantur
295 insolido. Censuque nefas suasura fugatur
pauperies. Liceat: est ipsa pecunia sanctis

"Democritus, too, when on his way to Athens inspired by 280
the same zeal for learning, cast away his riches, the shrines
and idols of the greedy man. He gave away his ancestral
estate, and his knapsack, stuffed with books, swollen by the
infusion of Phoebus, drank its fill of Minerva. Full of mor-
sels of wisdom, albeit lean in worldly goods, it waxed great
in the Muses' gifts, pregnant with Pallas as it bounced 285
against his back."

Chapter 10

Democritus's oration: riches should be possessed only to be spent

After this, Democritus spoke: "The riches which bear dam-
nation as their fruit bring pleasure to none. All such things
will last for a short time, offering a false image of boundless
delights to him who lacks them, but making a man less
happy the more he possesses. Be the wish rebuked and the 290
thirst for wealth extinguished; let not the burning desire for
property crack the vessel of the spirit.

"And yet by means of wealth it is possible for anyone to
impose anything upon anyone; through wealth an uneasy
love is extorted from an enemy, and opponents are linked
by its insecure bond. The poverty which draws one into 295
wrongdoing is banished by possession. So be it: money

accipienda viris licite quesita; datores
magnanimos habeat, et dantibus affluat, arcae
non inserta diu, rara et brevis hospita, numquam
300   incola, nec turpe loculi questura sepulcrum.
　　"Collige sparsurus, mete quae discretio dextrae
seminet; et summum dandi prudentia nomen
germinet, et meritis fructum producat in astris.
Invidiosa Titi sit dextera, munera tanto
305   a simili sparge. Quo dives splendeat astrum
esse puta munus, oblitam dona memento
amisisse diem. Loculos signasse ruborem
inferat, et census quae pondere sudat anhelet
distribuendo manus. Fudit Fortuna, refundat
310   dextra; nec ardorem dandi respectus avari
congelet. Ille tibi Romani maximus auctor
muneris occurrat, immo quem fausta dedere
tempora Normannis, qui dandi sidere mundo
et superis fulget; cui, qua non praebuit, haec est
315   visa nefasta dies; ille est cui Copia cornu
fundendique vicem ieiuno tradidit orbe."

legitimately acquired should be acceptable to virtuous men; let it be held by magnanimous donors, and accrue to these givers, not to be long stored in chests, but as a brief and fleeting guest, never a resident, who would complain of the sordid tomb of a coffer.

"Gather in to spread abroad, reap only what your hand may considerately sow again: wise husbandry will bring forth the lofty title of donor, and bear the fruit of a reward among the stars. Make the hand of Titus himself seem grudging, by strewing gifts in a way so similar to his. Think of a gift as a star that makes a rich man shine, and remember that you have wasted the day on which you have forgotten to give. May you blush to have sealed up a moneybag, and let that hand which sweats under the weight of its wealth exhaust itself in bestowing that wealth. What Fortune grants, let your hand grant anew; let not the concerns of the greedy man cool your ardor for giving. Be mindful of that greatest agent of the bounty of Rome, still more of him whom a blessed time bestowed upon the Normans, whose generous star shines on earth and in heaven; to him the day on which he has not made a grant is profaned; to him Abundance has entrusted the office of showering forth her fruits on a starving world."

Capitulum 11

Oratio Ciceronis de prodigalitate vitanda

Hic Cicero verbis instantibus ora resolvens:
"Dando tamen praefige modum; substringe solutos
muneris excursus. Iusto Moderantia fine
320 temperet expensas; cedatque improvida caeci
ebrietas luxus, moderandi limite dandi
luxuriem praecinge. Pati largitio frenum
noverit; et quantum permittit Copia, funde
largus. In exhibitis habiti modus arbiter esto,
325 meta sit expensae dandique auriga facultas.
 "Luxus opum consumit opem, dandique potestas
carpitur et carpit. Non est insania maior
quam quod posse cupis niti non posse. Daturus
et dans esse nequis, si luxum consulis. Ille
330 hoc illo perimit; dare quod manus ebria spargit
ire datum tollit. Sumptu consumeris; urges
quod doleas; spernis hodie quod crastinus optes.
 "Prodige de pleno vacuum concludis, amarum
de sapido, de luce lutum, de Caesare Codrum,
335 ludibrium de laude, nihil de quolibet. Istud
prodiga prodigium novit manus: amplius aequo
amplificans sumptus, habitisque licentius utens
quam liceat; Natura petit, Fortuna ministret.

Chapter 11

Cicero's oration on avoiding prodigality

Then Cicero gave forth these earnest words: "Yet establish a limit for your giving; control the flowing forth of your bounty. Let moderation keep your expenditure within proper bounds, avoid the reckless drunkenness of blind excess, and confine indulgence within the limits of well regulated giving. Largesse will learn to submit to restraint; give as generously as your resources permit. Let moderation govern your displays of wealth; let your means set a limit on expense, and guide your chariot in giving.

"Excess in the use of wealth consumes wealth; the capacity to give is fed by it and devours it. There is no greater madness than striving to make yourself unable to do what you desire to do. If you pursue excess, you cannot both give and continue to give. Such giving dies by its own act: the gifts that a drunken hand strews abroad cancel future giving. By such expense you expend yourself; you do eagerly what you will regret; you make light today of what you will wish for tomorrow.

"By prodigality you create emptiness out of fullness, bitter out of sweet, gloom from light, a Codrus from a Caesar, mockery from praise, nothing from anything. The prodigal hand knows this one prodigy: the expansion of expense beyond measure, and the use of possessions with illicit license; Nature asks one way of life, Fortune provides another.

"Carptor opum vilescit inops. Dum divite dextra
340   dat, redolet; post munus olens mendicat ubique,
inveniens nusquam. Queritur dum quaerit amaros
non praescisse dies, cum dulcibus usus amico
fideret in Fato. Pudet illis esse pudori
quos dives decuit; fusi reminiscitur aeris,
345   amissique piget, et opes fluxisse refluxum
non habuisse dolet. Fati resilire favorem
ingemit, et vellet, Fortuna dante, dedisse
parcius, et dextrae male praecavisse sinistram
devovet. Et sero quem laeserit alea ludi
350   paenitet; elususque manum qua luserit odit."

Capitulum 12

Oratio Plinii quid sequatur ex luxu

Talibus annectit redolenti Plinius ore:
"Prodigus es, sequitur: eris indigus. Huius Egestas
est vitii vindex, meritaque ulciscitur ira
Pauperies luxum, tenui contracta cubili,

"He who pares away his wealth becomes worthless in poverty. While he gives with lavish hand his scent is sweet; but when the giving is over he is foul smelling, everywhere begging, nowhere receiving. As he begs he laments that he did not foresee these bitter days, while he enjoyed life's sweets, and trusted Fate as a friend. He is ashamed to be an object of shame to those to whom when wealthy he was a fitting companion; he remembers his squandered money, grieves over its loss, and laments that for the wealth that has flowed away there is no flowing back. He bemoans the elusive favor of Fate; he wishes that Fortune had granted him the ability to give more sparingly, and he would sacrifice his left hand to have been forewarned of the evil tendency of his right. Too late does he whom the dice have ruined regret having played; only having lost does he hate the hand that made the cast."

Chapter 12

Pliny's oration on the consequences of excess

To this Pliny added his own sweet-scented words: "If you are a prodigal, it follows: you will be poor. Want is the scourge of this vice, and poverty avenges excess with justified wrath,

355 panniculo sordens, ventri ieiunia longo
indicens odio. Cereris Bacchique recedunt
accessus soliti; stomacho succedit inani
aegra fames ardensque sitis. Vacuumque rapinae
instruit, et dextram qua fuderit omnia furto
360 damnat, et aere manus alieno polluit, omne
pro modico suasura nefas, clausisse bilingues
ingeniosa dolos, ut, qua sibi deficit, alter
supplementa ferat. Omni quo pauper abundet
limite procedit; et primi rursus inundat
365 diluvium Luxus; solitumque refluctuat aequor;
et manus ad dandi revolat, quem noverat, aestum.
   "Cura prodigitur dando qui prodigit. Aeris
creditor occurrit, gravis, urgens, improbus, acer,
impatiensque morae, repetendi prodigus, irae
370 largus, avarus opum. Tantoque protervius haeret
quo magis aeris eges, quo plus sub mole terentis
laederis usurae. Pulsat, ferit, instat; oportet
quod petit ut solvas, nec solvere sufficit arcae
aut loculi macies. Quid ages? Te pessimus ille
375 undique divellit; et dandi si qua reliquit
primus amor, dantur. Sed eo dilatio dono
venit emisque moras, sed qui prius institit idem
maturat reditum dolor. Interrupta quievit
rixa, sed ad tempus redit in fervore tumultus
380 asperior maiorque furor.
                         "Mors sola dolores
sopitura venit, latura beatius esse
et miseris optata quies. Solatia poenae,
quae vita est, mors poena parit. Respirat Egestas

crouching in its narrow bed, wrapped in foul rags, proclaim-   355
ing with longstanding hatred the emptiness of the belly. The
accustomed visits of Ceres and Bacchus cease; faint hunger
and burning thirst take over the empty stomach. Poverty
teaches the man who has nothing to steal, condemns to
thievery the hand with which he had once showered forth
all things, and defiles it with the money of others, urging any   360
wrongdoing for a small gain, and ingeniously hiding her du-
plicitous wiles, so that where her own means fail another's
may supplement them. She travels every path by which a
pauper may grow rich; the flood of excess rises again; the sea   365
flows in as of old; and the hand reverts to the storm of giving
it had known.

"He who is prodigal in giving is visited by prodigal wor-
ries. The moneylender visits him, grim, importunate, per-
sistent, aggressive, impatient of delay, prodigal of petitions,
lavish of anger, covetous of his money. He clings to you so   370
shamelessly that you become still more needy, harassed still
further by the grinding weight of his usury. He knocks,
pounds, intrudes; you must pay what he asks, and the ema-
ciation of your chest or purse has not sufficient means. What
are you to do? This worst of evils tears at you from every   375
side; and if the old love of giving has left you anything, this
too is given. But while deferral comes of this, and it buys de-
lay, the same trouble that had formerly afflicted you soon re-
turns. When his wrangling was suspended there was quiet,
but soon the shouting returns, harsher in its intensity and   380
rage.

"Only death will lay these sorrows to rest, bringing a hap-
pier condition and a long-awaited peace for those in misery.
The pain of death produces a solace for the pain that is life.

mortis in amplexu; vitaeque molestia leto
385 tollitur; et vulnus curatur vulnere, poena
poena, dolore dolor. Ut te tot, prodige, tandem
eruat adversis, ut tot pulsantibus obstet,
supremi metuenda venit clementia Fati.
    "Parcius a loculis expensae audacia surgat,
390 ad census contracta modum, ne debita mensi
devoret una dies, mensisque ligurriat anni
suffectura morae. Si qua est improvida, non est
saepe datura manus. Nemo nisi parcus habebit,
unde diu largus effundat muneris urnam;
395 solaque munifico laudes cautela perhennat."

Capitulum 13

Oratio Cratetis de
aulae incommodis

Interea dubio versans in pectore Crates
quando mersit opes, longum meditatus: "En" inquit
"en memini. Loculos odi, mundumque daturas
Fortunae contemno manus. Erroribus ortum
400 divitiae praestant et opes delicta tuentur;
libertasque datur vitiis et semina culpae
praefecunda iacit, nec non altissima Fati.

Need finds relief in the embrace of death, and the trouble of life is removed by it; wound is cured by wound, pain by pain, suffering by suffering. The fearful mercy of the fated final day has come, O prodigal, to free you at last from so many ills, shield you from so many cruel blows. 385

"Let spending issue less boldly from your purse, and be kept to the limits of your resources, lest a single day consume what should suffice for a month, or a month lick up the supplies for a whole year. The hand that gives improvidently will not give often. No one who is not frugal will be able to maintain for long the flow of generous gifts from his urn; only caution can ensure an enduring reputation for munificence." 390

395

Chapter 13

Crates's oration on the ills of the courtier's life

Meanwhile Crates was anxiously mulling over the day when he had cast his wealth into the sea. "Yes" he said, after long reflection, "yes, I remember. I detest riches, and I scorn Fortune's hand though it should offer me the world. Riches provide an opening for error, and wealth shields our crimes; it gives free rein to vice, and sows the all-too-fertile seeds of wickedness, the abysses of Fate. A day of security never 400

Nulla venit sincera dies: maiorque potestas
saevius a ludo Fortunae laeditur, et plus
405 solliciti quam pacis habet, semperque beatos
altius, adversis labor inclementius urget.
     "Nulla quies aulae! Circumvenit improbus aulam
curarum populus, vexat congesta laborum
turba potestates, alienativa quietis
410 agmina concurrunt: regni custodia; iuris
sollicitudo minor; tractanda negotia; causae;
iudicis examen; lis decidenda, querelae;
pauperis instantis pulsatio crebra; rogantis
importuna manus; precibusque interflua rixae
415 asperitas quam pigra parit dilatio recti.
     "Rarus ibi somnus. Vigilatae taedia noctis
indolitura dies equitantis vexat ocellum
semita delicti, culpae via, strata reatus,
methodus inferni, Stygis orbita, limes Averni.
420 Nugarum lituus, falsi tuba, tibia ficti,
bucina rumoris: denso strepit aula tumultu.
Altiloquus quatit astra fragor, tollitque soporem
et superis, fessasque Iovis ferit arduus aures.
Undique garritur: hic verbum supprimit, ille
425 erigit; hic linguae tumidus tonat, ille susurrat;
hic socium tangit, vitium mordente cachinno;
publicat ille scelus, gravius laedente susurro.
Ille movet rixas, hic corripit; ille flagello
vapulat, hic lingua; contemnitur ille vel illa,
430 praevalet is vel ea.

comes: the greater the power the more fiercely it is harassed by Fortune's whims; it knows more of worry than of peace, and the burden always afflicts the favored few with troubles more deeply and severely. 405

"There is no rest at court! An unruly mob of troubles roams the halls, a dense crowd of tasks worries men of power, armies hostile to peace charge toward them: affairs of state, petty legal difficulties, business to be transacted, cases at law, judicial inquiries, disputes and complaints to be resolved, the continual clamor of the demanding poor, the importunate hand of the plaintiff, the harsh sound of anger interspersed with entreaties to which the slow dispensation of justice gives rise. 410 415

"Sleep is rare at court. Days, suffering the lingering effects of wakeful nights, trouble the eyes of the knight who travels the path of sin, the road of wrongdoing, the highway of guilt, an infernal scheme, winding path to the Styx, passage to Avernus. The court resounds with continual tumult: the clarion call of petty quarrels, the trumpet of falsehood, the pipes of deception, the great horn of rumor. The clash of loud voices makes the stars tremble, robs the very gods of sleep, and strikes the weary ears of Jove on high. There is chattering everywhere: when one stops speaking, another begins; one speaks out in inflated language, another whispers; one man criticizes a companion, nipping at his vicious conduct with laughter; another exposes a crime in the whisper that wounds more severely. One man provokes a quarrel, another takes it up; the first is attacked by a lash, the other by a tongue; one or the other is put down, one or the other prevails. 420 425 430

　　　　　"Raro tamen elicit aula
eloquio laudes, et se vix aulicus offert
laudandi studio; sepelit quod novit honestum,
denudat vitium, meritum sub criminis umbra
occulit, et Famae picturam moribus aufert.

435　　　"Hic scelus antiquum memorat, gaudetque relatum
non solus scivisse nefas. Nullique pudendum
commisisse pudet; socii submurmurat aurae
laudantis facinus, avidoque in crimina verbo
iactitat hic factum, deliberat ille futurum.

440　Non phaleris, non felle vacat fecunda malorum
lingua parens, omnisque pluit facundia nugas.

　　　　"O male felices, quorum nec purpura morbos
nec loculus curat; nec opes suprema morantur
Fata, nec ad nervum revocatur mortis harundo.

445　Dives apud Ditem veniam non impetrat auro;
nec cupidae vendit Cereris gener auctius aevum.
Non parcit trabeae subeunti Cerberus, illum
nec regni gladius nec mitrae cornua terrent.
Non homines humana beant. Similemque beato

450　forma, genus, praetexta facit, virtusque beatum."

"Yet rarely does the eloquence of the court issue in praises, and scarcely ever does a courtier show himself eager to praise; the court conceals what it knows to be honorable, and exposes what is vicious, covers over merit with the suggestion of wrongdoing, and thereby robs the character of its reputable appearance.

"Here a man recounts his past misdeeds, and is not the 435 only one to enjoy knowing of the wickedness he reports. No one is ashamed to have committed shameful acts; he confides his guilt to the ear of an applauding ally, and while he boasts of what he has done, in words that show his eagerness for crime, the other ponders what he will do. The 440 tongue, that teeming parent of evil, has no lack of ornate and poisonous words, and all its eloquence is showered on petty crimes.

"Cursed in their good fortune, no purple robe or full purse can minister to their disease; wealth will not defer the fated final day, and the mortal arrow cannot be recalled to the string. Dives for all his gold will find no favor in Dis; the 445 son-in-law of yearning Ceres will not sell an extended lease on life. Cerberus does not spare one who descends in stately robes, nor does he fear the royal sword or horned miter. Human things do not make men happy. Beauty, noble birth, 450 robes of office make one appear happy, but virtue that makes one happy."

Capitulum 14

Oratio Senecae de gloriae contemptu

"Sentit idem Crates quod sentio; novimus aulam,"
altitonantis ait Lucani patruus, ille
quo Nero defuncto quam vivo maluit uti.
"Optima paupertas possessio! Iulius orbem
455 sorbuit, et somnum vacui laudavit Amyclae.
Fulgor opum caecat; Fortuna miserrima, quid sit,
est homini factura fidem. Quid possit in alto,
cernit in oppresso; quo fructu prospera rident,
in lacrimis adversa vident. Quo gloria tollat,
460 inferiora docent. An virtus nana Gigantum
in superos esset, et debeat esse timori
Iupiter, an possit deitas impune lacessi,
Enceladi tandem rabies extincta probavit.
Et probat, iniectam quotiens demugit ob Aetnam,
465 alternatque latus humero nervoque sonanti,
aut manibus niti dorsoque assurgere temptat.
    "Occubuit temere surgens Titania Virtus,
et caret optato praesumens Gloria fine.
Tollo pedem fixumque ligo, nam lubricus ille
470 est locus; accessu facilis gressuque relato
difficilis. Raptisque Notis Elatio turget,
et subito quaevis tumet Excellentia vento;
et tenui novit illabi Gloria rima.

Chapter 14

Seneca's oration on scorning glory

"Crates's feelings are my own; for we know the court," says
the uncle of high-thundering Lucan, he whom Nero appre-
ciated better dead than alive. "The best of possessions is
poverty! Julius swallowed the whole world, yet praised the   455
slumber of impoverished Amyclas. The gleam of wealth
blinds us; the worst of ill fortune will make a man sure of
what he is. When cast down one sees what one might be if
raised up; weeping adversity sees the fruits that make pros-
perity smile for what they are. A lowered condition teaches
us how glory exalts us. When the madness of Enceladus   460
was finally extinguished, he had proof that the strength of
Giants was dwarfed by that of the gods, that Jupiter was to
be feared, that his godhead could not be attacked with im-
punity. And he proves it still, whenever he groans because of
Aetna heaped upon him, turns himself over with creaking   465
joints and muscles, or tries to stretch out his arms and arch
his back.

"The strength of the Titans, rising in folly, was cast down,
and their Glory-seeking presumption failed of its desired
goal. I turn my steps away and hold fast to my course, for the
place is treacherous; it is easy to enter and difficult to re-   470
trace one's path. Elation is puffed up by the winds it has
caught, and every sort of Excellence is swollen by their sud-
den blast; the love of Glory can enter our minds through a
mere fissure.

Capitulum 15

De Alexandro

"Altius ingenio raptus quam corpore, mundos
475 innumeros potuit animo numerasse suosque
Pythagoras superos. Stupidus narrante dolebat
Magnus Anaxarcho; nec aperto lingua dolori
defuit, et morbum gemitu testatus anhelo:
'Ha miser!' exclamat 'vacuos rectoris inermes
480 tot video mundos, mihi nondum serviat unus;
nec mea dignatur casa mundus sceptra, nec unum
exaequasse Iovem Pellaeis glorior armis.'
    "O nimis excurrens Praesumptio! Nescia votis
Ambitio praeferre modum, quae sola iubendi
485 anxia, diis solis regnantibus invidet orbem.
Fixum non habuit successum gloria: Magnum
parvula, qui mundos sitiebat, sorbuit urna.

Chapter 15

Alexander

"Borne aloft more in understanding than in body, the mind of Pythagoras was capable of enumerating innumerable worlds, each with its gods. Stupefied by Anaxarchus's account, great Alexander grieved; speech was not lacking to express his grief openly, and he revealed his suffering in a painful groan: 'Wretch that I am!' he cries, 'for I behold so many worlds, lacking rulers and defenseless, but as yet not a single world owes service to me; not even the world where I dwell acknowledges my scepter, nor may I glory in having made myself the equal of even a single Jove by force of Pellaean arms.'

"O too unrestrained Presumption! Ambition that knows no limit to its hopes, tormented by the desire to command, looks jealously on a world ruled only by its gods. But the pursuit of glory attains no lasting success: a little urn swallowed the great Alexander, who had thirsted for entire worlds.

Capitulum 16

De morte Homeri

"Quaestio quam praedo fluvialis movit Homero
institit ad mortis lacrimas, nervosior ultra
490   quam quae Maeonii posset succumbere luctae.
Plus aequo doluit vulgo vilescere, Famae
laudibus incisis inconsolanter adauctae
iacturam gemuit. Qui non est passus, ut ampli
nominis arduitas modica pro parte labasset,
495   nec tulit, ut nomen tenui nubesceret umbra."

Chapter 16

The death of Homer

"A question which a plunderer of the river put to Homer, one too knotty to yield to the efforts of the Maeonian, drove 490 him to mortal sorrow. He grieved beyond measure at appearing commonplace to common people, mourned inconsolably the damage to his Renown from the cessation of praise. He could not endure that the loftiness of his glorious name be diminished in the least, nor suffer it to be clouded 495 by the slightest shadow."

BOOK SEVEN

Capitulum 1

Quam diligenter audiat Architrenius philosophos loquentes

Rivos eloquii prono succedere cursu
et videt, et mentis bibit Architrenius ore;
et riguas capitis et cordis inebriat aures.
Dumque bibendo sitit, nec sentit hydropicus unde
5 congestos calyces; nisi fesso vase bibendi
continuetur item. Vix respirarat, et ecce
iam decimum rursus eiusdem pocula Bacchi
pectoris a plena Symmachi gener extrahit urna,
Nec de divitibus timet integrasse querelas.

Capitulum 2

Oratio Boethii de potentum inclementia

10 "O meritos extrema pati, quos ardua tollit
ala potestatis; quorum clementia numquam
hospita divertit, sed mortis larga tyrannis,

Chapter 1

How intently Architrenius listens to the philosophers' speeches

Architrenius perceives the stream of eloquence moving steadily forward, and the mouth of his mind drinks it in; its intoxicating effect flows through the ears of head and heart. Since he is made thirsty by drinking, he does not notice, in his dropsical state, how the goblets are accumulating; unless 5 the vessel is weary of drinking, let it continue in the same way. Scarcely has he caught his breath when lo, Symmachus's son-in-law for a tenth time draws a goblet of the same wine from the brimming urn of his heart, and fearlessly renews the complaint against the wealthy.

Chapter 2

Boethius's oration on the harshness of rulers

"Deserving of the most extreme punishment are those 10 whom the soaring wings of power bear aloft; their kindness never entertains a guest, but the tyrant is generous with

iustorum risura neces, factura flagello
quod pietatis erit. Ha, nulla potentia rebus
15   oppressis tranquilla venit; non sumit ab illa
pauper opes vel opem. Gravis est flexisse favorem
inferius, qui summa potest; aciesque laborat
ardua, pressa videns. Raro qui surgit in aulam
respexisse casam placido dignatur ocello.
20   "Spernit anhelantis animi suspiria, surda
praeterit aure preces, lacrimis insultat easque
ridet habere dolos. Clamosaque pectora planctu
exaudire vetat, gemitusque adversa loquentes
vix recipit vultu, faciem pallore minantem
25   horridiore fugit, domitas regnante repellit
paupertate genas, fluidos maerore tumenti
nauseat ore sinus, senio rumpente solutos.
Non iuvenum cautela minor, non fracta senectus,
non levior sexus quam longa intorsit egestas,
30   non oris ferrugo movet, non sordida vultus
ariditas, non cura genis scriptura senectam,
non exesa fames, maciesque domestica leto,
non quicquid Siculos posset movisse iuvencos.
Pauperis haud umquam fatum lugubre potentis
35   extorquet lacrimam; tenuis Fortuna beatos
nescit in affectum tenuem flexisse. Minorum
damna minus maiora movent; soliique facultas
non meminit fragmenta casae, non sarcit hiantes
paupertate sinus, non aegri exterminat oris
40   attritam maciem, vacui non expedit usum
pauperis. Angustis saties angustior aulae,
plenius ad plenos opibus venit.

death, laughs at the slaying of just men, performs his acts of
mercy with a whip. Power never enters gently into the lives 15
of the oppressed; the poor man derives from it neither
wealth nor aid. It is difficult for one who commands the
heights to direct his favor downward; to observe the down-
trodden is a hardship for his sight. Rarely does one who
attains the court deign to look back with a kindly eye on the
cottage.

"Power ignores the sighs of the exhausted spirit, turns a 20
deaf ear to prayers, mocks at tears and laughingly suggests
that they are false. It refuses to hear the loud cries of the
complaining spirit, barely acknowledges with a glance sobs
that tell of adversity, flees a face frightening in its terrible
pallor, rejects the cheek whose bloom has been overcome by 25
the tyranny of poverty, sickens at the sight of garments
made damp by the welling up of grief, or tattered by ravag-
ing age. Unprotected youth, crippled age, feminine weak-
ness long tormented by need, the blighted complexion, the 30
withered and filthy face, do not move the powerful, nor the
worry that inscribes the cheeks with the signs of age, wasted
hunger, the leanness that is near companion to death, things
that could move Sicilian bullocks to pity. Never does the
pauper's grim Fate exact a tear from the man of power; his 35
meager lot cannot draw those blessed ones to a meager
show of feeling. The greatest disasters of small people move
them not at all; he who possesses a throne does not notice
the destruction of a cottage, mend garments torn open by
poverty, eliminate the worn emaciation of the sick man's 40
face, or provide for the needs of the utterly destitute. The
abundance of the court is penurious toward those in penury,
but gives itself amply to those of ample means.

"Ipsa potestas
extorquet sibi cuncta dari. Maioraque magnis
accedunt, peiora bonis; si pluris habundes,
45   dantis plura feres; si quis caret, ipse carebit.
Maior opum maiora capit, maioris egenti
fit minus; et quaerit manus errantissima dantis,
non qui plus egeat, sed qui plus possit habere.
Dantis apud dextram non intercedit Honestum,
50   non animae vernantis odor; non impetrat ipsis
proxima diis Virtus, nec Famae cognita morum
Canities, nec fixa gravi Constantia vultu,
nec corrosa genas, marcenti livida labro
Religio, non fracta malis, nulloque tumultu
55   flexa voluptatis, animi vallata rigore.
   "De tot divitibus nulli datur uncia Codro.
Dilapidantur opes, Gula sic disponit et ultor
Luxus Avaritiae, violens exactor Honesti,
lenaque nec morum minus exactiva Libido."

Capitulum 3

Oratio Xenocratis de Libidine

60   Ad suprema gemit Xenocrates verba, nec ultra
protrahit excitum reticendi lingua soporem:

"Power takes all by force to bestow it upon herself. Greater gifts are bestowed on the great, lesser ones on the good; the more amply you are endowed, the more gifts you will receive; if one is in need, he will remain in need. The great man receives the greater portion, while less is done for him whose need is greater; so erratic is the hand of the giver that he asks, not who is most in need, but who may possess the most. Worthiness does not intercede to guide the hand of the donor, nor the freshness of the springlike spirit; Virtue, that godlike quality, gains no favor here, nor the Ripeness of character that Renown acknowledges, nor firm Constancy with her grave face, nor Religion, her cheeks worn, her lips dull and withered, yet unbowed by misfortune, unmoved by any tumultuous desire, secure in her strength of spirit.

"Out of such riches, not a penny is bestowed on Codrus. Wealth is squandered as Gluttony decrees, and Luxury, the avenger of Avarice, who violently demands Probity as her price, and Lust, a bawd equally adept at extorting virtue."

Chapter 3

Xenocrates's oration on Lust

At these last words Xenocrates groans, and his tongue prolongs no further its reticent slumber: "Here is an evil which

"Ecce malum, quo cuncta dolent, quo terra laborat,
quo superi languent, quod Tartara movit et ipsum
saepe Iovem torsit. Quicquid vel surgit ad Euros
65 vel cadit ad Zephyros, quicquid vel despicit Arctos
vel Notus abscondit, urtica Libidinis urit.
     "Castra Pudicitiae furor hic praedulcis amara
obsidione ligat, facula contentus et arcu,
fracturusque levi votorum pondera risu.
70 Huius in amplexu vis plectitur, huius ab usu
Threicii morbi manavit abusio, cuius
Thracem paeniteat frustra, cum iudicis urna
venerit et fornax, si quos non coxerat ante
Orpheus, aeterno mores coctura camino.
75 Hora nimis properata malis, sed tarda beatis,
cum tandem Croesi fracto diademate, sceptrum
quod feret orbigenae dextrae clementia Codrus
induet. Et nostri Iovis ampla palatia paucos
accipient, nec erit populus quod peccat inultum.
80   "Haec satis est; hucusque licet meminisse profanam
morphosin, infaustum Naturae Protea, Thracum
Tisiphonen. Audire ipsum mihi fascinat aures
osque loqui, maculatque sacram conceptio mentem.
Quod decet, id sermo sapiat, fugiatque loquela,
85 quod Natura fugit. Satis est tetigisse, quod oris
inquinat officium nec conciliatur honesto.
Est satis ad vires in nostra pericula dandas
coniuga Naturae mundo concessa Libido,
quantum prolis amor et sacra iugalia poscunt.

all things suffer, through which the earth labors and the gods lose their power, which stirs Tartarus and has often tormented Jove himself. Whatever rises in the East or sinks in the West, whatever the Bears behold or the South conceals from us, burns with the nettle of Lust.

"This madness, surpassingly sweet, holds the forces of chastity under a bitter siege, content with mere torches and bows, yet able to overcome the power of prayer with a mere smile. Its power is involved with embracing, and from this practice stems that abuse known as the Thracian disease; for this let the Thracian repent in vain, when the urn and furnace of the judge shall be at hand to blast in eternal fire whatever such habits Orpheus himself has not already burned away. The hour is coming, too quickly for the wicked, slowly for the blessed, when the diadem of Croesus will finally be broken, and Codrus will assume that scepter which the mercy of the world-creating hand will bring. The spacious palace of our Jove will admit the few, and the sins of the many will not go unavenged.

"Enough of that; it is right to have said this much about the profane mutation, the ill-omened, Protean transformer of Nature, the Thracian Tisiphone. To hear such things and speak of them is an enticement to my ears and lips, but to dwell on them taints the sanctity of the mind. Let our speech be of what is fitting, and let our utterance shun what Nature herself shuns. It is enough to have touched on a thing which defiles the office of the lips and cannot be reconciled with decency. Suffice it to say that among these powers bestowed to our peril, Lust has been granted to the world as Nature's partner, to the extent that the love of offspring and the rites of marriage require.

90   "Ha, Cypri rabies! Quam dulci pace salutat,
      quem sibi venatur hominem; primoque propinat
      dulce, sed ex dulci tandem concludit amarum.
      Sic est blanda Venus; sic, quos melliverat ante,
      edidicit fellire favos; sic ultima taxo
95   toxicat et verna veniens hiberna recedit.
      Quam placida mentis oculos omnemque soporat
      nube diem, dum clausa sacri sub pectoris aula
      fervet, et irriguum fontem desiccat honesti.
      Tutius est gelida vitam glaciasse sub Arcto
100   quam semel in praeceps flexa rationis habena,
      Lotophagos Veneris libasse et pocula Circes;
      tutius aestiferae radiis ardere Syenes
      quam cesto posito Veneris sudasse camino;
      tutius indomitis animam fudisse lacertis
105   Herculis et Siculo rursus mugire iuvenco,
      quam iecur omnicremo fricuisse Libidinis igne.
      Vix ullo reprimo lacrimas adamante, quod ista
      blanda fames, quod grata sitis, quod mulcebris ardor
      carnem consumat, animam bibat, urat utrumque.
110   "O vere studio degentibus optima vitae
      forma foret, supraque deum secreta viderent,
      haec nisi trabs oculis obiecta studentibus esset.
      At sub sideribus deitas decisa beatis;
      non exacta datur; minor est quam plena bonorum
115   integritas, raroque venit sincera venustas.
         "Combussit Phrygium pastorem, Pergama, Graecos
      a Veneris surgens faculis amor, ignis et ira.
      Canduit Alcides Veneris Nessique veneno,
      Et Veneris Nessi conclusit in ignibus ignes,
120   dum quos interula teneros vestivit amores

"O Cyprian madness! How sweetly and gently she greets 90
the man she pursues; at first she offers him sweet delight,
but in the end bitterness comes of this sweetness. Such is
charming Venus; thus has she learned to make bitter those
honeycombs which she had first filled with honey; thus does
she finally make them as poisonous as the yew berry, and 95
what had come as spring departs as winter. With a calming
mist she lulls to sleep the eyes of the mind and dims the very
light of day, while the inner chamber of our blessed spirit
seethes, and dries up the brimming fount of decency. It is
safer to expose one's life to the icy Pole than once to impul- 100
sively tug the rein of reason, and taste Venus's lotos food and
the goblets of Circe; safer to burn under the rays of the hot
Egyptian sun than to unbuckle and sweat in the furnace of
Venus; safer to risk one's life in the invincible grip of Hercu- 105
les, to make the Sicilian bull roar once again, than to wear
away the liver in the all-consuming fire of Lust. Scarcely can
I restrain my tears by any sternness, when this enticing
hunger devours our flesh, this gratifying thirst drinks up our
spirit, this soothing fire burns both together.

"Truly the life of those dedicated to study would be the 110
best of all, and they would behold the mysteries of the gods
on high, if this beam did not obstruct their scholarly vision.
But far below the blessed stars divinity is diminished; a full
measure is not granted to us; the integrity even of good men
is less than perfect, and purity of spirit rarely appears. 115

"Love, fire and wrath, arising from the torch of Venus,
destroyed the Phrygian shepherd, Troy, and the Greeks. Al-
cides burned with the poison of Venus and of Nessus, and
Venus's fires led to those of Nessus, when she who clad him 120

vestiit interitu. Temere dum credidit hosti,
et fuit Alcide, Nesso, sibi Deianira
raptoris dolitura dolo: rogus, ultio, poena.
Alciden pudeat, quod eodem pollice pensum
125 Antaeique necem, nunc vir, nunc femina, nevit.
    "Novimus ut Circes gremium molliret Ulixem,
Penelopes rigidos cum nemo flecteret arcus.
Hoc sale, sal hominum, Salomon insulsus amari
demeruit, morem quod amaro gessit amori.
130 Infractum Samsona Venus confregit et ipsum
fortia rumpentem molli certamine rupit.
Occidit ad Colchon ortus Sulmone, Corinna
dum male delituit velati nominis umbra.
    "Sed quid in immensum cedit labor? Ut quid abyssum
135 metior? Incertas nullus definit harenas
calculus et numerus vaga vix amplectitur astra.
Nulla dolos Veneris capit area, nulla dolendi
sufficiunt exempla modis, ubi vulnus in alto
sedit, et igne Venus nocuit, nervoque Cupido.
140   "Ha, Venus imperii, quod nullos excipit annos;
quo senii lascivit hiems, inflexa virorum
mollescit gravitas, iuvenum calor uritur, annis
solvitur integritas teneris; quo mollior aetas,
ductilis in cunctas species, transumitur usus
145 in geminos, dum mas nubit vel femina ducit.

she tenderly loved in a shirt clad him in death. Since Deianira foolishly trusted her enemy, through the guile of the ravisher she was soon to mourn for Alcides, Nessus, and herself: Hercules's pyre, Nessus's revenge, her own suffering. Let it be Alcides's shame that with the same hand he both plied the distaff and wrought the death of Antaeus, a woman 125 at one moment, a man the next.

"We know that the embrace of Circe soothed Ulysses, while none might bend Penelope's rigid bow. The cleverest of men, Solomon, foolishly let himself be caught by love in a clever way, for he subjected himself to a love with bitter consequences. Venus destroyed the indestructible Samson, and 130 broke with a tender kind of warfare the strength that could break strong bonds. He who was born at Sulmona died at Colchis, for his Corinna concealed herself badly beneath the shadow of a veiled identity.

"But why should one labor at so vast a task? Why do I seek to measure the abyss? No reckoning can enumerate the 135 infinite sands, and number can hardly comprehend the wandering stars. No space can contain the wiles of Venus, no examples suffice to show her deceitful ways, when the wound is deep-seated, when Venus has stricken us with fire, Cupid with his bow.

"O dominion of Venus, which exempts no age; under it 140 the winter of the elderly grows wanton, the unbending gravity of manhood becomes soft, the blood of youth burns, the purity of tender years is undone; our malleable time of life, lending itself to behavior of all kinds, adopts ambiguous 145 customs, for males put on the bridal veil, and women take men in marriage.

"Ha, Venus, ad nutum trahis omnia numina celi,
astra moves alioque rotas errore planetas.
Accendis gelidam sine fratris lampade Phoeben
mutato coitu. Quin totus inardeat isto
150 sidere Mercurius, non temperat astra galero.
Iustius ipsa tuo percussa Cupidine Martis
laederis amplexu. Per te turbatus oberrat
Sol oculus mundi. Respirat Martius ardor
languescens ardore tuo. Suspirat ad Arcton
155 Iupiter et fixam radios declinat ad Ursam.
Fax tua Falciferi glaciem liquat. Ecce supernae
religio sedis caveat sibi, si quis utrisque
axibus ulterior latuit deus; imminet hostis
quem vix afficiat omnis satis impetus, in quem
160 fulminis et tonitrus omnis natura laboret.
      "Nec tamen hac miror iecur incandescere flamma,
quod gula fermento Veneris corrumpit; honusta
plus aequo saties Cypraeum ventilat ignem,
Idalioque rogo stomachi succendit abyssum
165 et luteo renes iubet exundare fluento,
talis enim tales effundit Aquarius imbres."

"Venus, you subject all the powers of heaven to your will, make the stars move and send the planets whirling in new and erratic ways. You set cold Phoebe afire without the aid of her brother's lamp, by a new conjunction. Mercury indeed burns inwardly for this planet, and his helmet no 150 longer contains his radiance. You yourself, deservedly stricken by your own Cupid, suffer the harsh embrace of Mars. The Sun, the world's eye, wanders, unsettled by you. The fire of Mars pants and grows weary in fiery desire for 155 you. Jupiter sighs for the Pole, and directs his rays toward the steadfast Bear. Your torch melts the icy chill of the Scythe-bearer. Yes, let the sacred power of the heavenly region be on guard, and any deity who may be hidden beyond the two poles; for an enemy is at hand whom all your force is hardly sufficient to control, against whom the full power of 160 thunder and lightning might grow weary.

"And yet I do not wonder that the liver burns with this flame, for gluttony contaminates it with the ferment of Venus; an appetite excessively indulged fans the Cyprian flames, kindles the Idalian pyre in the abyss of the belly, and 165 commands the loins to discharge their murky stream, for such an Aquarius pours forth such showers."

Capitulum 4

Invectio Pythagorae
contra Ingluviem

Sermones hucusque trahit, Samiusque loquendi
reliquias linguae facundo pectine texit:
"Aeriae regionis opes, opulenta profundi
170 vitrea regna dei, quicquid praelarga beato
dulce dedit Natura solo: cur perditis omne,
obsequium praestare Gulae? Cur gloria mensae
lascivit, tot lauta cibis? O perdita Luxus
ambitio, cui tota suis elementa laborant
175 deservire bonis, immo coguntur ad omnem
delicias vomuisse famem, dapibusque potentes
explicuisse sinus. O compressura ciborum
omne genus, nulloque Gulae suppressa libido!
Cura quidem cunctis animantibus instat et unus
180 anxius ardor inest, fragilis ieiunia vitae
quaesito posuisse cibo. Sed nescia rerum
luxuries servasse modum, diffunditur ultra
quam licet, et libitum liciti transformat in usum.
    "O Saties nullo violata Libidinis aestu!
185 Augustis augusta viris angustia! Felix
Copia, Paupertas, factura beatius aevum
deposito Luxu paritura que saecula rursus
aurea, calcato, quod mundum ferreat, auro.

Chapter 4

Pythagoras's invective against Gluttony

Xenocrates carried his discourse to this point, and the Samian fashioned the rest with the fluent lyre of his speech: "The riches of the regions of the air, the gleaming, splendid realm of the god of the deep, all the delights that most bountiful Nature has bestowed on this blessed earth: why do you despoil all this, to offer service to Gluttony? Why does the splendor of the table run riot, garnished with so many kinds of food? O ruinous ambition of luxury, to whom all the elements labor to offer their goods, nay are compelled to spew forth delicacies for every craving, and open out their vast depths to provide feasts! O irrepressible, gluttonous lust, that forces together every kind of food! A care that impends on every living thing, one anxious desire present in all, is the need to allay the hunger of our fragile life by seeking out food. But this luxury, unable to keep a limit on its consumption, goes far beyond what is fitting, and makes indulgence perform the office of propriety.

"O Sufficiency, unsullied by the seething of lustful greed! Venerable austerity of venerable men! Poverty, a happy abundance, will make life more blessed by casting luxury aside, and give birth once again to an age of gold, while treading underfoot that gold which turns the world to iron!

Capitulum 5

Conquestio eiusdem de nova vestium petulantia

"Haec doleo. Sed adest iterum dolor, altera mentem
190 non minor urget acus; animo subtexitur aegro
poena, labor gemitum vomit intimus, alta serenum
pectoris in nubem premit indignatio: vestis
ambitione nova nudaque libidine cultus
saecula dissolvi. Veterum vilescit amictus
195 religio, rerumque placet petulantior usus.
Succumbunt antiqua novis; circumfluit orbem
luxuries; folio levitatis cedit honestum
maturusque rigor. Ridetur sobria vitae
simplicitas, morumque viros infantia mollit.
200 Pronius ad vestes huius sollertia maior
temporis inspexit, proprio male sedula damno
et temere sollers, urbano rustica cultu.

Chapter 5

The same philosopher complains of a new wantonness in dress

"I grieve over these things, but grief visits me again, another point no less sharp goads my mind; buried deep in my weary spirit there is pain, an inner struggle that pours forth in sobs, a deep-seated indignation that keeps my peace of mind under a cloud: our age has abandoned itself to a new ostentation in dress, a naked lust for finery. The reverence of olden times for decent attire is scorned, and a more wanton practice is in favor. Ancient customs yield to new ones; luxury overruns the world; stern maturity yields the place of honor to trifling inconstancy. The life of sober simplicity is mocked, and childish behavior enfeebles grown men. These times devote their most serious attention to dress, sinfully eager, recklessly devoted to their own ruin, boorish in their very urbanity.

Capitulum 6

Quod mundus exundet vitiis,
et de VII sapientibus qui in Graecia
moribus et scientia floruerunt

"Quid moror? Est mundus res immundissima, labis
alveus, exundans vitiis, ut nubibus aer,
205 aequor aquis, caelum radio, caligine tellus,
fructibus autumnus, ver floribus, aestibus aestas,
frigoribus bruma, nitro Pharos, India nardo,
chameleonte Phryges, basiliscis Africa, Nilus
hypotamis, Ganges hebenis, sturionibus Helle,
210 Tartara tormentis, Styx nocte, Megaera venenis,
seditione furor, gemitu dolor, ira tumultu,
fulmina terrore, Mars ictibus, alea rixis,
garrulitate merum, Venus igne, Cupido sagittis,
ingluvies luxu, gula sorde, bitumine venter,
215 curia fabellis, fora litibus, histrio nugis,
paelex blanditiis, lupa quaestu, lena susurris,
fastu nupta, socrus odio, livore noverca,
sors dubiis, Fortuna dolo, velamine Fatum,
spe miser, opposito felix, utroque Iohannes.
220   "Cleobolus Lycios, Mitylenen Pittacus auxit
consiliis; Spartae Philon illuxit; Athenis
sol hominum, Solon; Periandro summa Corinthi

Chapter 6

The world teems with vices. Seven wise men who adorned Greece with their character and learning

"Why should I say more? The world itself is the basest of worldly things, a perilous pit, as overflowing with vice as the air with clouds, the sea with waters, heaven with light, earth with shadow, autumn with fruits, spring with flowers, summer with heat, winter with cold, Egypt with soda, India with nard, Phrygia with chameleons, Africa with basilisks, the Nile with hippopotami, the Ganges with ebony, the Hellespont with sturgeons, Tartarus with torments, Styx with night, Megaera with poisons, madness with mutiny, grief with sobbing, wrath with confusion, thunderbolts with terror, Mars with blows, gaming with quarrels, wine with loose talk, Venus with fire, Cupid with arrows, greed with luxury, gluttony with foulness, the belly with waste, the court with gossip, the forum with debate, an actor with trifles, a mistress with enticements, a whore with haggling, a bawd with whispers, a bride with haughtiness, a mother-in-law with hatred, a stepmother with envy, chance with uncertainty, Fortune with guile, Fate with obscurity, misery with hope, happiness with its opposite, Johannes with both.

"Cleobolus enriched the Lycians with his wisdom, and Pittacus Mitylene; Chilo brought light to Sparta; Solon, the Sun of humankind, to Athens; the ruling house of Corinth

205

210

215

220

paruit; et valuit Bias famulante Priene.
Hos sibi cum magno gaudet peperisse Thalete
225 Graecia, quos senior sapientes iactitat aetas.
Mundus ne titubet, ne caecus et invius erret,
hos habeat servetque duces. Stillabit Ulixem
lingua, senex Pylius animi purgabit amurcam."

Capitulum 7

De lamentatione Architrenii propter poenam aeternam ex vitae immunditia secuturam

Dixerat. Et fuso gemitu praecordia rumpit
230 et querulo planctus tonat Architrenius ore:
"Hoc miser, hocne salo semper iactabere? Numquam
Sirenes poteris has declinasse, tuoque
per modicum servire Iovi? Poterisne sub axe
Tartareo calicem Mortis gustasse perennem?
235 Quis poterit volvisse tuum revolubile pondus,
Sisyphe? Quisve polos et eosdem Ixionis axes
circinet, et totiens uno nugetur in orbe?
Viscera quis reparet totiens peritura? Quis undis
perditus impendat operam, quam perdat ut undas?
240 Quis totiens lusus pomi cedentis inane
mordeat, et sitiat in quo fit naufragus amnem?

gave birth to Periander; and Bias grew to manhood in the bosom of Priene. Greece rejoices to have borne these men, along with great Thales, men whom an ancient time extolled   225 as wise. If the world is not to falter, or wander blindly and at random, it must acknowledge and cherish these guides. Then the tongue will speak like Ulysses, and the old man of Pylos will clear away the dregs of the mind."

Chapter 7

Architrenius's lament over the eternal punishment that must result from the uncleanness of our life

Pythagoras had ended. Architrenius broke into a burst of sobbing, and in plaintive tones uttered this lamentation: 230 "Wretched man, must you be forever tossed about on this ocean? Will you never be able to turn away from these Sirens, and offer some small service to your Jove? Will you be able to drink the cup of Death without end in the depths of Tartarus? Who will be able, O Sisyphus, to roll your ever-   235 returning rock? Who will turn Ixion's axletree, and be whirled like a toy, again and again, in the same circle? Who will restore entrails so often destroyed? Who is so abandoned as to devote to drawing water labor that will be wasted along with the water? Who that has been so often   240 mocked by the elusive fruit can keep snapping at air, and thirsting for the stream in which he founders?

"O quam triste sedet ad nigri iudicis urnam
concilium, dum iura movet firmissima Minos,
dum superum vindex cunctis excessibus aequat
245 poenas, et rigido leges exasperat ore!
Heu quam terribilis iudex immobilis, heu quam
difficiles Minos, Rhadamanthus et Aeacus umbris!
Quam dubio fluitat animus terrore, metuque
contrahitur, quotiens meditanti pectore fundo
250 Cocyti lacrimas, Phlegethonteosque caminos!
Heu, quis Titanum laqueos communicet? Heu, quis
suspenso poterit vitam suspendere saxo?

"Dira sibi triplex hominem partitur, et omnes
distrahit humanos affectus, facta, loquelas.
255 Inquinat Alecto servae praesepia mentis
affectusque pios, sacrumque forinsecat ignem.
Iuris praecipitat aequum in declive Megaera
errantesque manus enormibus implicat actis.
Tisiphone linguas agitat, scelerumque palude
260 inficit eloquii currus, auriga loquendi.

"Nativum video iam caligasse serenum
involvique diem tenebris, quem Iupiter annis
commisit teneris. Divum Deus optimus ille
corporeae purum casulae commiserat ignem.
265 Sed iam nubifera fumi pallescit in umbra;
nativae sacras animas mundique minoris
sidera noctiferum sepelit caligine peplum.
Criminis obnubor tenebris; his intus opacor
noctibus; hoc laedor oculos, hoc lippio caepe.
270 Hae sorbent animam Syrtes; hiis pectus anhelat
pestibus; hoc mortis sub pondere vita laborat;
his rotor in praeceps Furiis. Haec vincula pessum

"O how grim is the council seated before the urn of the dark judge, while Minos imposes his unalterable decrees, and the supernal avenger assigns punishments to all our transgressions, exerting the harsh power of law with impas- 245 sive face! Alas, how terrible is that unyielding judge, how obstinate toward the shades are Minos, Rhadamanthus, and Aeacus! How my soul quavers in uncertain terror, how it shrinks in fear, whenever in my mind's imaginings I shed the 250 tears of Cocytus, and burn in the furnace of Phlegethon! Alas, who would share the bondage of the Titans? Who could let his life hang suspended from a hanging rock?

"The three Furies divide a man among themselves, and separate out human desires, deeds, and words. Alecto defiles 255 the precincts of the obedient mind and its virtuous impulses, and banishes the sacred fire. Megaera casts down the sense of right, and involves our hands in terrible acts. Tisiphone, taking the reins of speech, drives the tongue, and 260 fouls the chariot of eloquence in the swamp of wickedness.

"I see that the clear, natural light of day with which Jupiter endowed my tender years has grown dim, obscured by shadow. That best of gods entrusted his pure fire to my humble bodily dwelling. But now it is dimmed by the 265 shadow of a smoky cloud; the shroud of night has buried in darkness the sacred powers of my nature, the stars of my lesser universe. I am enveloped by the shadows of sinfulness; I am covered within by their night; this onion mars my vision and makes me blear-eyed. These quicksands draw 270 down my spirit; my chest heaves with this disease; my life labors under this burden of death; I am hurled about by these Furies. These chains draw downward a man's uplifted

os homini sublime trahunt, ne patria visat
sidera, ne superos oculis et mente salutet.
275   In declive caput trahitur, ne glorier umquam
affectum superis animo mandasse benigno."

Capitulum 8

Oratio Thaletis de timore Domini

Conquestiva Thales exhaurit dicta, propinquus
sede, querelanti reserasse domesticus aurem:
"Quisquis es, hunc nostrae cyathum libato Minervae.
280   Parce puer lacrimis, fletus agnosce virilem
dedecuisse genam; pudor est hoc imbre rigorem
immaduisse virum. Lacrimae planctusque loquuntur
degeneres animos. Riguumque facillima flendi
femina pectus habet; didicitque cadentibus ultro
285   in lacrimis clausisse dolos, reserasse dolores.
     "Ianua virtutum, purumque Aurora sciendi
allatura diem, et quo primo acceditur astris
cardo, timor Domini; sine quo fraudatur in omni
proposito votum. Nulla est statura potestas
290   ad subitum lapsura nihil; non purpura murum
divitibus praestat, nec sontem protegit auri
ambitiosa lues; et nullo pro aggere surgit
circumfusus opum cumulus nullumque tuetur.

gaze, lest he behold his native stars, and in thought and
vision acknowledge the gods. My head is bowed low, that I   275
may never rejoice to have offered my love to the gods in
peace of mind."

Chapter 8

Thales's oration on fear of the Lord

Thales, seated close by, took in these plaintive words, lend-
ing the ear of a friend to the sorrowing one. "Whoever you
are, drink this cup of our wisdom. Cease your tears, my boy;   280
know that weeping does not become the face of a man; it is
shameful to drench manly dignity with this shower. Tears
and laments bespeak degenerate spirits. A woman, readily
inclined to weep, has a breast ever damp; she has learned to   285
conceal her wiles and reveal her sorrows with falling tears.

"The gateway to virtue, the Dawn which will bring on the
clear day of knowledge, the crucial rule by which one as-
cends to the stars, is the fear of God; without this, prayer for
any undertaking is worthless. No power is so stable that it   290
may not suddenly collapse into nothing; no purple splendor
can provide safety for the wealthy, nor the favor-seeking
plague of gold protect a guilty man; and a pile of riches sur-
rounding a man is not a sufficient bulwark and will not make

Sceptri nulla salus, si quo mandaverit ictum
295 Iupiter, haud iaculo cogit lorica repulsam,
nec clipeo telum galeaque repellitur ensis.
   "Pone leves animos, temereque audacibus obsta
principio votis, et cui parere necesse est,
sollicitus sollersque time. Nam cuncta videntem
300 nil celasse potes, nec eum, qui totus ubique
excubat, evades; et qui Deus omnia novit,
falli non poterit. Iovis insopita lucerna
in tenebris lucet, secreti conscia, clausum
non sinit esse nefas; non occultatur opertum
305 hypocrisi crimen, nec sub lodice sepultum
Zoi chai sichen. Indignas Sole Mycenas
sensit; adulterio nodatam Cyprida Marti
Sol superum vidit; mensae conviva cruentae,
arguit Arcadicum, nec eum mansueta fefellit
310 oris ovis mentisque lupus. Vultusque recepit
cognatos animis, totus fera factus, aperto
mentis in ore lupo; ne pectore blandior esset
vultus, utroque fera. Faciem mens saeva cruentam
sumpsit et humano iugulo polluta tyrannis.
315 "O quem nulla fides mundi tutatur, in omni
robore quassari facilis, nullaque reniti
libertate potens; nec, solo nomine felix,
inter opes sensurus opem, timuisse potentem
cuncta necesse puta. Nam quo venisse voluntas
320 oderit, ipse trahet supremae calculus urnae;
vindictamque pati Iovis inconcussa potestas
cogit, et extremam tandem non differet iram."

him safe. The scepter itself will not be secure when Jupiter has determined to strike; no breastplate withstands his 295 javelin, and his spear and sword cannot be warded off by shield or helmet.

"Cast idle thoughts aside, boldly confront the author of things with bold prayers, yet give care and concern to fearing one whom it is necessary to obey. For you can conceal nothing from one who sees all things, nor elude him who 300 keeps watch always and everywhere; a God who knows all cannot be deceived. The light of Jove shines undimmed amid the shadows, knows secret thoughts, and permits no wicked act to remain hidden. The veiled crime of hypocrisy 305 is not hidden from him, nor the 'ah, my life and soul,' shrouded in a coverlet. He knew that Mycenae was unworthy of sunlight; Sun of heaven as he is, he saw the Cyprian fettered to Mars in adultery; invited to a bloody feast, he accused the Arcadian, and the mild sheep's face and the wolf- 310 ish mind did not deceive him. Lycaon received a face akin to his thoughts, became wholly bestial, his wolf's mind proclaimed openly in his countenance; lest his face be gentler than his spirit, he was bestial in both. The cruel mind, the tyrant spirit polluted by human bloodshed, took on a bloodthirsty aspect.

"O you whom no trust in worldly power may protect, so 315 easily shaken for all your strength, powerless to stand firm by any assertion of freedom; you who, happy only in name, do not know security amid your riches, consider that the powerful man must always live in fear. For where your will is loath to go, the sentence of the urn of heaven will drag you; 320 the unassailable power of Jove compels you to suffer retribution, and in the end he will not withhold his utmost wrath."

Capitulum 9

Oratio Biantis quod Deus
sit totis intimis diligendus

Vix ea, cum Bias simili de fonte propinat:
"Ecce time, quo tutus eris, solidusque timendum
325 amplectatur amor. Totis enitere votis
dilecto placuisse Iovi cui sufficit omni
gratia pro merito. Satis est ad praemia dantis
accipientis amor, nec gratis praestita doni
inquinat alterni pretio; munusque relato
330 munere non vendit. Absolvit libera dono
dona relativo, nec, quod dedit, auferet auctor
muneris et praedo. Nulli data gaudia laeva
invidiae tollit, ut eodem nunc sit avarus,
quo nunc largus erat. Pleno sua munera cornu
335 plus cumuli quam vallis habent; munusque volenti
exhilarat dextra, nec vultus pondere doni
gratia succumbit.
                "Tot dantem dilige! Si qua
magna dedit, maiora dabit. Meritisque tot unum,
dilexisse, refer. Qui se tibi poscit amari,
340 non sibi, totus ama. Non est quod prosit amato
collaturus amor, sed amanti. Dilige, si te

Chapter 9

Bias's oration on the duty to make God the sole object of our deepest love

Scarcely had the speech ended when Bias proffered a cup from a similar source: "See, and be fearful of that wherein you will be secure, and let steadfast love embrace him whom you must fear. Strive in all your prayers to be pleasing to that beloved Jove whose Grace is sufficient to reward all deserving. The love of the recipient of this grace is sufficient reward for the bestower, and he will not taint the generosity of his giving by exacting the price of a gift in return; he does not sell his favor in return for favors. His free bestowal absolves us of the need to reciprocate, and the author of this gift never turns robber and snatches away what he has given. From none does he take away with grudging hand the joys he has bestowed, growing covetous at one moment of that with which he had been generous at another. The gifts from his full horn partake more of the hill than of the valley; to give with willing hand is his joy, and the grace of his countenance is undiminished by the amount of his gift.

"Love him who gives so much! If he has bestowed great gifts, he will grant still greater ones. In return for so many favors, offer the one gift of love. Love him totally who demands to be loved for your sake, not for his own. The love to be offered is one that benefits not the beloved, but the lover.

325

330

335

340

non odisse velis. Mundum seseque daturus,
his ut ametur, emit. Non est deceptus amator
qui recipit quod amat, superum conviva futurus,
345   aeternamque Stygis non descensurus in Aetnam.
    "Dilige, dilecti grato venare favorem
numinis obsequio; partum tenuisse labora
immotumque liga; mentis fervore refixum,
ne labet, astringe, ne gratia sumpta relabi
350   diminuive queat. Habitam servare voluntas
obsequiosa potest; cupidis attende volentis
imperio votis; animos impende iubenti.
Mandati ne differ opus, ne langueat actu
gratia dilato; placitura citatius urge,
355   ne meritum perdas, nam suspendisse volentem
est meruisse minus. Maturo nitere facto;
plenius ad meritum praesens quam crastinus imples."

Capitulum 10

Oratio Periandri quod
Deus colendus est

"Non satis est," inquit Periander. "Tertia sume
pocula, de nostro placeat sorbere fluento.

Love him, unless you would show hatred toward yourself. He paid a price to give us the world and his very self, that he might be loved for this. The lover who obtains the thing he loves is not deceived, for he will come to partake of the feast of the gods, and not descend to the eternal fires of Styx. 345

"Love, and pursue the favor of the beloved power by that obedience which pleases him; strive to retain what he has bestowed and hold it fast; cling tightly to it with eager mind, lest it elude you, lest the grace obtained be lost or diminished. An obedient will can preserve what it possesses; acknowledge his rule with the eager prayers of a willing spirit; submit your mind to him who commands. Do not put off the task assigned you, lest grace grow weak from the deferral of action; do quickly what will be pleasing to him, lest you lose merit, for to have deferred what one is willing to do is to have been less deserving. Seek to act while the time is ripe; you will prove more fully deserving by immediate than by deferred actions." 350 355

Chapter 10

The oration of Periander on the duty of offering worship to God

"This is not enough," declared Periander. "Take up a third bowl, and be pleased to drink from my stream. Strike the 360

360 Tange precum laudumque lyram, geminaque Tonantem
sedulitate lita. Superum cultura loquatur
te caeli cupidum, complecti numina mente,
et toti nupsisse Deo. Ne flecte tenendos
hic vigiles sensus, et ei servire memento
365 quo solo regnare potes. Ne cetera tollat
cura, Deum cura. Quaecumque negotia tractes,
providus ad superos oculum mentemque reducas.
Nam vacat humanis studiis impensa, nihilque
est lucri latura dies et inutilis exit
370 exclusi secura Dei; cui vivere soli
est toti vixisse sibi. Sine numine frustra
est operosa manus, studio marcescit inani
in vacuum tractura moras; sterilisque laborat
actio quae nulla superis pro parte ministrat.

375   "Quae nocuos laesura tonat, quae fulmina tractat,
sit semper suspecta manus; non parcit inultis
Criminibus. Tonitruque minas et fulmine poenas
mandat, et ad Stygias urget properantius undas
quos Phlegethon exasset aquis; Cocytus adustis
380 elixet lacrimis; habeatque Ixionis axis
quos rotet aeternum; versentque reductile pondus
Sisyphium, poenamque levent consortia poenae,
communisque minus habeat iactura querelae.

    "Impermixta malis, bonitas Iovis omne timeri,
385 omne coli meruit. Solida virtute cavendum
luctandumque puta, ne quid deliret in illam
error ad offensam. Pudeatque offendere quem te
offendisse pudet, illumque lacessere cuius
libertas est summa iugum; cui cedere pondus

lyre of prayer and praise, and propitiate the Thunderer with
redoubled zeal. Let your worship of the gods declare that
you are eager for heaven, that you have embraced the divine
powers inwardly, and wedded yourself wholly to God. Do
not stray from maintaining constant awareness, and remem-
ber that you serve him through whom alone you may come
to rule. Lest other cares draw you away, give your care to   365
God; whatever tasks you undertake, prudently draw your
eyes and thoughts back to heaven. For time spent on human
pursuits is idle; a day from which God is carelessly excluded
passes without profit or purpose; to live only for him is to   370
live wholly for oneself. Without divine aid the hand exerts
itself in vain, falls into useless pursuits, spends long hours on
nothing; any activity will prove sterile that makes no provi-
sion for the gods.

"Be ever fearful of the hand whose thunder threatens   375
wrongdoers, which wields the lightning; he does not suffer
crimes to go unavenged. He declares his menace in thunder,
his punishments in lightning, and drives swiftly to the Sty-
gian stream those whom the waters of Phlegethon will burn;
whom Cocytus will steep in boiling tears; whom the wheel   380
of Ixion will claim and whirl about eternally; who will roll
the ever-returning rock of Sisyphus, and alleviate his suf-
fering by sharing it, that a common disaster may provide less
occasion for lamentation.

"Untainted by evil, the goodness of Jove deserves wholly
to be feared, wholly reverenced. Consider that you must be   385
aware and ready to fight with steadfast virtue, lest some reck-
less error offend against that virtue. And think it shameful
to give offense to him to whom it would be abhorrent to of-
fend you, or provoke him whose yoke is the highest free-

390 maiestatis habet; cui mendicare potestas;
servire imperium; flere est non flere; dolere
non dolor est; mors absque mori, sitis absque sitire,
esuriisse cibus. Et ei parere iubentis
est habuisse vicem. Levibusque occurrere votis
395 accurrisse deis. Animoque excludere mundum
inclusisse Deum, fierique a corporis umbra
sidus, et optatum superis annectere civem.
   "Nec minus invigiles, inconcussoque rigore,
si potes, evincas, ne vitae larva coloret
400 hypocrisis mendas, virtutum littera, prava
pectoris interpres—utinamque incognita claustro
et mitrae et baculo!—vultus cautela professi
mentis honestatem, verum occultare diserta,
simpliciter falsum factura probabile, culpae
405 occulto patrona dolo, pictura reatus,
celatura notam. Vultusque reconditur umbra
mente latens ignotus homo, superumque favorem
excipit et mundi recipit, lucratus honores.
   "Dum simulat mores et morum nomine mundum
410 deceptus deceptor emit, perditque supernae
delicias mensae. Verum tollatur inane
hypocrisis velum, mundae sincera coruscet
integritas vitae. Refert fallentis in auro
occultasse lutum, fraudisque iniuria stagnum
415 palliat argento. Reverentior esto nihilque
deliquisse velis; Davumque a pectore tolle,
nec vultu mentire Numam. Concordia vultum
affectumque liget, pudeatque abscondere culpam
quam pepulisse potes, illumque accersere testem

dom; to submit to him is to partake of majesty; to beg of him   390
is power; to serve him is to rule; to weep before him is to
weep no more; to grieve is not grievous; to die is not death;
to thirst is to be without thirst; to hunger is to be fed. To
obey him is to become one who commands. To run to him
in swift prayer is to come quickly among the gods. To ban-   395
ish the world from your mind is to install God there, to be
turned from a shadowy body to a star, and to join oneself to
the cherished company of the heavens.

"If you can be ever on guard, with unwavering firmness,
you may ensure that the surface of life does not become a
mask for the deceits of hypocrisy, the mere letter of virtue,   400
the corrupt representation of the mind—would that it were
unknown to the cloister, the miter, the pastoral staff!—, the
guarded face that asserts the honesty of the mind within,
well schooled in concealing the truth, rendering falsehood
plausible by its simplicity, endorsing crime by hidden guile,   405
embellishing guilt, concealing the traces. The man's mind
lurks unknown, concealed by the shadow of appearance,
while he grasps at divine rewards and purchases the worldly
honors he receives.

"While he pretends to good character, and garners
worldly success in its name, the deceiver is deceived, and   410
forfeits the delights of the heavenly feast. But let the thin
veil of hypocrisy be removed, and the pure integrity of the
uncorrupted life will shine forth. It becomes clear that mud
has covered itself in gold, that injurious fraud has covered a
swamp with silver. Be reverent and seek never to transgress;   415
banish Davus from your heart, and show no false image
of Numa on your face. Let concord unite face and feeling,
and think it shameful to conceal, invoking that witness

420 delicti, quem nulla latent; oculisque sopori
occultis occulta videt, nullisque tenetur
obicibus, quem nulla tenet distantia, visus.
  "Est tamen ut vitiis mens obluctata ruinam
declinasse nequit; et nervo saucia labi
425 cogitur in labem. Nec vincere libera, frustra
carnis anhelat opem, certaminis impos, inermis,
victa cadit. Cecidisse dolet, sed dulce cadenti
est vitii pondus; blandaque indagine cingit
torquendas animas carnis mansueta tyrannis."

Capitulum 11

Oratio Philonis de occultandis delictis

430 Hic Philon: "Vitiis quotiens victoria cedit,
fas esto latuisse nefas, tenebrisque notatam
dissimulasse notam, clausaque excludere mundi
excubias culpa, cynicosque evadere morsus
et satirae serras, Flaccique eludere ludum
435 insipidosque sales. Nam si sordere necesse
est animam, satius est mundae parcere Famae,
nec vitae maculis oculos laesisse bonorum.

of your guilt from whom nothing is hidden, the guilty act 420
which you could have repudiated. He sees with secret in-
sight things hidden from our dull vision, and as no amount
of distance can keep him from us, so no obstacle can restrict
his vision.

"And yet it is true that the mind assailed by vice cannot
withstand ruin; stricken by its arrow, it is forced into ruin. 425
No longer capable of prevailing, it yearns in vain for succor
from the flesh, and falls, incapable of resistance, a helpless
victim. It grieves at having fallen, yet as it falls the burden
of vice seems sweet: the mild tyranny of the flesh binds in
a gently beguiling way those spirits that will suffer its tor-
ments."

Chapter 11

The oration of Chilo on the need to conceal our misdeeds

Here Chilo spoke: "Whenever victory is ceded to vice, be it 430
right to keep the wrong hidden, to cover the evidence of in-
famy in darkness, avoid the watchful eyes of the world by
concealing guilt, evade the carping cynic and the barbs of
satire, and escape the mockery, the insipid wit, of Flaccus. 435
For if it is inevitable that the spirit be defiled, it is right to
spare the untainted reputation, and not offend the eyes of
good men with the imperfections of the life.

"Pullulat in vulgi facinus vulgata voluptas
derivatque notam; dum plebis caeca libido
440 imbibit aure scelus, sunt internuntia culpae
scire, videre, loqui; scelerisque audacia multo
crescit in exemplo, surgitque impune reatus
a simili; notumque trahit contagia crimen.
     "Haec rerum dominis caveat sollertia, Famae
445 deludens oculos. Horum nota latius orbem
inquinat exemplis. Populi delicta regentis
absolvit facinus; maiorum forma minores
pressius informat. Avidusque in funera morbus,
quo caput elanguet, reliquos depascitur artus;
450 praelatique parit labis consortia labes.
     "At sceptri facinus latebris caret; ardua nubis
excedunt latebras. Nulla praetexitur umbra
imperii sidus, noctisque excludit amictum
principis illa dies. Fama penetrante trahuntur
455 regnorum secreta palam, scelerique potentum
lux adhibet lucem; nec molli purpura sordes
occulit in ruga. Culpae latuisse volenti
maiestas peccantis obest; maiusque videri
maiorum facinus consuevit et auctior auget
460 gloria delictum. Nec sic censura togatos
ut regni trabeas, plebi minus aspera, mordet.
     "O igitur, quem nulla facit praetexta beatum,
O miser in laetis: tibi delituisse negatur.
Deliquisse nega! Vitiorum terge lituras;
465 nec labem sincerus habe; stabilemque nefandis
pone modum votis. Morum candore nivescat

"A carnal sin, made public, branches out, becomes a commonplace sin, and spreads its infamy abroad; when the blind, lustful mob takes in the news of the crime, knowledge, observation and word of mouth become panders of guilt; sin grows more bold with an abundance of examples, and guilt thrives secure with a precedent; a well known crime has contagious effects. 440

"This concern should keep men of power on their guard, deceiving the eyes of Reputation. A fault in them, too widely known, pollutes the world by their example. The transgressions of rulers absolve the crimes of common people; the pattern of great men's lives exerts a shaping influence on lesser men. A raging, deadly disease, when the head has grown feeble, feeds on the rest of the body; the lapse of a prominent figure spawns a communal decline. 445

450

"But the crime of the ruler has no hiding place; they stand out high above cloudy cover. No shadow cloaks the star of ruling power; the daylight of a prince rejects the mantle of night. The secrets of rulers are dragged into the open by probing rumor, and the radiance of power illumines its crimes; a purple robe does not conceal foul deeds with its soft folds. The high rank of the sinner thwarts his wish to conceal his guilt; the crimes of great men commonly appear greater, and their larger glory only enlarges their fault. Public opinion, less severe with common people, does not tear at the humble toga as it does the kingly robe. 455

460

"Thus for you whom no sumptuous trappings make happy, you who are wretched amid your good fortune, concealment is denied you. Refuse to sin! Wipe away the stain of your vices; be pure and admit no lapsing; impose a firm control on your wicked desires. Let your mind, purged of 465

a vitii mens pura luto, mundique favorem
extorque meritis, accensaque pectore virtus
ferveat. Haec animae tenebris intacta lucerna
470 splendeat exterius, nullo dilanguida fumo.

"Nec permitto nefas, sed quem cecidisse necesse est,
occulto nutasse volo scelerisque latendo
evasisse notam. Prave ne intellige, si quid
instruit ad mores; non ultra sedulus esto,
475 quam licet, interpres. Temere volat ocior aequo
impetus ingenii; distortaque littera culpae
promittit veniam, scelerisque occasio surgit
ex male distinctis. Nostris sollertia simplex
accedat monitis, animo quid araverit Auctor,
480 indecepta videt. Ponat praesumptio limae
lectorisque vicem, studii dementia caeca
desinat erroris auctorem quaerere, si qua
imperat enodis servandos pagina mores."

Dixit; adhuc patula stetit Architrenius aure,
485 eloquiique fores tacito Philone resolvit.

the taint of vice, gleam with the candor of virtue, lay claim
to the world's favor by your good actions, and let the fire of   470
virtue be kindled in your breast. Let your soul's lamp shine
forth, unhindered by shadow, dimmed by no smoky cloud.

"I do not condone wrongdoing, but I urge that whoever
is forced to fall should keep his weakness secret and avoid
notoriety by concealing his crime. Do not read a wicked
meaning into anything that promotes morality, and be no   475
more zealous a critic than is fitting. The impulses of human
understanding are random and overhasty; a badly written
version of the facts can give rise to an indulgence of sin, and
the occasion for wrongdoing arises from faulty reasoning.
May honest good sense accept my advice, for it will see,
undeceived, what the Author has engraved in the mind. Let   480
presumption abandon the role of sleuth and herald, and
cease to search for malefactors in a mad excess of blind zeal,
while there exists a page that clearly enjoins the preserving
of moral standards."

He had spoken. Architrenius still stood with open ear,
but as Chilo fell silent, he opened the gates to his own   485
eloquence.

BOOK EIGHT

Capitulum 1

De commendatione antiquitatis et mundi negligentia circa mores

"Omne bonum veterum labiis distillat. Et imbres
Pegaseos senior aetas exundat, et orbi
ubera centenni puero distendit, honesti
lacte fluens nutrix. Nec maturatur, anilis
5 criniculo, mente puerescens, mundus, et aucto
corpore non adhibent crementum moribus anni.
Lactativa bibit veteris praecepta Minervae,
nutritiva parum, nam vix libata vomuntur
pocula; nec prosunt, quae nunc data nausea reddit,
10 nec satis auricula vigilas, si pectore dormis.
    "Area delicti, scelerum domus, excipit omnes
mens hominum sordes. Has egessisse paludes
virtutis vis nulla potest, vitiique revelli
non didicit ruscus. Patiatur cetera tolli,
15 spina tamen restat; solidamque Superbia sedem
immota radice, ligat, truncoque recisa
stirpe manet fixo. Nihil est illime nec ista
Alcidae potuit faculis arescere Lerna."

Chapter 1

In praise of ancient times,
and on the carelessness of our world
regarding morality

"All good doctrine flows from the lips of the ancients. It is an earlier age that gives rise to the Pegasean stream, and swells its breasts, a nurse abounding in the milk of probity, to feed a world which, though centuries old, is still a child. For the world, though it shows the outward signs of age, is childish in understanding, and does not mature, and though its body is full grown, the years do not bring growth in moral wisdom. It drinks in the nurturing precepts of ancient wisdom, but they provide little nourishment, for the drink is no sooner taken in than vomited forth; what nausea gives back the moment it receives it can do no good; your ear cannot be sufficiently awake if your mind is asleep.

"The mind of man, a place of transgression, home of wickedness, admits every sort of foulness. No virtuous power can drain these swamps, none knows how to clear the dense thickets of vice. Though it be granted us to remove the rest, a bramble still remains; Pride, its roots immovably deep, remains firmly in its place, and though the trunk be cut away the stump remains fast rooted. Nothing avoids its taint, and this Lernaean monster cannot be burned away by the torch of Hercules."

Capitulum 2

Oratio Pittaci de mansuetudine
appetenda et elatione vitanda

"At licet ista filix sit inextirpabilis" inquit
20 Pittacus "et nulli valeat succumbere falci,
quin nocuo fetu populosa repullulet Hydra,
tu tamen assiduus animae luctare colonus.
Mollescant animi dulces vitiumque tumoris
cedat; et asperitas nullo silvescat in actu
25 obicibus laedens, inconsultique rigoris
robora lentescant. Adsit clementia sceptris
indivisa comes, gladiique coerceat ausus
mitior, et iuris quantum permittit habena
imperio parcens, prohibens punire flagello
30 deterrenda minis. Fluvios exosa cruoris
non lacrimae, si quam regnis extorsit Egestas
et solium movere casae, si quando potentum
arentes oculos tenero Compassio fletu
impluit et latuit sceptro rorante tyrannis.
35 "Corruit elatus, luci sublatus et umbris
Lucifer illatus, vanoque a numine venit,
quo Numa devenit. Tumidusque inventus, ab alto
detumuit ventus, et Lucifer esse coactus

Chapter 2

Pittacus's oration on the duty of pursuing gentleness and avoiding vainglory

"But even granting that this growth can not be plucked out," said Pittacus, "and will yield to no blade, though indeed this Hydra may teem with a whole tribe of baneful progeny, you must still fight zealously as keeper of your soul. Let the spirit grow sweet and gentle and the vice of pride give way; in none of your actions let the rough thickets of harshness offend by their aggression, but let the obduracy of ill-considered severity be softened. May clemency become the inseparable companion of rulers, and gently control the boldness of the sword, asserting its authority as sparingly as the rule of law allows, forbidding punishment by the lash for crimes which should be prevented by strong words. Let it deem abhorrent the flow of blood, though not the flow of tears, if need has ever extorted tears from kings, or the plight of the cottager moved the throne; if ever compassion has caused the dry eyes of the mighty to well up with tender weeping, or a tyrant concealed himself as tears bedewed his scepter.

"Lucifer fell from on high, banished from light and relegated to shadow; from an empty dream of divine power he came to where Numa too has come. Having been found puffed up with pride, his windiness dwindled as he descended from on high; and he whose duty was to be Bringer

371

Letifer est factus, astrisque parentibus orbus
40 luteus in luteum cadit, in pigrum impiger orbem.
  "Vicit in humano spolio Deus. Exulis exul
hospitis hospes erat. Ad Ditis inhospita venit,
Tartareasque fores caelorum ianua, Christus,
Lucifer Aeternus, infractaque dextera fregit.
45 Ecce, quod amisit incauta Superbia, caelum
Maiestas submissa dedit, Dominusque ministrum
induit, et meruit humilis vicisse potestas.
  "Fortius insudes humili mansuescere mente
et placido vultu. Socia dulcedine linguam
50 affectumque riga. Superum mundique favorem
captet uterque favus; pacemque extorqueat orbis
illa vel illa quies. Animi depelle tumorem
Luciferique Notos, tollatque Superbia flatus
praecipites Boreamque suum; tumidique rigoris
55 subsidat rabies, et sola in pectore toto
pax Zephyri vernet, florumque potentior illa
pullulet aura crocos animaeque superserat ortis.
  "Oderit ulcisci gladio censura. Nec illum
consulat in poenam, nec eum tortore cruentet,
60 quem liceat torquere minis; pudeatque regendos
imperii fregisse iugo, semperque venenum
et numquam fudisse favum, ferroque dolorum
subsecuisse vias, crudisque extinguere morbos
ignibus; alterutro levius curantibus herbis!

of Light now became Bringer of Death. Banished from the 40
starry realm of his birth, his brightness was cast into murky
darkness; his restless energy into the sluggish material
world.

"God, assuming human flesh, was the victor. An exile was
the guest of an exile host. For Christ, Bringer of Eternal
Light, came to inhospitable Dis, and his undaunted right
arm smashed open the gates of Tartarus, now a gateway to 45
heaven. Behold, that heaven which reckless pride had lost,
submissive majesty restored; the master took on the office
of servant, and his power prevailed by humbling itself.

"Strive boldly to be gentle, with unassuming spirit and
peaceful countenance. Steep your words and thoughts in 50
sweet sociability. Such twofold sweetness will win you the
favor both of gods and men; the one gentleness and the
other will exact a peaceful response from the world. Rid
yourself of the puffed-up spirit and windy thoughts of Luci-
fer, and let pride withdraw her gusting blasts and northern
chill; let the madness of unbending haughtiness subside, the 55
vernal calm of Zephyrus take sole possession of your spirit,
and its more efficacious breath produce a rich flowering and
strew the garden of your soul with blossoms.

"Let judgment think it hateful to punish by the sword.
Let it not seek this recourse in assigning a penalty, nor
bloody by torture any whom it is possible to sway with stern 60
warnings; and be it held shameful to destroy with the yoke
of power those who should be governed, to offer a drink
that is always bitter poison and never honey, to carve out a
path with the instruments of torment, and purge every
infection with harsh fire; far better than either of these are
curative herbs!

65 "Tutior est regnis gladio tranquilla iubentis
Nec fraudis suspecta quies. Haec mente favorem
Extrahit, hic lingua. Feritas dirumpit amorem,
mansuetudo ligat. Hauritque incauta venenum
effera maiestas vinoque ulciscitur enses;
70 unaque tot flendi claudunt convivia rivos.
Fictaque subridens iterat suspiria plebes,
dum domini laeto producit funera planctu,
et tenero sudant oculo velantia risum
pectora, quae modico praetexunt gaudia fletu.
75 "Pax ad opus mandata rapit; stimulique potestas
non perdit sub pace vicem; violenta trahuntur
iussa minusque movent, segnesque ingrata ministros
Ingratosque trahunt, nec habent extorta volentem.
Est ubi mandatum violenta potentius urgent,
80 servilesque docet animos servire flagellum.
"Nec satis est mandantis amor, positoque voluntas
mandativa iugo, precibusque innixa potestas.
Pollicitis instare vacat, mollire rigorem,
blanditiis condire minas; saevire necesse est
85 et virga mutasse preces, pressumque domandis
inseruisse iugum. Clementia Caesaris auras
verberat; est tauro Phalaris mandanda voluntas.
At iuri praecisa velis! Praemordeat aequi
lima voluntatem, quo solo invita trahatur
90 laeva potestatis gladio committere poenam."

"Mild tranquility untainted by any suspicion of coercive   65
betrayal ensures a kingdom's safety better than the sword.
The one elicits approval from the mind, the other only from
the tongue. Brutality destroys the bond of love, gentleness
strengthens it. Cruel majesty drinks poison unawares, and
its woundings are avenged in wine; in one instant a feast   70
ends the flowing of many streams of tears. The people,
laughing inwardly, sigh repeatedly in feigned grief, as they
perform the funeral rites for their lord with joyful lamen-
tation, and the breasts which conceal their smiles grow
damp with tender weeping, cloaking their joy in moderate
weeping.

"It is peace that compels the carrying out of orders; the   75
force of a command does not lose its effect through mild-
ness. Harsh orders are obeyed slowly and have less force,
and disagreeable orders result in sluggish and unwilling ser-
vants: forced labor is not performed willingly. For when vio-
lence imposes the assigned task too forcefully, it teaches the   80
servant's spirit to deserve the lash.

"It is not enough that he who commands be loving, that
he make his will known without coercion, mingling force
with appeal. There is a time for relying on promises, for
softening sternness and softening threats with sweet words.
But it is also necessary to grow angry, to exchange such ap-   85
peals for the whip, and to impose the yoke firmly on those
who must be controlled. Caesar's clemency beat the air in
vain; such kindness should be consigned to the bull of
Phalaris. But adhere strictly to the law! Let the file of equity
so trim the will that the arm of power is drawn only reluc-   90
tantly to entrust punishment to the sword."

Capitulum 3

Oratio Cleoboli de Fortitudine

Hic Lycius: "Quicumque iubet dulcescere raro
edidicit; torquere potest, sed parcere nescit.
Imperii moles subiectos emolit. Anceps
hic gladius cladis est illativus, et ira
95 principis in populos fulmen populatur; et orbem
hinc dominus pulsat, illinc Fortuna, Charybdis
saevior inque bonos crudescens vipera. Verum,
si tumidum praesaeva tonet, si nauseet iras
pectore flammato, vultu crudescat, et axem
100 torqueat in lacrimas, versumque exasperet orbem
descendente rota, miseris oppone rigorem
mentis inattritae, nubesque expelle sereno
pectoris obiecti. Veniat tutissima Virtus
obvia Fortunae, Fati evasura procellas
105 naufragiique minas, ut non nisi prospera fiant
fata. Scias adversa pati! Felicia numquam
Magnanimo desunt; animo Fortuna virili
omnis laeta venit. Fatum lugubre videri
debilitas infirma facit. Quae saevius instant,
110 materiam virtutis habent, certissima sunt haec
argumenta viri, virtusque abscondita laetis
prodit in adversis. Fatoque obscura sereno
lucet in obscuro. Dum voto accommoda fiunt

Chapter 3

Cleobolus's oration on Fortitude

Here the Lycian spoke: "Those who command are rarely schooled in kindness: they can punish, but know not how to be sparing. The weight of ruling power grinds its subjects down; its double-edged sword conveys the threat of slaugh- 95 ter, and the wrath of the prince assails his people like a thunderbolt; and as rulers attack the world from one side, from the other attacks Fortune, a fiercer Charybdis, a viper striking harshly at the good. But though she fiercely thunders her proud taunts, spews forth rage from her fiery breast, cruelly distorts her face, forces the very heaven to weep, and 100 goads a whirling world to madness as her wheel descends, you must withstand her with the firmness of a mind unwearied by suffering, and banish all clouds by the serenity of spirit you present. Let the full surety of Virtue confront Fortune, Virtue that can escape the storms of Fate and the 105 menace of shipwreck, so that none but favorable Fate may befall you. Learn to accept adversity! Happiness never forsakes the greathearted; all Fortune is favorable to a manly spirit. It is faltering weakness that makes Fate appear dismal. What bears hardest upon us provides the means for vir- 110 tuous action, the most decisive proof of manhood; and the virtue that lies hidden in happy times serves us in adversity. Clouded over when Fate is serene, it shines forth when Fate is cloudy. When all things adapt themselves to our wishes, it

omnia, noctescit, miserisque diescit; et umbram
115   prospera virtuti faciunt, adversa lucernam.
        "Ardua dum surgunt pendente Ceraunia fluctu,
eversumque suas pelagus spumescit in iras,
attollique fretum superis contendit, et audax
fluctus in astra volat, Lunamque extinguit et ipsos
120   Falciferos axes; nunc trudit ad ultima navem
Tartara, nunc raptam superis nolentibus offert,
nunc prora nunc puppe cadit, nunc surgit utroque
saepe bibente ratis, trepida nunc claudicat alno
luctanti cessura freto, dum pugnat et aurae
125   fluctibus et ponti, fervetque in funera toto
Mors armata mari. Tunc remigis arte fruendum;
tunc laus est vicisse fretum; tunc, si qua potestas
est nautae fit tota palam; nec deside tutum
est languere mora. Venienti occurrere Fato
130   uniusque manu populi servasse salutem
expedit, ut pelagi victorem Fama coronet.
        "Virtuti expediunt aditus adversa; virorum
sarcina, torporis prohibens languescere somno
degeneres animos. Nescit felicia Virtus,
135   mollibus utenti raro comes. Induit omnem
prosperitas labem: nulloque innoxia facto,
non sentit consueta nefas. Temerarius ausis
ignovisse solet, solidator criminis, usus.

remains in darkness, but it shines forth for those who suffer; happy times cast a shadow over virtue, but hardship is her 115 lamp.

"When the steep Ceraunian mountains pour forth their downward-rushing streams, when the storm-tossed ocean foams in its rage, when its swell struggles to reach the heavens, and its surge rises boldly toward the stars, extinguishing the Moon and even the far-off Scythe-bearer, the sea thrusts 120 the vessel down to the depths of Tartarus at one moment, and at the next thrusts it aloft as an offering to the unwilling gods: first the prow is submerged, then the stern; now the boat struggles forward, frequently awash at either end; now it staggers with creaking timbers, on the point of succumbing to the violent tide, while it fights against the surge of 125 wind and water, and Death itself takes up arms and rages over the sea in search of victims. It is then that the oarsman's art must be put to use; then it is praiseworthy to conquer the waves; then whatever strength the sailor possesses shows plainly; and it is not safe to succumb to idle delay. Now is the time for the hand of some single man to confront 130 oncoming Fate and ensure the people's safety, that Fame may crown him victor over the sea.

"Adversity provides the occasion for virtue; it is a burden for men, and forbids even degenerate spirits to languish in a drowsy torpor. Virtue does not know happy times, and 135 rarely attends those whose situation is easy. It is always prosperity that lapses: none of its actions are blameless, and being accustomed to wrongdoing, it is unaware of it. Thoughtless habit, accustomed to overlooking its own boldness, strengthens the guilty impulse.

"Qui flet in adversis pueriles errat in actus;
140 et lacrimas perdit et Famam polluit. Auget
litus arans adversa dolor, nescitque rigorem
quo solidat Natura viros. Doluisse dolenda
non redimit, nec damna levant, qui damna queruntur.
Hic dolor elusas lacrimas serit, irrita mandat
145 semina; nam sterilis nullaque puerpera messae
fit seges, et fallit vacuum cultura colonum.
    "Si miser es, spera! Veniet felicior annis
horula, meta malis. Aperit solatia maestis
Fortunae levitas: verni praenuntia plausus
150 maeroris praesaevit hiemps, praeludit amaris
mox latura favos. Miseris Fortuna secundos
adiectura dies; subitosque miserrima laetis
promittunt aditus; Fortunae lubrica nescit
mobilitas fixisse rotam, sceptroque minatur
155 solaturque casas. Varios fastidit honores
Caesaris et tandem solii spem mandat Amyclae."

"He who weeps at hardship has strayed into childishness; he squanders his tears and taints his good name. Grief, plow- 140 ing the barren strand, increases his hardships, and never knows that firmness with which Nature emboldens men. To grieve at one's grievous plight does not make it better, and those who complain of their suffering do not suffer less. Such grief strews futile tears, sows seed in vain; for grief is 145 sterile and produces no corn yielding a harvest, and his farming leaves the farmer deceived and empty-handed.

"If you are unhappy, be hopeful! A happier hour will come, an end to hard years. The very capriciousness of Fortune af- fords comfort to the sorrowful: the winter of sorrow is a har- 150 binger of the favor of spring, preluding with bitterness the sweets she will soon be bringing. Fortune is bound to bring a happier day to those in misery; the unhappiest times prom- ise the sudden arrival of happiness; for Fortune, slippery and unstable, can never stay her wheel. A threat to the ruler offers solace to the cottage dweller. For she tires of Caesar's 155 array of honors, and finally permits even Amyclas to hope for a throne."

Capitulum 4

Oratio Solonis circa Prudentiam et vitae optimam compositionem

Dixerat. At Solon: "Minor est praecognita Fati
asperitas; adversa minus praevisa flagellant.
Et quia Fortunae laqueum Prudentia solvit,
160 semper ubique tibi caveas, teque omnis in omnes
cautela eventus praemuniat, et tibi toti
sis oculus totus. Animi sollertia, lampas
praevia, noctifugam ferat insopita lucernam.
Haec tibi dictatrix operum cunctisque magistra
165 prima rudimentis, ne qua laedatur honestum,
invigilet, nulloque tibi non consulat actu.
     "Rem male provisam dubius manet exitus. alis
evolat insolidis si quem rapit impetus ausu
non bene pennato. Melior nisi navita clavum
170 torserit et velo biberit Prudentia ventos,
tam mare quam mortem poturae crederis alno.
     "Si datur indemnis voto dilatio, votum
differ, ut inspicias. Properatum velle volentem
fraudat, et audaces maturo paenitet ausi.
175 Tarda venit subitis successus gloria; damnum
praecipitat qui vota rapit. Facienda diserte

Chapter 4

Solon's oration on Prudence and the best way of ordering one's life

He had finished. But Solon followed: "The harshness of Fate foreknown is less severe; adversity strikes less cruelly when it is foreseen. And since Prudence loosens the knots of Fortune, be always and everywhere on your guard, take every 160 precaution to protect yourself against every eventuality, and be for yourself an all-seeing eye. Let alertness of mind, a forward-looking, unquenchable lamp, provide a beacon to dispel the darkness. Let Prudence prescribe your tasks and teach you how to begin in all that you do; let her be watch- 165 ful, lest your character be damaged in any way, and let there be no undertaking in which she does not advise you.

"When a thing is badly planned, the outcome is uncertain. He who is caught up by impulse to an act of unfledged boldness flies on unsteady wings. If Prudence, the best of sailors, has not taken the helm and controlled the filling of 170 the sail with wind, you have entrusted yourself to a vessel that is bound to drink its fill of both seawater and death.

"If what you seek to do can be delayed without harm, defer your plan, so that you may consider it. The too-hasty pursuit of a thing hoped for betrays him who hopes, and those who act rashly soon regret their rashness. The glory of 175 success is slow in coming for work abruptly begun; to snatch at what one wants is to bring on disaster. If a thing is to be

sunt studio tractanda morae. Festina iuventam
plus redolent, praevisa virum; praecepsque volendi
plurima praesumit infantia, pauca secundat.

180   "Circumspecta tamen oculo scrutante, labora
impiger officii, nec honesto languidus actu.
Ignavo torpore veta mollescere nervos,
nec sub fasciculo fascem laturus anhela.
Sordida, tersa minus, vulgo cognatior, absit
185 cura, relinquatur aliis, aliena sit omnis
actori paritura notam. Vilescat oportet
libertatis honor, serviles si induat usus.
    "Est tamen ut quotiens locus aut vis temporis urget,
maiorum deceant plebaea negotia mores.
190 Quicquid ages, virtus illud praemandet; et orsus
perfice! Nam coepti qui finem praeterit errat
turpius admittens quam qui non inchoat. Illud
accusat levitas, hoc disquisitio recti
excusare potest, opera nil ausa repenti,
195 propositi longo trutinans examine metas.
    "Si qua tamen coepisse pudet, clausisse pudori
et culpae est, scelerumque licet rescindere cursus.
Imperfecta solent veniam delicta mereri,
et levius laedit qui parcius institit error.
200   "Quas adhibes curas, vix interrumpe. Laboris
difficilem rursus capit intercisio nodum.

done with skill it must be done with a due regard for time. Haste is the way of youth, foresight of manhood; and the childishly wishful impulse to undertake many projects accomplishes little.

"Look about you, then, with probing eye. Labor tirelessly 180 at your task, and never weary of honest toil. Do not allow your sinews to grow soft in idle dullness, and if you would bear the fasces do not let a fascicle weary you. Put far away those base and impure concerns that are the property of the 185 mob; let these be left for others, and have no part in anything that will bring censure on the doer. The honorable status of a free man must needs grow base if it takes on servile pursuits.

"But it may happen that when circumstances or the pressure of time require it, plebeian tasks may be appropriate for men of noble character. Whatever you do, let virtue pre- 190 scribe it; and once embarked, complete it! For he who leaves unfinished what he has undertaken commits a more shameful error than he who does not begin. One is the fault of idleness; the other can be excused through the discovery of a legitimate motive, a task not to be rashly or hastily taken up, a decision requiring a long and careful consideration of 195 the object of the enterprise.

"If, however, one is ashamed of having begun some task, and it seems shameful and blameworthy to bring it to completion, one may declare the guilty undertaking null and void. Unaccomplished crimes are commonly treated indulgently, and a wrong action does less harm if its effect remains tentative.

"Whatever concerns occupy you, avoid interruption. 200 When a task is broken off it is difficult to grasp the problem

Fax, sopita nisi moveatur, mota soporem
excitat in flammas vigiles, motuque remisso
languet et amissos iterum vix integrat ignes.
205   "Crescat, et in ramos Virtus fundatur et alta
evolet, et penitus fixis radicibus orbem
occupet; egregiis factis vulgata, tibique
mane bono cumulet meliori vespere Famam.
Assiduo fructu pariant hanc saecula messem,
210   nec nisi cum morum veniat lux crastina luce.
    "Si qua tibi vitio sordet vicinia, labem
effuge, ne spargant similes contagia mendae.
Dilexisse bonos et eis devinctius uti
innuit esse bonum, ratioque probabilis urget
215   esse malum coluisse malos. Accedit eisdem
unanimes nectens studiis devotio; blanda
stringitur in simili convictus copula voto;
et Marti Venus est, et Marcia grata Catoni,
nec Phariam Caesar refugit, Cornelia Magnum.
220   "Livoris pudeat rastro verrisse bonorum
magnificos actus; alienas auribus aequis
non corrosivus, non invidus accipe laudes.
Sunt quos immeritus honor indignatur, et illud
non attingit humi serpens ignavia culmen,
225   pigra, nec accedens, quem tollit gloria, monti.
Hi, quos erexit probitas odere, favoris
non habitos plausus aliis fluxisse dolentes,
alteriusque favent animo successibus aegro.

again. A torch grows faint unless it is moved about; once moved it arouses its drowsy light into wakeful flames, but when movement ceases it grows faint and can scarcely re-muster its wasted fires.

"Let Virtue flourish, let it spread its branches and grow 205 tall, and grip the earth with its deep-set roots; may it be widely known through your outstanding deeds, and increase your reputation from good dawning to still better evening. May future ages bring this harvest to continual fruition, and 210 let no day's light arrive unattended by the light of your good deeds.

"If proximity to vicious conduct causes you to appear tainted, flee from the danger, lest your associates spread the contagion of their error. To cherish the good, and engage yourself closely with them is a sign that you are good, and a plausible deduction suggests that to cultivate bad compan- 215 ions is bad. It is a devotion to common pursuits that joins together those of like mind; the sweet bond of intimacy is made fast by a common desire: it is thus that Venus is pleas-ing to Mars, and Marcia to Cato, that Caesar does not reject the Egyptian queen, nor Cornelia Pompey.

"Think it shameful to seek to sweep away the splendid 220 deeds of good men with the rake of envy; be neither caustic nor envious, but accept praise of another with impartial ear. There are those who are angered by honor they consider un-deserved; their own poor spirit, hugging the ground, does not attain these heights, too indolent to approach the lofty 225 mountain of glory. Such men hate those whom worthiness has exalted, aggrieved that the favor and acclaim which they do not receive should flow to others, and they are sick at heart as they commend another's successes.

"Parce tuae laudi! Si quid bene gesseris, alter
230   te tacito laudet. Aliis dicenda, silendum
est tibi; nec vacua sunt laude silentia laudis.
Absit, ut a propriis iactandi gloria factis
exeat et Famam praeco sibi polluat actor.
Plus egisse, loqui minus: id decet. Amplior actis
235   esto, minor tumidam solvat praesumptio linguam.
    "Absit, ut externi vitii te illaesa voluptas
ad scelus invitet, impunitumque timeri
non perdat facinus; populus delinquere regum
a simili nolit. Non est defendere culpam
240   ostendisse malos; scelus est absolvere crimen
crimine, nec magna redimunt exempla reatus.
    "Sit tibi pro lima sapiens, auriga regendi
pectoris excessus inhibens; suppresset habenam
ad medium tendens, laterum vitando paludes.
245   Hic tibi sincerae ferat exemplaria vitae;
hic praecepta tuos domet in moralia sensus,
hic paleas purgans excussos ventilet actus,
albaque mundandae tribuat tersoria menti.
    "Prudentum speculo mores compone, disertos
250   dilige, philosophis impende libentior aures.

"Avoid self-praise! If you have done something well, let another praise it while you say nothing. It is for others to 230
speak, and for you to be silent; silence about one's own merit is not devoid of merit. Far be it that your glorious praises should be the result your own efforts, that the doer of the deeds should mar his reputation by becoming his own herald. To do much, to say little: this is seemly. Be expansive in your actions, but do not presume to flaunt yourself in 235
inflated speech.

"Let not another's unscathed pleasure in vicious conduct induce you to a guilty act; let not an unpunished crime remove your own fears; a people is not bound to follow the guilty example of their king. To point out that there are malefactors is not to condone their wrongdoing; what is 240
wicked is to give legitimacy to use crime to excuse crime; that great men provide the example does not redeem the guilt.

"Let a wise man be your standard, a charioteer controlling the spirit and curbing errant tendencies; let his hand on the reins impose a middle course, avoiding the mire on either side. Let this man provide you with the example of a 245
pure life; let him conform your understanding to moral precepts; let him purge away chaff, expose your actions to a winnowing scrutiny, and provide a white cloth to cleanse your mind.

"Order your character on the model of prudent men, cultivate the wise, and lend a willing ear to the philosopher. 250

Capitulum 5

De subita morum mutatione circa
Atticum Palaemonem

"Auribus hortatus bibulis hausisse peritos,
quos habeat fructus, satis est monstrasse Palaemo
Atticus, effusi suadente libidine luxus,
qui non illecebris modo lascivire, sed ipso
255 luxuriae noto plebescere nomine vellet.
    "Hic, matutinis Phoebo candente caminis,
morbida nocturnae liquit dispendia cenae,
marcidus unguentis, sertis redimitus, honustus
ora ligante mero, petulanti pictus amictu.
260 Aspectuque vagus, Xenocratis limen apertum
cernit et accedit, plena sapientibus ausus
consedisse domo, salibus risuque faceto
divitis eloquii morsurus dogma. Sed illum
indignata virum gravitas matura recessum
265 maturare iubet. Xenocratis sola morandi
indulget veniam bonitas tranquilla; manuque
pacis signa movet, et quod tractabat omisso
proposito cursu, vires formamque modesti
disserit, ut iuvenem, luxu qui sordet, honesti
270 urat in affectus, aliosque inflammet amores,
et vitae in melius revocandae spiret odorem.

Chapter 5

On the sudden transformation in the character of Polemo of Athens

"To show what benefits he may gain whose thirsty ears have taken in the exhortations of the wise, it is enough to cite Polemo of Athens, who not only loved to indulge wanton appetites, seduced by a desire for prodigal excess, but wished his reputation for wantonness to be common knowledge. 255

"As Phoebus was brightening his morning path, Polemo was leaving the unwholesome excesses of an all-night banquet, heavily perfumed, crowned with garlands, full of wine which impaired his speech, and adorned with a gaudy robe. His unsteady gaze fell on Xenocrates's open door, and he approached, making so bold as to take a seat in a house filled with wise men, and mock the theme of their rich discourse with jests and idle laughter. The company, their mature gravity outraged, ordered him to make a hasty withdrawal. Only the tranquil goodness of Xenocrates himself granted him permission to stay. He made a peaceful gesture with his hand, and departing from the subject under discussion, spoke about the power and character of moderation, in order to kindle in this young man, so tainted by excess, an attraction to probity, make him burn with love of another kind, and inspire him to the appeal of recalling his life to a better way. 260 265 270

"Nec mora, primitias capienti fronte pudoris
erubet et molles habitus damnasse Palaemo
sustinet, et vultus accusat purpura crimen.
275 Ecce voluptatum pudet et piget, ecce coronam
decerpit capiti, leviumque insignia vellit,
dispersaque comam serie conturbat et hirtam
maturat tenero iuvenilem pectinis usu.
Effusasque manus inconsulteque vagantes
280 contrahit et clamidis fugientibus inicit umbram.
"Succedente mora, succedit gratia morum,
inque dies cedit Venus accedente venusto.
Rectificatque virum declivem regula virtus,
philosophumque facit facundia philosophantis,
285 Socraticosque bibit Xenocratis alumnulus imbres."

Capitulum 6

Quod Architrenius Naturam viderit in loco floribus praelascivo, et de Naturae habitu eminenti et comitatu eiusdem

Sic loquitur Solon, et prona funditur urna
eloquii torrens, non arescente loquendi
aequore nec liquidis intermiscente paludes.

"At once Polemo blushes, his forehead receiving the first tokens of his shame, and as his flushed face declares his sense of guilt, he agrees to destroy his effete garments. Indeed he feels shame and disgust for his pleasures, snatches the crowning garland from his head, tears away all the tokens of frivolity, shakes out the scattered locks of his hair and by the delicate exercise of the comb disposes its youthful bushiness in a mature way. He draws back his hands, outflung and moving at random, and compels them to flee to the shadow of his cloak.

"With the passage of time, the appeal of morality increases, and Venus yields, day by day as its charm gains the ascendancy. The rule of virtue rectifies the fallen man, fluency in philosophic discourse makes him a philosopher, and he becomes Xenocrates's nursling, imbibing drafts of Socratic wisdom."

Chapter 6

Architrenius beholds Nature, in a place luxuriant with flowers. Nature's noble attire and her companions

Thus Solon spoke, and the flood of eloquence poured forth from his inclining urn, a tide of discourse that neither ran dry nor interrupted its steady flow with stagnant pools.

Proclives oculos levat Architrenius: instar
290 sideris ardescens mulier spectatur, et igni
latius educto rutilum procul explicat orbem,
ingeminatque loci radios; nam Vere marito
praegnativa parit rosulas et lilia Tellus,
splendoresque serit alios fecundula florum
295 Flora, perennantis iubar effusiva diei.
Non hiemis faecem queritur tersissima Veris
area, nec recipit Zephyrus consortia brumae.
　　Haec mulier vultu roseo phoebescit, ephebis
defaecata genis, senio matura. Virentis
300 servat adhuc laurum faciei, temporis aevo
non minor, ut Pylios longe praecesserit annos.
Non marcente cuti vetulatur fixa iuventae
floriditas; anus est aetas faciesque puella.
Nec speculum longi nebulescit temporis umbra.
305 Praeminet in specie maiestas; sobrius oris
matronatur honos; levitatem nulla fatetur
portio nec quatitur gestu petulante. Gravescit
tota: brevisque suum non perdit fimbria pondus.
Illasciva sedet, quovis reverenda, chorusco
310 imperiosa throno, quem lactea crine coronat
turba senum, dominae genibus minor. Ardua sedes
est illos aequasse pedes; plenaque licentur
nobilitate deae summum contingere calcem.
Innituntur humo, cancellatisque sedentes
315 cruribus, insternunt pro pulvinaribus herbas.
　　Miratur solito magis Architrenius, ardet
agnovisse deam. Novitas blanditur et urit

394

Architrenius raises his downcast eyes: he beholds a woman, 290
whose starlike brilliance, blazing forth on every side, spreads
a circle of glowing light far abroad, and redoubles the splen-
dor of the place; for Earth, made pregnant by Spring, her
bridegroom, brings forth rosebuds and lilies, while prolific
Flora spreads abroad the splendors of other blooms, diffus- 295
ing the brilliance of endless day. The flawless expanse of this
Spring is not troubled by the dregs of winter, nor must
Zephyrus endure the company of frost.

This woman, Phoebus-like in the rosy glow of her face,
has the unblemished cheek of youth, though of mature age.
She preserves the freshness of a flourishing complexion, 300
though her age is not less than that of time itself, so that she
has far surpassed the years of the old man of Pylos. By no
wrinkling of the skin does her unchanging youthful bloom
appear aged; an old woman in years, her face is a young girl's.
The traces of a long lifetime do not cloud her mirror. Maj- 305
esty predominates in her appearance; the sober dignity of
her face is matronly; none of her features suggests levity or
is disturbed by a wanton gesture. Her dignity is complete:
even the brief fringe of her garment does not lose its down-
ward tendency. Grave, revered by all, she sits in majesty on a 310
gleaming throne, about which the throng of old men, seated
below the knees of their mistress, form a crown of white
hair. To have attained the level of those feet is to enjoy a
lofty station, and it is because of the ample nobility of the
goddess that they are permitted to approach this highest
place. They lower themselves to the ground, and sitting with
crossed legs, make the grass serve them in place of cushions. 315

Architrenius is amazed beyond measure, and longs to ap-
proach the goddess. The novelty of her appearance beguiles

in desiderium. De qua, Solone docenti,
ut primum didicit quod erat Natura, citato
320 advolat excursu, fletum derivat, adultae
laetitiae testem, comitatu gaudia dulci
producunt lacrimae. Venit, affandique negatur
copia, de mundo Genesi texente loquelam.

Capitulum 7

Sermo Naturae de obsequio quod mundus homini exhibet et situ eiusdem et motu

"Omnigenae partus homini famulantur. Eique
325 et domus et nutrix ancillaque, machina mundi,
omne bonum fecunda parit; maiorque minori
obsequitur mundus. Tibi discors unio rerum
aeternum statura coit, fractoque tumultu
pax elementa ligat. Gaude tibi sidera volvi;
330 defigique polos; mundique rotatilis aulae
artificem gratare Deum; Dominumque ministro
erexisse domum cuius molitio summum
actorem redolet. Excelsi dextera tantis
dotibus excoluit opifex opus omnia posse
335 disputat illud eam; nec enim decisa potestas
est ea, qua numquam lapsurus volvitur orbis

him and he burns with desire. As soon as he has learned by
the prompting of Solon that this is Nature, he rushes head-   320
long toward her, summons forth weeping to witness the full-
ness of his happiness, and a company of tender tears attends
his joy. A rush of words emerges, but is stayed, as Genesis
herself fashions a discourse about the universe.

Chapter 7

Nature's speech on the service that the universe offers to man, and on its structure and motion

"Creatures of every kind attend on man. For him this uni-   325
versal frame, home and nurse and handmaid, brings forth
every good in its fertility; the greater world obeys the will of
the lesser. It is for you that that the union of its discordant
parts coheres in eternal stability, that peace has put down
the conflict of the elements and united them. Be glad that
the stars revolve for you; that the poles stand firm; that they   330
are pleasing to God, the maker and ruler of this whirling
court, the universe; that the Lord has constructed for his
minister a home whose very composition tells of its supreme
author. The shaping hand of that lofty being has endowed
his handiwork with such gifts that it declares his omnipo-   335
tence; for that power is unlimited through which the

raptibus aeternis, totusque volubilis axem
circuit immotum, paribusque rotatibus actam
praecipitat sphaeram, dum sola immobilis ima
340 pondere vergit humus. Nullo conamine surgens,
se nulla levitate rotat, centroque cohaeret
impatiens motus, medio pigrescit in axe
infima, si veteres verum cecinere. Modernae
at melior, famosa minus, sollertia pubis:
345 vel nihil est imum vel quaelibet infima.

                                                   "Mundus
ne labet, immenso circummordetur inani.
Terra vicem puncti recipit collata supremo,
unde modum terrae visus punctum aestimat, unde
fraudari radios positis procul imputat astris.
350   "Terrae forma teres, teretisque supernatat undae
curva superficies, terramque amplectitur arcu
imperfecta maris, prohibenti litore, sphaera,
quae medium centri contingit cuspide mundum.
    "Ardenti spolio vestitur sidere caelum,
355 multifidaque face tenebris occurrit, et orbi
exhibet excubias, oculis populosior Argus.
Astra pluunt radios, et caligantibus usum
Lampadis indulgent; et pessum nata superne
flamma peregrinat, sordentibus hospita tectis.
360   "Contrahitur terrae stella globus artior. Illum,
visa minor, superat astri rota plenior; infra
sunt Cytherea, soror Phoebi, Cyllenius ales.

universe, never faltering, is turned with eternal force, and all circles in rotation about an unmoved axis, that power which impels the firmament to move in a constant orbit, while the Earth alone, unmoved, is borne downward by its weight. Powerless to raise itself, it lacks the buoyancy to rotate, and clings to the center, admitting no movement, the inert low point on the central axis, if what the ancients sang is true. But the astuteness of our modern youth, though less renowned, is superior: either there is no lowest point, or the low point can be anywhere.

"Lest the universe should fall away, it is contained by a boundless void. The Earth has the role of a centerpoint in relation to the heavens, and thus the viewer deems the Earth no larger than a point, and blames the distant placement of the stars for having deceived his sight.

"The Earth is round in form, and the curving surface of the rounded ocean swims over it. The sphere of ocean, incomplete because of the intruding landmass, embraces the Earth in its arc, and its center point corresponds to the center of the Earth.

"The sky is clad in a blazing array of stars, challenges the darkness with this many-faceted torch, and keeps watch over the world, an Argus more fully endowed with eyes. The stars rain down their beams, and grant the use of their lamps to those in darkness; born in heaven, their fire descends to travel abroad, a welcome guest in lowly dwellings.

"The globe of the Earth is more limited in size than a star. The circle of a star, though it appears smaller, far exceeds it. Cytherea, the sister of Phoebus, and the winged Cyllenian are smaller.

340

345

350

355

360

Capitulum 8

De duplici stellarum genere

"Scinditur in geminum stellans genus: altera fixus
impetus astra movet, error premit altera flexu
365 multivago torsisse vias. Interque planetas,
falce Senex, sceptroque Iovis, Marsque ense coruscat;
Sol arcum, Cytherea facem, Cyllenius harpen
et Phoebe pharetram venandi fervida gestat.
        "Astri Luna vicem Phoebi mendicat ab astro;
370 sideris obscuro naturam eliminat orbe.
Iacturam redimit et Solis imagine Solem
induit et damnum fraterna lampade pensat.
Parte iubar recipit, partem ferrugine texit,
nec Stygium perdit partim Proserpina peplum.
375 Nunc tamen et toto fraudatur luminis usu,
cum Phoebi radios terrae ferit obvia nubes,
et caput aut caudam lunamque intercipit umbra
et soror a fratris vultu declinat amato,
totaque sulphureo nubit Proserpina Diti.
380   "Nec minus et fratris homini iubar invidet, arcens
obiectu radios, noctem mentita reciso
luminis excursu. Visusque excussus, ut axes
Phoebeos feriat, lunari offenditur orbe,
nec placitam celeri defigit harundine praedam.

400

Chapter 8

The two kinds of stars

"The starry race is divided into two kinds: a fixed course governs the movement of one kind, while the other is compelled to pursue a random, winding course of continual change. Among the planets, light flashes from the scythe of aged Saturn, the scepter of Jove, and the sword of Mars; the Sun brandishes his bow, Cytherea her torch, the Cyllenian his curved blade, and Phoebe, that avid huntress, her quiver.

"The Moon borrows the property of a star from the star of Phoebus; because her orb is dark, she does not possess the natural property of a star. She compensates for this failing by imitating the Sun and assuming his appearance, offsetting her own defect with her brother's light. In one part she receives his light, while cloaking another in dusky darkness, for Proserpina does not cast off a portion of her Stygian mantle. Yet at times she is robbed of all access to light, when the shadow of the Earth obstructs Phoebus's rays, and intercepts the Moon at the head or tail of its path, so that the sister is withdrawn from the sight of her beloved brother, and Proserpina gives herself up to sulfurous Dis.

"But she also begrudgess her brother's light to mankind, concealing his rays by intruding herself, and creating false night by cutting off the emission of his light. As our vision goes forth, aiming to strike the center of Phoebus's circle, it is obstructed by the orb of the Moon, and its swift arrow does not reach its intended target.

Capitulum 9

De quorundam circulorum caelestium descriptione

385 "Figit utrumque polum, paribusque utrumque diei
respicit aequator spatiis. Mundique tumorem
dividit et partes in sphaera maximus aequat.
Nec minor obliquo signorum circulus arcu
ad Boream surgit et ad Austrum vergit; et illum
390 aequator mediumque secat, mediusque secatur.
Nec minor et mediae qui nocti ascribitur orbis,
dimidiumque diem metiri dicitur arcu
stante, ceniz capitum mundique supermeat axes.
Nec minor et medius medium partitus, utrumque
395 percutit axe ceniz, visus finitor, orizon,
et Styga cum superis communi limite nodat.
Linea solstitii mundi curvatur ad axes
orbe paralello; Phoebi sensura recursus,
proxima fit capitum vel distantissima puncto.

400 "Et tamen aequator directo figit in orbe
solstitium, quo cernit Aren simul Arcton et Austrum.
Deprensum est hunc esse locum, tumor ille duobus
solstitiis ardet, totidemque recessibus idem
friget, et aequator solem statione reflectit
405 aequidiemque facit. Etenim sol cogitur omni

Chapter 9

A description of certain
celestial circles

"The equator defines the two poles, and looks upon each   385
during an equal interval of daylight. It cuts across the world's
swell at its widest point, and divides its sphere into equal
parts. The circle of the constellations, no less great, rises to-
ward Boreas and bends its slanting course toward Auster;
the equator intersects it at its midpoint, and is intersected   390
by it at its own. No smaller is the circle of the meridian,
which is used to calculate the midpoint of night and divide
the day in half by its steady circle, encompassing the zeniths
and the equatorial poles. Nor is that circle smaller which is
divided in half by the meridian, and whose poles mark the
midpoint between the two zeniths, the horizon, which sets   395
a limit to sight, and draws the heavens and the Stygian realm
together at a common border. The line of the solstice inter-
sects the poles in its circular course; it registers the recur-
ring shifts of the sun, and is at one time close to the zenith
point, at another far from it.

"But the equator, too, where Aren beholds both the   400
Northern Pole and the Southern, marks a solstice in its own
level circle. It has been determined that in this region the
swelling earth grows hot at its two solstices, while at the two
withdrawals the same region grows cold, until the equator
turns the Sun back to its stable path and creates an equinox.   405

stare paralello, qui Cancri interiacet altum
depressique situs caput Aegocerontis. Et illa
sunt loca, Zodiacus ubi plus declinat ad Austri
Arcturique polos, et ab aequatore recedit.

410   "Amplior includit egressae cuspidis orbem
area Zodiaci, quo sol raptatur ad ortum
ingenito motu, centroque amplectitur arcum.
Nunc terrae propior, nunc elongatus, et augis
figitur in Geminis, et pigra rotatur ad ortum,
415 fixis tarda comes in eisdem raptibus astris.

Capitulum 10

De eis quae accidunt
ex varia positione horizontis

"Dividit innumerus sphaeram declivis horizon,
augeturque dies Cancri, contraque minorem
deprimit Aegoceron, quanto est erectior Arctos
fit brevior brevior et maior maior, eamque
420 nox recipit formam, similique revolvitur arcu.
Hic situs est declivis, ubi producitur absque
nocte dies Cancri, nec nox contractior arcu
languet in opposito; surgitque Aurora diei

For the Sun is compelled to dwell in every latitude that lies between the high point of Cancer and the zenith of low-lying Capricorn. And these are the places where the Zodiac inclines most toward the North and South poles, and withdraws most from the equator.

"Insofar as the Sun is drawn toward its rising by its own inherent motion, a broader portion of the Zodiac encompasses its eccentric course, and makes its orbit conform to its center. Passing close to the earth at one moment, it withdraws from it at another, at its apogee it is located in Gemini, and returns slowly to its rising point, a sluggish companion to those stars that are fixed in constant orbits.

410

415

Chapter 10

Things which occur because of the changing position of the horizon

"The shifting horizon divides its circle in innumerable ways. Daytime is increased in Cancer, whereas the weight of Capricorn makes it shorter; and in proportion as the Polestar ascends, the shorter grows shorter, the longer longer, while night assumes a corresponding form and passes through a similar cycle. At the point of extreme deviation, daytime in Cancer is prolonged by the absence of night, while at the opposite extreme night is just as long; Aurora appears,

420

promissura facem, sed non latura, vel instans
425 cogitur esse dies; nam idem complectitur ortum
punctus et occasum. Superisque revolvitur orbe
dimidio Phoebus, Thetidisque recolligit undis
surgentes radios, pascitque soporibus artus
insomnes alias, udisque cubilibus ardet.
430   "Est ubi nox piceo mensem non vestit amictu,
est ubi per geminos eadem non texitur umbra,
est ubi luna tribus fraterna lampade pallet,
est ubi bis duplici sol insopitus anhelat,
est ubi per quinque Phoebi vigil excubat ignis,
435 est ubi sex solito caret hospite mater Achillis.
    "Nec minus extendi brumae contingit ad arcus
oppositos noctes, totoque rotabitur anno
una una cum nocte dies. Ubi meta videnti
sternitur aequator, et mundi figitur axe
440 indeclive ceniz, mediique est nulla diei
linea, vel quaevis situi cuicumque diurnam
partitura moram, Boreae quia subiacet. Illa
in longum regio non tenditur, omnibus ipsa
latior. Occiduis numquam decurritur astris.

promising the lamp of daylight but not producing it, or else day is reduced to an instant; for the same point of time embraces both rising and setting. Phoebus is borne through the heavens in a diminished orbit, and draws his beams back to the depths of Thetis even as they rise, granting sleep to limbs which are otherwise sleepless, and eager for a watery bed. 425

"There is a place where for a month night does not spread her pitchy mantle; another where her shadow is not cast for two months; one where the Moon is dimmed by her brother's lamp for three months; one where the Sun labors without slumber for twice two months; one where the watchful fire of Phoebus keeps vigil for five; and one where Achilles's mother is deprived of her accustomed guest for six. 430 435

"Nor are the frosty nights any less protracted at the opposed poles, where the cycle of an entire year consists of a single day and a single night. At the point where the extended plane of the equator marks the limit of sight, and an unshifting zenith is defined by the axis of the earth, there is no meridian line, nor anything such as would divide the day into regular periods in other places, for it lies at the very north. This region is not defined by longitude, and its latitude is greater than at any other place. The stars that pass over it never set. 440

Capitulum 11

De ortu signorum

445   "Semper ab Eoo consurgit cardine mundus
axibus immotis. Signorumque erigit orbem,
errantesque trahit stellas. Totumque revolvit
in paritate morae; nec idem mutatur eodem
mutatove situ. Nec surgit segnior arcus
450   quam cadat oppositus; et Cancri semper in ortu
Aegoceron vergit; et rursum, si qua propinquant
Phrixei capiti vel Librae signa, paresque
interhabent arcus; neutrum deductius ortu
surgit. Et Astraeam qui Chelas impetus urget,
455   Haemoniique moras Hydrae sibi vendicat ultor.
     "Omnibus hoc sphaeris. Sed qua directus orizon
ustam cingit Aren, aequalis dirigit ortus
Zodiaci quartas, tropicas ubi flectit habenas
sol, noctique diem punctis finalibus aequat.
460   Quilibet hic arcus aequales protrahit ortu
occasuque moras, oriturque aequaliter omne
opposito signum. Nam Librae suscipit horas
portitor Helleus, nec Tauro Scorpio cedit.
Permittitque Chiron gemino sua tempora fratri;
465   Aegoceron Cancro par enatat, Urna Leoni;

Chapter 11

The rising of the constellations

"The motion of the heavens on their unmoving axis always 445
arises from the eastern portal. Here rises the circle of the
constellations, here the wandering stars are drawn forth.
The whole firmament revolves at a uniform rate; nothing is
changed from its constant state, nor does its location
change. One portion of the circle does not rise more slowly
than the opposing portion declines; Capricorn always de- 450
scends at the rising of Cancer; likewise the constellations
that border the Phrixean Ram or Libra maintain equal in-
tervals between them; none moves forth too tentatively
from its rising. The same force drives both Astraea and
Libra, and the avenger of the Hydra adopts for himself the 455
behavior of the Haemonian.

"This is true for all the spheres. But where the horizon
centers on burning Aren, when the Sun guides his teams
away from the tropics, and makes day equal to night in ex-
tent, an equal rising governs the sections of the Zodiac.
Here every portion of the circle will enjoy an equal interval 460
of rising and setting, and every constellation will arise in
exact correspondence to its opposite. The ferrier of Helle
claims the hour of Libra, and Scorpio yields nothing to
Taurus. Chiron allows the twin brother his due interval;
Capricorn floats aloft like Cancer, the Urn like the Lion; the 465

Erigonesque moras aequant dispendia Piscis.
Aequis a tropico spatiis distantia surgunt,
tractu signa pari; tropicoque propinquius ortum
plenius extendit. Et Libra tardior exit
470   Scorpius, Erigone Cancer, Vectore Lacones."

time allotted to Pisces equals that of Erigone. The constellations arise at an equal distance from the tropic, in an identical path; in proportion as their rising is closer to the tropic the interval is extended. Thus Scorpio emerges more slowly than Libra, Cancer more slowly than Erigone, the Spartans than the Carrier." 470

BOOK NINE

Capitulum 1

De admiratione Architrenii super
verbis Naturae

"Mirari faciunt magis haec quam scire, rudisque
ingenii non est" ait Architrenius "astris
intrusisse stilum vel, quae divina sigillant
scrinia, deciso dubii cognoscere velo.
5 Trans hominem sunt verba deae. Miracula caecus
audio, nam lampas animi subtilia pingui
celatur radio. Nec mens sublimia visu
vix humili cerni;, nec distantissima luce
fumidula monstrat. Tamen haec ut maxima credam,
10 maiestas dicentis agit; caelumque legentem
miror, et ignotis delector, et aure libenti
sollicitor, si magna loquens maiora loquatur."

Chapter 1

Architrenius's amazement at Nature's words

"These things create wonder rather than knowledge," says Architrenius. "It is not for the rude intellect to impose a pattern on the stars, or rend the veil of doubt and learn what divine caskets keep sealed. The words of a goddess are beyond human understanding. I hear of such miracles as if blind, for the lamp of my mind obscures subtle matters by its dull light. My mind can scarcely discern sublimity with its lowly gaze; its smoky little lamp cannot reveal things so remote. Nevertheless the majesty of the speaker compels me to believe these great utterances. I marvel at your reading of the heavens, take delight in things unknown, and wait eagerly with ready ear, should she who speaks of great matters speak of matters still greater."

Capitulum 2

De residuo ortus
signorum

Interea coeptum Genesis non segnior urget,
sermonisque rota properante diutius addit:
15 "Qua vero inclinat sphaeram declivis horizon
deprimiturque Notus, ibi quarta citatior exit,
quam caput alterutro Phrixeum limite claudit.
Tardior ad Librae caput est, pariterque remotis
a tropico signis, celerem rapit ocius ortum,
20 cui magis accedit trepidantis portitor Helles.
Pisce magis Libra surgendi protrahit arcum,
Aegoceronte Chiron, Tauro Leo, Scorpius Urna.

"Aegoceronta sequens declivi contrahit arcus
orbe moras ortus, rectoque diutius instat
25 segnities signi. Recipit contraria Cancri
posteritas: rectumque citus superevolat ultor
Alcidae, sphaerisque piger declivibus exit.
Tempora si sumas una quibus elicit ortus
oppositos arcus, recto labuntur in orbe
30 tanta ut declivi. Nec segnius una Lacones
Haemoniumque simul quam quaevis sphaera revolvit.
Proximitate quibus tropicus accedit eadem,

Chapter 2

What remains to be said about the rising of the constellations

Even as he speaks, Genesis, unflagging, presses forward, continuing further on the whirling wheels of speech: "Where the circle of the horizon is tilted and the southern 15 region is thrust downward, there the quarter of the Zodiac which the house of Aries contains with its two boundaries emerges more swiftly. The pace approaching the house of Libra is slower, as it is also for constellations that are equally distant from the tropic, while a constellation takes its rise more swiftly that is located closer to the bearer of trembling 20 Helle. Libra protracts her upward movement longer than Pisces, Chiron longer than Capricorn, Leo than Taurus, Scorpio than the Urn.

"Those constellations that follow Capricorn along the slanting path reduce the time of their ascending arc, and on the upright circle they move forward more gradually. Those 25 constellations that follow Cancer experience the opposite effect: the attacker of Alcides flies swiftly over the upright circle, but is slow to depart from the inclined. If you take together the lengths of time required for the rising of opposed constellations, as much time will elapse in the upright circle as in the inclined. One circle does not revolve the 30 Spartans and the Haemonian more slowly than the other. The same movement governs those constellations which

accidit illud idem; nam quantus pignora Ledae
elevat et Cancrum, visus ubi limitat Arctos,
35   tantus ubi Borea surgenti vergit orizon.
      "Nec citius, qua fervet Aren, mundique tumorem
occupat, excurrunt signi cuiuslibet una
ortus et occasus sumpti quam qua eminet Arctos
occuliturque Notus; unde in declivibus ambos
40   si simul annectas, directo fiet in orbe
alterutri duplum. Nam qua raptissima torret
ardua Libra ceniz, signo properatur ad ortum
occasumque pares; et eodem tempore, visum
quo fugit, Idaeam Ganymedes detegit Urnam.

Capitulum 3

Quod signa apud
quosdam oriuntur inversa

45   "Qua magis a fixo Boreali distat orizon
quam tropicus Cancri, qua nescia vere remitti
aequora bruma ligat, oriuntur versa caduntque
signa: priorque venit quam Piscis portitor Helles,
posterior Tauro Phrixeus, Piscibus Urna.
50   Haud secus opposita vergunt: Libraque sequenti

draw equally close to the tropic; for whatever the angle to which Leda's children and Cancer rise, where the Northern Pole defines the limits of sight, the same angle is attained 35 when the horizon shifts with the elevation of the Pole.

"The rising and setting of any given constellation do not run their course more swiftly where Aren burns, placed at the swelling center of the world, than where the Northern Pole is at its height and the Southern is hidden; thus if you 40 combine the two movements in the inclined circuit, it will amount to twice the amount of one or the other in the upright circle. For at the zenith where Libra, at her height and moving swiftly, grows hot, the length of rising and setting is identical for each constellation; Ganymede displays his Trojan Urn for the same period that he evades our gaze.

Chapter 3

The constellations appear in reverse order in certain regions

"Where the Horizon diverges from the fixed Northern 45 Pole further than the tropic of Cancer, where ice locks up oceans that never know the release of spring, the constellations rise and set in reverse order: the Phrixean bearer of Helle comes before Pisces and after Taurus, and the Urn follows Pisces. And the setting of their opposite constellations 50

Scorpius inversus decumbit, ad aequora Libra
Virgine descendit prior hospita, Virgo Leone.

Capitulum 4

De portione terrae quae tota et sola
secundum Alfraganum inhabitatur

"Circulus aequidiem librans, Austrumque colurus
qui secat et Boream, Zephyri sub cardine mundum
55   Auroraeque ligant. Quartisque aequaliter orbem
sectio distinguit, et fixo stante coluro
scinditur ad rectos terrae fixissimus orbis.
Iunctior Arcturis habitatur quarta; situsque
reicit humanos extremi frigore limbi;
60   oppositoque gelu torpescit inhospita paulo
ulterius Tyle, quam despicit hora Bootes.
Quod riget aeterna glacie, curtatur ad Arcton
orbe paralello.
          "Quartae pars cetera tractu
Mitior incolitur; Boreali limite Sclavos
65   Metatura sinus, ut Fama fante fatetur
filius Admeti. Zephyrique a follibus aequor
verberat occiduum, qua nomine celsius Atlas
quam dorso erigitur. Eous limes ad Eurum

is no different: Scorpio falls backward with Libra following; Libra descends into the welcoming ocean before Virgo, Virgo before Leo.

Chapter 4

The only portion of the earth that is fully inhabited, according to Alfraganus

"The circle that determines the balance of night and day and a colure that intersects both the Southern and Northern Poles contain the world within eastern and western boundaries. Their intersection divides the world into equal quarters, and the unvarying circumference of the Earth is intersected at right angles by the fixed position of the colure. One quarter that borders on the Arctic is inhabited. At its upper border the cold forbids human habitation; a little beyond, unwelcoming Thule, over which Bootes always lowers, is numbed by hostile frost. The region fixed in perpetual ice is terminated at the Pole by the colural circle.

"The milder remaining portion of this quarter is inhabited; along its northern border it has been settled as the haven of the Slavs, as the slave boy of Admetus could attest, if report be true. A sea driven by the bellows of Zephyrus pounds the western coast, where Atlas stands, loftier in name than in elevation. The Orient extends to the east as

finibus exit Atin, ubi Gades orbis habena
70 fixit Alexander. Cuius famosior aram
Hypanis attollit, medioque opponitur orbe
Gadibus Alcidae—si fas est credere, Fama
quod scivisse putat. Sed ad Austrum porrigit Indos,
et sitientis Aren sepelit sub sole recessus,
75 quae medios signat in adusto limite fines,
oppositisque pari discedit Gadibus arcu.

Capitulum 5

De inaequalitate dierum naturalium et arcu diei et arcu noctis

"Sol, iubar astrifugum, mundum circummeat et, quo
dimidius candet, geminum complectitur ortum
nocte sua comitata dies; verum incipit ille,
80 terminat ille diem. Sed nec mensura diebus
omnibus una facit; distinguitur illa, nec omnes
par mora distendit, cum nec rapiantur ad ortus
tractu signa pari, nec in aequo permeat aequos
tempore sol arcus orbis, qui cuspide mundi
85 centratur, medium dum terrae immobile centro
percutit, et summo distinguitur orbita signis.

far as the territory of Acin, where world-ruler Alexander 70
founded his own Cadiz. At his more famous Hypanis he
raised an altar, a counterpart, halfway round the world, to
Hercules's altar at Cadiz, if it is right to believe what Fame
deems to be certain knowledge. But India extends to the
south, and distance conceals Aren, thirsting beneath the
Sun, which marks the midpoint of the burning path, and is 75
equidistant from the opposed Cadizes.

Chapter 5

The inequality of the natural day, and the arc of day and the arc of night

"The Sun, whose radiance puts the stars to flight, circum-
navigates the universe, and where he shines for half the
time, a day, accompanied by its night, spans two sunrises, for
one rising begins each day and the other concludes it. But a 80
single standard of measure does not suffice for all days; one
is distinct from another, and all do not endure for an equal
length of time, since the constellations are not drawn to
their rising always by the same path, and the Sun does not
move in the same amount of time through equal arcs of its
orbit, which is oriented to the zenith of the firmament,
when its rays strike directly on the unmoving center of the 85
Earth, and its orbit at its highest point emerges from the
circle of the constellations.

"Volvitur in mundum mundoque revolvitur orbe
paene paralello Phoebus, nam signa relatas
declinant oblique vias. Arcusque diei
90 dicitur occasum qui claudit et exerit ortum,
oppositusque moras nocturnae limitat umbrae.
Et quia maiores declivis sphaera diei
suscipit ad Borean arcus, stratique minores
amputat hora Noti, Borealis crescit, ad Austrum
95 contrahitur devexa dies; haec plenior, illa
aequidie brevior brumalibus evolat horis.

Capitulum 6

De eccentrico et motu epicycli in eo et de circulo Draconis et de motibus planetarum

"Circulus eccentris egressa cuspide mundum
non figit medium; complectitur orbita terram
et mediam centro quam totam circuit exit.
100 Volvitur eccentri brevior epicyclus in orbe
excluditque solum, superos succinctus ad axes,
vectorisque sui cuspis non deserit arcum.

"Phoebus revolves now in opposition to the firmament, now is revolved by it in an almost parallel orbit, for the constellations descend obliquely along related paths. What is called the arc of day concludes with sunset and opens out at 90 sunrise, and the opposing arc defines the limits of the darkness of night. And because the slanted circle attains a larger diurnal arc in northern regions, while in the sprawling southern region the days are cut short, the northern day grows longer, and day is diminished in its southward de- 95 scent; the one grows larger than the equinox while the other flies more quickly through its frosty hours.

Chapter 6

The eccentric circle and the motion of the epicycle within it, the circle of the Dragon, and the motions of the planets

"An eccentric circle, whose centerpoint has shifted, does not center on the midpoint of the universe; its orbit embraces the Earth, and departs from the center of that body which it completely encircles. A smaller epicyclical revo- 100 lution is contained within the eccentric orbit and this rejects the earth, bound to the greater orbit as its axis, and its centerpoint never departs from the arc of the circle that carries it.

425

"Zodiaci nullo tractu declinat ab orbe
cuspide concentris mundo. Scinditque Draconis
105 circulus eccentrem, quisquis declinat ad Austrum
sidereosque boves, et qua transitur ab orbe
signorum ad Boream, caput est ea sectio; nodus
oppositus cauda, per quam vergente planeta
ad Noton urget iter, nautarum Plaustra relinquens.
110   "Fertur ad Auroram pariter festina planetae
cuspis in orbe brevi; brevis eluctatur ad ortum
cuspis in eccentri. Sed et hunc Draco volvit eodem
segnior eccentrem, fixis non ocior astris.
Ad Zephyrum mundo non obvia Cynthia cuspis
115 serpit in orbe brevi; praeceps excurrit eodem
impetus eccentris. Cui parvo cuspis in orbe
concentri rapitur mundo, motusque Draconis
non alio raptat egressae cuspidis orbem
eccentremque bigam, sed eadem segnior urget.
120 Reptat in occasus omni Proserpina centro;
solus in eccentri mundo brevis obviat orbis.
Non secus et Stilbons rapitur, si eccentris agatur
cuspis in occasus, infixae cuspidis orbe,
qui minor angusto sic cuspide distet ab arcu,
125 ut procul a medio mundi secat orbita mundum.
Nec minus et Stilbons comes est et Cynthia fixis
sideribus, fixaeque trahunt utrumque Draconem,
qui rotat eccentrem secum torpentibus astris.

"The concentric circle is never drawn to deviate from the orbit of the Zodiac with the earth as its center. The circle of the Dragon intersects any eccentric circle that descends toward the south and the starry oxen, and where departure from the circle of the constellations is toward the North, that intersection is called the head; the opposite point of intersection is the tail, through which the path of a descending planet leads southward, leaving behind the Wagon known to sailors.

"A planet moves swiftly toward the East in its epicyclical movement, but the epicycle labors toward its rising point in its eccentric course. The more stable Dragon, however, moves the eccentric circle at the same rate, not slower than that of the fixed stars. Cynthia, acquiescent to the Earth, creeps westward in her epicyclical course; in her eccentric movement on the same path she rushes headlong. Her movement in its epicyclical motion is controlled by the earth as its center, and the motion of the Dragon does not force the orbit of her eccentric chariot to adopt a displaced center, but slowly impels her along a constant path. Proserpina creeps toward the west wherever her orbit is centered; in her eccentric course only her epicyclical orbit resists the influence of earth. Mercury is borne along in the same way, when his eccentric course is drawn toward the west by the orbit of the unfixed center; thus his lesser circle distances its center from that of the arc by a slight eccentricity, so that his orbit centers on the earth away from the earth's center. Mercury and Cynthia are likewise companions to the fixed stars, and these determine the movement of both in respect to the Dragon, who impels their eccentric movement by his own in relation to the slow-moving stars.

Capitulum 7

De retrogradatione et statione et progressione planetae a Zodiaco versus Austrum et Septentrionem

"Retrogrados nescit errores Cynthia; nusquam
130 stat biga cum Phoebi curru, contraria mundo.
Impetus errantis fit progressivus in orbe
quem rotat eccentris, quotiens, vicinior augi,
praecipiti luctatur equo; retrogradus infra
augis in opposito, dum stellis exit Eois
135 occiduasque petit, mundoque citatior illas,
oppositos inter motus staturus, anhelat.
    "Ad Boream numquam signorum surgit ab orbe
Mercurius; contraque Venus non vergit ad Austrum;
Luna, Iovis, Mavors et iniquus Falcifer Austri
140 nunc secreta petunt, nunc sidera tarda Bootis.
Cuspis in eccentri defertur Delia nusquam
devia, Zodiaci numquam declivia mutat.
    "Ecce creatoris quid maius dextera mundo
indulsisse queat homini? Cui sidera volvit,
145 continuat lucem, fervoribus obicit umbram,
alternoque gelu sitientem submovet aestum,

Chapter 7

The retrogradation, stasis, and progression of the planets to the north and south of the Zodiac

"Cynthia knows nothing of retrograde wandering; never does her team come to a standstill with Phoebus's chariot,   130
resisting the influence of the earth. The pace of a wandering planet is progressive in the orbit that its eccentric motion pursues, whenever, drawn close to its apogee, it must struggle with its impulsive steeds; at the point opposite to its apogee, when it leaves the eastern stars and seeks those that   135
have set, its retrograde, inward movement pursues them more swiftly than the firmament, though it will come to a standstill between its two opposing motions.

"Mercury never ascends northward beyond the circle of the constellations; Venus in contrast never diverges to the south; the Moon, Jove, Mars, and the wicked Scythe-bearer seek the hidden regions of the south at one moment, the   140
slow-moving stars of Bootes at another. Delia's motion in her eccentric course never diverges, never alters in relation to the declivity of the Zodiac.

"Behold! What greater thing than the universe could the Creator's hand have bestowed on mankind? For him he moves the spheres, renews the light of day, opposes dark-   145
ness with warming beams, dispels parching summer with

et noctis somnique vices fomenta laboris
adicit, et noctis sepelit dispendia somno."

Capitulum 8

Quod Architrenius Naturae genibus obvolvitur

"Quam procul eloquii fluvius decurret et aures
150 influet exundans," ait Architrenius, "utre
iam duplici pleno? Satis est hausisse referto
vase; nec auriculae pelagi capit alveus undam."
Haec fatus rumpitque moras, pedibusque loquentis
irruit, et genuum demissos complicat artus,
155 et cubitos sternens, iunctis iacet infimus ulnis.

intervals of cold, provides the recompense of night and sleep to alleviate his toil, and buries the idle hours of darkness in slumber."

Chapter 8

Architrenius embraces the knees of Nature

"How much longer," says Architrenius, "will this river of eloquence run on, filling my ears to overflowing though the sack has already been filled twice over? Enough has been swallowed when the vessel is full; the little channel of my ear cannot contain an ocean's flood." Having said this, he delays no longer, and rushes toward the speaker's feet, folds the joints of his lowered knees, and spreading his elbows, lies prostrate with his arms together.

Capitulum 9

Oratio Architrenii ad Naturam

"Hoc nihil, immo minus nihilo, dea, respice! Fletus
fonticulos, stagna lacrimae, maeroris abyssos
extenues, et plena malis vivaria sicces.
Torqueor; et planctus animi tormenta fatetur
160 garrulus, et morbi latebras suspiria clamant.
Nec lacrima fraudo; veris a nubibus imber
solvitur, et nimbos oculi pluit intima nubes.
Ducitur ex animo luctus; certissima flendi
causa subest, et vera movent adversa querelas.
165 Nam tot inexhaustis anima languente procellis
concutior, totusque dolor circumfluor omni
peste, quod in lacrimas Phalarim siccumque moverem
Democritum, scopulosque novus suffunderet humor.
Sic mundi Boreis agitor, sic Syrtis harena
170 naufragor humanae, sic impacata Charybdis
me sorbet, sic Scylla freto latrante flagellat.
His mihi naufragiis peregrino Tartara fletu
compassura reor; et flecti posse Megaeram
suspicor, et saevos alias mansuescere crines.
175 Omnis in hoc casu feritas admissa nocendi
cederet; inflexi pietas adamanta rigoris
molliret, praecepsque Iovis lentesceret ira.

Chapter 9

Architrenius's prayer to Nature

"Look, O Goddess, upon this nothing, nay less than nothing! Reduce these fountains of weeping, these pools of tears, abysses of misery, and dry up these ponds that teem with evil. I am tortured; my speaking grief declares the torments of my mind, and sighs proclaim the disease that lurks within. 160 My tears are not feigned; the spring rain issues from clouds, and a cloud within makes showers rain from my eyes. My grief is wrung from the heart; most definite reasons for weeping give rise to it, and true hardships provoke my complaints. For I am assailed in my weary breast by so many un- 165 relenting storms, I flounder, consumed by pain, amid such disease, that I might move Phalaris or dry-eyed Democritus to tears, and cause an unwonted moisture to suffuse the cliffs; so harassed am I by the chill wind of the world, so wrecked on the sands of a human sandbar; such an implaca- 170 ble Charybdis draws me down, such a Scylla's barking straits attack me. Tartarus, I think, would weep in compassion for my outcast, shipwrecked condition; I dare say Megaera could be moved, and her fierce locks learn a gentler manner. All savage things would give over their hurtful wickedness in 175 this sad case; pity would soften the hardness of unbending rigor, and the precipitate wrath of Jove himself would grow mild.

"Compaterisne tuam scelerum, Natura, flagellis
affligi sobolem? Quae sic in pignora pacem
180 maternam turbavit hiemps? Odiumne novercae
matris amor didicit? O dulces ubera numquam
exhibitura favos! Heu pignora semper amarum
gustatura cibum! Pietas materna rigorem
induit et scopulis Prognes induruit Ino.
185 "Sed quid ego? Dubito, luctusne refundere culpam
in matrem liceat: matrem vexare querelis
exhorret pietas, prohibet reverentia matris,
imperat ira loqui. Rabies in turpia solvit
ora, pudorque ligat. Sed iam declino pudoris
190 imperium, maiorque mihi dominatur Erinys.
"Torrenti, fateor, irae non impero: de te,
pace tua, Natura, queror. Tibi supplicat omnis
maiestatis apex, et nobis semper avarum
obliquas oculum, nulla dulcedine clausas
195 scis reserasse manus. Homo praeda doloribus aevum
tristibus immergit; nec amicis utitur annis,
nec fruitur laetis, nec verna vescitur aura.
"Humanos statui numero strinxisse reatus,
sed metam desperat opus. Nec finis apertum
200 principium clausisse potest; nam cedit harenae
turba malis, humana quibus dementia bellum
indicit superis. Divumque et fulmen et iram
in se cogit homo. Lipares Iovis eicit ignem
dextra, magis candens ira quam fulmine. Vindex
205 Hostibus exoptans veniam, tonitruque minanti

"And can you, Nature, feel pity for your offspring, tormented by the scourge of wrong? What winter storm has so aroused your motherly gentleness against your charges? Has 180 a mother's love learned a stepmother's hatred? Alas, that your breasts will never impart their honeyed sweetness! Alas, that your charges will always taste bitter food! Motherly devotion has cloaked itself in severity, and Ino has grown as hard as rocklike Procne.

"But what am I to do? I doubt whether it be right to place 185 the blame for my suffering on my mother; piety shrinks from assailing a mother with complaints, reverence for a mother forbids it, but wrath commands me to speak. Madness gives rein to foul speech, though shame resists it. I now reject the rule of shame; the Fury who dominates me is too 190 strong.

"I cannot. I confess, stem the tide of wrath. By your leave, O Nature, my complaint is of you. The crowning glory of your realm entreats you, yet you always turn a grudging eye upon us, unable to open your clenched hands in kindness. 195 Man is a prey to hardship, lives his life immersed in sorrow; he knows no favorable years, enjoys no delights, never feels the breeze of spring.

"I decided to set a number on the instances of human guilt, but the task of counting them was hopeless; no end could have been imposed once a beginning had been made, 200 for the multitude of the sands must yield to that of the wicked means by which human madness makes war against the gods. Man has drawn their wrath and lightning upon himself. Jove's own hand has hurled the fire of Liparaean Vulcan, his wrath hotter even than the thunderbolt. But the avenger, wishing to be lenient toward his enemies, curbs his 205

435

Parcit, et admissos clementia praepedit ictus,
audacesque facit scelerum dilatio poenae.
   "Tolle, parens, odium! Tandem mansuesce, novercam
exue, blanda fave! Morum bona singula mater
210   possidet, et nato nec libra nec uncia servit."

Capitulum 10

De responsione Naturae
et promissione subsidii

Dixerat et verbum lacrimarum reppulit aestus,
et stetit opposito singultus obice lingua.
At dea: "Nec matris feritas est illa, nec illa
fellificor taxo. Semper tibi sedula grates
215   et meritum perdo. Gratamque, ingrate, bonorum
indulsi satiem, misero felicia fudi
non merito, donumque tenes donoque teneris.
   "Sollicitis hominem studiis limavit et orbem
officiosa dedit, cumulato larga favore
220   nostra Iovi bonitas cognata et cognita. Numquam
plenior exhibuit veram dilectio matrem.
Non aegresco datis, dare non fastidio; rerum
continuans partus, nec rumpit dextera fluxum

thundering menace; clemency withholds those blows, and his deferral of punishment makes men bolder in crime.

"Withdraw your hatred, O Parent, grow mild at last, put off stepmotherly cruelty and be gentle and kind. A mother possesses every good quality, and does not deal with her child in terms of pounds and pennies." 210

Chapter 10

Nature's reply and her promise to provide for him

He had said this much when a flood of tears thwarted speech, and his tongue grew still, confronted by a barrier of sobbing. But the goddess replied, "This cruelty is not your mother's, and no such poison embitters me. Ever zealous on your behalf, I gain neither thanks nor reward. I have gra- 215 ciously allowed you, ingrate, an abundance of good things, and showered happiness on your undeserving wretchedness. What you possess is my gift, and by my gift you are sustained.

"Our goodness, closely akin to Jove's, and sanctioned by 220 him, fashioned man with attentive care, and in our abundant largesse we generously bestowed the universe upon him. Never did a more loving act reveal the true mother. And my power to give has not grown feeble, nor am I reluctant to give; constantly bringing creatures to birth, my hand

muneris incisi, nec dandi rustica donum
225 diminuit torpendo manus. Sed dona minoris
credis, ubi dono est plus quam contenta voluntas.
Occulit ubertas pretium, satiesque sapori
derogat et tenuat accepti copia grates.
At quia sedulitas homini mea servit eique
230 fundit opes et opem, meriti secura, malorum
radicem fodiam, morbos a sedibus imis
eiciam. Paucis—cupias scivisse—docebo.
Iam lacrimae deterge lutum, limoque remoto
post tenebras admitte iubar. Rorantia mores
235 Ubera nutricis senio lactandus anhelas;
annosusque puer nec pectore canus ut annis,
imberbique senex animo. Iam debita menti
canities aderit et maturabitur intus,
ne viridis putrescat homo; dabiturque petenti
240 dulce, quod ad satiem sitiens delibet alumnus,
quo puer ex animo sordensque infantia cedat.

never interrupts the flow of an incomplete gift, and mine
is no ignoble hand that diminishes the value of the act of 225
giving by its listlessness. But you consider that an inferior
gift by which your wishes are more than fulfilled. What is
plentiful appears of less worth, sufficiency loses its savor,
and abundance reduces the gratitude of him who receives it.
But since it is my constant care to be of service to man, to 230
shower him with my wealth and succor with no concern for
reward, I will dig out the root of these evils, cast out the dis-
ease from your innermost being. I will offer a brief lesson.
Take pains to understand it. Wipe away the stains of your
tears, and when their taint is gone let light enter in place of
shadow. In your old age you are still eager to draw streams of 235
moral wisdom from the breasts of your nurse; you are a boy
full of years, hoar in age but not in spirit, an old man with
the mind of a beardless youth. Now the mind will assume
the white-haired gravity that befits it, and grow inwardly
mature, lest the man should grow rotten while still green;
to him who seeks it a sweetness will be granted which the 240
eager nursling may taste until satisfied, so that boyhood and
the messiness of childhood depart from his mind.

Capitulum 11

De sanctione Naturae
in rerum genituris

"Sanctio nostra virum sterili marcescere ramo
et fructum sepelire vetat, prolemque negantes
obstruxisse vias. Commissi viribus uti
245   seminis, et longam generis producere pompam,
religio nativa iubet, ne degener alnum
induat aut platanum, semper virguncula laurus,
aut salicem numquam parienti fronde puellam,
aut si qua est vacuo folio vel flore pudica.

Capitulum 12

De ancillae amplexibus
aspernandis

250   "Nec facit ad sapidos amplexus nubile multis
ancillae gremium. Variis haec bobus aratur
terra, nec indecores scit fastidire colonos.
Vulgi cimba rapax; carpentum vile palustri

Chapter 11

Nature's decree concerning procreation

"Our decree forbids a man to wither on the barren bough, give fruit to the earth, and prevent conception by blocking its channels. Natural religion bids a man exercise the seminal power entrusted to him and give rise to a long procession 245 of offspring, lest he be reduced to the state of the barren alder or plane tree, the ever-virgin laurel, the maiden willow whose boughs never bear, or any other chaste plant devoid of leaf or blossom.

Chapter 12

The embraces of maidservants are to be spurned

"But the body of a maidservant, which has performed a 250 wife's office for many men, does not make for pleasurable embraces. Such ground is plowed by oxen of all sorts, and does not know how to reject disgraceful farmers. Her skiff is

accurrit populo; vix plena inviscerat alno
255 vectorem quemcumque ratis. Nauloque frequenti
quot capit expilat, iteratis omnia carpit
navigiis; usuque vices impendere gratis
dememinit longo. Nulloque innaufraga fluctu
occumbit, tumidam ridens concussa procellam.

Capitulum 13

De adulterio devitando

260 "Turpis adulterii labes redimicula morum
vellit, et obscuram trahit in contagia famam,
in varias suspecta neces. Pretiumque pudendi
hospitis, a loculo Naturae malleus exit
et Lachesis gemino succiso pollice, Parcis
265 tollitur una colus. Laribus depellitur exul
amittitque Venus vacuos exclusa penates,
arentique vado solitam sitit alveus undam.

greedy for passengers eager to take the rabble on board; her common carriage serves a filthy clientele; her vessel filled with much ado, she stuffs in any and all steersmen. And as 255 many as she takes in she fleeces by her frequent tolls, robbing them of everything over the course of repeated voyages; over her long career she has forgotten how to give a free performance. Immune to shipwreck, she never founders in the waves, but as she is buffeted laughs at the swelling storm.

Chapter 13

Avoid adultery

"The foul disgrace of adultery plucks away the girdle of good 260 character, and afflicts a shadowed reputation with diseases that lead to ruin in various ways. As the price of a shameful night's lodging, Nature's hammer forsakes its pouch, its twin is cut away by the hand of Lachesis, and the distaff, too, is 265 severed by the Parcae. Venus is driven from her abode, an exile, excluded from the empty chambers, while the channel, its bed grown dry, thirsts for its wonted stream.

Capitulum 14

Persuasio Naturae ut Architrenius ducat uxorem

"Rumpe moras thalami! Maturo contrahe! Sunt haec
illativa tori. Solido nectatur oportet
270 connubium nodo, riguo dum flamma iuventae
fervet adhuc suco, nondumque infundit aniles
brumula prima nives, nec vellera verticis albent
crine pruinoso; nec serpit ruga, senectae
verior interpres, ubi crispo fimbria vultu
275 pallet et in facie numeratur Nestoris annus.
    "Est mihi dilecta nivei signata pudoris
clave nec attrito marcens virguncula flore;
iam vicina toris, culmo solidata iuventae,
primaque lanigerae texens velamina pubi.
280 Blanda comes thalami sapidoque tenellula tactu;
obnubit splendore diem, noctisque profundae
Peplum siderei vultus carbunculus urit.
Cum sit adulterii promptissima laena, Diones
pronuba corruptae, Venerisque ancilla solutae
285 gloria, sollicito species suspecta pudori,
non tamen haec recipit alienos innuba nexus.
Nec Ledaea tenet animos, Lucretia vultum;
solaque Penelopen gremio gerit, ore Lacaenam.

444

Chapter 14

Nature persuades Architrenius
to take a wife

"Cease to put off nuptial rites! Marry in good season! This is the right time for marriage. It is fitting that marriage should be made firm by a strong bond while the flame of youth is   270 still hot in your blood, while early winter has not yet showered you with the snows of age, and the fleece of your head does not gleam with white frost; while wrinkles, a surer sign of age, have not crept forth, the fringe around your pinched cheeks has not become white, and the years of Nestor can-   275 not be numbered in your face.

"There is a maiden, dear to me, protected by the key of pure chastity, a maiden whose virgin flower is unwithered; she is ready for marriage, sustained by the sturdy plant of youth, and putting forth the first fleecy growth of puberty. She will be a sweet companion in the marriage chamber, del-   280 icately soft to the appreciative touch. Her splendor dims the light of day and the gemlike glow of her starry face burns through the mantle of the darkest night. Though the most persuasive of procuresses should present herself, corrupt Dione's very matron of honor, the most brilliant handmaid of dissolute Venus, that race so mistrusted by anxious chas-   285 tity, this maiden would never accept the embraces of a stranger. She does not harbor a Ledaean spirit nor the face of Lucretia; in her heart she is all Penelope, though her face is Helen's.

"Flammativa viri sunt omnia, prona medullis
290   Inseruisse faces, hilarem factura iuventam
iocundumque senem. Longo Moderantia nobis
cognita convictu, rerum cautissima, morum
ingenio felix, Virtutis filia, natu
nobilis et thalamos meditanti nubilis anno.
295   Pulchra, pudica tamen, dabitur tibi, sacra ligabo
foedera; quae nulla caveas diffibulet aetas.
Ipsa quidem vitii pravos exosa susurros,
haud immunda pati poterit consortia; semper
expavit tetigisse picem. Contagia toto
300   pectore declines, alioquin vincula rumpet
coniugii, passum maculas non passa maritum.

Capitulum 15

De cesto, cingulo Veneris

"Nupta tibi ceston Veneris dabit. Ille Diones
baltheus, illa tuos praecinget fascia lumbos.
Incudis studio sponsae lucratus amorem,
305   Lemnius hanc cocto solidavit sedulus auro,
follibus eluctans vigiles excire caminos
non minus ardescens Lipares quam Cypridis igne,
dum Venus emollit operam mirando laborem.
Dum tamen insudat operi manus, oscula morsis

"Her every feature is sure to arouse a man and infuse his marrow with fire, promising a joyous youth and a happy old age. She is Moderation, well known to me from long intimacy, prudent in all things, blessed with keen moral sense, a daughter of Virtue, nobly born, and of an age to consider the marriage bed. Beautiful yet chaste, she will be yours, and I myself will tie the sacred knot; take care that no length of time undo it. For she so detests the lewd whisperings of vice that she will never be capable of accepting an impure relationship; she has ever shuddered at the thought of touching pitch. Keep your mind wholly free of any taint of sin; otherwise she will break the bond of marriage, not accepting a husband who could admit such a stain. 290 295 300

Chapter 15

The girdle of Venus

"Your bride will present you with the girdle of Venus. Let this Dionean belt, this band, gird your loins. The Lemnian smith, laboring at the anvil to purchase the love of his spouse, carefully fashioned it from molten gold, straining with the bellows to heat his ever-glowing forge, and growing hot with both Liparaean and Cyprian fire, when Venus lightened his labor by marveling at his handiwork. Even as his hand applied itself to the work, his mouth was snatching 305 310

310 lingua rapit labris plus quam fabrilia. Vultu
sit licet obscuro, claudo pede, basia carpit
dulcia; nec plure saturantur adultera melle
nec, Pari, plus Phrygiis poteras pavisse Lacaenam.

Capitulum 16

De caelatura eiusdem
facta a Vulcano

"Sollicito quaedam digito caelavit, amata
315 dictantis rapiente vicem; manuumque Minervam
spectatrix acuit et cotis suscipit usum,
ingenii supplens laudato coniuge vires.
    "Hic vomit Hippolytus animam ne Phaedra pudorem
sorbeat, intactus generis morumque novercae.
320   "Expositum Phrynes gremio vinoque perustum
nulla Xenocratem Venus ebriat: innuba nusquam
integritas nutat; scorti luctamina ridet
indomitus, frigetque mero candente libido.
    "Non potitur Lais dubio Demosthene; nec quem
325 moverat evellit; perdendo prodigus auro,

from her delicious lips kisses that were not at all forged. Though his face was blackened, and his gait halting, he fed on these sweet kisses; the kisses of adulterous love are no more steeped in honey, nor could Paris's Phrygian kisses have tasted sweeter to Helen.

Chapter 16

The engraving done by Vulcan on the girdle

"With careful hand he carved certain figures, while his beloved took on the office of dictation; by looking on she 315 sharpened the skill of his hands, and performed the function of a whetstone, making her husband's imaginative powers greater by praising them.

"Here Hippolytus pours forth his spirit lest Phaedra consume his chastity, unyielding to her who was stepmother both to his family and to his virtue.

"Though he is subjected to the embrace of Phryne and 320 stimulated by wine, no power of Venus can intoxicate Xenocrates: his virgin integrity never wavers; undefeated, he laughs at the efforts of the harlot, his lust remaining cool as the wine grows hot.

"Lais does not overcome wavering Demosthenes; though 325 she had moved him, she does not fleece him; prodigal in

non emit amplexus. Thalamos qui vendit, ementem
fallit, et emptorem mox paenitet empta voluptas.

"Inguina Democritus castrat, sexumque virilem
exuit et neutrum recipit. Fratresque togatos
330 detogat et Veneris geminum depellit avito
mancipium tecto, lumbique incendia ferro
ingelat et nervi succisus apocopat usum
renibus.

"Antiquo Pharius de more sacerdos
excubat et palmae de fronde cubilia sternit;
335 et sibi secretus alios latet incola phani.
Femineae labis vacuus, temereque vaganti
non sitit aspectae speciei nectar ocello.

Capitulum 17

De monili quod nupta fuerat delatura

"Ipsa pudicitiae testem castique monile
argumenta tori, pectus clausura, retruso
340 intrusore feret, prohibens ne iuncta dehiscant
limina, neve sinus vilescat ianua, quovis
trita viatore nec, quo delectet honestos
coniugis attactus, oculus delibet adulter.

squandering his gold, he does not buy her embraces. For she who sells her bed deceives the buyer, and pleasure that is purchased soon makes the buyer ashamed.

"Democritus cuts off his private parts, abandons the male sex and becomes neuter. He divests the robed brothers of their male robes, banishes Venus's twin servants from 330 their ancestral home, quells with cold steel the fire in his loins, and cuts short the work of that organ by severing it from the loins.

"By ancient custom the Egyptian priest sleeps out of doors, and spreads himself a bed of palm fronds; secluding 335 himself from others he lives concealed in the sacred precincts. Free of the contamination of women, he never thirsts with wantonly roving gaze for the sweet sight of a comely body.

Chapter 17

The necklace which the bride would wear

"As attestation of her purity and proof of the chastity of her bed, the bride will wear a necklace, clasping it about her breast to fend off intrusion, preventing the joined portals 340 from gaping open, lest access to her bosom seem cheap, a path to be trod by any wayfarer, and so that what attracts the honorable caresses of a husband may not gratify the eye of the adulterer.

"Pectoris hic nodus signis intexitur. Artis
345 me, fateor, vincente manu; pictura pudicam
praedicat, et sacrum perhibent exempla cubile.
Hic animo victrix, lecti Lucretia ferro
dedecus excusat; riget expectator Ulixis
Penelopes arcus. Navem plus Claudia morum
350 quam manuum virtute movet. Religatque solutum
Marcia nupta fide thalami, non carne Catonem.
Prima sacerdotis vice Flacci dedicat uxor
Idaliae sacrum, monitis instante Sibylla.
   "Frustra Maeoniis vates sub Apolline Fati
355 praecinit ambages. Pretio Cassandra negato
nec pactum recipit thalamo, sed pectore Phoebum,
plenaque non tollit gremio, sed mente magistrum.
   "Risus et lacrimas sponsi partitur, utroque
iuncta comes Fato. Nec deserit integra fractum
360 Hypsicratea virum, consors immota pericli
ut thalami. Regis nusquam secura suique
Mithridatis, fragiles bellis accommodat artus:
loricata latus, alienis degener armis,
exulat in clipeos, strictos peregrinat in enses,
365 belligeros transumit equos, sexumque virili
occulit in cultu, galeato mascula crine.
   "Mausole, viva tibi dat Mausolea, virumque
Artemesia bibit; quos pavit aromate, sponsi
sorbet amans cineres, sparsumque in melle maritum

"This band about her breast is worked with images. The artist's hand, I confess, is superior to mine; his representation proclaims her chaste, and his other examples enforce the sanctity of the marriage bed. Here Lucretia, victorious in spirit, absolves by the sword the dishonor of her bed. Penelope's bow remains unbent, awaiting the return of Ulysses. Claudia causes a ship to move by the power of her virtue rather than her arms. Marcia rejoins her sundered bond with Cato, devoted to marriage in her fidelity, though not in carnal union. The wife of Flaccus before all the others performs a priestlike office in dedicating a temple to Venus, as the Sibyl's warnings had enjoined.

"In vain does Cassandra the priestess of Apollo sing to the Maeonians of the windings of Fate. Having refused Apollo's offer she receives him not, as agreed, in her bed, but in her breast, suffering him not to fill her womb, but to instruct her mind.

"Hypsicratea shares both the laughter and the tears of her spouse, an inseparable companion in good times and bad. She remains loyal to her husband in defeat, a companion as steadfast in time of danger as in the marriage bed. Lest she ever be separated from her royal husband Mithridates, she equips her frail body for war: clad in armor, unfit for the strange business of fighting, she is an exile amid the clash of arms, strays among drawn swords, rides a charger and conceals her sex in male garments, manlike with her hair bound by a helmet.

"Mausolus, your Artemisia provides you with a living mausoleum by drinking you. For she lovingly swallows the ashes of her spouse, which she has preserved with with

370 haurit, utrumque favum. Nec Fatis foedere rupto
connubium servat uteri torus alter et una
coniugis est coniunx tumulus, pira, piramis, urna.

Capitulum 18

De loculo puellari
et contentis in eo

"Hoc feret, inque tuis vigilabit zonula lumbis,
excuba, ne morum penetret lascivia murum.
375 Florida picturae pretio vernante brevemque
ampla puellarem loculum demittit, amoris
nuntia laturum sponsae munuscula sponso.
Clauditur in dando: lecti Concordia, Pacis
foedus, Amicitiae nodus, Correctio voti,
380 Integritas Recti, Virtutis serrula, Morum
lima, Rigor mentis, Maiestas oris, Honesti
pondus, habena Modi, Scelerum succisio, Culpae
meta, Minerva Boni, Medii via, methodus Aequi,
Munditiae pecten, vitae Fragrantia, Famae
385 gratia, Solamen miseris, Cautela secundis."

spices, and consumes her husband mixed with honey, both   370
equally sweet to her. Thus Fate cannot sunder their bond;
her stomach, a second marriage bed, preserves their mar-
riage, and she is at once her husband's wife, tomb, pyre,
monument, and urn.

Chapter 18

The maiden's purse
and what it contains

"This she will bring, and her girdle will stand guard over
your loins, watchful lest wantonness penetrate the barrier of
virtue. From this broad belt, sumptuous in the springlike   375
richness of its decoration, there depends a girl's small purse,
to bear those little gifts which betoken the bride's love for
her husband. Included among these gifts are the Union of
the marriage bed, the pledge of Peace, the bond of Friend-
ship, the Guidance of prayer, unwavering Rectitude, the saw   380
of Virtue, the file of Moral Character, Firmness of mind,
Dignity of bearing, solid Worth, the curb of Restraint, a di-
vorce from Wrongdoing, an end to Guilt, Knowledge of the
Good, the path of the Mean, the lesson of Justice, the comb
of Cleanliness, Sweetness of life, the grace of Reputation,
Solace in time of sorrow, and Caution amid good fortune."   385

Capitulum 19

De contractu coniugii et dote

Dixit. Et a lacrimis redit Architrenius. Aegra
maestitiae caligo fugit, nec laetior umquam
foederis instanter nodum petit. Illa capacem
consilii laudat, optata citatius urgens.
390 Curia contrahitur, legitur locus, apta iugandis
omnia tractantur; producitur ultima virgo,
Phoebigero plus quam praefulgentissima vultu.
Dos datur a nupta: vigil observantia Recti;
casta Quies linguae; Facundia passa soporem;
395 Eloquii pondus; os in sermone pudicum;
faece carens pectus; mens labis inhospita naevo;
munda domus cordis; animae laudanda supellex;
Pacis Amor frater; germana Modestia nuptae;
Iuris Norma comes; Pietas vicina Favori;
400 ara Pudor Morum; Fidei Dilectio pignus;
Famae sponsor Honos; Maiestas Nominis obses;
Spes pugil adversis; dubiis Fiducia pugnans;
Consilii libra; resecans Censura reatus;
Nestoris examen; polientis lima Catonis,
405 Sollicitudo fori, solidi Cautela senatus;
illimis Bonitas, manuum mundescere curis;
circumcisa loqui studiose tersa voluntas;
maior egestate, minor exundante facultas.

Chapter 19

The marriage contract and dowry

She concludes, and Architrenius emerges from his weeping.
The cloud of sickly misery is dispelled, and happier than
ever before he demands at once the bond of union. The
goddess commends his acceptance of her counsel, and sets
quickly to work to fulfill his hopes. A council is convened, a
site is chosen, and all things pertaining to the union are ar-
ranged. At last the maiden is brought forward, her Phoebus-
like face more than surpassingly brilliant. The bride's dowry
is presented: a clearsighted adherence to the Right; a
modest Softspokenness; a Fluency which accepts intervals
of rest; a grave Eloquence; a mouth pure in its speech; a
breast devoid of foul thoughts; a spirit that rejects any
marks of dishonor; a heart that harbors purity; an admirably
well-stored mind; Love, the brother of Peace, and Modesty,
sister to the bride herself; sound Precept, the companion of
Justice; Pity, near neighbor to Favor; Purity, the shrine of
good Character; Love, the pledge of Trust; Honor, guarantor
of Reputation; Dignity, surety for Good Name; Hope, the
foe of adversity; Confidence, at war with doubt; balanced
Judgment; Severity in restraining guilt; the reflectiveness of
Nestor; the acumen of keen-minded Cato; Concern for the
common weal; the Prudence of a united senate; untainted
Goodness, cleansed of the work of the hands; a careful con-
cern to speak briefly and concisely; a style that is not impov-
erished yet not fulsome.

Capitulum 20

De donatione et
instrumentis musicis

A tenui sponso tenuis donatio: dantur
410   obsequium carnis, animae tractabilis usus.
    Connubii tandem solidatur nodus, et ecce!
Laetitiam spargit solemnis prodiga applause:
Solis opus cythara; studium lyra Mercuriale;
dulce Pharo sistrum; requies pastoris harundo;
415   canna vocans somnos, faciens syringa sopori;
lite graves aulae; iocundula nabla querelis;
folle chorus rauco; petulanti cymbala tactu;
pauper avena sono; modulatu fistula dives;
buccina scabra modos; veterum sacra tympana sacris;
420   tibia vulgaris; regina fidicula cantu;
murmur onusque tuba; lituus citator edendi.

Chapter 20

The bridegroom's gift and the wedding music

From the frail bridegroom, a meager contribution: obedi- 410
ence in fleshly appetite and a spirit willing to be guided are
his gifts.

At last the bond of marriage is made firm, and lo! Music
full of festive celebration spreads joy abroad: the Sun god's
lute; the Mercurial art of the lyre; the rattle dear to the
Egyptian; the flute, pastime of shepherds; the drowsy sound 415
of the reed pipe, preparing an inlet for sleep; the pipes that
sound so stern in battle; the harp, so pleasing in its lament;
the organ with its coarse bellows; the wantonly tinkling
cymbal; the meager sound of the oaten flute; the panpipe, so
rich in its melodies; the war trumpet with its harsh strains;
the timbrel, hallowed by ancient rites; the common flute 420
and the regal song of the cittern; the tuba's growling burden;
the clarion which summons to the feast.

Capitulum 21

De avibus verba usurpantibus

Nec minus et mima nemorum circumsonat ales
et modulos crispat nativi pectinis arte:
ruris alauda chelys; lyricen Philomena rubeto;
425   per vada cantor olor; citharoeda per aequora Siren;
corvus "ave" dicens; homo linguae psitacus usu;
pica salutatrix; lasciva monedula fando;
turdula prompta loqui; facundo gracculus ore;
et quaecumque stilum valet usurpasse loquendi.

Capitulum 22

De ancillis sponsae

430   Sponsae lecta manus thalamis ancilla ministrant:
virginis Integritas; vidui Castratio lecti;
matronae Gravitas; Levitas immota puellae;
Simplicitas vultus; redolescens oris Honestas;
tuta Fides lecti; nuptae Venus invia culpae.

Chapter 21

Birds appropriate the power of speech

The winged pageant of the surrounding groves is no less
musical, warbling melodies with natural artistry: the lark,
lyre of the countryside; the nightingale, lyrical among the
thorns; the swan, songster of the shallows; the Siren, carol-   425
ing across the deep; the raven, crying "Hail!"; the parrot,
manlike in his power of speech; the magpie's cheerful greet-
ing; the lewdly chattering chough; the thrush, ever twitter-
ing; the fluent jackdaw; and every bird that can assume the
appearance of speech.

Chapter 22

The bride's attendants

A chosen band, handmaids to the bride, have charge of the   430
bridal chamber: Inviolate Virginity, the Chastity of an un-
shared bed, matronly Dignity, a maiden's stable Liveliness,
Naturalness of demeanor, a countenance redolent of Honor,
sure Fidelity to the marriage bed, a love immune to conjugal
misbehavior.

Capitulum 23

De clientela pro diversis officiis obsequenti

435 Ordo clientelae varius discurrit, ubique
servit, et ad vota famulatum sedulus explet:
firma viri Virtus; teneri Timor intimus anni;
Cura Senectutis; operum passiva Iuventus;
dandi cauta manus; meritorum dextra beatrix;
440 dona Modus librans; inhibens Prudentia luxum;
expensae Ratio; reminiscens Calculus asses;
sollers auricula; vitiis inapertus ocellus;
pesque reformidans molli iuvenescere passu;
lascivaque timens dematurescere culpa.

Capitulum 24

De ferculis in nuptiis Architrenii et Moderantiae

445 Tempus adest mensae, quam mundo Copia cornu
sarcinat; et morum locupleti funditur urna:

Chapter 23

The retainers carrying out
various duties

A varied array of retainers bustle about, assisting every- 435
where, and eagerly perform their duties on command:
strong, manly Virtue; the inner Fear of tender years; the
Cares of Age; Youth, capable of labor; a hand cautious in its
giving, but prompt to reward merit; a Restraint that weighs 440
the value of each gift; a Prudence that curbs luxury; Reason-
able Expenditure, and Accounting of moneys disbursed; an
attentive ear; an eye undistracted by vice; feet fearful of ap-
pearing too youthful by the lightness of their step, and wary
of lapsing from maturity by straying into wantonness.

Chapter 24

The banquet at the wedding of
Architrenius and Moderation

The time is come for the festive board, which Plenty heaps 445
with a seemly abundance, and an urn well filled with virtues

sobrietas mensae; saties angusta paratus;
ventre minor potus; epuli contracta libido;
pauca petens guttur; combustio nulla palati;
450 mansuetudo gulae; stomachi tranquilla Charybdis;
limes in effusis dapis artans meta volumen.

Capitulum 25

Quod Fortuna favit nuptiis

Respicit et blandis epulas percurrit ocellis
et vultus adhibet animi cum melle favorem:
Sors inopum vindex, regum Tuchis ulta tumores,
455 Rhamnus opum terror, Nemesis suspecta tyrannis,
Casus agens mitras, tribuens Fortuna curules.
    O data vel raro vel nulli fercula, solis
degustanda viris! O felix mensa, Catoni
forsitan et nostro vix aevo nota! Beatis,
460 immo beativis, indulge sumptibus! Absit
meta deum clausura dapes; connubia Virtus
sanctiat et dempto convivia fine perhennet!

                        * * *

is poured out: sobriety at table; a modest sufficiency of dishes; less drink than the belly can bear; a restrained desire for rich food; a throat whose demands are modest; a palate that does not burn with greed; moderateness of appetite; peace in the Charybdis of the stomach; a limiting of expenditure that sets a limit on the quantity of dishes.

450

Chapter 25

Fortune blesses the marriage

There is one looking on who surveys the feast with kindly eyes, and matches the favor in her expression with the sweetness of her thoughts: Chance, that protects the poor and avenges the overbearing pride of kings, the Rhamnusian scourge of wealth, the Nemesis feared by tyrants, the Accident that creates Prelates, the Fortune that allots high office.

455

O feast so rarely granted, if at all, to be enjoyed by a few chosen men! O blessed board, familiar perhaps to Cato but to our age almost unknown! Vouchsafe them your blessed, nay your beatifying abundance! Let that term be far off which will bring to an end this feast of the gods; let Virtue hallow their marriage and perpetuate their feasting without end!

460

* * *

465

Hic igitur suspendo stilum. Procedere ruptis
erubeo mensis, quarum producere tempus
465 non breviasse decet. Metari prandia nolo,
quae Deus assiduo faciat succedere gustu,
nec satie nutet epulandi fixa voluptas.
    O longum studii gremio nutrita, togati
ingenii proles rudis et plebaea, libelle,
470 incolumis vivas, nec te languescere cogat
invidiae morsus; quo morbificante bonorum
febricitat nomen, et eo tortore modernis
aegrescit titulus. Forsan, tibi si qua favoris
uncia debetur, peplo livoris amicta
475 non poterit venisse palam, dum sorbeat auras
vivificas auctor. Ortum lux illa Iohannis
sumat in occasu, Sol ille a funeris urna
surgat, inextincto semper spectabilis igne.
Sub Fati tenebris me noctescente, diescat
480 hic liber et Famae veterum feliciter annos
aequet, in aeternum populis dilectus et ultra!

Here, then, I stay my pen. I blush to go further after interrupting a feast whose duration it would be more fitting to 465 prolong than curtail. I am loath to set a limit to a meal which, God willing, will so prolong their eager appetite that the pleasure in feasting will be constant, and not grow drowsy with satiety.

O little book, nursed so long at the breast of study, rough and lowborn offspring of the wit of a common man, may you 470 survive intact, and may the carping of envy never make your voice grow faint; her baneful power blights the names of good men, and through its cruelty the renown of modern writers languishes. It may be that if you are deemed worthy of some scrap of favor, it must come shrouded in the cloak of envy rather than appearing openly, since the author still 475 breathes the breath of life. Let this light dawn as Johannes's light is setting, let this Sun rise from his funeral urn, and let its undimmed fire be visible forever. As I enter the dark night of shadowy Fate, let this book emerge into daylight: 480 let it know a favor as enduring as the fame of the ancients, and be cherished by all people to eternity and beyond!

Note on the Text

In Paris in 1517 Jodocus Badius Ascensius (Josse Bade) published the first printed edition of the *Architrenius,* based on a single fifteenth-century manuscript, Troyes, Bibliothèque municipale 2263, or a copy of that manuscript. The text preserved in the manuscript contains many errors, and these are compounded, first by the editor's use of other, unknown manuscripts, and then by his attempts to "correct" the author's prosody. Kuno Francke, "Der *Architrenius,*" 477–78, reports searching in vain through German libraries for a copy of that edition, and finally discovering one in Copenhagen, only to find it severely flawed by "senseless punctuation, reckless emendations, and typographical errors." Major errors are listed by Schmidt, 110–11.

Wright's Rolls Series edition (1872) is based on the Paris edition (acknowledged only by the letter *P* in Wright's critical apparatus) and on three London manuscripts, identified only as *A, B,* and *C:* (*A*) British Library MS Harley 4066; (*B*) B. L. Royal 15.C.V (closely related to the Troyes manuscript used by Badius, which, however, according to Schmidt, preserves a better text); and (*C*) B. L. Cotton Vespasian B. XXIII, which is seriously damaged. These are *E, G,* and *H* in Schmidt's detailed survey of the manuscripts. As Schmidt rightly remarks, the two London manuscripts not used by

Wright, British Library Royal 13.A.IV and Westminster Abbey 19, are far superior.

Carlucci's translation is based on Wright's text. He knew of both Francke's study and Schmidt's edition but did not heed Francke's warning about the Paris edition, with which he "corrects" Wright at many points, and he makes only limited use of Schmidt's text in establishing his own.

Schmidt's excellent edition, which I used with gratitude as the basis of my Cambridge edition, reproduced here, and have departed from only by a few cautious emendations and changes in punctuation, is based on a careful examination of all the twenty-six known manuscripts.

Except where a specific page reference is given, citations of Schmidt refer to his notes on the passages cited. Most of the manuscripts of the *Architrenius* contain glosses, mainly explanations of mythological references and the meanings of words. Schmidt's notes include a generous selection of the glosses, and I have cited a number of these in the notes to my translation, identifying manuscript sources by Schmidt's sigla: C = Edinburgh, University Library, MS 20; D = Leiden, Rijksuniversiteit, MS Vulcanius 94; E = London, British Library, MS Harley 4066; F = London, British Library, MS Royal 13.A.IV; K = Munich, Staatsbibliothek, MS 237; P = Oxford, Bodleian Library, MS Digby 64; Q = Oxford, Bodleian Library, MS Digby 157; V = Rome, Biblioteca Apostolica Vaticana, MS 370; X = Rome, Biblioteca Apostolica Vaticana, MS 1812.

Notes to the Text

2.221   delicit *Minkova, Carlucci*: delicat *Schmidt*

2.478   haut *Minkova*: aut *Schmidt*

3.347   Cirrhae *Wetherbee*: Cirres *Schmidt*

4.151   haud *Wetherbee*: ad *Schmidt*

4.405   dominique *Minkova*: domuique *Schmidt*

6.286   nulli *Minkova*: nullum *Schmidt*

7.103   posito *Wetherbee*: posita *Schmidt*

8.274   ne *Wetherbee*: nec *Schmidt*

Notes to the Translation

Prologue

1   The Prologue appears in fewer than half the manuscripts, often in a later than the text, provides only obvious information in a stereotypical form, and can hardly be by Johannes. As Schmidt, 117, observes, it is important mainly as evidence that the *Architrenius* was well known in the schools of the thirteenth century.

the ferment of this resentment . . . uncontaminated love: The opposition of "ferment" to "uncontaminated" (*azymus*, literally, "unleavened") feeling echoes 1 Corinthians 5:7.

2   *Whom God has joined . . . asunder*: Matthew 19:6; Mark 10:9.

Manuscripts *C, F,* and *Q* provide the marginal gloss, *Architrenius*: *archos*: *princeps*; *trenos*: *lamentum*. Architrenius is the prince of sorrows or arch-weeper. As the title of Johannes's poem, his name follows the twelfth-century fashion, noted by Gervase of Melkley, *Ars poetica* 94, of ornate titles loosely derived from Greek: *Didascalicon, Cosmographia, Policraticus, Metalogicon*.

3   *his name is Johannes*: Luke 1:63.

Book I

1   The reference is to the digging of a canal through the Athos peninsula and the bridging of the Hellespont, in preparation for Xerxes's campaign against Greece in 480 BCE, cited also by Walter of Chatillon, *Alexandreis* 6.188–91. *Velificatur Athos* echoes Juvenal, *Sat.* 10.174, and show Johannes identifying him-

self with the satirist. Gervase observes that the pentasyllable is a distinguished beginning for a hexameter (*Ars poetica* 210) and that in the opening two lines a "paradigmatic" placement of exemplary material achieves a strongly hortatory effect enhanced by hypozeuxis, each of a series of clauses having its own subject and verb (*Ars poetica* 36, 151).

3   *Thetis*: The mother of Achilles. She was a sea nymph, whose name is often used of the sea itself: Virgil, *Ecl.* 4.32; Claudian, *Rapt. Pros.* 1.150. In 2.386 and 3.34 she stands for water. In 3.263, 4.287, she is again the sea.

4   *Salmoneus*: Brother of Sisyphus, who used torches to imitate the thunderbolts of Zeus. He was struck by a thunderbolt and cast into Tartarus: Virgil, *Aen.* 6.585–94; Hyginus, *Fabulae* 61.

41–64   This chapter develops a common topos, the modern writer's deprecating comparison of himself to great authors of antiquity. Chapter 3 presents the answering topos, resentment of the prejudice, which denies value to modern writing: Echard, "Map's Metafiction," 294–99.

51   *ordinary people*: *Togatus* denotes an ordinary citizen as opposed to members of the equestrian or consular class, the *trabeati*. In Johannes's epilogue, 9.468–69, his poem is the "offspring of the wit of a common man" *(togati ingenii proles)*.

52   *lower note*: *Succentus,* translated here as "lower note," is a musical term denoting an accompaniment or second part; Martianus Capella, *De nuptiis Philologiae et Mercurii* 1.11.

53   *Amyclas*: The poor boatman of Lucan, *De bello civili* 5.520–677, who is a stock figure for poverty in twelfth-century school poetry.

        Croesus: King of Lydia, famous for his vast wealth.

54–55   Lucan, *De bello civili* 5.527–28.

57   *death-song of the swan*: The swan was traditionally supposed to sing beautifully at the time of its death: Ovid, *Her.* 7.3–4; Bernardus Silvestris, *Cosmographia* 1.3.449–50. Pliny, *Nat. Hist.* 10.32.63, reports the tradition, but is skeptical.

71   *Deucalion . . . Pyrrha*: The only survivors of the great flood created by Jupiter; they restored the human race: Ovid, *Met.* 1.313–415.

73   *charioteer of the horses*: That is, Phaethon, named again in 5.24.

75   *the old Maeonian*: That is, Homer: Ovid, *Ars Am.* 2.4.

81   *Atin*: Atin, or Acin, signifying the eastern limit of Johannes's
         world (as Atlas in the same line signifies the far west), denotes
         a region corresponding roughly to Sind in modern Pakistan.
         Schmidt, 289, notes that the name is drawn from Chapter 9 of
         the *Differentiae* of Al-Farghání, source of Nature's astronomi-
         cal discourse in Books 8 and 9. Acin and Atlas are opposed
         again in 9.66–76.

82   *Syene*: Modern Essouan, in southernmost Upper Egypt.

87   *downy white*: Gervase, *Ars poetica*, 136–37, complains at length
         about the *dura transumptio* (difficult metaphor) in *olore senectae*
         (literally, "the swan of old age"). *Candor,* or whiteness, is in
         question, and he considers that snow *(nix)* or the lily *(lilia)*
         would be a more appropriate vehicle.

89   *China's purple robes*: The *Seres* are the Chinese, famous for silken
         fabrics. Roman authors seem to have been unsure of the loca-
         tion of their homeland; Lucan, *De bello civili* 10.292–93, places
         it at the headwaters of the Nile: Emanuele Berti, ed., *M. Annei
         Lucani Bellum civile liber X* (Florence: Le Monnier, 2000), 228.

92   *a book, not a balance*: As Schmidt notes, the opposition of *libri*
         (books), and *librae* ("pounds" in the monetary sense, or "scales"
         used to weigh money and goods), is a commonplace. It appears
         again at 5.333.

93–94   *Cirrha*: An ancient town near Delphi, sacred to Apollo: Lucan,
         De bello civili 1.64; Statius, *Theb.* 3.474–75.

         Phoebus: Here and throughout, both patron of the art of poetry
         and, with Pallas/Minerva, patron of learning in general.

95–99   *Zoilus*: A grammarian and philosopher (ca. 400–320 BCE) known
         for his severe critical judgments, which included an attack on
         Homer. In the likely source of this anecdote, Vitruvius, *De ar-
         chitectura* 7.Praef.8–9, Zoilus is rebuked not by Alexander, but
         by Ptolemy II.

100   *Pergama*: Pergama or Pergamum is a poetic name for the citadel
         of Troy: Virgil, *Aen.* 1.466, 651, etc.; Ovid, *Met.* 12.445, 591; 13.169.

103–8   *Danai,* from Danaus, legendary founder of Argos, and *Pelasgae,*
         traditionally the original inhabitants of Greece, denote the

Greek army at Troy. *Phryges,* from Phrygia, where Troy was lo-
cated, and *Dardanios,* from Dardanus, legendary ancestor of
the Trojan royal house, denote the Trojans. Virgil makes fre-
quent use of these four names.

110   *Ida*: A high mountain near Troy and an important landmark: Vir-
gil, *Aen.* 2.801; 10.158. "Idaean" often denotes the Trojans in Au-
gustan poetry.

117–19   *Britain, freely giving . . . absolved the Greeks*: These abruptly digres-
sive lines, the first of Johannes's several allusions to the legend-
ary history in the *Historia regum Britanniae* of Geoffrey of Mon-
mouth (ca. 1100–1154/55), refer to the conquest of Britain by
Brutus and the Trojans.

125   *Tempe*: The beautiful valley of the river Peneus in Thessaly. Its
name was used of beautiful valleys elsewhere: Ovid, *Am.* 1.1.15;
Statius, *Theb.* 1.485.

126   *Hybla*: The name of a mountain and a city in Sicily, known for
flowers and bees: Pliny, *Nat. Hist.* 11.13.32.

130–31   *a second Olympus rises . . . toward the orient*: The suggestion is per-
haps that whereas the classical Olympus was the home of the
pagan gods, the Olympus that represents Johannes's patron,
Walter of Coutances, is defined by its orientation toward the
east and Jerusalem. Schmidt cites a gloss in *Q* that reports that
while pregnant with Walter his mother dreamed of giving birth
to a scroll that, when opened out by Walter, extended far to the
east.

135   *Walter*: Walter of Coutances, newly named Archbishop of Rouen,
to whom the poem is dedicated. The first letters of the poem's
first eight books form the acrostic *VVALTERO*. The first let-
ters of the final lines of these books form a corresponding
IOHANNES. Johannes's lavish praise of Walter and his lin-
eage, unlike most such gestures, is not confined to this dedica-
tion, but recurs at length later (5.384–480; 6.311–16).

141   *Glorious Aetna*: The "glory" imputed to Aetna is probably that of
Henna, where Proserpine was captured by Pluto; its hillside
gardens are described by Claudian, *Rapt. Pros.* 2.71–136. Henna
is not close to Aetna, but Claudian describes the mountain in
1.153–78, and perhaps for this reason the mythographers report

that it was from Aetna that Proserpine was stolen: Vatican Mythographers, 2.93; 3.7.2.

159   *northerly*: The adjective *arctous* is derived from *Arctos,* the double constellation Ursa Major and Minor, the great and Lesser Bear, located close to the north pole. Johannes uses both terms as equivalent to "north" or "northern," or to denote the pole itself.

159–60   Johannes changes his metaphor here, or treats manna as liquid.

172   *Maecenas*: Wealthy and cultured, he was a friend and advisor to Augustus, and patron of Virgil, Horace, and Propertius.

173   *my rough understanding*: Johannes, like Alan of Lille in the *Anticlaudianus,* uses the name of Minerva to denote understanding, intelligence, or learning.

175   *measure out the hidden course*: *harenae* (literally, "sands") are the multiplicity of human fates *(fata),* which only God can number. Johannes echoes Lucan, *De bello civili* 10.308, but has altered the sense of Lucan's *metiris* (traverse).

188   *Clotho, Lachesis, and Atropos*: The Fates, or *Parcae,* who determine the length of each human life, Clotho spinning a thread, which Lachesis extends, and which is finally cut by Atropos: Fulgentius, *Mitologiae* 1.8; Isidore, *Etym.* 8.11.90–93; Bernardus Silvestris, *Cosmographia* 2.11.7.

193–95   These lines recall the conclusion to the first book of Ovid's *Amores* (1.15.33–42), a boast that his book will outlive the gold-bearing Tagus and the gnawing of envy.

193   *Tagus*: A river that rises in Spain and flows through Portugal to the Atlantic, famous for the gold dust in its sands.

194   *Tantalus*: Invited to dine with the gods, he disclosed their secrets. He stands under a tree whose fruits recede as he reaches for them, and in a pool of water that drains away when he tries to drink: Horace, *Sat.* 1.1.68–69; Ovid, *Met.* 4.458–59.

223   *ruling spirits*: On Johannes's use of *lares* to evoke the powers that govern the inner life, Piehler, *Visionary Landscape,* 87–89, and Owen Barfield's review, *Medium Aevum* 42 (1973): 88–90. Johannes elsewhere uses *lares* as a simple metonymy for "chambers" of whatever kind (e.g., 3.61).

240   *Olympian firmament*: Because of its great height and the fact that

its summit was often hidden by clouds, Olympus was associ-
ated with heaven, and its name was often used as an equivalent
to *caelum:* Virgil, *Ecl.* 6.86; *Aen.* 9.106; Servius, *ad Aen.* 4.268;
6.782; 8.280; 10.1.

241   *Whatever you behold is nature*: Lucan, *De bello civili* 9.580.

248–319   It is hard to know what function to assign to this bizarre cata-
log, but *pace* White, *Nature, Sex, and Goodness*, 101–4, I do not
think it should be read as calling into question the benignity of
Nature.

250   *of both sexes*: There is no ancient testimony to the bisexuality
of Cornelia. Schmidt suggests that Johannes may have misun-
derstood Pliny, *Nat. Hist.* 7.36.122: two snakes were caught in
the house of the Gracchi, and when it was foretold that the
father, Titus Sempronius Gracchus, would live if the female
snake were killed, he urged that "his" snake be killed, since
Cornelia was still young and able to bear children. In 7.15.69,
Pliny cites Cornelia as evidence that it is bad luck to be born
with the genitals closed *(concreto virginali)*.

    little hammers: On the hammer as an image for the male organ
or testicles, J. N. Adams, *The Latin Sexual Vocabulary* (Balti-
more: Johns Hopkins University Press, 1982), 43, cites only the
twelfth-century Latin comedy *Lydia,* but hammer and anvil are
an image of sexual union at several points in the *De planctu na-
turae* of Alan of Lille.

251–   On Arescon, "whose name had been Arescusa," Pliny, *Nat. Hist.*
7.4.36. Much of the point of the passage is in the use of the
terms *ducere,* "to take in marriage," properly used of the bride-
groom, and *nubere,* "to put on the marriage veil," used of the
bride. The terms are reversed again in 7.145. As Schmidt points
out, Johannes has evidently created the nominative *Aristonte*
on the basis of the accusative *Aristontem* in his text of Pliny.

256–57   Pliny, *Nat. Hist.* 7.15.68; Solinus, *Collectanea rerum memorabilium*
1.70. Both give the name as Curius.

257–58   Pliny, *Nat. Hist.* 7.15.69; Solinus, *Collectanea rerum memorabilium*
1.70.

258–59   Solinus, *Collectanea rerum memorabilium* 1.74.

258–61 Solinus, *Collectanea rerum memorabilium* 1.74, reports Lygdamus's victory at Olympus but does not mention the tradition central to Pindar, *Olympian* Odes 3 and 10, and perhaps invented by him, that the Olympic games were founded by Hercules; see Jerome, trans. Eusebius, *Chronicon,* ed. Helm, 59b1; Vatican Mythographer 1.192. Aulus Gellius, *Noctes Atticae* 1.1.1–3, reports Hercules pacing out the dimensions of the first Olympic stadium. The patron of the games is Zeus, at whose shrine they took place.

262–64 Pliny, *Nat. Hist.* 6.35.187; Isidore, *Etym.* 11.3.18.

265–69 Schmidt notes the similarity of these lines to a passage in an anonymous poem on Pyramus and Thisbe printed by Faral, *Les arts poétiques,* 334, lines 123–25.

265 Pliny, *Nat. Hist.* 6.35.188; Isidore, *Etym.* 11.3.18. *Iactura* here is "lack," "absence," rather than "loss."

270–71 Pliny, *Nat. Hist.* 6.35.188; Isidore, *Etym.* 11.3.18.

274 *tiny teat*: As Schmidt notes, *mamillula,* which reappears in 2.17, is found elsewhere only in a letter of Matthew of Vendôme (*Epistolae* 2.4.69, ed. Munari, 2:128).

275 Pliny, *Nat. Hist.* 7.2.22–23; Solinus, *Collectanea rerum memorabilium* 52.26. Johannes treats *Nulo* as indeclinable.

276–78 Pliny, *Nat. Hist.* 7.2.23; Solinus, *Collectanea rerum memorabilium* 52.29.

279–80 Pliny, *Nat. Hist.* 7.2.23; Solinus, *Collectanea rerum memorabilium* 52.32.

279 *governed by Libra*: Schmidt sees here a reference to "astrological geography," which views each region of the earth as influenced by a particular constellation. Libra governs North Africa. Several manuscripts give *Libiae* in place of *Librae*.

281 Pliny, *Nat. Hist.* 7.2.24.

281–82 Pliny, *Nat. Hist.* 7.2.23; Solinus, *Collectanea rerum memorabilium* 52.27; Isidore, *Etym.* 11.3.15.

283–84 Pliny, *Nat. Hist.* 7.2.28; Solinus, *Collectanea rerum memorabilium* 52.28.

285 Pliny, *Nat. Hist.* 7.16.74; Solinus, *Collectanea rerum memorabilium* 1.90.

286–87   On Gemagog and his battle with Corineus, see Geoffrey, *Historia* 1.16. On Corineus, see below, 5.385–429 and note.

288   Pliny, *Nat. Hist.* 7.16.74; Solinus, *Collectanea rerum memorabilium* 1.89. Both give the giant's name as *Gabbara* and his height as nine feet, nine inches.

289–91   Solinus, *Collectanea rerum memorabilium* 1.91. His source is unknown, but he refers to Quintus Metellus Creticus, who, with Lucius Flaccus as his lieutenant, subjugated Crete in 69–67 BCE.

292–95   Pliny, *Nat. Hist.* 7.2.16–17; Solinus, *Collectanea rerum memorabilium* 1.101.

296   Pliny, *Nat. Hist.* 7.19.79; Solinus, *Collectanea rerum memorabilium* 1.72; Cicero, *De fin.* 5.30.92.

297–98   Pliny, *Nat. Hist.* 7.19.80; Solinus, *Collectanea rerum memorabilium* 1.74.

299–300   Pliny, *Nat. Hist.* 7.19.79; Solinus, *Collectanea rerum memorabilium* 1.73; Cicero, *De off.* 1.26.90. I take *letos* as one of Johannes's fanciful attempts at a Greek genitive.

301–7   Pliny, *Nat. Hist.* 7.2.25; Solinus, *Collectanea rerum memorabilium* 52.30.

308–11   Pliny, *Nat. Hist.* 7.2.14; Solinus, *Collectanea rerum memorabilium* 27.41; Lucan, *De bello civili* 9.906–11.

308   *nature has so steeled*: I assume *Natura* as the subject of *loricavit,* since the Psyllian is contrasted with Architrenius himself as described in 312–13, where *Natura* is clearly the implicit subject of *exponit.*

313   *Hydra*: A seven-headed serpent; when one head was cut off, two new heads grew in its place. In Boethius, *Cons.* 4, pr. 6.3, Philosophy uses the image of the Hydra to express the difficulty of understanding the relations of Fate and Providence; in 4, m. 7.22 she cites Hercules's destruction of the Hydra in exhorting the Prisoner to aspire to higher understanding.

315   *Chalybes*: The territory of the Chalybes, near the Black Sea, was famous for its iron mines, and their work in steel included armor consisting of small scales known as *plumae,* from their resemblance to feathers: Statius, *Theb.* 11.543.

318   *Stymphalides*: Monstrous birds who infested the lake Stymphalus in Arcadia, destroyed crops and humans with their bronze-tipped feathers, until slaughtered by the arrows of Hercules: Claudian, *Rapt. Pros.* 2.Praef.37; Ovid, *Met.* 9.187.

318–19   The bow and arrows are apparently the resources of Architrenius's inner nature, which fail to defend him against the impulse to sin.

350–52   *poetic Philomena*: The poetic nightingale is Claudian, who describes the palace of Venus, its setting, and the life of Venus's court, in his *Epithalamium* for the emperor Honorius, 49–85.

353–56   It is hard to see Johannes's point in speaking as he does of Claudian's powerfully satiric *In Rufinum* and his eulogizing poems on the campaigns and consulship of Stilicho. A gloss in *Q* suggests that Claudian has falsified the characters of the two men, but while modern historians have arrived at markedly differing views of their careers, Johannes is unlikely to have had historical grounds for questioning Claudian's accuracy. He may be suggesting that the contrasting portraits are politically motivated.

360   Godman, *Silent Masters,* 320–22, claims to see in the description that begins here a parody of Alan's portrait of Prudentia (*Anticlaudianus* 1.270–302) but offers no evidence; his view is questioned by Roling, "*Moderancia*-Konzept," 196.

363   *defers to her radiance*: *subradio,* attested in Tertullian, *De resurrectione carnis* 29, could be translated as "illumine" or "illustrate." My rendering here assumes that Johannes regarded the prefix *sub-* as indicating subordination or deference.

385   *its white bloom has received . . . berry juice*: *Ligustrum,* or privet, was a conventional image for whiteness: Ovid, *Met.* 13.789, and especially Virgil, *Ecl.* 2.15–18, where fair Corydon and dark Menalcas are contrasted as *ligustrum* and *vaccinium,* which here, as in 1.348 above, probably connotes only dark coloration.

389–92   Joined eyebrows often indicate a defect of character in medieval texts: Nathaniel Griffin, "Chaucer's Portrait of Criseyde," *Journal of English and Germanic Philology* 20 (1921): 39–40. Schmidt quotes a gloss in *V* that asserts that a man with joined eyebrows must be good for nothing.

410   Ovid mentions the proverbial virtue of Sabine women: *Am.* 1.8.39–40; 2.4.15; 3.8.61. *Met.* 14.829–51 tells of Hersilia, the Sabine wife of Romulus, whose grief at his death led Juno to transform her into the constellation Hora.

421   *happy air*: *aera*, the Greek accusative singular of *aer,* appears in several Latin authors known to Johannes.

447   *rubric*: The play on "rubric," the heading of a chapter or the major division of a text, commonly written in red lettering, is part of an elaborate medieval metaphorics based on scribal practice: 2.50n, and Ernst R. Curtius, *European Literature and the Latin Middle Ages,* trans. Willard R. Trask (Princeton and Oxford: Princeton University Press, 2013), 315–16.

448   *customary biting*: A gloss in *V* explains this as the practice of young women who bite their lips to make them red.

451   *warm glow*: "Warm glow" is less vivid than "glowing coal," but may give the intended effect.

473   *Parthian Lion*: The Lion is the constellation Leo, "Parthian" because in astrological geography it governs Asia (279n).

474   *firmament*: I take *arcu* as referring to the curvature, the vault of the heavens, as again at 9.124.

483–84   This passage plays on the opposition of the grammatical terms *epenthesis*, the insertion of a letter into a word, and *syncope*, the removal of a letter.

BOOK 2

3   *too-vivid*: *praesentior* is probably borrowed from Ovid, *Met.* 3.658, where it is used of the immanent power of a god.

19   *slender*: For *castigata,* compare Ovid, *Am.* 1.5.21.

33   *empty court*: The implications of archetypal purity in this description are enhanced by the echo of Bernardus Silvestris, *Cosmographia* 1.1.56, where Noys, the wisdom of God, is depicted as presiding over "an empty court," since God has not yet decreed the union of form with primordial matter. Bernardus's line is echoed ironically at *Architrenius* 5.151.

49   *full*: Minkova, "Textual Suggestions," 381, suggests replacing *plena* (full) with *plana* (flat), the reading of several later manuscripts, as complementing *pagina*.

    smooth skin: As *pagina* (literally, "sheet" or "page") indicates, the image is of a sheet of parchment, scraped with pumice to provide a clear and smooth surface for writing.

65   *armed*: *Cristatam* is "crested" or "plumed," neither of which describes the buckthorn. The word is used of armor: Virgil, *Aen.* 1.468; Statius, *Theb.* 3.223. Bernardus Silvestris, *Cosmographia* 1.3.279, describes the *rhamnus* as "armed."

73   *inclinations*: I take *pectore* (in the sense of "desire") as an ablative of means; it is by exploiting the feelings of young men that Cupid achieves his deceptions.

74   *Idalian deceptions*: That is, the arts of Venus. Idalium was a city in Cyprus sacred to the goddess.

93–164   At 93 the passage apparently abandons Cupid and becomes the portrait of a self-indulgent young man of fashion. Johannes's description and the denunciation with which it ends reflect the concern of clerical commentators with the excesses of court fashion, particularly that of men: C. Stephen Jaeger, *The Origins of Courtliness: Civilizing Trends and the Formation of Courtly Ideals, 939–1210* (Philadelphia: University of Pennsylvania Press, 1985), 76–94; Bond, *Loving Subject*, 107–9.

121   *at the open end*: That is, at the wrist.

165–66   This transition provides a good illustration of Johannes's narrative method, in which progression is wholly absent.

178–79   C. Fabricius Luscinus, Roman statesman and military hero, was consul in 282 and 278 BCE, whence the reference to the fasces in line 177. His proverbial poverty and austerity are recalled again at 2.391 and 5.288. C. Atilius Serranus was summoned from his farm to Rome and served as consul in 257 and 250 BCE. Fabricius and Serranus are paired in Virgil, *Aen.* 6.844; Claudian, *In Rufinum* 1.201–2, *De quarto consulatu Honorii* 414–15; and possibly in Lucan, *De bello civili* 10.151–54, though there the hero "summoned unwashed from his plow" is probably Cincinnatus.

182   *Ceres and Nereus*: Ceres, goddess of agriculture, and Nereus, god of ocean, are here bread and water.

189   *swim*: To "swim" is to be served in a sauce or broth.

190   *infraction*: *iactura* is apparently the possible consequence of swallowing food not lubricated by sauce.

219   *kitchen of Baucis*: Baucis and her husband, Philemon, old and poor, were the only mortals who offered hospitality when Jupiter and Mercury descended into the world disguised as mortals; the gods transformed their cottage to a temple, where the couple served as priests until, at death, they were transformed to trees: Ovid, *Met.* 8.611–724.

220   *Codrus's cottage*: Codrus, in twelfth-century poetry a stock figure for poverty (3.54; 6.334; 7.56), is named repeatedly by Virgil, *Ecl.* 5.11; 7.22, 26, and Juvenal, 1.2; 3.203, 208, as a rival poet, apparently inferior, and by Juvenal as impoverished. (In modern editions the name of Juvenal's victim is "Cordus," but Johannes undoubtedly knew him as Codrus.) A second tradition names Codrus as the last king of Athens (11th century BCE). When the Dorians invaded Attica, and the Delphic oracle declared that they would conquer if Codrus's life were spared, he went forth disguised as a peasant and provoked a fatal quarrel with a Dorian, thereby saving Athens: Valerius Maximus, *Memorabilia* 5.6.ext.1.

224   *Amyclas*: See above, 1.53n.

229   *wicked toil*: *labor improbus* echoes ironically Virgil's account of the life of toil imposed on man by Jupiter at the end of the Golden Age: *Georg.* 1.121–46.

235   *the burning pole*: A gloss in *D* identifying *ardentem polum* as the Antarctic pole is confirmed by 245–46 below.

240   Pharos, here a metonymy for Egypt, is the island near Alexandria where Ptolemy Philadelphus built the famous lighthouse. The reference to star-gazing Memphis may simply acknowledge the Egyptians as pioneering astronomers, but the ap-

pended clause suggests a particular man, probably the mathematician and astronomer Ptolemy (fl. ca. 127–170 CE), who apparently spent his entire life in Alexandria, but is called *Ptolomaeus Memphiticus* by Bernardus Silvestris, *Cosmographia* 2.5.20.

243   *Aren*: Aren, or Arin, was the name assigned by Arab astronomers to an imaginary city located on the equator and considered the center of the world: Schmidt, 74–75, 303.

244   *colural band*: The colures are circles, intersecting at the poles, one of which passes through the points in Cancer and Capricorn that mark the solstices, the other through the points in Aries and Libra that mark the equinoxes.

245   *Eastern spices*: Eoas, from *Eos*, "dawn," "morning," or, as here, "east," "orient."

245–46   *the torrid south*: *perusti/Axis* denotes the Antarctic pole, which Johannes assumes to be hot, in contrast to *Arctos*, the north pole.

251   *drawn into the service of the feast*: *epuli peregrinat in usum* echoes Alan of Lille, *Anticlaudianus* 3.135, which refers to the translations of Boethius, through which logic leaves Greek, its native language, and *nostri peregrinat in usum*. This is one of several appropriations of Alan's phrases that indicate Johannes's knowledge of the *Anticlaudianus*.

254   *Crassus*: M. Licinius Crassus Dives (d. 53 BCE), a Roman general and political ally of Julius Caesar, and a man of immense personal wealth, was killed in battle by the Parthians. According to Florus, *Epitomae* 1.46 (3.11).11, they sent his head to their king, who had it filled with molten gold. In medieval accounts Crassus himself is made to drink the gold while still alive; *Architrenius* 2.253–56; Bernardus Silvestris, *Cosmographia* 1.3.239–40; Alan of Lille, *Anticlaudianus* 2.227–28. Crassus reappears at *Architrenius* 5.491 as a general in the army of Avarice.

   other Crassi: Rigg, Review of *Architrenius*, 498, sees in *Crassos* a likely pun on *crassus* (fat, gross).

265   *divine protector*: I take *alumnum* in its late Latin meaning, "nourisher," "educator," "protector."

286   *Bacchus*: *Lyaeus* (relaxer, deliverer from care) is a name of Bacchus: Virgil, *Georg.* 2.229; Ovid, *Met.* 4.11.

290   *Megaera*: One of the three Erinyes, or Furies, who is traditionally the cause and punisher of jealousy or envy, but in the *Architrenius* arouses "madness" of all kinds.

294   *Paeonian herbs*: Virgil, *Aen.* 7.769. Paeon, or Paean, was a god of healing, whose name became a title of Apollo in his role as healer, and gave its name to a song, the paean, originally sung to the healing gods.

303   *the sevenfold bowl*: *paterae septemplicis*: As Homer's Ajax bears a sevenfold shield: Ovid, *Met.* 13.2. Schmidt sees the English Ajax as a type ("der ungestüme Engländer"). Chesley M. Hutchings, "L'*Anticlaudianus* d'Alain de Lille: Étude de chronologie," *Romania* 50, no. 197 (1924): 11, suggests that Nero, Midas, Ajax, Paris, and Davus in Alan of Lille, *Anticlaudianus* 1.169–81, represent Henry II and his sons. Ajax would correspond to Richard Coeur-de-Lion.

371   *consume more*: With Schmidt I take *esse* in line 371 as the infinitive of the contracted form of *edo, edere*, "eat," "consume."

380   *white cowl*: The Cistercians, still at the height of their influence a generation after the death of Bernard of Clairvaux in 1153, are distinguished by their white habits.

389–90   These lines define at once the virtues of cabbage and those of the Cistercian life.

406–80   Johannes borrows freely from Ovid's account of the meal prepared by Baucis for the disguised gods Jupiter and Mercury, *Met.* 8.641–78.

411–13   *water was mixed . . . earthen jug*: I assume that this is a kind of beer. Ovid's Baucis serves the gods "not very old wine," *Met.* 8.672.

478   *or*: For Schmidt's *haut* a number of manuscripts give *aut,* which Minkova, "Textual Suggestions," 383, prefers, and which I have adopted with some hesitation: if *Lascivia* cannot be banished, at least let *Copia* extend to all.

484–93   A version of these lines in a treatise praising French culture pro-
voked Petrarch's attack on the *Architrenius*; see above, Intro-
duction, "Fortunae."

484   *Chrysaean*: Pliny, *Nat. Hist.* 6.23.80, and Solinus, *Collectanea rerum
memorabilium* 52.17 cite reports of two islands at the mouth
of the Indus river, Chryse and Argyre, whose mines, as their
names suggest, produce only gold and silver.

488–92   These lines, in which Paris becomes a sort of Paradise, recall
Pliny's concluding encomium on the natural endowments of
Italy, *Nat. Hist.* 37.77.201–2.

Book 3

46–48   Boreas, Eurus, Zephyrus, and Auster are the North, East, West,
and South Winds, respectively.

82–83   Geta and Birria are the names of slaves in comedies of Terence,
borrowed by twelfth-century authors of elegiac comedies and
appropriated by Latin school poetry generally to denote low or
buffoonish types. See also 5.342 and the reference to "Davus"
at 3.341.

105–6   The winged horse Pegasus by a stroke of his hoof brought forth
on Mt. Helicon the fountain Hippocrene, sacred to the Muses:
Ovid, *Met.* 5.256–63. The Castalian spring is on Mt. Parnassus.

131   Minkova, "Textual Suggestions," 384, proposes substituting *un-
guibus* (nails) for *ignibus* (fires, heat), but it is found in only a
single late manuscript.

137   *in a direct path*: That is, from east to west.

142–43   *bonds of harmony*: The phrase *musica vincla* recalls Bernardus Sil-
vestris, *Cosmographia* 1.1.22.

156   Euclid, *Elementa* 10, Appendix 27.

158   *lyre*: *cheli* is Johannes's plausible ablative singular of *chelys*. This
form is not found in ancient Latin.

163–67   Hegesias of Cyrene (early third century BCE.) advocated suicide,
and was banished from Alexandria because of his teachings. Jo-
hannes's vivid picture embellishes the brief accounts in Vale-
rius Maximus, *Memorabilia* 8.9.ext.3, and Cicero, *Tusc.* 1.34.84.

165   *Lachesis*: See 1.188n.

168–72   These lines describe dialectic, the art that distinguishes truth from error.

173   On Grammar as "nurse and mother" of the Arts (whence the *cunis* of line 173), John of Salisbury, *Metalogicon* 1.13.

174–76   *transitive relation*: If *transitio* denotes the transitive relation between nouns or pronouns, as in Priscian, the grammatical rules here set forth would seem to be false. Two nominatives *(recta)* can be related only by equivalence, and any relationship between a nominative and a word in a different case *(obliquum)* is in some sense transitive: Priscian, *Institutiones* 14.14–15, cited by Schmidt; also 13.25–26; 17.153–55. Minkova, "Textual Suggestions," 385, suggests that Johannes is using *transitio* in the sense of "conjunction," and cites *Ad Herennium* 4.35.

214   *mute babbling*: I have tried to suggest the punning effect of *infantia,* speech at once unspoken and like that of a preverbal child.

229   *traveler*: I assume that the *hospes* is the Sun, but *stellis . . . mutato* may just be a way of setting an early morning scene.

249–50   As Schmidt notes, Johannes has treated *fontis . . . Cirrhaei* as parallel to the two preceding infinitive clauses.

260   *quos* refers to *ocellis* in 259, but I have treated them as a metonymy for the lover.

285   *line of Libra*: I take this to be the equinoctial, the circle that passes through the signs of Libra and Aries, and thus provides a fixed point in relation to which the hour of sunrise can be estimated at other times of the year.

287   *the swell*: Ovid uses *arcus* of cresting waves: *Met.* 11.568; and there is perhaps a play on "arch," which, with *ianua,* would suggest that day begins with the Sun's grand entry as if through a triumphal arch.

       Tethys: The wife of Oceanus and mother of the sea nymphs and river gods. In Ovid, *Met.* 2.69, and Lucan, *De bello civili* 1.414, her name stands for the sea itself.

289   *Minerva*: Also known as Pallas Athena, notorious for her love of battle.

Cirrha: Here, and in 3.347 and 383, stands for learning or wisdom.

300   *evening*: I take *roscidus*, "dewy," "wet with dew," which can hardly apply to the sun, as a somewhat far-fetched indication that it is evening.

306–313   These lines are largely imitated from Claudian, *In Rufinum* 1.251–56, which mentions all the villains named by Johannes with the exception of Nero.

306   *Sciron*: The robber Sciron was killed by Theseus. Neither earth nor ocean would admit his bones, and they were transformed into a rocky cliff: Ovid, *Met.* 7.443–47.

308   *Diomede*: This Diomedes is not the Homeric hero, but the barbarous Thracian king, who owned a team of man-eating mares: Claudian, *Rapt. Pros.* 2.praef.12. Hercules destroyed the king's stables and taught the mares to feed on grass, having first, in one version of the story, fed them their master: Vatican Mythographers, 1.61, 63; 2.151.

    Busiris: An Egyptian ruler who sacrificed strangers on the altar of Zeus, and was himself killed by Hercules: Virgil, *Georg.* 3.5; Ovid, *Met.* 9.182–83; Statius, *Theb.* 12.155.

310   *Sinis*: Another robber killed by Theseus, he bent pine trees to the ground, tied captives to their tops, and released them, catapulting the victims into the air: Ovid, *Met.* 7.440–42.

311   *Sulla*: Lucius Cornelius Sulla Felix (138–79 BCE) was a Roman general who twice invaded Rome, establishing himself as dictator in his last years.

312   *Phalaris*: A Sicilian tyrant (ca. 570–549 BCE), held to have possessed a brazen bull in which his enemies were roasted alive: Valerius Maximus, *Memorabilia* 9.2.ext.9; on his cruelty, Cicero, *De off.* 2.7.26.

313   *Cinna*: Lucius Cornelius Cinna (d. 84 BCE), a Roman general and statesman, sought to restore and maintain ordered government in Rome after the Social Wars and the first invasion of Rome by Sulla.

    Spartacus: A Thracian gladiator (d. 71 BCE) who led a revolt and won several victories against Roman generals in southern Italy, before he was defeated by Marcus Licinius Crassus.

314   *the Stygian dog*: The three-headed Cerberus, who, on the far bank of the river Styx, guards the entrance to the underworld: Virgil, *Aen.* 6.417–23.

315–16 Cocytus, the river of weeping, and Phlegethon, the river of fire, are located in the lower depths of the underworld: Virgil, *Aen.* 6.132, 323, 550–51.

318   *thread*: *filo* refers to the thread provided by Daedalus to Ariadne that enabled Theseus, having made his way to the center of the Labyrinth and killed the Minotaur, to retrace his path to the entrance: Virgil, *Aen.* 6.27–30.

319, 321 Charybdis, a whirlpool, and Scylla, a large rock, are the traditional perils of the passage between Sicily and Italy: Homer, *Od.* 12.73–110, 234–59; Virgil, *Aen.* 3.420–32. Scylla, originally a beautiful maiden, was transformed to a monster, beautiful down to the waist, but with the heads of fierce dogs or wolves below: Ovid, *Met.* 14.59–74; hence *latratus* in *Architrenius* 3.320 and *cane* in 5.270.

322   *Syrtis*: Literally, "sandbank"; commonly denotes an area of shoals off the north coast of Africa. It appears again in a similar catalog of perils in 9.169.

341   *Davus*: Like Geta and Birria, the name of a slave in Roman comedy. In Horace, *Sat.* 2.7, he is a ne'er-do-well, and it is in this role that he reappears in 5.334 and 7.416. Schmidt cites several twelfth-century references to his bad character.

351   *mitra*: A turban or headdress, here presumably the miter of a bishop.

383   *Cirrha*: *Cirrhen* is evidently Johannes's version of the Greek accusative. At 3.347 Schmidt gives *Cirres,* the reading of a single late manuscript, as the genitive, though at 3.289 it is *Cirre.*

407   *Nysa*: A city in India, traditionally the birthplace of Bacchus: Virgil, *Aen.* 6.805; Pliny, *Nat. Hist.* 6.23.79.

435   *a double sun*: With Schmidt I take *geminum Solem* as referring to Phoebus in his double aspect, as Sun and as god of wisdom, but other interpretations are clearly possible.

443   This line is perhaps corrupt. What seems to begin as a conventional opposition between generosity in one instance and avarice in another seems awkwardly broken off, and Schmidt's concluding question, *Cui larga tenetur?*, is hard to construe, though Johannes is apparently playing on different meanings of *teneo* (withhold, obligate). My translation conveys what I assume to have been the intended meaning of the line.

471   *an actor*: *histrio* here may signify the courtier who abandons his own character to adopt the self-serving role of flatterer. The equation of the client or courtier with the actor, common in Roman satire, is developed by John of Salisbury, *Policraticus* 3.4, 8.3.

Book 4

9   *Pella*: A city in Macedonia; the birthplace of Alexander the Great.

14   *opposite to the apogee*: *Aux* or *augis* is the term used by the ninth-century Arab astronomer Al-Farghání, or "Alfraganus," Johannes's chief source for astronomical data, to denote the apogee of a planet. Hence the *oppositio* or *oppositum augis* is the perigee.

16   *quartered surface*: The *quadratura* is one half of one of the Moon's hemispheres, hence the phase described is half-moon.

17   *One face of the mountain*: My translation assumes that the mountain of line 9 is reintroduced as subject at the midpoint of line 16. It would perhaps be possible to construe *partem . . . vergit* as referring to the Moon, but *arduus* in 18 must refer to *mons,* and the use of the enclitic *-que* to link the two clauses suggests that they have a common subject.

34   See Ovid, *Her.* 5.21–30, where Oenone recalls verses carved by Paris on the bark of a poplar tree declaring their love and his fidelity.

39   *cinnamolgos*: A legendary bird that makes its nest in the cinnamon tree: Pliny, *Nat. Hist.* 10.50.97; Solinus, *Collectanea rerum memorabilium* 33.15; Isidore, *Etym.* 12.7.23.

43   *thirsting for the early rain of Bacchus*: The notion of a "thirsting"

peach *(persicus)* involves a play on *persiccus* (very dry). The "rain of Bacchus" may refer to a method of preserving peaches in wine, perhaps new wine (which might explain *primaevum,* otherwise puzzling to me), or mixing their juice with wine. Pliny, *Nat. Hist.* 23.66.132. recommends the latter.

44   *quince: Coctanus,* a corruption of *cottanum,* is the name of the Syrian fig, often confused with quince *(cotaneus)* by medieval writers. The *Dictionary of Medieval Latin from British Sources* assigns both.

46–51   The pear hallowed with the name of Regulus in 46 is presumably, as Schmidt notes, the *pirum Sancti Reguli* cited in the *Dictionary of Medieval Latin from British Sources.* That in 47, named for the hollow of the palm, is probably the *volema* of Virgil, *Georg.* 2.88, and Pliny, *Nat. Hist.* 15.16.56. Du Cange cites a *pirum angustiae* called in French *poire d'angoisse;* this must be the pear associated with *matrina angustia* (the narrow passage of motherhood) in 48: in both cases the pear-like shape of the womb will have suggested the association. (Du Cange notes that the name seems to be derived *a vulgari notione.*) For the pear of 49, sponsored by Augustus, Schmidt cites Valerius Cordus, *Historia plantarum ac stirpium* (Strasburg, 1561), p. 178, who names a *pirum Augusti,* which ripens *tempestive* (seasonably) in the month of August. The pear fathered by Robert in 50 is glossed in X as "pere Robert." Various varieties named by Pliny are identified by French editors with the "poire de St. Jean," presumably the pear baptized by "another John." I see no evidence that this other is the Evangelist rather than the Baptist, as Schmidt suggests; Johannes may simply intend to denote a "John" other than himself.

58–59   The pallor known to lovers is perhaps that prescribed by Ovid, *Ars Am.* 1.729, and by Andreas Capellanus, *De amore* 2.8, where the fifteenth of the Rules of Love declares that "every lover normally grows pale under the gaze of his beloved."

60   *only:* I take *solum* as an adverb rather than a noun (soil) because of the similar use of the adjective *solis* in 67.

63   *berries, which, black though they are:* Perhaps the whortleberry.

102   Hypocrisy's unpainted cheeks are intended to feign simplicity or innocence: Rigg, Review of *Architrenius,* 498.

109   *creeps*: Minkova, "Textual Suggestions," 385, objects that *repto* is not a deponent verb, but the participle *reptatus* is used by Statius, *Theb.* 5.581, and Claudian, *In Rufinum* 2.180, in ways that would readily suggest the impersonal *reptatur.* (In translating I have altered the construction to make *Ambitio* the subject of the verb.)

118   *Sun and Moon*: I assume with the glossator of *X* that sun and moon stand for day and night.

130   *Pyrrhus*: King of Epirus (319–272 BCE), who warred against Rome on behalf of the Greek colonies in Italy, winning several battles before abandoning the campaign.

147   *Olympus*: For Olympus as the heavens, 1.240n. It is perhaps because of the mountain's double role that Johannes calls the mountain of Ambition a third Olympus.

153   *Phlegra*: The site of the battle of the Giants against the gods.

154   *a sky-born race*: Though *caelestis homo* suggests a particular figure, I take the phrase as referring generally to the Titans, "sky-born" in that they were born of the union of Earth and Sky. Johannes seems not to have made a clear distinction between Titans and Giants: 5.36–39n.

171–72, 175–76 As noted in Introduction, n. 54, these lines appear in Gibbon's *Decline and Fall.*

215–18   Arachne, a maiden skilled in weaving, declared herself equal in skill to Pallas Athena. The goddess appeared to her disguised as an old woman, and when Arachne refused to retract her boast, she revealed herself, and they competed. When Arachne produced a flawless tapestry depicting gods disguising themselves to ravish mortal women, Athena destroyed the work and turned Arachne into a spider: Ovid, *Met.* 6.1–145.

218   *Hermus*: A gold-bearing river in Asia Minor, now the Gediz, which flows into the Mediterranean near Izmir, Turkey.

227–29   The language and imagery recall Bernardus Silvestris, *Cosmographia* 1.1.39–40.

240   *the son of Atreus*: Here, Menelaus. In 250 it is Agamemnon.

244   *Pyrrhus*: The son of Achilles and ancestor of the Pyrrhus named
        in 4.131, he captured and later married Andromache, widow of
        Hector, and founded a kingdom in Epirus: Virgil, *Aen.* 3.292–
        97, 325–29.

260–64 The frequent appearance of Pyramus and Thisbe (Ovid, *Met.*
        4.55–166) as a theme in twelfth- and thirteenth-century school
        poetry is traced by Glendinning, "Pyramus and Thisbe in the
        Medieval Classroom." That Johannes composed a poem on this
        theme is suggested by Schmidt, 25–26, on the basis of Gervase,
        Ars poetica 119.

265–67 The incestuous loves of Byblis for her brother Caunus, and Myr-
        rha for her father Cinyras, are narrated by Ovid, *Met.* 9.447–
        665; 10.311–502. Gervase, *Ars poetica* 29, 83 cites lines by Jo-
        hannes that may be from a poem on Byblis and Caunus.

265–66 *herself a stepmother*: Myrrha is stepmother to herself in that she
        succeeds her own mother as "wife" to her father and both
        causes and suffers the cruelty with which stepmothers are com-
        monly associated in medieval Latin poetry.

267–71 In Ovid, *Her.* 9.55–80, Deianira, Hercules's neglected wife, re-
        ports the rumor that he had put on female dress and worked at
        spinning wool, though at the bidding of Omphale, rather than
        Iole.

268   *Alcides*: That is, Hercules, grandson of Alceus, king of Tiryns.

274–76 The artist-weaver, identified as Arachne in 4.215, is now mascu-
        line.

279   *he brings forth*: The subject of *parit* is not clear. The glossator of
        X questions whether *ille* in 276 refers to the tapestry or to the
        artist *(pannus vel pictor?)*.

289   For *Pharius* in the broader sense of Egyptian, see 2.240n.

291   In *X* this passage is glossed as *commendatio Maioris Britanniae*
        (praise of Great Britain), but while a later encomium on King
        Henry II (5.85–93) seems straightforward, in the present con-
        text Johannes's praise of the luxury of his court is surely ironic.

296   Tyre was an island city of the Phoenicians off the southeast
        Mediterranean coast, famous for a purple dye derived from a

shellfish, the murex: Pliny, *Nat. Hist.* 9.60.125. In Latin poetry "Tyrian" often refers to this elegant color.

303–5 These lines echo Alan of Lille, *Anticlaudianus* 6.486–88, where Prudentia returns from Heaven bearing the divine gift of a new soul for humankind: *miratur in illo / Artificis Natura manum, munusque beatum / laudat.* As at 2.251, I take the similarity as evidence that Johannes knew Alan's poem.

310–11 The "fellow human" is the little man at the bottom of the goblet, whom Gluttony, by distracting the feaster with food, spares from being drowned in drink. The bird, the serpent, the angel, etc. in other goblets are not spared.

334 *outward expression*: Minkova, "Textual Suggestions," 386, suggests emending Schmidt's *operto* (concealed) to *aperto* (open), which, paired with *occulto* (secret), would bring it into line with the series of antitheses that runs through this chapter. I have preserved *operto* as making better sense with *animo* (mind), though its relation to what precedes and follows is awkward.

366–67 *has no use for promises unless to betray them*: There is an untranslatable pun here on *foedus* (pledge, promise) and *foede, foedius* (foully, basely).

387–88 *sweeps away that dust*: This gesture, part of the stock in trade of Ovid's attentive lover (*Ars Am.* 1.151), is standard courtly behavior in medieval satire: Murray, *Reason and Society*, 107–9.

393 *against his lord's interest*: The subject of *volenti* is unclear; the point may be that the flatterer gives his own misfortunes a favorable appearance to avoid disturbing his lord.

404–5 *the punishing of wrongdoing . . . of his lord*: I assume that the *facinus* entrusted to the flatterer is not a crime he is to commit, but rather the punishment of crime: what follows suggests that he has been made responsible for policing the household, but instead betrays his trust by warning wrongdoers and winking at their crimes. I have replaced Schmidt's *domuique* with the well-attested *dominique*, since I assume that it is the lord, rather than his household, who is betrayed. In 4.470–71, *domus* is said to have betrayed *dominum*.

440 *vessel*: *alnus* (alder) was a wood frequently used in ancient ship-
building.

chap. 17 The argument of this chapter closely resembles that of Boe-
thius, *Cons.* 2, pr. 8.

468 *friendships*: The antecedent of *quos* is not clear; "friendships" is a
conjecture suggested by *amico* in the previous line.

Book 5

11 In the Aesopian fable a jackdaw decks himself in peacock feath-
ers and pretends to be a peacock. Horace, *Epist.* 1.3.19–20, in
alluding to the story, substitutes a crow *(cornicula)* for the jack-
daw. The jackdaw is the example in Phaedrus, *Fabulae* 1.3.

13–14 Isidore, *Etym.* 12.2.30, describes the ape as *facie foeda* (foul-
faced). Solinus, *Collectanea rerum memorabilium* 27.56, speaks of
apes copying a deliberately deceptive gesture by men, daubing
their eyes with birdlime, and thereby rendering themselves
easy to capture.

15 *eager*: *Admissam* means ready to breed, accept a male sexual part-
ner.

16 *unbending sluggishness*: The elephant's rare and secret matings
and its avoidance of promiscuity, reported by Pliny, *Nat. Hist.*
8.5.13, together with the sluggish sexual nature of the male, be-
come a standard topic in bestiaries: *Physiologus latinus (Versio
Y)*, edited by F. J. Carmody, University of California Publica-
tions in Classical Philology 12.7 (Berkeley: University of Cali-
fornia Press, 1941), p. 117; *Theobaldi "Physiologus,"* ed. P. T. Eden
(Leiden, 1972), pp. 64–65.

 the Molossian hound: Considered by some the ancestor of the
modern mastiff, it was known for its fierceness: Horace, *Sat.*
2.6.114–15; Statius, *Theb.* 3.203.

17 *Lycaon*: When Lycaon, king of Arcadia, offered to the disguised
Jupiter a meal of human flesh, he was transformed to a wolf:
Ovid, *Met.* 1.163–243.

21 *Pasiphae*: The wife of King Minos of Crete. Her passion for a
snow-white bull led her to persuade the master artisan Daeda-
lus to create a wooden cow within which she concealed herself.

When the bull mounted the false cow, the Minotaur was conceived: Ovid, *Ars Am.* 1.295–326; Virgil, *Aen.* 6.24–26.

22–23 Niobe pridefully compared her seven sons and seven daughters to the mere two children of Latona. Latona's children, Apollo and Diana, slaughtered the children of Niobe, and she herself, as she wept, was turned to stone: Ovid, *Met.* 6.146–312.

24–30 Ovid, *Met.* 2.1–271. See 1.73n.

26 *the straying sun*: I take *diem* as the sun, but I cannot explain its relation to *urit,* and my translation is conjectural.

27 Ovid, *Met.* 2.176–77.

31–32 The child of Ceres is Proserpina. As bride of Pluto she dwells in the underworld for half the year, and during the other half is restored to the world and her mother to ensure the regular continuance of agriculture: Ovid, *Met.* 5.332–661; Claudian, *Rapt. Pros.* 3.18–54.

32 On Pyrrhus, see 4.245n. His kingdom in Epirus took its name from Molossus, his son by Andromache.

33–34 The centaur Nessus was killed by Hercules when he sought by a trick to abduct Deianira: Ovid, *Met.* 9.101–28.

34–35 *the Lemnian, a blot on the heavens*: Fulgentius, *Mitologiae* 2.11. Vulcan is *Lemnius* from Lemnos, an island in the Aegean, traditionally the site of Vulcan's forge.

36–39 The assault on the gods to which Johannes refers here was that of the Titans, rather than the Giants: Virgil, *Georg.* 1.279–83; Ovid, *Met.* 1.151–62. (In 150 Ovid misleadingly refers to the Titans as giants.) The Titans appear again at *Architrenius* 5.318–21, and the Giants' attack is recalled at 6.461–66.

40–41 For the anecdote of Aristotle's allowing his pupil to publish certain writings of his on rhetoric, Valerius Maximus, *Memorabilia* 8.14.ext.3.

44–45 The contest of the Pierides and the Muses is related by Ovid, *Met.* 5.294–678.

47 *the stolen name*: Johannes apparently refers to the fact that the Muses are the original Pierides: Cicero, *Nat. D.* 3.21.54; Virgil, *Ecl.* 8.63, 10.72. The Ovidian Pierides, he suggests, have stolen the name.

55, 58 *God*: I take *superum* and *superis* as denoting God.

66   *undisciplined speech*: *circumcisa* recalls Exodus 6:12 and 6:30, where
      Moses protests the Lord's command that he speak to the Isra-
      elites, claiming that his lips are "uncircumcised." See also 9.407
      and Alan of Lille, *De planctu Naturae* 16.11.

69   Schmidt notes other twelfth-century plays on *ara*, "pigsty," and
      ara, "altar."

71   Avernus ("without birds") was a lake south of Rome which
      exhaled vapors that killed birds who flew over it: Pliny, *Nat.
      Hist.* 31.2.21. It was traditionally the entrance to the under-
      world.

72   *low creature*: *vulgus* seems to refer to a single figure, the *puer in-
      solidus* (unstable boy) of the preceding twenty lines.

80   *teacher*: *Rabbi* is here equivalent to *magister* (teacher): Matthew
      23:7–8; John 1:38.

88–89 *Leader in war and peace*: Henry is *dux*: "general" in war and "duke"
      in peace.

99   *eagerly acquisitive*: I read *ardens* here as transitive, with *loculos* as
      its object, as in Virgil, *Ecl.* 2.1: *Corydon ardebat Alexin* (Corydon
      burned for Alexis).

103–4 *on earth . . . in heaven*: I assume that Johannes is treating *terris* and
      caelo as locatives.

105   *toes*: On *articulos*, Alan of Lille, *Anticlaudianus* 7.145–46, where
      this way of walking is criticized.

129   *two winds*: The two winds, as a gloss in *X* explains, are the effects
      of pride and of feasting.

152–53 *uniquely worthy*: The subject of *unam . . . dignam* is *belua* (mon-
      ster) in 149.

161   *sails both black and white*: These are the habits of Benedictine and
      Cistercian.

164–68 My translation of these lines has been guided by Placanica, Re-
      view of *Architrenius,* 748, and Minkova, "Textual Suggestions,"
      387.

165–66 On these lines Placanica, Review of *Architrenius,* 748, aptly cites
      the gloss of Peter Lombard on Psalm 18:14 (*Commentaria in
      Psalmos, Patrologia Latina* 191.213D): "I will be cleansed from the

greatest fault, the fault of pride, which is the last for those re-
turning to God and the first for those withdrawing."

169–73   The ironic tone of this passage is emphasized by the allusion in
169 to Juvenal, *Sat.* 2.47, on the *magna concordia* (great bond)
among those *molles animos* (degenerate spirits) united by a com-
mon pursuit of debased sexual practices.

181   *North*: On *Arctos*, 1.159n.

183–84   The reference to "northern" and "southern" regions of Heaven
is ultimately based on Isaiah 14:13, where Lucifer declares that
he will place his throne *in lateribus Aquilonis*. On this and re-
lated questions of heavenly geography, Thomas D. Hill, "Some
Remarks on 'The Site of Lucifer's Throne,'" *Anglia* 87 (1969):
303–11.

186–87   *reduces his pride to nothing . . . grow slack*: I take *irritat* here in its
late Latin sense of "nullify," "render vain." Though *lentescere* is
perhaps ambiguous, my rendering of the line is prompted by
Schmidt's citation of the monostich, *Redditur invalidus, nimium
si tenditur, arcus* (if the bow is drawn too far, it is rendered inef-
fective), no. 26448 in Hans Walther, *Lateinische Sprichworter und
Sentenzen des Mittelalters,* 5 vols. (Göttingen: Vandenhoeck and
Ruprecht, 1963–1969).

199–200   *let the high realm of the gods beware*: The point of *caveat . . . sedes* is
apparently that any angel privileged to dwell in the *summa sedes*
might be susceptible to a fatal pride like that of Lucifer.

206–19   On this passage, Catherine Klaus, "De l'Enfer au Paradis . . . et
Retour," 27–29.

218   *He . . . he*: I read both occurrences of *ille* in this line as referring
to Lucifer.

242–43   A gloss in *Q* explains that Phoebe is identified with the monster
"because she conceals powers *(virtutes)* from us." The portion
of her brother's fires that she conceals is evidently a metaphor
for the spiritual power of the Church; the monster is plainly
identified with the papal court at Rome in 5.482.

247   *she creates . . . she will see*: I have treated *factura* and *visura* as verbs,
and made *visura* also the understood main verb of a new sen-
tence beginning with *mollesque* in 249.

247–48   *depths . . . daytime*: The *recessus Antipodum* represent deeply hid-
den motives, and *noctis dies* is the dark time when only thieves
and other malefactors can see their way.

251   *Thule*: An island in the extreme north, perhaps Iceland or one
of the Shetlands, traditionally the northernmost point of hu-
man habitation. It is *ultima Thule* in Virgil's praise of Augustus,
Georg. 1.30. Here it stands for the extreme west, the point fur-
thest from the rising Sun.

255   *realizing what she is*: As Schmidt observes, in *noto quid erat* an ab-
lative absolute construction incorporates a subordinate clause.

269   *Ceraunian waves*: Ceraunia is the name of a mountain range in
Epirus. In associating it with *fluctus* Johannes may partly mis-
read Lucan, *De bello civili* 5.650–53, where the huge waves of a
sea storm are described hyperbolically as threatening to dash
Caesar's ship, not just against the rocky coast, but against the
tops of the neighboring Ceraunian mountains. In *Architrenius*
8.116 the *ardua Ceraunia* are associated with downward-rushing
streams.

270   *Phorcis*: (gen. *Phorcidis*) identifies Scylla as the daughter of Phor-
cus, best known as the father of the Gorgons, but often as-
signed various sea monsters as progeny.

271   *a single day*: I take *diurna* here as in Ovid, *Her.* 6.36, where Hyp-
sipyle recalls Jason's tales of men born through the sowing of
the serpent's teeth, sprung full grown from the ground only to
die immediately in battle, *aetatis fata diurna suae,* "their lives
fated to last a single day."

275   The Hesperian (i.e., Western) stream is the gold-bearing Tagus
(1.193n).

    Hebrus: *Bessique meatus* refers to the river Hebrus, in a region
of Thrace where there were gold mines. The Bessi were a peo-
ple of the region who worked the mines. Johannes, apparently
misreading Claudian's *Panegyric on the Consulship of Manlius The-
odorus* 38–41, has taken *Bessi* as the name of a river.

276   *Macrobian's chains*: The Macrobians, an Aethiopian people, were
said to bind their criminals with chains of gold: Solinus, *Collec-
tanea rerum memorabilium* 30.10.

Chryse: See 2.484n. Nero is reported to have fished with golden nets: Suetonius, *Nero* 30; John of Salisbury, *Policraticus* 7.2, 8.18.

277   *the tree of Hesperus's daughters*: The daughters of Hesperus were the keepers of a tree that bore golden apples: Servius *ad Aen.* 3.113; Vatican Mythographers 1.38; 3.13.5. Statius, *Theb.* 7.43–44, describes the home of Mars as made entirely of iron, but in Claudian, *Magnes* 22–24, Mars and Venus dwell together in a temple of gold. Jupiter took the form of a shower of gold to mate with Danae: Ovid, *Met.* 4.610–11; Hyginus, *Fabulae* 64; Vatican Mythographers, 1.157; 2.110.

278   *tomb of Bacchus*: As Schmidt observes, this reference is perhaps due to a misreading of Jerome's version of Eusebius's *Chronicon* 7.1, where the tomb of Bacchus is said to be visible at Delphi *iuxta Apollinem aureum* (alongside golden Apollo), but is not itself said to be made of gold.

278–79 *the Egyptian tyrant*: Ptolemy XIII, who drowned in the Nile in 47 BCE, was reported to have been wearing a golden breastplate: Florus, *Epitomae* 2.13.

279   *the infancy of Jove*: Glosses in *P*, *Q*, and *X* suggest that "Jove's tender years" is probably an oblique reference to the Golden Age when Jove's father, Saturn, ruled the world. But Robert Babcock has suggested to me that the phrase alludes to Juvenal, *Sat.* 6.14–16, in which a still-beardless Jove is seen as the youthful ruler of the Silver Age.

280   *reward from the wise men*: On the wise men's gift to Apollo, Valerius Maximus, *Memorabilia* 4.1.ext.7: A fisherman's net drew up a golden tripod. He had agreed to sell his catch to another man, and it was unclear which had a right to the tripod. Apollo at Delphi ruled that it should be given to him who excelled all others in wisdom, and it was offered to the Seven Sages, one by one: each deferred to the next, and finally Solon offered the trophy to Apollo himself.

281   *the twin poles*: I accept the suggestion of Placanica, Review of *Architrenius*, 748, who sees the two *axes* as the two poles, and cites Claudian, *De consolatu Stilichonis* 3.138, which is echoed by Johannes's line. Schmidt suggests that the *axes* are the axles

of the chariot of the Sun, described by Ovid, *Metamorphoses* 2.107–8, as made of gold.

288 On Fabricius, 2.178–79n. On Crassus, 2.254n.

312 *Philomena*: The nightingale (1.352n), that is, a sweet singer.

314 On the singing of the swan, 1.57n.

315–16 *the two sunrises and both daytimes*: Greed embraces both hemispheres, as implied in line 281.

332–33 *the altar would not now . . . greed to godhead*: Gervase, *Ars poetica* 25, cites line 333 as an effective instance of *additiva correctio:* the point made first by the opposition *ara–auro* is clarified, and rendered progressively more meaningful, by the subsequent oppositions *liber–libra, numen–nummus.*

336 *Simon*: Simon Magus, who attempted to buy from the Apostles the power of the Holy Spirit (Acts 8:9–24), and gave his name to simony, the buying and selling of spiritual things, especially, as here, ecclesiastical preferment.

346 *astonished way*: The use of *stupidum* to modify *iter* is odd; Minkova, "Textual Suggestions," 387, suggests *stupidus,* attested in one early manuscript, to modify the sentence's subject, though Johannes is quite capable of transferring a mental condition to an *iter.*

361–62 *a tide of blood soaks the earth . . . clarion of their neighing*: The accusatives *terram* and *aera* are puzzling: *terra*, it would seem, should drink *undam,* and *aer* seems the likely subject for *mugit.* My translation follows this line of reasoning.

384–442 This portion of Gawain's narrative is based on Geoffrey of Monmouth's *Historia regum Britanniae.* As Echard suggests, *Arthurian Narrative*, 108–12, it is mainly a frame for the appended account of the lineage of Johannes's patron, Walter of Coutances, but it also identifies Arthur with the cardinal kingly virtue of generosity.

384 *Lodonesia*: That is, Lothian in southeastern Scotland, ruled by Loth, father of the speaker, who at 6.4 will identify himself as Gawain: Geoffrey, *Historia* 8.21, 9.9, 11.

387–429 On Corineus, Geoffrey, *Historia* 1.12–13, 15–16. He is the leader of a group of descendants of exiles from Troy who are discovered "beyond the Pillars of Hercules" by Brutus (407n) and join

him to invade first France and then England, where Corineus
becomes the ruler of Cornwall, which takes its name from him.

387   *the second Tirynthian*: That is, second Hercules, whose youth is
        associated with the Argive town of Tiryns.

393   *Cornubia*: Cornwall.

395   The Tyrrhene shore, the Italian coast from Tuscany to Calabria,
        here stands for Italy. On Corineus's domination of "Tyrrhene"
        or "Etrurian" giants, Geoffrey, *Historia* 1.12.

399–400 On the conquest of Aquitaine, Geoffrey, *Historia* 1.12–14. The
        cities of the Franks are sacked much later by the Roman gen-
        eral Maximianus: Geoffrey, *Historia* 5.10.

407   *Brutus*: Lineal descendant of Aeneas and leader of the main body
        of survivors from Troy, who will become king of Britain: Geof-
        frey, *Historia* 1.3–18.

        Achates: The faithful companion of the hero of Virgil's *Aeneid*.
        Though the Latin phrase is ambiguous, Johannes seems to have
        diverged from Geoffrey and made Corineus, rather than Bru-
        tus, the Aeneas figure.

411   *guided by Diana*: Journeying westward, Brutus visits a temple of
        Diana; the goddess appears and prophesies that he will found a
        kingdom on an island in the sea: Geoffrey, *Historia* 1.11.

412   *Albion*: The name of the island of Britain before the arrival of
        Brutus: Geoffrey, *Historia* 1.16.

412   *vessels*: On *alno*, 4.440n.

425–29 1.286–87n.

426–27 The giant Antaeus was the son of Tellus, the goddess Earth, and
        drew his strength from contact with the earth. Hercules de-
        feated him by lifting him off the ground: Ovid, *Met.* 9.183–84;
        Lucan, *De bello civili* 4.593–655.

431   *Iulus*: Iulus, or Ascanius, was the son of Aeneas and the grandfa-
        ther of Brutus.

433–34 After the fall of Troy, Pandrasus, king of the Greeks, had taken a
        number of Trojans to Greece as slaves. Defeated in battle by
        Brutus, he gave him his eldest daughter in marriage: Geoffrey,
        Historia 1.3–11.

434   *Silvius*: Ebraucus, great-grandson of Brutus and King of Britain
        ca. 1000 BCE, sent his thirty daughters to Italy where King

Silvius Alba provided them with Trojan husbands: Geoffrey, *Historia* 2.7–8.

437–42 Uther Pendragon, king of Britain, desired Ygerna, wife of Gorlois, duke of Cornwall. Merlin transformed him into the likeness of Gorlois, and in Gorlois's absence he lay with Ygerna, and Arthur was conceived: Geoffrey, *Historia* 8.19–20. As Echard notes, *Arthurian Narrative*, 109, Geoffrey had emphasized Arthur's legitimacy. Johannes's brief, anticlimactic account of Uther's adulterous act, which does not reflect on the character of Arthur, is perhaps intended to set off by contrast the glorious lineage of Ramofrigius and Walter.

443–74 Here Gawain abandons Geoffrey and embarks on an elaborate compliment to Johannes's patron, Walter of Coutances. The genealogy linking Walter and his father, Rainfroy, to Geoffrey's mythical Corineus may be the sort of family tradition that led other members of the Norman nobility to claim Trojan ancestry, but Johannes's elaboration is very much in the spirit of Geoffrey's fictions in the *Historia*. If Johannes is responsible for the linkage, his invention was tacitly acknowledged as *ben trovato* by Giraldus Cambrensis, who declares that Walter was "born in Cornwall of the family of Corineus, and stemmed from the noble British race and its original Trojan stock": *Vita S. Remigii* 25, in *Opera*, ed. J. S. Brewer and J. F. Dimack, Rolls Series 21 (London: 1877), 7:38. There are similar Geoffreyesque inventions in Walter Map, *De nugis curialium* 2.17.18.

446 *Scythe-bearer*: Saturn is called the Scythe-bearer from his use of a scythe to castrate his father, Caelus, whose genitalia, cast into the sea, gave birth to Venus: Cicero, *Nat. D.* 2.24.63–64; Macrobius, *Saturnalia* 1.8.6–8; Servius, *ad Aen.* 5.801; Vatican Mythographers, 1.104 (a version in which Jove castrates Saturn); 2.30; 3.1.7. For the epithet *Falcifer*, Ovid, *Ibis* 218.

451 *hides in eclipse*: I assume that the *nodus* is the point on the ecliptic at which the moon suffers eclipse.

453 *Ramofrigius*: That is, Ranfroy, the father of Walter of Coutances.

454 *Tydeus*: Notorious for fierceness in battle, he was one of the seven Greek champions who fell at Thebes: Statius, *Theb.* 1.401–16; 2.527–681; 8.659–766.

455   *Numa*: Numa Pompilius, the second king of Rome (715–673 BCE), was credited with wise governance and the establishment of religious and political institutions.

467–68   *just as a contingent angle of curvature . . . right angle*: The basis for this comparison is apparently Euclid, *Elements* 3, Prop. 16. The angle *quem contingentia curvat,* or "angle of contingency," is formed by the arc of a circle and a line tangent to the circle; whether this could be considered a measurable angle was debated in the later Middle Ages and the Renaissance: Morris Kline, *Mathematical Thought from Ancient to Modern Times* (New York, 1972), 67–68.

482   *the Latian monster*: That is, Avarice, associated here, as often in twelfth-century satire, with the papal court at Rome (Latium): Murray, *Reason and Society,* 74–75.

491   On Crassus, 2.254n.

492   When the Consul Opimius demanded the head of Caius Gracchus, and offered its weight in gold as a reward, Septimulus decapitated Gracchus, his close friend, and may have filled his skull with molten lead: Valerius Maximus, *Memorabilia* 9.4.3.

493   When Silius and Calpurnius were caught on the point of assassinating Quintus Cassius, he released them in return for payments totaling eleven million sesterces: Valerius Maximus, *Memorabilia* 9.4.2.

494–96   Ptolemy, king of Cyprus, fearing that enemies would rob him of his vast wealth, loaded it onto ships, intending to sink them and drown himself rather than surrender his gold to others. But in the event, he could not bear to sink the gold and sailed home, bringing "the future reward of his own death": Valerius Maximus, *Memorabilia* 9.4.ext.1.

BOOK 6

1   *army*: *cuneus* (wedge) can denote a formation of soldiers drawn up for battle.

2   *Round Table*: Arthur's Round Table first appears, not in Geoffrey's *Historia*, but in the *Roman de Brut* of Wace (ca. 1155).

13   *Bears to sink*: The Greater and Lesser Bear, which in the north-

NOTES TO THE TRANSLATION

ern hemisphere never sink below the horizon, do so when viewed from below the equator.

ern hemisphere never sink below the horizon, do so when
viewed from below the equator.

20 *Tylos*: With its perpetual spring, Tylos is distinct from Tyle, the
name Johannes employs twice (5.251, 9.61) to refer to the far
northern region known to ancient poets as Thule. Tylos seems
to be the island called Tylos or Tyros by Pliny, *Nat. Hist.* 12.21.38–
22.39, and Tylos by Solinus, *Collectanea rerum memorabilium*
52.49, who report that trees on this island never lose their
leaves. Tylos, "full of forests," is said to be located with Chryse
and Argyre (2.484n) in the eastern ocean, "between the east
and the southeast," in the *Descriptio mappe mundi* attributed to
Hugh of St. Victor, ed. Patrick Gautier Dalché (Paris: Études
Augustiniennes, 1988), 135.

25 *a deity native to the place*: The "native deity" of this line is evi-
dently Nature herself, who will appear as Solon, the last of the
philosophers to speak, concludes the story of Polemo: 8.289–
323. On the debt of Johannes's Tylos to the *domus Naturae* of
Alan of Lille, *Anticlaudianus,* and the *Gramision* of Bernardus
Silvestris, *Cosmographia,* Roling, "Das *Moderantia*-Konzept,"
203–4.

28 When Archytas of Tarentum (fl. ca. 400–350 BCE), Pythag-
orean philosopher and mathematician, returned from a jour-
ney to discover that his overseer had neglected the upkeep of
his lands, he refused to punish the man, lest his anger make
the punishment unjustly harsh: Valerius Maximus, *Memorabilia*
4.1.ext.1; Cicero, *Tusc.* 4.36.78.

55 *A faithful retinue*: I take *ancilla* to be functioning as an adjective,
modifying *manus*.

81 *Erebos*: Originally the name of the god of darkness, it is often a
name for the lower world in Latin poetry: Virgil, *Geo.* 4.471,
Aen. 4.510; Ovid, *Met.* 5.543, 10.76.

93 *Bellona*: The Roman goddess of war: Virgil, *Aen.* 8.703.

101 *Tyrian dye*: See 4.296n. Placanica, Review of *Architrenius,* 749,
notes that *virus* can mean "color" or "tincture" as well as "poi-
son": Servius, *ad Geo.* 1.129. Claudian, *Phoenix* 20, refers to the
purple legs of the phoenix as painted with *Tyrio veneno.*

115   *Celaeno*: The queen of the Harpies, monstrous, voracious birds with the faces of women, who spread filth on those whom they attacked: Virgil, *Aen.* 3.210–58.

123   *Cato*: Though Johannes could have known of Cato the Censor from Cicero's *De oratore, De senectute,* and other works, the Cato introduced here is probably Cato of Utica (95–46 BCE), whose fierce Stoic austerity finds eloquent expression in Lucan, *De bello civili* 2.239–325; 9.186–214, 379–406, 564–84.

131   On Croesus, 1.53n.

132   *gods*: I assume with the glossator of *X* that *deos* refers to riches, as at 6.281.

135   *Corruption*: *ambitus* can denote bribery or illegal canvassing for office, condemned in several orations of Cicero.

153–54   *no Dives will evade Dis*: *Dis* originally meant simply "god" but came to specify the god of the Underworld, or the underworld itself: Virgil, *Geo.* 4.519, *Aen.* 4.702; Ovid, *Met.* 4.438, 511. *Dites* is the plural of *dis,* the contracted form of *dives,* "rich," which becomes a conventional name for a wealthy man, often with the implicit suggestion that he is ungenerous with his wealth.

162   On Atropos, 1.188n.

197   On Diogenes: Jerome, *adv. Jovinianum* 2.11; Cicero, *Tusc.* 5.32.92.

198   *Phoebus's double arc*: that is, the Sun's passage over both the known and the unknown hemisphere of the world.

209   The version of the birth of Alexander in which the deposed Egyptian ruler and sorcerer Nectanabus (here *Neptanabus*), rather than King Philip of Macedon, is his father, is a feature of many medieval versions of the Alexander legend. It apparently originated in a Greek romance translated circa 950 by Archpriest Leo of Naples. This work became the basis for the widely influential *Historia Alexandri Magni de preliis:* George Cary, *The Medieval Alexander* (Cambridge: Cambridge University Press, 1956), 9–11, 38–58; Richard Stoneman, "Primary Sources from the Classical and Early Medieval Periods," in *A Companion to Alexander Literature in the Middle Ages*, ed. Z. David Zuwiyya (Leiden and Boston: Brill, 2011), 2–19.

219–20   *the fourth generation*: My translation is prompted by Placanica,

Review of *Architrenius,* 749–50, who sees an allusion to Nestor's having lived through three generations of men (*Iliad* 1. 250–52); Cicero, *Sen.* 10.31; Hyginus, *Fabulae* 10.

226   On *Tyrius,* 4.296n. *Pecten,* "comb," suggests the shell from which a comb might be made, which in turn suggests the murex from which the Tyrian dye was derived.

227   Sidon, the mother city of Tyre, is imagined sewing purple thread into Chinese silk (for *Serum,* 1.89n).

229   *a single robe*: Matthew 10:10.

230   In Roman cult, Rhea is identified with Cybele, the Great Mother, and with fertility.

238   On Socrates as the founder of moral philosophy, Cicero, *Tusc.* 3.4.8, *De fin.* 2.1.1; Augustine, *De Civ. Dei* 8.3; John of Salisbury, *Policraticus* 7.5.

241   *water-drinking*: Schmidt, citing a gloss in *K* on *rigui*: "because Diogenes always wept," notes that Diogenes, rather than Heraclitus, is paired with laughing Democritus in later twelfth-century texts. But the reference to drunkenness in the next line suggests that here Diogenes is "watered" or "watery," not as weeping, but as drinking only water.

253   *Alexander*: As a gloss in *X* suggests, *Magni* (the Great) may refer specifically to Alexander, as at 6.486. Cicero, *Tusc.* 5.32.92, and Valerius Maximus, *Memorabilia* 4.3.ext.4, report the famous anecdote in which Diogenes refuses every gift offered by Alexander, asking only that he move so as not to block the light of the sun.

259–60   See John of Salisbury, *Policraticus* 5.17; Jerome, *adv. Jovinianum* 2.14.

261–63   On the twelfth century's predilection for this sort of grammatical metaphor, see Paul Lehmann, *Die Parodie im Mittelalter,* 2nd ed. (Stuttgart: A. Hiersemann, 1963), 49–54; Jan Ziolkowski, *Alan of Lille's Grammar of Sex: The Meaning of Grammar to a Twelfth-Century Intellectual* (Cambridge, Mass.: Medieval Academy of America, 1985), 51–76.

262–63   *declinitive of vice . . . dative of virtue*: *declinativa*: "avoiding," "turning away"; *ablativa*: "removing"; *genetiva*: "generative"; *dativa*: "prone to give."

265–66   See John of Salisbury, *Policraticus* 8.8; Jerome, *adv. Jovinianum* 2.9.

266–69   See Valerius Maximus, *Memorabilia* 4.3.ext.4b; also Horace, *Epist.* 1.17.13–24, where, however, Aristippus is said to get the better of his exchange with Diogenes. In *Carmina Burana* 189 Diogenes firmly rejects Aristippus's attempt to make him a flatterer.

269   *Aristippus*: Aristippus of Cyrene, whose writings do not survive, was a friend of Socrates, but was evidently known for his luxurious mode of life.

273–79   See John of Salisbury, *Policraticus* 7.13; Jerome, *adv. Jovinianum* 2.9.

274   *Crates*: Crates of Thebes (368/65–288/85 BCE) was a follower of Diogenes.

279–85   On Democritus (b. 460/57 BCE), Valerius Maximus, *Memorabilia* 8.7.ext.4; John of Salisbury, *Policraticus* 7.13.

284   *morsels of wisdom*: *sophisma* in classical Latin has the negative implication of sophistry or fallacy, but here *sophismatica* are apparently "nuggets of wisdom."

286   *to none*: With Minkova, "Textual Suggestions," 389, I have substituted *nulli* for Schmidt's *nullum*. Schmidt points to several pairings of a neuter singular adjective and an infinitive: *tuum scire*, "your knowledge," 6.215; *properatum velle*, "a (too-) hasty wish," 8.173. But the perfect infinitive makes such a construction unlikely.

304–5   On Titus's generosity, Suetonius, *Titus* 8; John of Salisbury, *Policraticus* 3.14. Titus's assertion that a day on which he did not perform an act of charity was wasted is noted in lines 306–7. In lines 314–15 a similar generosity is credited to Archbishop Walter (or King Henry?).

311   *agent of the bounty of Rome*: That is, Titus.

312–16   Probably yet another tribute to Walter of Coutances but as Schmidt notes, possibly a reference to Henry II.

317–95   Much of Cicero's speech is drawn from the discussion of the use of riches in Cicero, *De off.* 2.15.54–16.56.

334   On Codrus, 2.220n.

358–63   The subject of this sentence is the *pauperies* (poverty) of line 354, as confirmed by the feminine *suasura* (urging) and *ingeniosa* (ingenious) of lines 361–62.

358   *who has nothing*: I take *vacuum* as denoting one who has lost everything, who is "empty" of possessions.

372   *you must pay*: I have altered Schmidt's punctuation, which gives the misleading suggestion that the impersonal *oportet* is part of the sequence of parallel verbs *pulsat, ferit, instat*.

396–97   See above, lines 273–79.

417–19   *the knight who travels . . . passage to Avernus*: I have departed from Schmidt's punctuation and followed his suggestion that *equitantis* (which seems an unlikely substitute for *equitis*) in 417 can be read as transitive, with the otherwise paratactic sequence of phrases in 418–19 as its objects.

445   *Dives . . . Dis*: 6.153–54n.

446   *the son-in-law of yearning Ceres*: That is, Pluto, god of the underworld and husband of Proserpina: 5.31–32n.

451–60   Much of the argument of these lines can be traced to Seneca's *Epistulae morales* 2.5, 4.11, 18.8, 27.9, 31.10, 44.5–6, 76.16.

452–53   John of Salisbury, *Policraticus* 8.13, notes that Seneca's suicide was treated as martyrdom by Jerome, *De vir. illustr.* 12. Both John and Jerome assume the authenticity of the supposed correspondence between Seneca and Saint Paul.

454–55   See above, 1.53, and Lucan, *De bello civili* 5.526–31, where not Caesar but the narrator praises Amyclas's tranquility.

461–66   Enceladus was one of the Giants who fought against the gods. His fate was to be buried beneath Mount Etna: Virgil, *Aen.* 3.578–82; Statius, *Theb.* 3.594–95.

467–68   5.36–39n.

475–82   Anaxarchus (fl. mid-fourth century BCE) was a philosopher in the tradition of Democritus, who accompanied Alexander on his campaigns. For the anecdote: Valerius Maximus, *Memorabilia* 8.14.ext.2; John of Salisbury, *Policraticus* 8.5. Both identify the philosopher whose teaching Anaxarchus reports as Democritus, rather than Pythagoras.

488–95   See Valerius Maximus, *Memorabilia* 9.12.ext.3; John of Salisbury, *Policraticus* 2.26, 7.5. I take *praedo fluvialis* as "river-plunderer," corresponding to Valerius's *piscatoribus* (fishermen). Valerius does not reveal the question put to Homer, and John speaks only of *nescioquam nautarum quaestionem* (some sailors' question). According to Heraclitus, DK 56 (Hippolytus, *Ref* 9.9.6), the question was a riddle: "What we saw and caught we leave behind, and what we neither saw nor caught we take away." The solution to the riddle was "lice."

BOOK 7

33   *Sicilian bullocks*: This is another reference to the bull of Phalaris (3.312n).

44–45   These lines apparently recall ironically Matthew 13:12.

57–59   The price of trafficking with luxury and lechery is the loss of good character.

70–71   *practice . . . abuse*: John of Salisbury also plays on *usus* and *abusus* with reference to sodomy and pederasty: *Policraticus*, 3.13. Sodomy/pederasty is the "Thracian disease" because associated with the Thracian bard Orpheus (the *Thracem* of line 72), who after his loss of Eurydice foreswore the love of women and taught Thracian men to transfer their love to adolescent boys: Ovid, *Met.* 10.83–85. As with the *De planctu naturae* of Alan of Lille, we cannot determine the focus of Johannes's criticism here, though lines 70–86 suggest that a specific person is implicated.

90   *Cyprian*: Cyprus was a center of the worship of Venus, the "Cyprian."

101   *lotos food*: Johannes apparently understands *Lotophagos* as referring, not to the Lotus-eaters themselves, but to the lily eaten by them.

102   *Egyptian*: On Syene 1.82n.

103   *to unbuckle*: Though *posita* is the reading of most manuscripts, I can make sense of this line only by emending to *posito*.

105   On the Sicilian bull, 3.312n.

112   *beam*: For *trabs,* see Matthew 7:3.

116–17   Gervase, *Ars poetica* 82–84, cites these lines as an instance of *synthesis*, or *hyperbaton ex omni parte confusum,* a figure liable to be carried to "inexcusable" extremes, and even in this relatively clear instance misleading because of the singular verb.

118–23   *the poison of Venus and of Nessus*: The Centaur Nessus was killed by

Hercules for attempting to abduct his wife, Deianira. As he died he gave Deianira a garment tainted with the poison of the Lernaean Hydra, telling her that it was a love charm. Hearing that Hercules had become the lover of Iole, Deianira sent him the shirt, which caused his death, though he was then deified by his father, Jupiter: Ovid, *Met.* 9.101–271.

118, 124–25 Gervase, *Ars poetica*, 138, cites these lines as illustrating aspects of the "transumptive" or metaphorical use of diction. In 118 *veneno* (poison) is used literally *(proprie)* in respect to Nessus, metaphorically *(transumptive)* in respect to Venus. In 125, though the passage is corrupt in Gräbener's edition, the point is clearly that *naevit* (wove) is used in a similarly "equivocal" way in reference to *pensum* (measure of wool) and *necem* (death).

122–23 As the unwitting cause or means of Hercules's death, Nessus's revenge, and her own suffering, Deianira is identified with *rogus, ultio,* and *poena.*

128 *cleverest of men . . . foolishly*: *sal* here stands for "wit" or "cleverness"; *insulsus* is literally "unsalted."

129 Solomon's bitter love is presumably his devotion to foreign women, which cost him the favor of the Lord: 1 Kings 11.

132–33 Ovid refers to a mistress by the code name of Corinna: *Am.* 2.17.27–30; 3.1.49–52; *Ars Am.* 3.538. Sidonius Apollinaris (*Carmen* 23.158–61) cites Ovid's intimacy with a *Caesarea puella* as the cause of his exile, and this seems to have led to the supposition, reported in twelfth-century *accessus,* that Corinna was the *puella* in question and that she was the wife of the emperor: John C. Thibault, *The Myth of Ovid's Exile* (Berkeley and Los Angeles: University of California Press, 1964), 24–25, 42–46. A gloss in *X* identifies Corinna as *uxor Cesaris.*

132 Schmidt explains Johannes's making *Colchon* the accusative of *Colchis* as due to his assumption that the accusative plural *Colchos* was nominative singular.

140 *dominion*: Robert Babcock has suggested to me that *imperii* is a rare Latin use of the Greek Genitive of Exclamation. Compare Propertius, *Carmina* 4.7.21; Plautus, *Mostellaria* 912.

145 On *nubere* and *ducere*, 1.251–55n.

149   *a new conjunction*: Though there is an obvious pun, *coitus* also de-
       notes the "conjunction" or apparent coming together of two
       heavenly bodies.

150   *his helmet no longer contains his radiance*: An echo of Statius, *Theb.*
       1.305, where Mercury dims his radiance in preparing to de-
       scend into Hades.

155   *the steadfast Bear*: That is, Ursa Major, once the nymph Callisto
       whom Jupiter ravished and who was transformed to a bear by
       Juno. She is *fixa* in that her constellation never sinks below the
       horizon.

156   On Saturn the Scythe-bearer, 5.446n.

163   *Cyprian flames*: These are the symptoms of the power of Venus
       (7.90n).

166   *such an Aquarius*: An allusion to the identification of Aquarius
       with Ganymede, cupbearer and favorite of Jove, a common fig-
       ure for sodomy and pederasty in school poetry.

167   *the Samian*: That is, Pythagoras, born on the island of Samos.

189–202 On Pythagoras's concern over female dress, Justinus, *Epitoma
       historiarum Philippicarum* 20.4; John of Salisbury, *Policraticus* 7.4.

207   On Pharos as a metonymy for Egypt, 2.240n. Pliny describes the
       soda beds of Egypt, 31.46.III, and Indian nard, 12.26.42.

208   On chameleons, Solinus, *Collectanea rerum memorabilium* 40.21.
       On African basilisks, Pliny, *Nat. Hist.* 8.33.78, Lucan, *De bello
       civili* 9.724–26.

209   On hippopotami in the Nile, Pliny, *Nat. Hist.* 8.39.95; Solinus,
       Collectanea rerum memorabilium 32.30. On Indian ebony, Pliny,
       12.8.17; Solinus, 52.52. Schmidt suggests that the association of
       the Hellespont with sturgeons was prompted by Pliny, 9.11.34,
       who remarks on the similarity of dolphins to *thursiones,* or por-
       poises. Johannes may have mistaken *thursiones* for *sturiones*
       (sturgeons) and identified these with dolphins, which accord-
       ing to both Pliny, 9.20.52, and Solinus, 12.3, were plentiful in
       the Hellespont.

219   *misery with hope, happiness with its opposite, Johannes with both*:
       That is, Johannes is full of both hope and its opposite, fear.

221   Since the group Pythagoras has named are clearly the Seven

Sages, "Philo," here and in line 430 below, is Johannes's version of the name of the sage Chilo.

228   *the old man of Pylos*: That is, Nestor.

235–37   Sisyphus, robber and trickster, must eternally push uphill a huge rock which then rolls down again. Ixion, whose impieties included an attempt to ravish Hera, wife of Zeus, is stretched on an endlessly turning wheel, Ovid, *Met.* 4.460–61; 10.42, 44.

238   The Giant Tityos, who assaulted the Titaness Leto, or Latona, lies stretched on the floor of Hades, while two vultures tear at his liver. See Virgil, *Aen.* 6.595–600; Ovid, *Met.* 4.457–58.

238–39   The reference is to the Danaids, the fifty daughters of Danaus. Claimed in marriage by the fifty sons of Aegyptus, all except Hypermestra murdered their husbands on their wedding night. Their punishment is to endlessly pour water into a leaking vessel: Horace, *C.* 3.11.21–28.

240–41   This is Tantalus, on whom 1.194n.

242–43   Virgil, *Aen.* 6.432–33.

246   Gervase, *Ars poetica*, 17, cites this line as an instance of *leonitas,* or internal rhyme, somewhat more "commendable" than the more extended exercise of 8.36–39.

246–47   On Rhadamanthus, Virgil, *Aen.* 6.566–69; on Aeacus, Horace, *C.* 2.13.22; Ovid, *Met.* 13.25–28.

249–50   *burn*: Since *lacrimas* (tears) seems the only likely object of *fundo,* I have added a second verb to govern *caminos* (furnace).

250   On Cocytus and Phlegethon, 3.315–16n.

251–52   *Who could let his life hang suspended from a hanging rock?*: Schmidt suggests that this is Prometheus, but it is apparently the rock, not the man, that is suspended, and the line applies better to Tantalus, one version of whose story adds to his punishment a huge rock that threatens to fall on him; Lucretius, *De rerum natura* 3.980. Virgil, *Aen.* 6.601–2, does not name Tantalus, but it is frequently suggested that his punishment is here treated as a representative form of torment. The forbidden feast of lines 603–7 also recalls Tantalus (1.194n).

253–60   The characterization of the Furies recalls the common scheme in which Allecto represents unremitting anger, Megaera vio-

256   lent action, Tisiphone hostile speech: Fulgentius, *Mitologiae* 1.7; Vatican Mythographers 1.109; 2.12; 3.6.23.

256   *banishes: forinsecat,* apparently coined by Johannes, and glossed in X as *foris expellit,* "drives out," seems to me to make better sense if read as occurring *from* without, as suggested by its derivation from *forinsecus.*

282   *to drench manly dignity:* Minkova, "Textual Suggestions," 391, proposes replacing *virum* with *viri,* attested in a single manuscript.

306   *ah, my life and soul:* See Juvenal, *Sat.* 6.195, where this phrase *(zoe kai psyche)* is cited as an example of Roman women's affected use of bedroom Greek.

307–8   The sun turned back in its course after Atreus, king of Mycenae, tricked his brother Thyestes into eating the flesh of his own children: Lucan, *De bello civili* 1.543–44.

307   For the famous episode of Vulcan's entrapment of Venus and Mars in adultery, Ovid, *Ars Am.* 2.561–86.

308–314 Lycaon, king of Arcadia, when Jupiter in disguise visited his country, refused to believe in his divinity and tested it by attempting to serve him human flesh, for which he was transformed to a wolf: Ovid, *Met.* 1.196–239.

417   On Numa, 5.455n.

424   *arrow:* In rendering *nervo* very loosely as "arrow," I am recalling the use of *nervo* to denote the bow of Cupid in 7.139.

434–35   Johannes's respect for the satires of Horace is attested by his many borrowings, and he uses Horace as a standard to rebuke the "presumption" of Persius in 5.48–49. Thus *Flacci* here should probably be taken as referring to satire in general (perhaps with a play on its literal meaning, "flabby," "flaccid," hence lacking the force and firmness of effective satire).

Book 8

3   *a world which, though centuries old, is still a child:* As Schmidt notes, Isaiah, 65:20 speaks of a time when one who has lived a hundred years will be considered a boy, but whereas Architrenius

18   The marsh of Lerna was the home of the Hydra (1.213n). But
      Johannes almost certainly knew an alternative myth, related by
      Servius, *ad Aen.* 6.287, in which the Hydra is identified with the
      swamp itself, which frequently flooded the surrounding region
      with waters that emerged through many channels. Hercules
      used fire to clear the land and was then able to close off the
      channels.

rebukes the immaturity of a world grown old, in Isaiah longev-
ity is one of the wonders of the "Jerusalem of exultation" envi-
sioned by the prophet.

19   *this growth: filix* is a kind of fern (Pliny, *Nat. Hist.* 27.55.78–79),
      evidently invasive. For Virgil, *Geo.* 2.189, and Horace, *Sat.* 1.3.37,
      it obstructs the work of the plow and must be burned off.

36–40 Gervase, *Ars poetica* 17, finds the *leonitas*, or internal rhyme, in
      these lines "commendable," though carried too far.

37   *where Numa too has come*: See Horace, *Epist.* 1.6.27. As at 5.214–19,
      the juxtaposition of Lucifer with a virtuous figure from classi-
      cal tradition seems incongruous. On Numa, 4.55n.

40   *his brightness was cast into murky darkness*: The effect of Lucifer's
      fall is conveyed by an untranslatable play on *lūteus,* "golden,"
      and *luteus,* "muddy," "dirty."

68–70 By effecting the death of the tyrant, the feast eliminates the
      many ways in which he had made his subjects weep.

86–87 *Caesar's clemency beat the air in vain*: Caesar, when he returned to
      Rome having defeated the armies of Pompey in the east and in
      Africa, and the son of Pompey in Spain, granted clemency to
      all who had borne arms against him, but was nonetheless assas-
      sinated: Velleius Paterculus, 2.56–57; John of Salisbury, *Policrat-
      icus* 8.19.

87   On the bull of Phalaris, 3.312n.

123, 171 On *alno*, 4.440.

219   For *Pharius,* "Egyptian," 2.240n.

251–85 The length of this narrative, based on Valerius Maximus, *Memo-
      rabilia* 6.9.ext.1 and John of Salisbury, *Policraticus* 8.9, seems in-
      tended to suggest its significant bearing on the experience of
      Architrenius.

300   That Nature's perpetually youthful complexion is called *laurum* recalls the laurel's perpetually green foliage, Apollo's final tribute to Daphne: Ovid, *Met.* 1.565.

312   *they are permitted*: With Minkova, "Textual Suggestions," 392, I have replaced Schmidt's *licemur* (we are permitted), which he acknowledges to be very unusual, with *licentur.* The first-person interjection would have a certain attractiveness, but nothing in the surrounding lines seems to support it, and it seems clear that it is the philosophers whose actions are being described. In two of the earliest manuscripts, *E* and *Q, licemur* is corrected to *licentur* by a second hand.

313   *goddess*: As Placanica suggests (Review of *Architrenius,* 751), *deae* can be connected with *calcem* (the heel/feet of the goddess), but this makes *nobilitate* somewhat ambiguous. (Is it her nobility or that of the philosophers?) In fact, I think *deae* must be understood with both *nobilitate* and *calcem,* but I have linked it with *nobilitate,* and assumed that the link to *calcem* is sufficiently clear.

324   Here begins a long discourse, extending to 9.148. It is based on the translation by Johannes Hispalensis of the *Differentiae* (i.e., "Chapters"; in early printed editions the title is commonly *De rudimentis astronomie*) of the ninth-century Arab or Persian astronomer Al-Farghání, or "Alfraganus." I have also provided references to the early thirteenth-century *Tractatus de spera* of Johannes de Sacrobosco, which Johannes could not have known, but which is largely based on Al-Farghání and provides less technical explanations (not always accurate) of most of the features of his system that appear in the *Architrenius.*

341–46   The difference between ancient and "modern" ways of defining the position of the Earth is not clear. The point is perhaps that whereas an ancient cosmologist like Macrobius can speak of Earth as the "lowest" point in the universe, *ima* or *infima* (*Somn. Scip.* 1.19.10; 1.22.1), Al-Farghání, in Chapters 3 and 4 of the *Differentiae,* emphasizes its central position within a spherical universe, where it can be viewed in relation to both zeniths and nadirs. One can then speak of *quaelibet infima,* the low point relative to an arbitrarily chosen position on earth or on the outermost sphere: an imaginary perspective, like the *visus* in 348 that enables us to see the Earth as a mere point.

347–49   On the relative smallness of the earth compared to any of the fixed stars, Al-Farghání, *Differentiae* 4.3; Sacrobosco, *Tractatus de spera*, 1.

350–52   Al-Farghání, *Differentiae* 3; Sacrobosco, *Tractatus de spera* 1.

360–62   Al-Farghání, *Differentiae* 3–4, 22.

374   For Proserpina as the Moon, Fulgentius, *Mitologiae* 2.16; Vatican Mythographers, 1.7; 2.100; 3.7.2.

377   *head or tail*: The two points at which the Moon's eccentric orbit intersects the plane of the ecliptic, thus making possible an eclipse, are called the "head" and the "tail" of the "Dragon": 9.107–8; Al-Farghání, *Differentiae* 28; Sacrobosco, *Tractatus de spera* 4.

385–415   This chapter is based on Al-Farghání, *Differentiae* 5; Sacrobosco, *Tractatus de spera* 2.

396   *Stygian*: *Styga* perhaps recalls Virgil, *Geo.* 1.242–43, imagining the pole of the Earth that is "beneath our feet," which looks on "black Styx and the infernal shades."

397–99   *The line of the solstice*: One of the two "colures" (2.244–45n); the other, which marks the equinoxes, intersects the solstitial colure at right angles at the poles.

401   On Aren, 2.243n.

401, 403   Johannes here seems to use "solstice" in a broad, literal sense as referring to any "standing" or "station" of the Sun (*statione* in 404), hence denoting equinoxes as well as the summer and winter solstices. Lucan, *De bello civili* 9.531–32, refers to the Sun's path as the "circle of the high solstice," and describes the effect on Earth of its intersection with the Zodiac, equidistant from the poles.

402–3   *in this region*: The connection of the first clause (a verbatim quotation of Lucan, *De bello civili* 9.531) with the rest of the sentence is not wholly clear. If "this region" includes extremes of heat and cold, it cannot be the equator, where summer and winter are "of equal complexion" (Al-Farghání, *Differentiae* 6.10). "Region," like solstice, is apparently broadly defined.

403 *Recessibus* refers to the summer and winter solstices, when the Sun's path is furthest from the equator.

405 Since *equidies* has no English equivalent I have substituted "equinox."

407 *Aegoceron (Aegoceros,* Lucan, *De bello civili* 9.537; 10.213), equivalent in Greek to *capri-cornus* ("horn of the goat"), is Johannes's preferred term for the constellation Capricorn.

410–15 The Sun moves at a constant speed, but its orbit is eccentric; the *cuspis,* or center, is not the center of the Earth, so that its rate of movement through the sky appears to vary. At its perigee its movement through the signs of the Zodiac seems accelerated, while at its apogee *(augis,* 413) it seems to move at the same rate as the "fixed" stars: Al-Farghání, *Differentiae* 12.4–8; Sacrobosco, *Tractatus de spera* 4.

416–44 This chapter is based mainly on Al-Farghání, *Differentiae* 7.8–17.

432 *the Moon is dimmed:* Because the Sun shines continually, the Moon is obscured.

435 The mother of Achilles is Thetis, whose name here stands for the sea.

438–40 The point described is Arctos, the northern Pole.

445–70 This chapter is based on Al-Farghání, *Differentiae* 10.1–6.

452 *Phrixeus* is Johannes's name for the constellation Aries. Phrixus and Helle, children of the Theban king Athamas, fled from Thebes to Colchis, carried on the back of the ram with golden fleece, to avoid the wrath of their stepmother, Ino. Helle was drowned, and gave her name to the Hellespont. The same association is evoked by *portitor Helleus* in line 463 and *Vectore* in 470.

454 Astraea and Chele are the constellations Virgo and Libra. Astraea, goddess of justice, is sometimes identified with Libra, but here with Virgo, as at Lucan, *De bello civili* 9.535. Chele (claws) refers to the "arms" of Scorpio (Lucan, *De bello civili* 1.659); since these extend into Libra, the term is also an epithet for this constellation: Virgil, *Geo.* 1.33–35.

455 *the avenger of the Hydra:* That is, Cancer, which attacked Hercules at the instigation of Hera when he fought the Hydra: Hyginus, *Astronomia* 2.23.

the *Haemonian*: (i.e., Thessalian) is Sagittarius, identified as the centaur Chiron in 464.

460–65   Lucan, 9.533–37.

466   *Erigone*: The constellation Virgo. Erigone, daughter of the Athenian noble Icarius, hanged herself out of grief for his death and was transformed to a constellation. Her father became the constellation Bootes. See Hyginus, *Fabulae* 130. Erigone is identified with Astraea by Martianus Capella, *De nuptiis* 2.174.

470   The *Lacones* (Spartans) are the constellation Gemini, Castor and Pollux, twin sons of the Spartan princess Leda (9.33). The *Vector* is the constellation Aries, "carrier" of Phrixus and Helle (8.452n).

BOOK 9

15–17   The region described is the northern hemisphere. Nature here resumes her discussion of the rising of the zodiacal signs. Having devoted nearly all of 8.11 to the regularity with which signs ascend and descend at the equator, or "right" ascensions, she now follows Al-Farghání, *Differentiae* 10.6–11, discussing "oblique" ascensions that occur between the equator and the Tropic, which are necessarily unequal.

17   Aries's two boundaries are apparently the beginning and the end of the 180-degree arc of the six constellations beginning with Aries and ending with Virgo.

18–19   The rising of the constellations becomes slower as the cycle moves from Aries to Virgo, and faster as it returns from Libra to Aries.

23–24   *their ascending arc*: This is the region between the equator and the Tropic.

24   *upright circle*: *Recto* is the upright, or vertical, course in which the constellations ascend at the equator.

26–27   The attacker of Alcides (Hercules) is Cancer: 8.455n.

34   The limit referred to is the equator.

39–41   The equation holds true because the rate of ascent and descent in the "upright circle" (i.e., at the equator) is the same.

45–52   Al-Farghání, *Differentiae* 7.15–16.

53–76   Al-Farghání, *Differentiae* 6.9 (where Johannes has substituted his
         own few landmarks for Al-Farghání's elaborate gazetteer).

53   *circle*: This band is not one of the colures that mark the points of
         equinox and solstice, though it resembles them in that it inter-
         sects the equator at right angles (55–57). Al-Farghání, *Differen-
         tiae* 6.4, acknowledges that this circle is the product of his own
         "rational cogitation," an *ad hoc* way of defining the habitable
         portion of the earth.

66   *slave boy*: The *filius* (here in the broad sense of "boy" or "slave") is
         Apollo, whom Zeus compelled to serve as herdsman to King
         Admetus: Ovid. *Ars Am.* 2.239–41. The point of the reference
         seems to lie in the connection between Apollo's relegation to
         serfdom and the condition imposed on countless medieval
         Slavs (*Sclavos*, line 64).

67–68   Mount Atlas in Libya, supposed to be the highest mountain in
         the world, was the subject of many beliefs and legends; Pliny,
         Nat. Hist. 5.1.6–7.

69   On Atin or Acin, 1.81n. For Alexander's foundation, Solinus, *Col-
         lectanea rerum memorabilium* 52.7.

74   On Aren, 2.243n.

77–96   Al-Farghání, 11.

89–91   On the "arc of day" and "arc of night," Al-Farghání, *Differentiae*
         11.5–7.

96   See 8.405n.

97–128   Al-Farghání, *Differentiae* 12.

97–102   The eccentric circles are the orbits of the planets.

103–4   The concentric circle is that of the sphere of the fixed stars,
         which remains constantly centered on the Earth.

104–9   The "Dragon" is "the figure formed by the departure of the ec-
         centric orbit of a planet from the plane of the Zodiac." On the
         "head" and "tail" of the Dragon, 8.377n.

110–19   Al-Farghání, *Differentiae* 13–15. In this passage *cuspis* seems to
         denote the circle or orbit of the planet as well as the center of
         its orbit, and *mundo* is the Earth.

110–13   Al-Farghání, *Differentiae* 15.1–4. When a planet's epicyclical
         movement departs from the plane of the Zodiac to the north,
         it is moving from west to east and appears to move more

swiftly; when it departs to the south, its movement is from east to west and appears slower. The Dragon ensures that the two movements balance each other.

114–19 Al-Farghání, *Differentiae* 13.5–8.

120 See 8.374n.

122–25 On Mercury's adherence to the movement of the circle of the fixed stars, centered on the earth, Al-Farghání, *Differentiae* 14.7–11.

124 *arc*: *Arcu* is the firmament; the movement of the fixed stars.

125 *a slight eccentricity*: The circling of the fixed stars is constant and centered on the center of the earth. The center of the orbit of Mercury, like that of all the planets, is always to some degree distant from this center point.

129–48 Al-Farghání, *Differentiae* 15.

129–30 Al-Farghání, *Differentiae* 15.7–8.

136 On the seeming immobility of a planet while within the circle of the Zodiac, Al-Farghání, *Differentiae* 15.5–6.

137–42 Al-Farghání, *Differentiae* 18.13–15.

141 *Delia*: Diana, born on the island of Delos. Here the Moon.

167–68 *dry-eyed Democritus*: Democritus was traditionally known as the "laughing" philosopher and was paired with the "weeping" philosopher, Heraclitus; Juvenal, *Sat.* 10.28–30.

173–74 On Megaera's serpentine locks, Virgil, *Aen.* 12.848.

184 *rocklike Procne*: Procne's "rocks" are the stony ruthlessness she showed in killing her son Itys to avenge the rape of her sister Philomena by Tereus; 1.352n.

192 *By your leave, O Nature*: Schmidt, 61, cites Lucan, *De bello civili* 9.855, but Johannes is recalling Bernardus Silvestris, *Cosmographia* 1.1.55, where Nature accuses Noys, the wisdom of God, of showing too little love toward her offspring, the universe, which as yet exists only as chaotic primordial matter. Here it is Nature herself who stands accused.

198 *a number*: Placanica, Review of *Architrenius*, 752, sees here a possible play on *numero* in the sense of metrical form and cites Ovid, *Ex ponto* 4.2.30.

264 On Lachesis and the Parcae, 1.188n.

277–80 It is hard to see these lines as contributing to the portrait of

Moderation, or as providing edifying instruction for Architre-
nius.

287–88   The Spartan is Helen, daughter of Leda.

295   *Beautiful, yet chaste*: The phrase *pulchra, pudica tamen* is twice
cited by Gervase, *Ars poetica,* 17, 199, first as a felicitous use of
tamen to effect a simple *correctio* (for the more complex *additiva
correctio, Architrenius* 5.333n), and later as a successful *adversatio*
between two adjectives.

307   *Liparaean and Cyprian fire*: Lipari, one of several small volcanic
islands northeast of Sicily, known to Pliny as the "Aeolian"
or "Volcanian" islands: Pliny, *Nat. Hist.* 3.9.93; Isidore, *Etym.*
14.6.37. In one tradition Lipari, rather than Lemnos (5.35n), was
the site of the smithy of Vulcan, who is nonetheless identified
as the Lemnian in 9.305. The Cyprian is Venus (7.90n).

320–22   Valerius Maximus, *Memorabilia* 4.3.ext.3.

324–27   Aulus Gellius, *Noctes Atticae* 1.8; John of Salisbury, *Policraticus*
6.23; Walter Map, *De nugis curialium* 4.3.

328–32   In the traditional story, Democritus did not castrate, but blinded
himself: see Cicero, *De fin.* 5.29.87; Aulus Gellius, *Noctes Atticae*
10.17.1. Schmidt suggests that the basis for Johannes's substitu-
tion of castration is Tertullian, *Apologeticum* 46.11, where De-
mocritus is said to have blinded himself to avoid the stimulus
to lust provided by the sight of women. See Solinus, *Collectanea
rerum memorabilium* 1.126; Jerome, *adv. Jovinianum* 1.41.

332–33   If my repunctuation is accepted, the enjambment emphasizes
the shock of castration. Placanica, Review of *Architrenius,* 752,
connecting *Renibus* with what follows, sees the priest as lying
supine, perhaps, he suggests, evidently unfamiliar with Hor-
ace, *Sat.* 1.5, to prevent a nocturnal emission.

349–50   Claudia, a Vestal Virgin accused of unchastity, demonstrated her
purity by towing a ship that thousands of men together had
been unable to move; Jerome, *adv. Jovinianum* 1.41.

350–51   Lucan, *De bello civili* 2.326–80; Jerome, *adv. Jovinianum* 1.46.

352–53   See Valerius Maximus, *Memorabilia* 8.15.12; Pliny, *Nat. Hist.*
7.35.120; Solinus, *Collectanea rerum memorabilium* 1.126.

354–57   Virgil, *Aen.* 2.246–47. The reason for the rejection of Cassandra's
prophecies is given in Servius's commentary on these verses.

354   *Maeoniis* apparently refers to the Trojans, to whom Cassandra delivered her prophecies. *Maeonius* is often used of Lydia, the ancient kingdom that included Troy. It could also denote the "Maeonian" (i.e., Homeric, 1.75n) language that Johannes may imagine Cassandra as having spoken.

358–66   See Valerius Maximus, *Memorabilia* 4.6.ext.2.

367–72   See Valerius Maximus, *Memorabilia* 4.6.ext.1.

406   *cleansed*: I take *mundescere* as coined from *mundo, -are,* "cleanse," and as having the function of a verbal noun.

415   *an inlet for sleep*: I assume a play on *syrinx*, in the double sense of "reed" (or reed pipe) and "syringe," and an allusion to the story of the invention of the reed pipe, with which Mercury puts Argus to sleep in Ovid, *Met.* 1.682–721.

431   *Chastity*: As Schmidt notes, *castratio* must be intended as in some sense equivalent to *castitas*.

454–56   As the title of Chapter 25 suggests, the powers named here are all versions of Fortune. Schmidt notes that *Tuchis,* the Greek *Tyche,* is glossed as *fortuna* in Eberhard of Béthune, *Graecismus* 8.319. *Nemesis* is called *Rhamnusia* in Ovid, *Met.* 3.406, and, as *Rhamnusia*, equated with Fortune in Claudian, *De bello Gothico* 631–32. (Rhamnus, a town in the north of Attica, was famous for its statue of Nemesis.)

Bibliography

EDITIONS

Architrenius. Edited by Jodocus Badius Ascensius. Paris, 1517.

Architrenius. Edited by Thomas Wright. In *The Anglo-Latin Satirical Poets and Epigrammatists of the Twelfth Century.* Vol. 1, 240–392. Rolls Series 59. London, 1872.

Architrenius. Edited by Paul Gerhard Schmidt. Munich, 1974.

Architrenius. Edited and translated by Nicholas P. Carlucci. 2 vols. PhD diss., University of Minnesota, 1977.

Architrenius. Edited and translated by Winthrop Wetherbee. Cambridge Medieval Classics 3. Cambridge, 1994.

PRIMARY SOURCES

Alan of Lille. *Literary Works.* Edited and translated by Winthrop Wetherbee. Dumbarton Oaks Medieval Library 22. Cambridge, Mass., 2013.

Al-Farghání. *Differentie scientie astrorum.* Edited by Francis J. Carmody. Unpublished typescript, completed in 1943 and held by the Doe Memorial Library at the University of California, Berkeley.

Bernardus Silvestris. *Poetic Works.* Edited and translated by Winthrop Wetherbee. Dumbarton Oaks Medieval Library 38. Cambridge, Mass., 2015.

Eberhard of Bremen. *Laborintus.* In *Les Arts poétiques du xiiᵉ et du xiiiᵉ siècle,* edited by Edmond Faral, 336–77. Bibliothèque de l'École des Hautes Études 238. Paris: Champion, 1923.

Evrart de Conty. *Le livre des echecs amoureux moralisés.* Edited by Françoise Guichard-Tesson and Bruno Roy. Montreal, 1993.

Geoffrey of Vinsauf. *Poetria nova.* Edited by Ernest Gallo, *The* Poetria Nova *and Its Sources in Early Rhetorical Doctrine,* 14–129. The Hague, Paris: Mouton, 1971.

Gervase of Melkley. *Ars poetica.* Edited by Hans Jürgen Gräbener. Forschungen zur Romanischen Philologie 17. Münster: Aschendorff, 1965.

Henri d'Andeli. *The Battle of the Seven Arts.* Edited and translated by L. J. Paetow. Memoirs of the University of California 1.1. Berkeley: University of California Press, 1914.

Johannes de Sacrobosco. *Tractatus de spera.* Edited and translated by Lynn Thorndike, *The "Sphere" of Sacrobosco and Its Commentators.* Chicago: University of Chicago Press, 1949.

John of Salisbury. *Metalogicon.* Edited by C. C. J. Webb. Oxford, 1929.

——. *Policraticus.* Edited by C. C. J. Webb. 2 vols. Oxford, 1909.

Matthew of Vendôme. *Opera.* Edited by Franco Munari. 3 vols. Rome: Edizioni di storia e letteratura, 1977–1988.

Vatican Mythographers. *Scriptores rerum mythicarum latini tres nuper reperti.* Edited by G. H. Bode. 2 vols. Celle, 1834. Reprint, Hildesheim: G. Olms, 1968.

Walter Map. *De nugis curialium.* Edited and translated by M. R. James. Revised by C. N. L. Brooke and R. A. B. Mynors. Oxford: Clarendon Press, 1983.

Walter of Chatillon. *Alexandreis.* Edited by Marvin L. Colker. Thesaurus Mundi 17. Padua: Editrice Antenore, 1978.

SECONDARY SOURCES

Adler, Alfred. "The *Roman de Thèbes,* a 'Consolatio Philosophiae.'" *Romanische Forschungen* 72 (1960): 257–76.

Bond, Gerald A. "'Iocus Amoris': The Poetry of Baudri of Bourgueil and the Formation of an Ovidian Subculture." *Traditio* 42 (1986): 143–93.

——. *The Loving Subject: Desire, Eloquence, and Power in Romanesque France.* Philadelphia, 1995.

Camargo, Martin. "What Goes with Geoffrey of Vinsauf? Codicological Clues to Pedagogical Practices in England c. 1225–c. 1470." In *The Classics in the Medieval and Renaissance Classroom: The Role of Ancient Texts as Revealed by Surviving Manuscripts and Early Printed Books,* edited by Juanita Feros Ruys, John O. Ward, and Melanie Heyworth, 145–74. Turnhout: Brepols, 2013.

Conde Parrado, Pedro. "La recepción del *Architrenius* de Johannes de Hauvilla en el siglo XVI: Ravisius Textor." In *Poesia Latina Medieval (siglos V–XV): Actas del IV Congreso del "Internationales Mittellateinerkomitee,"* edited by Manuel C. Díaz y Díaz and José M. Díaz de Bustamante, 1007–18. Florence: Edizioni del Galluzzo, 2005.

Dunbabin, Jean. *France in the Making.* Oxford: Oxford University Press, 1985.

Echard, Sián. *Arthurian Narrative in the Latin Tradition.* Cambridge: Cambridge University Press, 1998.

———. "Map's Metafiction: Author, Narrator and Reader in *De nugis curialium.*" *Exemplaria* 8 (1996): 287–314.

Faral, Edmond. "Le manuscrit 511 du 'Hunterian Museum' de Glasgow." *Studi medievali,* n.s. 9 (1936): 18–119.

———. "Le Roman de la Rose et la pensée française au XIIIe siècle." *Revue des deux mondes* 35 (Sept. 1926): 430–57.

Francke, Kuno. "Der *Architrenius* des Johann von Auville." *Forschungen zur Deutschen Geschichte* 20 (1880): 473–502.

Gaselee, Stephen. "Notes on the Vocabulary of the *Architrenius.*" *Speculum* 8 (1933): 79–80.

Glendinning, Robert. "Pyramus and Thisbe in the Medieval Classroom." *Speculum* 61 (1986): 51–78.

Godman, Peter. *The Silent Masters: Latin Literature and Its Censors in the High Middle Ages.* Princeton: Princeton University Press, 2000.

Huizinga, Johan. "Über die Verknüpfung des Poetischen mit dem Theologischen bei Alanus de Insulis." In Huizinga, *Verzamelde Werken,* 4:3–84. Haarlem: H. D. Tjeenk Willink, 1949.

Jaeger, C. Stephen. *The Envy of Angels: Cathedral Schools and Social Ideals in Medieval Europe, 950–1200.* Philadelphia, 1994.

Jung, Marc-René. *Etudes sur le poème allégorique en France au Moyen Âge.* Romanica Helvetica 82. Bern: Francke, 1971.

Klaus, Catherine. "De l'Enfer au Paradis . . . et Retour, dans l'*Architrenius* de Jean de Hanville." In *Pour une mythologie du Moyen Age,* edited by

Laurence Harf-Lancner and Dominique Boutet, 27–42. Collection de l'École Normale Supérieure de Jeunes Filles 41. Paris: École Normale Supérieure, 1988.

Le Goff, Jacques. *Les intellectuels au Moyen Age.* 2nd ed. Paris, 1985.

———. "Warriors and Conquering Bourgeois: The Image of the City in Twelfth-Century French Literature." *The Medieval Imagination,* 151–76. Chicago: University of Chicago Press, 1988.

Lewis, C. S. *The Allegory of Love: A Study in Medieval Tradition.* Oxford: Oxford University Press, 1936.

Liebeschütz, Hans. "Das 12. Jahrhundert und die Antike." *Archiv für Kulturgeschichte* 35 (1953): 247–71.

———. *Medieval Humanism in the Life and Writings of John of Salisbury.* Studies of the Warburg Institute 17. London: Warburg Institute, 1950.

Meier, Christel. "Wendepunkte der Allegorie im Mittelalter: Von der Schrifthermeneutik zur Lebenspraktik." In *Neue Richtungen in der hoch- und spätmittelalterlichen Bibelexegese,* edited by Robert E. Lerner, 39–64. Schriften des Historischen Kollegs. Kolloquien 32. Munich: Oldenbourg, 1996.

Minkova, Milena. "Some Textual Suggestions on 'Architrenius' by Johannes de Hauvilla." *Filologia mediolatina* 19 (2012): 175–93.

Murray, Alexander. *Reason and Society in the Middle Ages.* 2nd ed. Oxford: Oxford University Press, 1985.

Norberg, Dag. *An Introduction to the Study of Medieval Latin Versification.* Translated by Grant C. Roti and Jacqueline de la Chapelle Skubly. Edited with an Introduction by Jan Ziolkowski. Washington, D.C.: Catholic University of America Press, 2004.

Pacca, Vinicio. "*De Thile insula (Fam.* III.1)." In *Motivi e forme delle* Familiari *di Francesco Petrarca,* edited by Claudia Berra, 591–610. Università degli Studi di Milano, Facoltà di Lettere e Filosofia. Quaderni di Acme 57. Milan: Cisalpino, 2003.

Payen, Jean-Charles. "L'utopie chez les Chartrains." *Le Moyen Âge* 90 (1984): 383–400.

Piaia, Gregorio. "La 'filosofica famiglia' nella poesia allegorica medievale." *Medioevo* 16 (1990): 85–130.

Piehler, Paul H. T. *The Visionary Landscape: A Study in Medieval Allegory.* London: Edward Arnold, 1971.

Placanica, Antonio. Review of *Architrenius,* edited by Winthrop Wether-bee. *Studi medievali* 40 (1999): 739–54.

Rigg, A. G. Review of *Architrenius,* edited by Winthrop Wetherbee. *Speculum* 72 (1997): 497–98.

Roling, Bernd. "Das *Moderancia*-Konzept des Johannes de Hauvilla: Zur Grundlegung einer neuen Ethik laikaler Lebensbewältigung im 12. Jahrhundert." *Frühmittelalterliche Studien* 37 (2003): 167–258.

Schmidt, Paul Gerhard. "L'ornatus difficilis' nell'epica latina." In *Retorica e poetica tra i secoli XII e XIV,* edited by Claudio Leonardi and Enrico Menestò, 125–38. Perugia: Regione dell'Umbria, and Florence: La Nuova Italia, 1988.

Sedgwick, W. B. "Some Poetical Words of the Twelfth Century." *Archivum Latinitatis Medii Aevi* 7 (1932): 223–26.

Semperena, Guadalupe Lopetegui. "El *Architrenius* de Johannes de Hauvilla: Apuntes para una caracterización genérica." *Studi medievali* ser. 3, 54 (2013): 263–303.

Stein, Elisabeth. "Bittere Medizin für verkommene Geistliche: Die *Hierapigra ad purgandos prelatos* des Aegidius von Corbeil." In *Epochen der Satire: Traditionslinien einer literarischen Gattung in Antike, Mittelalter und Renaissance,* edited by Thomas Haye and Franziska Schnoor, 73–93. Spolia Berolinensia 28. Hildesheim: Weidmann, 2008.

———. *Clericus in speculo: Studien zur lateinischen Verssatire des 12. und 13. Jahrhunderts und Erstedition des "Speculum prelatorum."* Mittellateinische Studien und Texte 25. Leiden, Boston, Cologne: Brill, 1999.

Strubel, Armand. *"Grant senefiance a": Allégorie et littérature au Moyen Âge.* Paris: Champion, 2002.

Takada, Yasunari. "The Brooch of Thebes and the Girdle of Venus: Courtly Love in an Oppositional Perspective." *Poetica* (Tokyo) 29–30 (1989): 17–38.

Tatlock, J. S. P. *The Legendary History of Britain: Geoffrey of Monmouth's Historia regum Britanniae and Its Early Vernacular Versions.* New York: Gordian Press, 1974.

Thomas, Hugh M. *The Secular Clergy in England, 1066–1216.* Oxford: Oxford University Press, 2014.

Uhlig, Claus. *Hofkritik im England des Mittelalters und der Renaissance: Studien zu einem Gemeinplatz der europäischen Moralistik.* Quellen und Forschungen zur Sprach- und Kulturgeschichte der germanischen Volker, N. F. 56. Berlin, 1973.

Velli, Giuseppe. "Petrarca, Boccaccio e la grande poesia latina del XII secolo." In *Retorica e poetica tra i secoli XII e XIV,* edited by Claudio Leonardi and Enrico Menestò, 239–56. Perugia, 1988.

von Moos, Peter. "The Use of *Exempla* in the *Policraticus* of John of Salisbury." In *The World of John of Salisbury,* edited by Michael Wilks, 207–61. Oxford: Blackwell, 1984.

White, Hugh. *Nature, Sex, and Goodness in a Medieval Literary Tradition.* Oxford: Oxford University Press, 2000.

Yunck, John A. *The Lineage of Lady Meed: The Development of Medieval Venality.* Notre Dame, Ind: University of Notre Dame Press, 1963.

INDEX OF PROPER NAMES AND PERSONIFICATIONS

PERSONIFICATIONS